D0107043

REFLECTION

A TWISTED TALE

ELIZABETH LIM

 DISNEY · HYPERION

Los Angeles • New York

If you purchased this book without a cover, you should be aware that this book is stolen property. It was reported as "unsold and destroyed" to the publisher, and neither the author nor the publisher has received any payment for this "stripped" book.

Copyright © 2018 Disney Enterprises, Inc.

Published by Disney · Hyperion, an imprint of Buena Vista Books, Inc. No part of this book may be reproduced or transmitted in any form or by any means, electronic or mechanical, including photocopying, recording, or by any information storage and retrieval system, without written permission from the publisher. For information address Disney · Hyperion, 77 West 66th Street, New York, New York 10023.

Printed in the United States of America
First Hardcover Edition, March 2018
First Paperback Edition, September 2019
5 7 9 10 8 6
FAC-025438-22046
Library of Congress Control Number: 2017950202
ISBN 978-1-4847-8218-7

Visit disneybooks.com

SUSTAINABLE
FORESTRY
INITIATIVE
Certified Chain of Custody
Promoting Sustainable Forestry
www.sfiprogram.org
SFI-01054
The SFI label applies to the text stock

To my family,
for teaching me the value of persistence
—E.L.

Chapter One

They had only one cannon left.

Mulan held her breath, digging her heels deep into the snow as she surveyed the valley ahead for any sign of the Huns.

Nothing.

From the heights above where, only minutes ago, a barrage of enemy arrows had rained down death upon them—also nothing.

All was still. Too still.

Mulan knew better than to hope the silence meant the Huns had retreated. No, with each passing second, her apprehension grew. None of the soldiers beside her—Yao or

Ling or Chien-Po, or even her dragon guardian, Mushu—said a word.

Something was wrong. She could feel it.

Her eyes focused on a plume of smoke curling across the top of the hill, moving like a dark and foreboding shadow. As it thinned into the air, Mulan's brow furrowed.

There was something behind the smoke. No, *someone.*

Dread twisted in her gut. Even from a distance, there was no mistaking the imposing form mounted on a black horse.

Shan-Yu.

The smoke lifted, revealing an endless line of Hun soldiers on horseback, rimming the hills and blocking their way. They were surrounded.

There were barely ten men left in Captain Li Shang's regiment against an overwhelming force of Huns. *And* the Huns had the advantage of attacking from above. Mulan knew what everyone must be thinking. How could they possibly survive?

Captain Li Shang tightened the collar of his red cape, then turned to face his soldiers. His expression was grim, but resolute. "Prepare to fight," he said. "If we die, we die with honor."

Her pulse pounding in her ears, Mulan clenched her fists and sucked in the cold, cold air. She didn't know whether her knees were buckling from fear or from hope-lessness. Or both.

She didn't want to be afraid. There was no dignity in fear. But there was no hope. After all, what could she do? It was clear Shang believed they could only stand their ground and fight.

Still, she drew her sword with hesitation. There had to be another way.

With a ferocious battle cry, Shan-Yu led the charge to war. His steed raced down the snow-covered slope, followed by his men. The sound of the horses thundering down the hill was a terrible counterpoint to Mulan's racing heart. She squeezed the hilt of her sword, trying to tune out the sound, but it was impossible. Her eyes froze on the storm of white cascading over the Huns as they ripped across the snow.

"Yao," Shang said calmly, "aim the cannon at Shan-Yu."

More like a firecracker than a cannon, Mulan thought glumly. *Too small to rest all our hopes on.* It was barely larger than her torso, with a red dragon's head at the tip.

Yao, the shortest soldier, swung the cannon left and right, trying to find the best position to fire at Shan-Yu.

She frowned. Eliminating their leader would likely throw the Huns into disarray and slow their invasion. But even if they killed Shan-Yu, the rest of the Hun army would slaughter them.

She forced her focus ahead, knowing she needed to prepare herself mentally for battle, but she couldn't take her mind off Shang's command to Yao. Something about it felt . . . wrong.

Her sword weighed heavily in her hand. She stared at the polished blade, wondering if its reflection would be the last sight she ever caught of herself. Would she die as Ping, the Fa son she'd made up so she could join the army in her father's place? If she died here, in the middle of this snow-covered mountain pass, she'd never see her father or her family again.

Mulan swallowed hard. Who would believe that only a few months ago, her biggest concern had been impressing the Matchmaker? She could barely remember the girl she'd been back then. She'd worn layer upon layer of silk, not plates of armor, her waist cinched tight with a satin sash instead of sore from carrying a belt of weapons. Her lips had been painted with rouge instead of chapped from cold and lack of water, her lashes highlighted with coal that she now could only dream of using to fuel a fire for warmth.

How far she'd come from that girl to who she was now: a soldier in the Imperial army.

Maybe serving her country as a warrior was truer to her heart than being a bride. Yet when she saw her reflection in her sword, she knew she was still pretending to be someone else. She'd never have a chance to find out who that person was, because she, *Mulan*, was about to die.

And the one thing she regretted most was that she'd never make her family proud of her.

The Huns drew closer. As Mulan raised her sword higher, a flash on the blade caught her eye again. Not *her* reflection this time, but that of a snowy overhang on a peak behind the Huns.

Her thoughts quickened as she tilted the blade from side to side, then glanced up, taking in the massive snow embankment.

She had an idea. It was crazy, and it would mean disobeying Shang's order. But if it worked . . .

Mulan's heart raced with a sudden burst of hope. What was there to lose? If she didn't try, they'd all die. Even if her plan succeeded, they likely wouldn't survive . . . but China—she could save China from the Huns.

No time for second thoughts.

Mulan sheathed her sword and lunged forward, grabbing the cannon from Yao.

"Hey!" he shouted after her, but Mulan was already racing toward the Huns.

It was the boldest, wildest thing she had ever done. She tucked the cannon under her arm, barely noticing as Mushu grabbed hold of her scarf so he could keep up. Up the hill she ran, and with each step she grew more determined and less afraid.

Behind, Shang shouted after her, "Ping! Come back! Ping!"

She ignored him. The Huns were descending fast. She had only moments before Shan-Yu was upon her and his army crushed what was left of Shang's troops.

Mulan stopped and planted the cannon into the snow, aiming it at the overhang, praying she had picked a good spot.

This could work—if Shan-Yu didn't kill her first. He was so close she could smell his horse's sweat, so close she could see his black eyes glaring at her.

Her blood thundered in her ears. Distantly she could hear Mushu telling her to hurry. She fumbled in her pocket for her pieces of flint and frantically tried to light the cannon's fuse.

She didn't see Shan-Yu's falcon soaring overhead. It swooped down, its powerful wing knocking her back into the snow and scattering the flint rocks behind her.

Mulan jolted up.

No no no, she thought as she swept the snow for the flint. She couldn't find it!

She looked up. Shan-Yu was charging straight for her.

She grabbed Mushu by the neck, squeezing until he choked a breath of fire. It was just enough to light the cannon. Sulfur burned into the air. Mulan crouched, holding the weapon steady as it shot off toward the overhang.

Shan-Yu's horse reared from the cannon's explosion, but Mulan was barely aware of the Hun leader. Her gaze was locked on the overhang, and on the rocket arcing smoothly toward it until it finally lodged itself into the snow.

A loud rumbling erupted. Snow plummeted off the precipice, washing down into the pass in fearsome white sheets. Avalanche!

Mulan grinned. She'd done it.

She stumbled, struggling to keep upright as the ground shook. She needed to get back to the others.

Suddenly Shan-Yu loomed above, and her grin faltered. Up close, he was like a mountain himself—broad and large, his fists alone the size of Mulan's head.

Shan-Yu's deep-set eyes narrowed with rage, and he lifted his sword with one powerful arm, ready to deliver her a crushing blow.

"Ping!" Shang shouted from behind. Before she could draw her sword to try to defend herself, Shan-Yu let out a furious cry and swung his blade.

Mulan braced herself for the blow.

It never came. Shang shoved her out of the way. It happened so fast. Before Mulan even tumbled into the snow, she heard a rush of wind, and the swipe of Shan-Yu's blade.

Then a low, pained grunt.

"No!" Mulan cried, lifting her head and pushing herself up. "Shang!"

The captain's red cape fluttered behind him, caught in the wind. For a moment, she couldn't see him, and she thought maybe, maybe it was the Hun leader's grunt she had heard. Maybe Shang had defeated him.

Then Shang's cape settled, sweeping over his back as before. And any hope Mulan had died.

She saw he was hurt, too hurt to even lift his sword. It fell from his hand into the snow with a thump. Shang staggered back, his boots grinding into the snow. He raised his fists, not about to give up.

"Is this the best China has to offer?" Shan-Yu said, laughing.

"Go, Ping," Shang rasped, as Mulan raced to help him. "Go."

She wasn't fast enough.

With one swift punch, Shan-Yu knocked Shang off his feet.

And the captain collapsed.

Chapter Two

"NO!" Mulan screamed.

Shan-Yu laughed again and jumped off his horse, blade in his hand. He stabbed it into the snow, wiping it clean of Shang's blood. Then he advanced toward Mulan, cleaving the air with such strong strokes that the wind whipped Mulan's cheeks.

Shan-Yu was a mere step away. She was next.

Don't panic, don't panic. Mulan drew her sword just in time to block Shan-Yu's blade before it sliced her chest.

He was strong, far stronger than she was. He overpowered her easily, and Mulan knew she couldn't hold him off for long. But she hoped she wouldn't have to.

Shan-Yu's back was to the bucking avalanche of snow that was rapidly flowing toward them.

Mulan gathered all her strength and resolve. Then, the moment she saw an opening, she lowered her sword and swept her leg at Shan-Yu's ankle. It surprised the Hun, and he stumbled back, thrashing to regain his balance in the snow.

That second was all she needed. Mulan whirled away and grabbed Shang by the arm to help him up.

The captain's face was very pale. The armor concealed his wound, but his hand, which clutched his side, was stained with bright red blood.

Act first, worry later. "Come on," she said between breaths, draping his arm around her shoulder. "We can do this."

Together, they ran. Shang breathed heavily at her side, but she wouldn't let him slow down. The bottom of the hill was so close. There was a large rock there where Yao and the others had taken shelter. If they could just reach it . . .

The wind bellowed, strong gusts pushing them forward. Mulan could feel the avalanche behind them. It had gathered speed, like a river released from its dam and gushing with full force and might. The cold whipped at Mulan's back, and heavy clouds of snow hurtled through the air above them. If they didn't move faster, the avalanche would swallow them.

She shouted for her horse, "Khan!"

Mulan stole a glimpse over her shoulder, just in time to see the mountain fall apart into large chunks of ice. Shan-Yu and the rest of the Hun army vanished into the snow, their shouts and cries smothered by the avalanche.

The ground roared and shuddered. Snow was everywhere, forcing itself into Mulan's eyes and nose and mouth. She clamped her mouth shut, only to have to gasp for air seconds later, the chill filling her lungs.

She focused ahead, widened her stride. *Keep going. Don't look back. We're halfway there.*

At her side, Shang was rapidly growing weaker, and they both knew it. Mulan was practically dragging him as she ran.

"I-I'm slowing you down," Shang said, wheezing. "Leave me and go ahead."

"Not a chance." She gripped Shang's arm so hard she could barely feel her fingers anymore. She wouldn't give up. She'd run until the end.

The avalanche thundered behind them, snapping trees and erasing everything in its path. A familiar neigh startled Mulan.

Khan!

Her horse powered toward her, his black mane powdered white with snow. Mulan leapt onto his back and reached down to grab Shang—but not fast enough. The avalanche had caught up with them, and it pulled Shang into its icy tide.

No no no, Mulan thought, watching the snow carry him farther and farther away. She kneed Khan into the flow and they drifted along with the avalanche's current, Mulan searching desperately for Shang. She couldn't tell which direction was north or south, east or west—there was only out of the snow and in it. The avalanche grew stronger by the second, washing down the hill with brutal force. Snow buried them, covering them in darkness. But each time they fell, Khan kicked and leapt clear of the snow, and Mulan resumed her search.

"Shang!" she yelled. "Shang!"

A flash of red caught her eye. She spotted the captain up ahead, unconscious and sinking into the snow. "Hyah!" she said, urging Khan toward him. Shang let out a groan as she pulled him up by his shoulders and folded him over Khan's back.

Mulan turned Khan back toward the rock. It was close now, but the pulsing waves of snow were too strong. They were impossible to navigate. From this distance, Mulan could see her friends watching her struggle.

Yao stood with his bow in his hand. He waved it at them, shouting something Mulan couldn't hear.

Ling, the slim and energetic soldier with Yao and

Chien-Po, pointed at the rope attached to one of the arrows. Now Mulan understood. They were going to try to pull her to safety!

Keeping one arm over Shang's unconscious body, Mulan waved her free hand to show she was ready.

Yao raised his bow and shot the arrow. It arced high into the sky, and for a moment Mulan feared that the roiling avalanche might devour it too. It landed just beside her and Mulan grasped it, tying the rope around Khan's belly. But the rope slipped through Yao's grasp!

Mulan gritted her teeth, but she didn't panic. Every second mattered now, and she had to figure out a way to save them all before they fell off the cliff.

Spotting the bow on Khan's pack, she reached for it and aimed the arrow back at her friends.

Please catch it, please catch it, she pleaded, watching the arrow and rope soar back toward Yao, Ling, and Chien-Po. She couldn't see them from the rush of the avalanche.

Mushu hollered in Mulan's ears as they swooped down with the snow, almost falling off the cliff. But she kept watching the rope, kept waiting—

Suddenly, the rope grew taut. The snow washed around them instead of with them, and Khan let out a loud neigh as he kicked against the current.

Mulan craned her neck, not daring to hope.

She could see her friends above, just along the edge of the cliff. And yes, they had caught the rope! She held her breath as the rope stretched, and the soldiers heaved together, pulling them to safety behind the rock.

Finally, Chien-Po, the strongest of her friends, lifted Shang off Mulan's lap.

They'd made it.

Mulan dismounted, pulled Khan by the reins, and grabbed Mushu. She pressed her back against the rock, squeezing her eyes shut as the tail end of the avalanche washed down the hill.

Finally, the ground stopped shaking, and the air grew still.

Mulan coughed and kicked her way out of the drifts. The others were doing the same. Mushu plucked Cri-Kee, their lucky cricket, out of the snow.

Mulan caught her breath. The sweat on her temples and neck had frozen, and she wiped the frost from her face and shook the snow from her uniform. She patted Khan's head, then turned to face her comrades. Yao, Ling, Chien-Po, and even Chi Fu, the Emperor's arrogant adviser—she could hardly believe they'd all survived. "Thank you. Thank you."

"Well, we couldn't let you die," Yao said, smiling.

Ling raised his fist in agreement. "You're the bravest of us all!"

Mulan exhaled, and slowly, her shoulders relaxed with relief. She and Shang had made it out of the avalanche alive.

Shang!

At once, her good spirits faded. She moved toward the captain, whom Chien-Po had managed to keep out of the snow. Shang's face was even paler than before.

"He's still unconscious," Chien-Po said. Outwardly, his expression was serene as always, but Mulan detected a hint of worry in his voice.

"He's wounded," said Mulan. "He needs medical—"

Shang stirred, clutching the cape wrapped over his chest.

Chien-Po brightened. "Look, he's waking up."

Shang coughed and wheezed, and Mulan squeezed his shoulder. "Easy, easy."

The captain blinked, then let out a labored breath. He turned to Mulan, his thick brows furrowing into an unreadable expression. "Ping," said Shang, trying to sit up.

Mulan straightened, preparing for a rebuke.

"Ping, you are the craziest man I've ever met." He paused. "And for that I owe you my life. From now on, you have my trust."

A slow smile broke out on Mulan's face.

"Let's hear it for Ping!" her friends cheered. "The king of the mountain!"

Shang opened his mouth to join in the cheer, then winced and exhaled harshly.

Mulan caught him by the arm. "Shang?"

"I . . . just need to . . . sleep." Shang closed his eyes.

Mulan shook his shoulders. "No, stay with us. Shang?"

But Shang didn't hear her. His hands, which had been clutching his cape, went limp, and he collapsed back onto the snow, unconscious.

"Shang!" Mulan cried. "Wake up!"

"Captain?" Yao said, nudging Shang's arm.

Shang lay still.

The soldiers looked at her hopelessly.

A lump hardened in Mulan's throat. Pleading with Shang to wake up wasn't going to do anything. It wasn't going to save him.

Mulan knelt beside the captain and touched his neck to search for a pulse. He was trembling.

"He's freezing," said Mulan urgently. "Someone, get him a blanket. We need to start a fire, keep him warm."

"Our supplies are buri—"

"There's a blanket on my horse," she interrupted.

Ling nodded and rushed toward Khan. When he returned, Chien-Po lifted Shang off the snow and carefully set him down on the blanket.

Kneeling beside him, Mulan gently drew back Shang's

cape. The soldiers gasped, and Mulan stifled a cry. There was a long, deep gash across Shang's abdomen, below his armor. Blood seeped through his uniform and dripped onto the snow, bright as his scarlet cape.

The color drained from Mulan's face. She stumbled back, barely noticing Mushu climb up her back and hide behind the green scarf over her armor.

"This is my fault," she whispered. "Shan-Yu was attacking me, and Shang took the blow."

"Hey, hey, it could've been worse," Mushu replied. "It could've been you, not him. At least you're still alive."

Mulan gave her guardian dragon a reproachful look. "You're not helping."

"What'd I—"

Mulan ignored him and untied her scarf. "Everyone, give me your scarves. We have to stop Shang's bleeding."

One by one, the soldiers passed her their scarves, and Mulan knotted them together into a long bandage. Carefully, she lifted Shang's armor, opened his tunic, and started wrapping his wound. His blood was warm, but his skin was cold—beads of frost dusted his cheeks and neck. When she was done, she reached to take his pulse again. Her hands shook.

Shang's pulse was faint. *Too* faint. But he was still alive.

"We need to make camp," she said finally.

"We need to go to the Imperial City," Chi Fu corrected her. The Emperor's adviser slid out of his corner by the rocks. Frost covered the tips of his thin mustache, making the hairs droop like whiskers on a catfish. He wrapped his robes tightly about him, clearly unhappy to be out in the cold and showing no gratitude that they were still alive. "We must inform the Emperor that the Huns have been defeated."

"We can't travel with Captain Li like this," Mulan argued. "He needs to rest."

Chi Fu gazed at the captain and wrinkled his nose. "He won't survive a wound like that. The captain is a man of honor. He'd understand."

"We're not leaving him," Mulan said firmly.

"Your duty to the Emperor comes first, soldier." Chi Fu frowned at her, his beady eyes unblinking. "Or must I document your insubordination?"

"Leave Ping alone," Yao growled.

"Yeah," Ling chimed in. "If not for Ping, we'd all be dead. He saved us all."

Chi Fu harrumphed and turned to face the group. "*All* this is Ping's fault. If not for his foolishness, your captain would still be alive."

"He *is* still alive," Mulan insisted stubbornly. "We're not leaving him behind."

"Who put you in charge?" Chi Fu retorted.

"No one," she replied. "But Captain Li Shang is our commanding officer."

"And the Emperor is our ruler!"

"Then we'll . . . we'll take Shang with us."

The other soldiers nodded in agreement.

"Impossible," Chi Fu snapped. "We don't have enough supplies to take our time. The longer we wallow in this . . . this blizzard, the sooner we'll all die. Besides, he wouldn't survive the journey."

"He will," said Mulan fiercely. "I'll care for him."

Chi Fu scoffed. "Lunatic boy."

"I will, too."

"So will I."

One after another, the soldiers pledged to help their captain.

"Order, people, order!" Chi Fu crossed his arms, and a crooked smile spread over his mouth. "Very well," he announced, "Ping will take care of the captain during the journey back. But if he falls behind, we won't wait for him. Getting to the Emperor is our top priority. If anyone else tries to help Ping, I'll report his name to the Emperor for insubordination." Chi Fu paused so his threat could sink in. "Understand?"

Yao opened his mouth to argue, but Mulan was quicker.

"I understand," she said. "Captain Li will be my responsibility. I don't want anyone to get in trouble."

"We can't let you do this alone," said Chien-Po.

Ling agreed. "Yeah, we all want to help the captain."

"I'm the only one left with a horse," Mulan replied, glancing about her sadly. The snow had buried Shang's and Chi Fu's horses, along with many of their fellow soldiers. Only now did she realize how drastically their numbers had dwindled. So many of the men she'd trained with had been killed—either by the Huns' initial attack or in the avalanche. She inhaled. "Khan can carry us both. I won't fall too far behind."

"But—"

"A wise decision," Chi Fu interrupted. "I am the Emperor's counsel. That means I'm now in charge. I see supplies in the snow that the Huns dropped. Retrieve as much as you can. Move swiftly. We leave in an hour."

No one dared argue with Chi Fu's orders, but as the soldiers glumly went about gathering provisions and gear from the snow, Mulan could read their thoughts. They knew Shang was gravely wounded.

Well, she refused to let Shang die.

She swore to herself then and there she would do whatever it took to save him.

Chapter Three

They might have won the impossible battle against Shan-Yu and the Huns, but it was a grim march to the Imperial City. Not one of the soldiers laughed or sang or smiled. Even Chi Fu didn't wear his usual smirk. A stranger passing by could have mistaken them for a funeral procession.

Mulan trailed the others, Shang slumped over Khan's neck in front of her. She kept her hand on Shang's shoulder, steadying him as Khan clopped along the icy pass. The Tung-Shao Pass, where they'd defeated the Huns, was hours behind them now, but there was no end to the snow. Worse yet, even as they plodded down the mountain, it seemed to only get colder, not warmer.

Worry festered in Mulan. Shang was getting worse.

More and more frequently, she and Khan stopped to let the captain rest. Yao and Ling and Chien-Po tried to hang back and keep her company, but with Chi Fu watching, she'd told them to go ahead with the others.

Over the day, she fell far behind the rest of the soldiers, but Shang needed the rest. What began to trouble Mulan was his temperature—every few hours, his skin glowed with fever.

Here she was, teeth chattering and skin rippling with goosebumps. Practically freezing, while Shang was burning up from inside. But she couldn't risk taking off his blankets and exposing him to the cold. Seeing him struggle against the heat, hearing him grunt with pain and mumble deliriously—they were punches to her heart.

Only once before had she felt so helpless: when Baba had been called to war. Desperation to save him had swelled in her chest, just as it did now. Desperation, then determination. But with her father, the way to save him had been clear: she'd gone to war in his place. With Shang—what could she do other than ease his suffering?

I'll think of something, she thought as she kicked at the snow. She trudged onward. Shang's mumbling faded, and worriedly, Mulan searched for his pulse.

"How's he doing?" Mushu asked, head hanging low. Seeing how heartsick Mulan had been the past day, the dragon looked sorry for the comments he'd made earlier about her surviving instead of Shang.

"Not great," Mulan said quietly. She brushed her hand across Shang's forehead. As the captain slept, the sweat on his skin dried into flakes of ice. "But his fever's down. A little."

"That's fantastic news," Mushu exclaimed. He added, "He looks way better. More color in his cheeks." To demonstrate his point, the dragon pinched Shang's skin.

The captain did *not* look better. His face stayed deathly pale. His lips were blue from the cold, and his hair was thick with frost. "Mmm . . ." he mumbled in his sleep.

"See?" said Mushu. "Even he agrees."

Mulan gritted her teeth. She didn't add that Shang's wound hadn't ceased to bleed. It'd slowed, but every time she checked his bandages, the blood was still warm, still fresh. There was nothing she could do to stop it.

Trying to hide her despair, she urged Khan to walk faster.

Her cricket, Cri-Kee, hopped onto her shoulder and chirped. It sounded consoling, but Mulan sighed and kept walking. The sun hung low on the west horizon; it was almost nightfall. The sooner they caught up with the others, the better.

She couldn't stop replaying that moment she'd shot the

cannon. She *should* have drawn her sword and been prepared to counter Shan-Yu right after she fired. But what had she done? She'd watched, grinning like an idiot—because her plan had worked.

Shang had paid the price for her mistake.

Stupid, stupid, stupid, Mulan berated herself. If she'd been a better soldier, they'd be marching to see the Emperor now while shouting to all about their victory. Instead, she'd gotten their captain gravely injured.

Shang let out another ragged breath, and his features contorted with agony.

Mulan touched his forearm. "I'm here," she said, even though she knew her words wouldn't help him with the pain. She couldn't bear seeing him suffer like this.

I'll never forgive myself if he dies, she thought miserably. *If there are any gods listening, please . . . please spare Captain Li's life. He's a good man. He doesn't deserve to die.*

Of course, she got no reply. She hadn't expected to.

Mulan blinked away her tears and wiped her nose on her sleeve. Crying over Shang wasn't going to help him. Getting him to warmth and safety, and to the Imperial City—that would.

The troops weren't as far ahead as she'd feared. If she squinted down the path, she could make out Chien-Po's burly figure marching down the hill. The end of the mountain path was near; she could see a forest not too far away. Past the forest, they'd meet the Yellow River, and they'd follow its course north toward the Imperial City. Even from where she stood, she could make out the Emperor's glittering palace.

So near, yet so far.

At best, it was two days' journey. But for Shang, each hour was a battle to live. She could hear the pain in his breath; she could see it whenever his chest rose and fell.

"Chi Fu was right," she said wretchedly. "This is all my fault."

"Don't listen to that catfish," Mushu said. "Chin up. You're strong, and you're smart. Heck, you defeated an army of Huns. You'll get the captain through this."

"I hope so."

"Keep talking to him," Mushu suggested. "Make your voice soothing, like a good cup of tea."

Mulan rolled her eyes, but she desperately wanted to believe the dragon's words.

"You can make it, Shang," she said to the captain. She touched his arm, then clasped his hand, warming his cold fingers with her own. "Whatever battle you're fighting in there, I'm going to help you."

"That's it," Mushu encouraged. "Keep going. Maybe you should give him a little kiss."

"Mushu!"

The dragon shrugged. "Hey, it works in all those folktales."

"That's enough," she said, turning away so Mushu wouldn't see the blush creeping across her cheeks. Of all the crazy ideas! "Let him sleep."

For a moment, Mulan was glad Shang was unconscious and probably hadn't heard the dragon's suggestion to kiss him. She squeezed his hand again. "Sleep, Shang. We'll catch up with the others soon."

They couldn't be more than an hour from the bottom of the hill. She tugged on Khan's reins with her free hand, but the horse wouldn't budge. Khan whinnied.

Then—

Shang's hand grew warmer, and his breath steadier.

Mulan jolted, relief swelling in her heart. "Shang?"

"Is it morning already?" he rasped, coughing.

"You're awake." Mulan instantly dropped his hand, remembering that he was her commanding officer. She fumbled for her canteen. "Here, have some water."

Shang tried to sit up.

"Easy," she said. "You're on my horse."

Shang winced, then laid his head back down on Khan's neck and let out a groan. "Where are we?"

"Half a day from the Tung-Shao Pass. Maybe less."

"Where are the others?"

Trust Shang to get straight to business, even when he was critically wounded. "Up ahead. Not far."

She paused, already dreading the answer before she asked, "Is the pain better?"

A shadow passed over Shang's face. Suddenly, he looked vacant and lost. "Is my father here? I heard him speaking earlier to Chi Fu. Tell him I'm almost finished with my training."

"Your father? But Shang, your father is—" Mulan stopped. Shang *knew* his father was dead. Chien-Po had found the general's helmet on a battlefield, strewn with the slaughtered soldiers of General Li's army. Shang had taken his father's helmet and hung it on his sword among the fallen in the snow. They'd all respectfully watched him do it. "Shang?"

Mulan put her palm against the captain's cheek. His skin burned with fever, much hotter than before. "Shang, wake up."

Mushu crept to Shang's side and waved a claw in front of the captain's face.

"I don't want my father to see me like this," Shang mumbled. He blinked drowsily. "Is that a snake on my stomach?"

"Who are you calling a snake?" Mushu said, offended.

Mulan snatched Mushu away. "Leave him alone," she whispered through gritted teeth.

"You might want to take a look at him," said Mushu. "Um, his eyes are looking glassy, and his skin's red. He's not looking too hot. Well, if you want to be totally accurate, he *is* looking hot—"

"Yes, I know," Mulan interrupted, a note of panic in her voice. She slipped off her horse and dragged Shang off Khan's back, lowering him onto the snow with a grunt. She peeled off the blankets Chien-Po had wrapped over his body, then gently lifted his head and carefully dribbled the water from her canteen through his parted lips.

"Shang," she said, tapping his cheek with her fingers. "Shang, it's Ping. I'm here. Wake up. Talk to me."

Shang's head bobbed to the side. "Ping?"

"Yes," Mulan said. "I'm here."

"You know," he murmured, "I was so frustrated with you at first."

Mulan tilted her head.

"You were the worst soldier I had ever seen, Ping. Do you remember? Always last in every exercise. You couldn't run, you couldn't shoot, you couldn't fight. I was so certain that you were completely unsuitable for war—I sent you home." Shang let out a dry chuckle, and for a moment, his eyes opened. "And yet, you surprised me."

Mulan inhaled. *Good, good. Keep him talking.* "Surprised you how?"

"You worked hard," Shang continued. He sounded far away, almost delirious. "You got better, and you got smart." He closed his eyes. "No, you were always smart. I didn't see that at first. But I did see that when *you* got better, everyone else wanted to improve, too. You inspired them to work hard, Ping." His voice drifted. "You had faith in them. But I . . . I didn't have faith in you."

His eyes opened again, surprisingly clear this time. Mulan could see her face reflected in his pupils, framed by pools of deep, deep brown. "I'm sorry."

"Shang, there's nothing to be sorry about."

Shang reached for the canteen. He held it himself, hands shaky, and took a long sip. Then he exhaled. "Ping, I know I'm dying."

"You're not."

"I can feel it." Shang set down the canteen, and his hand fell to his side on the snow. "You should leave me here."

"I'm not leaving you," Mulan said firmly. "You're coming with me."

Shang coughed, and the corners of his lips lifted into a wry but tired smile. "Still can't follow orders, can you, soldier?"

Shang coughed again, and Mulan reached for the stack

of blankets Yao and Ling had made as a pillow for him. She carefully arranged it under his head. Sweat beaded his temples, and she patted his skin dry before it froze. When he blinked again, this time his eyes were bloodshot.

"Shang, are you all right?"

He let his head sink into the makeshift pillow. "I thought I saw my father earlier."

"I know," Mulan replied quietly. "You called out for him. You must have been dreaming."

Shang turned his head, his gaze meeting hers. "In my dream, he was still alive." His voice was tight, and Mulan could tell that he hadn't yet had the chance to grieve for his father. The news of General Li's death had come too suddenly. "My father was a general for twenty years. He died protecting China. Ever since I was young, I wanted to follow in his footsteps." He managed a weak laugh. "But here I am, about to die after my first battle in command."

"You aren't going to d—"

"I wanted to become a general like my father," Shang interrupted. "I wanted to win battles and bring honor to my family name. Is it selfish—to wish I could keep living? Is it dishonorable of me, Ping? I want to continue protecting our country, our Emperor."

"No," said Mulan. "It isn't selfish or dishonorable at all."

Shang lay back, letting his head settle into the blankets.

"The Huns won't be the last of China's problems. The Emperor will always face new threats, new invaders. He needs to have strong, brave men at his side. Men like you, Ping."

"Shang," Mulan said, trying again, "stop talking like this."

"Now that it's all over, now that my time on this earth is done, do you know what comforts me the most?"

He waited, so Mulan gave in. "What?" she asked quietly.

Shang lowered his voice. "That I've made a friend like you, Ping. Someone I can trust completely."

Tears pricked the edges of Mulan's eyes. This time, she didn't try to hold them back. She knew she couldn't. She swallowed, choking on her words. "Stop talking like this. It's *my* fault you're wounded."

"I would never have thought of firing that last cannon at the mountain," Shang confessed. "I went after you to get the cannon back, but you—you saved us. It was an honor to protect you."

How strange, then, that Mulan's tongue grew heavy. There was so much she wanted to tell him. That it was her fault he was hurt; that if only she'd been more alert, she would have anticipated Shan-Yu's attack. She wanted to tell him he was the best leader their troops could have hoped for; a lesser man would have left her to die at Shan-Yu's hands, but

Shang was not only courageous—he believed in his soldiers, and treated them as part of his team. She remembered how proud he'd been during their training when she'd defeated him in one-on-one combat. The satisfied smile that'd lit up his face as he wiped his jaw after her kick—she would never forget it. She wanted to tell him that she admired him and had always wanted his friendship.

Yet not a word could crawl out of her mouth. Only a choke, and a guttural sound she barely recognized as her own, except that it burned in her throat. She turned away and fumbled with her canteen so Shang wouldn't see the tears sliding down her cheeks.

"What will you do now that the war is over, Ping?" Shang asked. "Will you go home?"

"Home?" Mulan repeated. She hadn't thought about that yet. Would things be different when she returned home, now that she'd served as a soldier in the army? Or would they go back to the way they had been? How could they, though, after everything that had happened . . . everything she'd done? "Yes. I would like to."

Shang reached for her arm. "Your family will be very proud of you, Ping. I heard that you'd taken your father's place. He was an esteemed warrior. My father always held him in high regard."

Mulan kept silent. How could she tell Shang that she

was really a girl? That she'd stolen her father's armor and conscription notice to join the army?

Yes, she'd done it to save her father from having to serve again. He was an old man now. He walked with a cane and had never fully recovered from his battle injuries fighting for China decades ago.

Just thinking about it made her heart heavy. The last night she'd been home, she'd stolen a glimpse at Baba practicing his battle stances with his sword. Not even a minute into his exercise, he'd collapsed, clutching his injured leg in pain. Seeing that, she knew he wouldn't survive. She *had* to be the one to go in his place.

But her reasons didn't matter. She'd disobeyed her parents, *dishonored* them. They must have been so angry when they found she'd left.

They had a right to be angry. She'd not only disobeyed them, but worse, she'd lied to them. She'd deceived them.

The same way she'd deceived Shang.

Oh, how she wanted to tell him the truth! But not now. Not like this.

The silence dragged on. Mulan knew she should say something, but what? Shang's words had been so honest, so sincere. He thought of her as a true friend, someone he trusted. Little did he know that she'd been lying to him this whole time.

You think he's a great captain, she reminded herself. *That was never a lie, and now . . . now you think of him as a friend, too.*

"I'm glad to be your friend," she said quietly.

Shang smiled again. A smaller smile than last time—Mulan could tell he was struggling not to show his pain. "Will you do something for me?"

"Yes, of course," she blurted. "Anything."

Shang stared up at the clouds drifting across the sky. Mulan looked up, too. Geese threaded the clouds, like they were sifting through snow.

"Take my ashes home to my mother," he whispered, "so I might be buried beside my ancestors. It will mean so much to her."

"Shang." His name clung to her throat. It hurt to speak. "You can't give up. You have to fight on. You have to live."

"Tell her . . . not to be sad. Tell her I'm with Father."

Mulan bit her lip. She was trembling, and not from the cold. The bleakness in Shang's face, the certainty in his words that he was going to die. It couldn't be!

A swell of heat burst in her throat, and she had to fight not to let the tears come. She would not let Shang's words shatter her, not without a fight.

She took his hand—his cold, limp hand—and entwined her fingers in his. She squeezed gently. "Yes," she whispered. "I promise. But you—"

"You, too, Ping," Shang interrupted. "Don't blame yourself." That small smile again. It pained Mulan to see it more than it comforted her.

She clenched her fists until her nails bit into her palms. A silent sob escaped her throat. Her lungs burned. "You have to keep fighting. We'll be in the Imperial City in a few days. Just hang on, Shang. Please."

"At least now I know. . . ." He stopped to gather his breath, then closed his eyes again. "Now . . . I know . . . that China will be in good hands."

Chapter Four

It was dark by the time Mulan made it down the mountain and caught up with the other soldiers. Lighting a lantern to help guide their way to the camp, Mulan saw Shang's breath curl into the cold air. She shivered. It was warmer down off the pass, but the air was still chilled, and she knew it would only get colder as night went on. She adjusted the blanket over Shang's body, then chirped to hurry Khan along.

"Almost there," she chanted, not sure whether the reassurance was meant more for her horse or for the sleeping Shang. "Almost there, almost there."

The soldiers had made camp along the outskirts of a small forest around the base of the mountain. The sight of a blazing fire with smoke unfurling into the sky, a pile of freshly cut wood, and a cluster of sturdy, wind-blocking tents lifted Mulan's heart. *And* Khan's, it appeared. Once the horse saw the fire, he picked up speed.

"Ping!" Yao and Ling hurried over to help her lift Shang off Khan's back. Chi Fu saw her, too. He crossed his arms and glared at Yao and Ling.

"Where do you two think you are going?" he shouted. "Come back here."

"We're going to cut some more wood," Ling responded. "Be right back!"

"Insubordinate ruffians!" Chi Fu harrumphed, then pushed open his tent flap to go back inside. He glanced back, fixing a stare on Mulan. "I knew Captain Li wasn't ready to lead. I knew he didn't deserve such a great responsibility. And look now; if his soldiers had learned to follow his orders, he wouldn't be dying."

Yao raised a fist at the Emperor's counsel. "The captain isn't dead!"

But Chi Fu had already swiveled on his heel and gone inside his tent.

Mulan bit her lip and turned to her friends. "Thanks for your help."

"We were worried you got lost," replied Ling. "How's Captain Li doing?"

Mulan shook her head. Her eyes were swollen, her voice raw. "Not great."

Yao's shoulders slumped. He was usually the most belligerent of the group, but even his bruised black eye looked sad. "We caught some pigeons. Chien-Po's making soup. I'll bring you some."

"All right," Mulan said tiredly. How long had it been since she'd eaten? How could she be hungry when Shang was fighting for his life? Still, she forced a smile. "Shang could use some good, hot soup. Are there any more tents?"

"Take mine," Ling offered, pointing. "We made it ready for you."

Mulan looked at her friends gratefully. "You guys are the best."

"It's the least we can do," Ling replied with a shrug. He picked up Shang by the shoulders, Yao lifted the captain's legs, and they walked with her to the tent.

"What are you doing?" Chi Fu cried, popping out to observe the soldiers carry Shang into Ling's tent. "I said no one is permitted to help Ping."

"We made camp," Yao argued. "What does it matter if we help him now or not? So report me."

"And me."

"And me," Chien-Po chimed in, holding up a soup ladle.

Chi Fu grunted, and he scribbled furiously on his scroll. "I will."

Chien-Po shrugged. "Dinner's almost ready," he said, as cheerfully as he could muster. A pot bubbled over the fire, and Mulan inhaled, savoring the delicious aroma of hot, freshly prepared soup.

As the soldiers crowded around the pot, eagerly slurping, Chien-Po helped Mulan and the others settle Shang into Ling's tent.

Most of the tents in the camp were patched together out of saddle blankets, capes, and animal skins, but Ling had managed to procure one of the Huns' tents. Several wooden poles propped up its triangular roof, and the material was thick muslin, like the tents in their training barracks at the Wu Zong camp. Chien-Po could barely fit inside.

"We made him a bed out of some wood," Chien-Po said, gesturing at the makeshift bed in the center of the tent, outfitted with a thin pallet of extra blankets. "He'll be more comfortable traveling that way. We will help you carry him tomorrow."

Mulan's heart warmed and her spirits lifted. Her friends had thought of everything. There was even a little stool and a bucket of clean water with a neat stack of cloths next to it.

She dipped one of the cloths into the bucket, wrung out the excess water, and started peeling away Shang's bandages to clean his wound.

Yao and Ling returned with two steaming bowls of soup.

"I'll eat later," Mulan said. *Too much to do now.* She filled another cloth with snow and placed it on Shang's forehead.

Ling crouched beside the captain and tried to feed him some soup. "He's still unconscious."

She nodded. "He woke up a couple hours ago, but he's been out since then." She swallowed, trying to stay positive. "He's stopped bleeding, so we won't have to cauterize the wound." She let out a small sigh of relief. "And I don't think it's infected, which is good news."

Her voice fell soft. "But I can't get his fever down."

The wind whistled outside, shuffling the tent's flaps. Mulan leaned against one of the wooden poles and started removing her armor. She hadn't realized how tired she was, how her muscles ached and her body demanded rest. She could hardly keep her shoulders up.

"You need to eat something," Yao said, observing her.

"You need to sleep," Chien-Po said, noting the dark circles under her eyes.

Mulan shook her head. "The only reason Shang is injured is because he saved me from Shan-Yu. It's my duty to take care of him."

"We could all take shifts."

"You three have been a great help already. We fought hard today, and we all need our rest."

Her voice was firm. No one dared argue.

Yao patted her shoulder. "All right, Ping," he said

reluctantly. "You got it. But let us know if you need any-thing. We'll be right outside."

"I will," Mulan promised.

Her friends left the tent, and Mushu crawled out of his hiding place in Mulan's pack and went to her side.

Mulan knelt and covered her face with her hands. "What if he doesn't wake up, Mushu?" she whispered. "What if he dies?"

Shang's request to have her take his ashes home to his mother haunted her. Even *he* thought he was going to die.

"This is all because of me."

"You've got to stop blaming yourself," said Mushu, climbing on top of the stack of cloths. "What happened to Shang is not your fault."

"If I had been a better warrior, if I'd been more prepared for Shan-Yu's attack, none of this—"

"Hey." Mushu reached out a claw to pat Mulan on the shoulder. "If not for you, *everyone* would be dead. You can't forget that. You protected your people. You saved your country. You can't save everybody."

Mulan didn't reply. Deep down, she feared Mushu was right.

Staying awake was hard. She rubbed her temples. They throbbed, the pain shooting up behind her eyes. She'd promised herself she'd watch Shang all night, but she was so, so tired.

The fire outside was dying, and Mulan left Shang's side briefly to feed its embers. The sky was black and starless; all was quiet in the camp. Yao and Ling, who were supposed to be on guard duty, had nodded off, and when she went back into her tent, she heard Mushu snoring. Even Cri-Kee was asleep, comfortably resting on top of Mushu's scaly stomach.

A pang of loneliness tugged at Mulan. She leaned against the tent pole and looked at Shang. He hadn't moved since they'd arrived at the camp; hadn't made a sound, either. The only reason she knew he was still alive was the slight rise and fall of his chest, the occasional flinch of his brow, and the faint tinge of color in his cheeks.

She'd had no success at all getting him to drink Chien-Po's soup. Every time she'd tipped the bowl to his parted lips, the soup just dribbled out of his mouth. Once or twice his teeth clenched, as if he were in terrible pain.

So she watched him, waiting for any sign that he might awaken. But he didn't.

The broth was cold now, almost frozen. She picked at it with a chopstick, then sipped the liquid dribbling from underneath the layer of ice on top. Once the ice cracked, she tilted the bowl toward her lips, forcing the broth down with one gulp.

As she drank, she closed her eyes and tried to imagine

she was drinking her grandmother's porridge. What she wouldn't give for a hot bowl of fish congee, sprinkled with green scallions and topped with a dollop of sesame oil! She'd even have willingly downed one of her mother's herbal soups; Fa Li used to make red sage soup almost every day when Mulan was growing up. How she'd hated the smell and pungent taste. She used to pick out the chopped pieces of the root and chew on the sweet wolfberries instead.

She missed home so much.

"If you wake up, Shang," she said aloud, "I'll take you home for dinner. No, not for my cooking. I still have a lot to learn. But my grandmother . . . my *nai nai*, she's the best chef on this side of China. Her pork dumplings would wake a dead man just to eat them." She cringed at the saying, but forced a laugh. "What do you say?"

She waited.

No answer, of course.

Feeling foolish as well as dejected, Mulan set the bowl aside. Her stomach still growled, but not as urgently as before.

She lay down by Shang's side, propping herself on an elbow, and gently swept his hair off his face. His jaw was still tight, but his forehead was smooth, and his breathing was quiet. He looked more peaceful than earlier.

Then she curled up and rested her head on her hands. She wondered if Shang was dreaming—of his home, his family, his friends back in his town. She hoped so. She hoped he was fighting to live.

She realized how little she knew about him. She knew nothing about his family other than that his father had been the Emperor's most trusted general. She didn't know anything about his life growing up, either; what he liked to eat or read, even where he was from.

As their leader, Shang had avoided socializing with the troops. He'd never joined in drinking games or jokes. After meals, he had always retreated to his tent to study battle plans and maps.

Then again, no one had ever sought him out. Now Mulan wished she'd gotten to know him better. She hadn't realized until now how dedicated Shang had been to ensuring the regiment became a team. Most other captains probably wouldn't even have known her name. But Shang would run alongside her and the other recruits to make sure no man was left behind, he sculpted each soldier's individual weaknesses into strengths, and he had even risked his life—for her.

Stop thinking like that, she thought miserably. *You sound like he's going to die.*

She watched his chest rise and fall, the movement so imperceptible she wondered if she imagined it. She couldn't even hear him breathe. Reaching for his wrist, she kept her hand over his, feeling for his pulse.

Still there. Still faint.

"Shang is not going to die," Mulan whispered aloud. She choked back a sob. "He's not."

But even she couldn't persuade herself. Moisture tingled in her eyes, and the swell in her throat hurt more and more as she tried to hold in her emotions. *He's not.*

Hot tears trickled down her cheeks as she unfolded her arms and sat up. She wiped her face, tasting the salt in her tears as they slipped into the corner of her mouth.

Her hands trembled at her side, and her head felt light. Fatigue was catching up with her, and she blamed it for her doubts.

Need to sleep, her body begged. *Just a little. Just for a few minutes.*

No. The world swayed. Her eyelids half closed. *Must watch Shang. Must. Watch.*

You can't take care of him if you don't take care of yourself. Sleep. Just a little.

Just a little. Finally, Mulan crawled away from Shang's side and retreated to the back corner of the tent, leaning against a pole. She hugged her arms against her chest and stretched out her legs over the frosted grass. Her breathing slowed.

She didn't know how long she slept—minutes or hours— before a burst of wind brushed her cheek and woke her.

Moonlight seeped into her eyes. Had the tent's flap

come loose? Mulan jerked upright with worry and started to get up to close the flap against the chill breeze.

But then she froze.

It wasn't moonlight at all, or a loose tent flap.

It was a man, leaning over next to Shang. He was dressed in a military uniform, but he wasn't one of Shang's soldiers, and they had to be days from the closest village. That was odd.

But even odder—he glowed. Was she dreaming? Mulan rubbed her eyes. He still glowed.

From his hair to his boots, he radiated a soft greenish blue, as if someone had put a lantern in the deepest part of the ocean. His ghostly face shone so brightly Mulan couldn't make out his features. His voice was low and soft. "Please don't die," he said to Shang. "It is not yet your time."

Careful to stay shrouded in the shadows, Mulan rose. She didn't recognize the stranger, and his uniform was blue like the rest of him, so she couldn't identify his rank. But she could tell his armor's quality was better than Shang's. A clue that he was an officer of high rank.

A general!

"My son," the general said, "can you hear me?"

Mulan held her breath. *My son?* If the man was Shang's father, then he was . . . General Li.

No, that's impossible. General Li is dead. I must be

dreaming. I must be so tired I even know I'm dreaming. She shrank back in her corner. General Li's body shimmered with watery blue light—and his boots, Mulan saw, barely touched the ground.

Definitely can't be real. I should go back to sleep.

But she couldn't. Not while General Li wept over his son's body. She watched his shoulders shake as he exhaled. It was a ragged, sorrow-ridden breath, one that touched Mulan to the core. If this ghost, this *spirit* truly was Shang's father, she had to do whatever she could to ease both their suffering.

She took a step toward him. If General Li saw her, he didn't acknowledge it. His attention was on his son.

"Do you remember, Shang, when you were a child?" he said. "Even then you were already my best student. Do you remember how your *ma* would scold you for studying military history instead of the classics, and how you turned her zither into a target for your shooting practice? I had to reprimand you, but inside, I was so proud. You weren't afraid of anything, except disappointing me. And when it finally came time for you to lead your own regiment into battle, I . . . I had such high hopes for you. But I should not have underestimated Shan-Yu's army. I failed you, my son."

Mulan pursed her lips, unsure how to address a ghost. "General Li?"

Shang's father turned to her, and a quiet gasp escaped Mulan's lips. The general's resemblance to his son was striking; they had the same probing, dark eyes, the same square jaw and earnest brow. But unlike Shang, gray streaked the general's hair along his temples, and a carefully groomed beard dressed the lower contours of his face.

Mulan composed herself. "I'm Ping. I'm your son's . . ." She stumbled over what to say. *Recruit? Soldier?* "I'm your son's friend."

At that, General Li's expression softened, and he bowed his head. "Ah, I see. Thank you for watching over him, Ping. You will be released from your duty shortly."

Mulan frowned at his words. What did he mean, she'd be released shortly? Was Shang going to die?

She started to ask him, but the question clung to her throat. So she said instead, "General Li, pardon me for asking, but—but how are you here?"

"Shang will not make it through the night," General Li informed her sadly, without answering her question. "He will join me in the Underworld."

"Sir," Mulan croaked, her voice crawling out of her lips, "what are you saying? You can't mean that Captain Li is going to d—"

"Yes," General Li cut her off. "I thank you for all you have done. But there is nothing that could have saved my son. Shang's spirit is already on its way to Diyu. In the morning, he will pass on."

Diyu. Her grandmother had told her stories about the Underworld when she was a girl. About how every person, good or bad, descended into Diyu upon death for judgment. There, King Yama, the ruler of Diyu, would judge one's time on Earth and determine how long one must stay in the Underworld as a ghost. Some would have to wait a year, others centuries. Some would never leave. They became demons.

Be a good girl, Grandmother Fa used to say, *or King Yama will turn you into a demon! Respect your ancestors—or none of their ghosts will greet you when you descend to Diyu and guide you through the Underworld.*

Mulan blinked. All those tales . . . they were just folklore. Legends. Weren't they?

"No," she whispered, shaking her head at General Li. "No. There has to be a way to save him."

"I'm afraid there is not."

"You're a spirit," she reasoned. "And yet, you've managed to break the boundaries between here and Diyu. You must know of a way I can save Shang."

General Li hesitated. His face was sorrowful. "I shouldn't be here. My family owes you its gratitude, Ping, for watching Shang over these last few hours—"

"No," Mulan said. "You don't." She curled her fists, sucked in a deep breath. "*I* owe Shang *my* gratitude. It's because of me he's dying. Your son saved me from Shan-Yu. If not for him, *I* would be dead. It is I who owe him a debt. And I will do whatever it takes to save his life."

General Li studied her. "Anything?"

"Yes," she whispered. "Tell me if there's a way to save him. I heard what you said—that it isn't his time to die yet. He is a good man, your son. Please help me save him."

General Li stroked the sides of his beard, considering. "There is a way," he said at last. "But it is impossible."

"Tell me."

"The only way is to change King Yama's mind," the general replied. "But Shang's name has already appeared in King Yama's book of judgment. He cannot be erased from it."

"It is only impossible if I don't try," Mulan said fiercely. "And I will."

"You are a man of unusual fortitude, Ping." A trace of hope lifted the general's voice, but only slightly. He nodded. "You will need it, if you are to save my son. Though I suggest you wake up first."

Mulan tilted her head. "What?"

Her vision blurred, and the sound of a large gong boomed. She jerked awake, hitting her head on the tent pole behind her as her ears buzzed and rang. She clutched her temples.

Hadn't she just been standing next to Shang? Now here she was back in the corner, her armor in a pile beside her.

She kicked the ground in frustration. *Was it really only a dream?*

She sat up, glanced at Shang. He lay motionless as before, but he was still breathing.

That was a relief. Then she remembered what General Li had said—that Shang would die in the morning.

Mulan peeked out of the tent, glimpsing the black, black night. Not one star in sight. Sunrise was perhaps several hours away.

She sat back down, clasped her arms together, and shivered. Mushu and Cri-Kee were asleep, and there was no sign of a gong.

Maybe I'm going crazy, she thought. *First, that dream about General Li. And now this.*

Then—

"*PINGGGGG,*" a beast roared. The gong sounded again. *BOOOMMMMMM!* Another roar. "*PINGGGGG!*"

Chapter Five

Mulan hastily put on her armor and grabbed her sword, then swept aside the tent's flap and went outside to confront whoever—or whatever—was yelling for her.

But there was no one. Nothing.

The camp was still as before. Even the embers in the fire had died out by now. All was dark, and only the rhythmic wheeze of sleeping soldiers accompanied her.

Mulan frowned. She could have sworn she'd heard something, but she must have been wrong. Still, as she turned back to her tent, something rustled in the distance.

"There you are," a deep voice rumbled.

Mulan immediately whirled and held up her sword. She half expected to see the Huns surrounding the camp, but she was still alone.

Or so it seemed.

"Stop dawdling." The intruder spoke so loudly he ought to have woken the entire camp, but no one stirred. Did they not hear his thunderous voice?

"Are you a soldier or a tombstone? Didn't anyone tell you we're in a hurry?"

Mulan ventured out into the camp, following the direction of the voice. She carefully stepped over her sleeping friends, then headed toward a thick tree trunk in a dark corner. "Who's there? Show yourself."

The intruder growled. "Show myself? I'm standing right in front of you. Look up."

Mulan raised her eyes, then jumped back, startled.

Not a tree trunk at all, but an immense stone lion! He was as tall as Khan and as wide as her tent. His round eyes were orange as persimmons, and an enormous, elegant jade pendant adorned his neck. He flexed his front paws into the snow, revealing dagger-sharp claws.

Mulan brandished her sword and opened her mouth to yell for her fellow soldiers, but the stone lion moved, stepping into the moonlight with one massive paw.

She gasped. "What . . . what are you?"

"I am ShiShi," the stone lion announced, proudly and regally. He peered at her, as if waiting for her to look impressed. Mulan remained silent.

"I am the guardian of the Li family, responsible for aiding every Li hero for over twenty generat—"

"So you're here to help Shang?" Mulan interrupted. She glanced back at her tent, where Mushu, her own guardian, was still fast asleep.

ShiShi frowned. "You didn't expect to do it alone, did you?" He squinted at her, then sniffed with disdain. "No wonder the general sent for me. You're punier than I expected. Small and unpunctual, two worrisome traits in a soldier."

Mulan overlooked the insults. Her eyes widened at ShiShi's words, and hope flared in her heart. "Shang's father sent you?"

"You promised him you would save his son, did you not? I'm here to help you fulfill that promise . . . although now I'm beginning to think it's a fruitless quest. You're no match for the Underworld."

"There's only one way to find out," said Mulan. "Will you take me there?"

"Climb on my back," ShiShi huffed. "Be careful when you take the braids, and don't pull on my mane."

His mane was thick and curly, despite being made of stone. She reached for one of the elaborate braids, then hesitated, wondering whether she should wake Mushu to bring him with her.

No, he'd just try to talk me out of going. He'd say it's too dangerous.

Dangerous or not, she'd made up her mind. She wouldn't let Shang die, not if there was a chance to save him.

"Hurry, little soldier," barked ShiShi. "We don't have much time."

Mulan grabbed ShiShi's braids and settled on his back. Before she could ask another question, ShiShi let out a terrible roar.

Suddenly the earth gave a terrible quake, and the ground beneath them split. As Mulan jolted back from the tremor, her sword fell out of her grasp and clattered onto the ground.

"My sword!" Mulan shouted, trying to jump off ShiShi to retrieve it. "Wait, it's my father's!" But the lion couldn't hear her, not as the earth trembled and his roar echoed across the camp.

"I hope you have a strong stomach, little soldier!" shouted ShiShi. Then, without any further warning, ShiShi leapt through the hole.

And down, down they fell into the depths of Diyu, the Underworld.

Chapter Six

Mulan clutched ShiShi's mane with both hands, holding on so tightly she was sure her knuckles turned white. Not that she could see anything. She might as well have closed her eyes—the fall into Diyu was so dark she couldn't tell whether they were actually falling, or whether ShiShi was bounding down an invisible tunnel.

It was probably a good thing she hadn't had much to eat. Even with an empty stomach, Mulan felt her insides twist and roil as they fell.

Be strong, she told herself. *Be strong for Shang.*

She didn't know how long she pressed her face against ShiShi's stone head, for time squeezed and stretched. It was all she could do to gasp for breath as they careened down and down.

ShiShi landed on his paws with a thump. "Still there, little soldier?"

Mulan caught her breath and waited a beat for her stomach to stop churning. "Still here."

The stone lion grunted, a sound that somehow indicated he was half impressed that she was still in one piece and half disappointed that the fall hadn't terrified her. "Most men get sick on the way down here."

I'm not most men, Mulan thought, but she kept quiet and climbed off ShiShi's back. It was still dark, so it took her a long moment before she realized the change in ShiShi.

"You're . . ."

Gone was his carved stone, replaced by a rippling coat of fur and a thick, coarse mane.

"Yes, yes," ShiShi interrupted. "This is how I would appear if I were normally your guardian. I know, I'm magnificent. You can thank the magic in this place for letting you see me this way. Otherwise, not being a member of the Li family, you wouldn't have the honor."

Mulan rolled her eyes in the shadows. Even Mushu wasn't *this* arrogant.

She dusted her pants and inhaled. The air was musty and dank, but it was warmer down here. After being in the snow for so many days, she had forgotten what it was like not to be cold.

Slowly, her vision adjusted to the darkness. Sharp,

pointed stalactites hung from the ceiling. In the dim light, they glinted like iron knives, but when she reached out to touch one—

"Limestone," she murmured. They were in a cave of some sort. "Is this Diyu?"

"Not quite," ShiShi replied, in a hushed but harsh tone. Ahead, deeper into the cave, was a vermilion gate, its color somehow bright against the cave's worn stones. ShiShi tilted his head toward it. "Move quickly now. It's best not to be—"

"Seen," Mulan whispered, finishing the warning for him. Shadows flickered from the near distance, and footsteps—that weren't their own—shuffled in the dark. Her jaw slackened as she realized she and ShiShi were most definitely not alone.

A horde of monstrous-looking creatures surrounded them. Their eyes bulged like yellow moons studded with blood-red pupils. Some had horns, others scales or fur thick as a bear's. Not one looked like another. Yet despite their beastly features, they stood on two feet and had two—or four—arms, almost like humans.

Demons.

"No trespassers," they hissed, pointing their spears and swords at Mulan's and ShiShi's throats. "No trespassers allowed."

ShiShi snarled at the demons. "I'm here on business."

"No trespassers. All trespassers must die."

"Well, I cannot," ShiShi said with a sniff. "I'm actually made of stone."

The demons were guards, realized Mulan. She flicked a glance at the gate's two vermilion-painted doors. That had to be the way into Diyu.

"This one's still living," one of the demons said, staring at Mulan. White hair protruded from his inky blue scalp, and unlike the others, he carried *two* weapons. He sniffed her, and Mulan wished she still had her sword. "Still fresh."

The rest of the demon guards turned to her now.

Great.

Surrounded, Mulan backed against the cave wall. Before the demons got too close, she leapt up and quickly twisted off a stalactite. She held the makeshift weapon above her head, ready to strike any demon that dared attack her. But there were so many of them!

They're probably stronger than men, she thought, taking in their swelling muscles, their curved nails, their rotten yet sharp teeth.

"We're here to see King Yama," she shouted. "Let us pass."

"No trespassers," the demons repeated. "And especially no *human* trespassers."

"Don't you know who I am?" ShiShi thundered, whipping his tail back and forth to keep the demons at a distance. He bared his teeth at them. "I am the legendary guardian of General Li's esteemed family. Now open the gates and let me pass with this boy—or King Yama will be furious."

A few of the guards hesitated.

"He will punish you all," Mulan agreed. "He'll . . . he'll—"

"He'll throw you into the Mountain of Flames," ShiShi said diabolically. "Or better yet—the river."

Mulan had no idea what ShiShi was talking about, but his threats clearly impressed the demons. Their yellow eyes wobbled with fear and uncertainty. Their hesitation grew, and they lowered their weapons.

"What about the living one?" the blue demon said, cocking his head at Mulan.

"This is my little soldier," ShiShi replied. "He's not . . . entirely human. There's a bit of fairy blood in him."

"But he's so small."

"I'm stronger than I look," Mulan spoke for herself. She kicked at the closest demon, smashing his wooden spear in two.

The blue demon didn't look convinced, but he withdrew his weapons. "Very well. We'll let King Yama decide. Open the gate and take them across the bridge."

Bridge?

The blue demon snatched the stalactite from Mulan's hand and crushed it in his fist. Someone tied a rope over her wrists, then pushed her toward the vermilion gates. The other demons followed, trampling behind and swiping their swords and spears at the stalactites as if it were a game.

Even in their dark surroundings, the paint on the gates was crisp and bright—a sharp contrast from everything around them. Neither door of the portal had bars or handles—no way of pushing or sliding them open—and round bronze casts of demon faces decorated the wooden panels. The eyes on the bronze medallions flickered with fire. Mulan could have sworn they were all watching her. Some faces smiled, a few frowned, and more than a few snarled.

"Behold," murmured ShiShi at her side, "the Gates of Diyu. The entrance to the Underworld."

Two demon soldiers stood on either side of the gates and stomped their feet. Then they each pressed one of the demon faces, so quickly Mulan couldn't tell which ones they touched. The gates let out a loud tremble, then began to slide open.

As soon as the opening was wide enough for her to pass through, the demons pushed her inside. ShiShi materialized beside her.

"Stop gawking," the blue demon said, snickering. "You're in the Underworld now."

The Gates of Diyu thudded shut behind them, but Mulan didn't look back. The view ahead nearly made her forget where they'd come from.

Mulan's breath caught in her throat as she stepped onto a ledge inside a cavernous chamber—so high the blue demon's taunt echoed for minutes, and so deep, she could hear a river gushing far below. The cave had expanded a thousandfold in height, depth, and width. She could hardly see the other side.

But it appeared the other side was where they were heading. For the demons prodded her forward, toward the mouth of a stone-paved bridge arching away from the ledge.

"The Bridge of Helplessness," ShiShi marveled. "Few have crossed it and been permitted to return to the other side. From here there's no turning back, little soldier."

ShiShi's warning didn't frighten Mulan. She was focused on holding her own against the demons, who seemed intent on tripping her. She watched her footing as she ascended the three steps that led onto the bridge. The stones were washed a bleak gray; they were smooth and flat, likely worn down by the demons' constant marching.

No structure such as the Bridge of Helplessness could have existed outside of Diyu. Mulan recognized the impossibility of it even before taking her first step. No ropes suspended it, and no poles supported it. Yet the bridge was so long Mulan couldn't see its end.

The demons made her step onto the bridge first. ShiShi followed, his shadow dwarfing hers. The lion was nearly as wide as the bridge itself, but Mulan hardly noticed. There was too much emptiness ahead—and below.

The railing was way too low for comfort. Mulan wasn't afraid of heights, but a glimpse of what lay beneath the bridge made the muscles in her legs tighten. It was impossible to gauge how high the bridge was, given that below were levels upon levels of harsh ridges and cliffs, stone deserts, and villages overrun with ghosts and demons. Somewhere far down, she thought she spotted the Mountain of Flames ShiShi had mentioned to the demons. Plenty of screams came from that direction. And she'd been right about the river. Its black waters surged, winding in a serpentine path across the craggy terrain below.

Wooden torches lit the bridge, the flames dancing like wild fireflies trapped in glass lanterns. Mulan tried to keep track of how far they'd gone by counting the torches, but after 108, she stopped counting.

It was hard to imagine that only hours ago, she'd been climbing the Tung-Shao Pass's snowy cliffs, firing cannons with Mushu on her shoulder. Her training as a soldier had not prepared her for the Underworld—for demons and magical caves and who knew what else!

Even with Shang's massive guardian now at her side, she was uncertain how she'd fare in Diyu or if they'd even be able to rescue Shang. She missed her own guardian. Yes, ShiShi had centuries of experience guiding China's greatest military heroes—but Mushu understood her, and he knew her secret. Mulan didn't know if ShiShi would still stand by her if he found out she was a woman. And a woman soldier, at that.

Would Shang? she wondered, remembering how much she'd wanted to tell him the truth when he'd woken up just before they had reached camp.

Something glinted to the side, catching the torchlight as well as Mulan's attention. It grew more brilliant as she progressed down the Bridge of Helplessness, but she couldn't figure out where it was coming from.

"ShiShi, do you see that?" she asked, glancing over her shoulder at the lion. "Those lights flickering on the cave stones."

"I don't see anything," the lion replied.

"The lights look like they're bouncing off something. Like large pieces of glass . . . or mirrors."

"Perhaps," ShiShi allowed. "But mirrors will be the least of our concern in Diyu, little soldier. They're not going to help us rescue Li Shang." He growled at the blue-faced demon behind them. "Omph. Stop pushing me."

Mulan lowered her gaze back to the demons, whose march had synchronized behind her and now slowed because there was something blocking their path.

Not something, Mulan realized as she got closer. Some-one. *Ghosts.*

Four of them sat cross-legged on the bridge, looking bored and playing a game of mah-jongg. Unlike General Li, they glowed orange and yellow instead of blue. Mulan wondered what the colors meant.

The ghost in the north position was the first to see her. A grin broke across his face, and he nudged his opponent on the left. All at once, they got up, crossed their arms, and floated toward Mulan.

"What do you think you're doing, boy?"

"You can't cross the Bridge of Helplessness if you're alive."

"I'm here on business," Mulan said, borrowing ShiShi's line.

"Business?" the ghosts exclaimed. They turned to the demons escorting Mulan and ShiShi across the bridge.

"Who is this?" one of the ghosts, a woman, demanded. "Who are you bringing into Diyu?"

"I am Ping," Mulan answered for herself. "I'm here to see King Yama."

She tried to slip past the ghosts, but they followed her.

"King Yama doesn't like visitors."

"Especially *living* visitors." A ghost leered at the demon guards through his spectacles. "You should know better, Languai."

Languai, the blue demon who appeared to be in charge, spat. "Go away and mind your business."

"We guard the bridge just as much as you do," the ghost reminded him.

"Perhaps we should throw him off the bridge," another ghost suggested. "Then he won't be living anymore. King Yama would like that better."

"You'll do no such thing," ShiShi growled from behind. "The boy's with me. I have an appointment with King Yama."

The oldest ghost's eyebrow rose. "An appointment? That's unusual." He circled ShiShi. "And with a guardian, no less."

"Stop giving the boy such a hard time," the female ghost urged. She smiled at Mulan, kindly yet sadly. "He reminds me of my son; he was a soldier, too. Let him cross."

"Yes, let him cross," agreed another ghost. "I want to know what King Yama thinks of him. Nothing ever happens here anyway."

The ghost with the spectacles frowned. His aura was the brightest of the four, as orange as ShiShi's eyes. He studied Mulan. "There's something different about this one."

"Jiao, you always say that."

"No, really. I don't know what it is."

"The guardian said he has fairy blood."

"That's not it," Jiao said. "There's something else. I can feel it."

"You don't feel anything. You're dead."

While the ghosts bickered, the demons pushed Mulan forward.

"Stupid gossips," Languai muttered under his breath. "Be happy. Now you've gotten the attention of the ghosts."

"Is that bad?" Mulan asked.

The demon laughed maliciously. "You'll see."

Jiao, the ghost with the spectacles, was still watching her, a curious expression unfolding over his translucent face. "Let's keep an eye on this one. It isn't every day we see an outsider visit Diyu. There *is* something different about him."

Mulan swallowed. She *knew* what was different about her, but there was no way the ghosts could sense that she was a girl, was there?

Languai poked Mulan's rib with the hilt of his sword. "Stop dallying. We don't have all night."

Mulan cringed from his jab. *All night,* she repeated to herself.

She craned her neck up until she could see the very top of the cave. There was a hole in the ceiling, just small enough to permit a soft beam of moonlight. When she squinted, she could make out a faint outline of the moon. It was full and bright, hanging like a golden pearl against the black sky.

It's still night, she thought. *I have until morning to save Shang.*

She quickened her pace, forcing the demons to hurry after her.

"I've never seen a mortal so eager to meet King Yama," Languai muttered after her.

Another snorted. "That's because he doesn't know any better. Look at him, rushing toward his doom. Even if King Yama doesn't kill him, he won't last long in Diyu."

Mulan ignored the demons. Their words didn't frighten her.

She'd crossed the point of no return knowing the price: that once she entered the Underworld, the world above would become a distant dream—one she might never wake and return to, ever again.

But fear, guilt, grief—she'd buried those emotions the moment General Li told her she had a chance to bring Shang back. Now, mere steps from the mouth of the Underworld, courage swelled within her. Courage and hope and determination.

She only hoped they would be enough.

Chapter Seven

Every time Mulan thought she'd reached the end of the bridge, she was wrong. The stone path seemed to extend forever. Every now and then she felt as though she were actually sprinting across the back of some stone-scaled dragon that kept growing and growing to keep her from reaching its tail.

If it was a test of her determination, Mulan didn't fail. Eventually, the number of torchlights on the bridge decreased, and no new ones appeared. *Twelve, eleven, ten lights*, she counted . . . then, *Finally!* Mulan spied the other side of this vast cavern.

She stepped off the Bridge of Helplessness and paused to catch her breath. She looked up, surprised to see the sky.

I guess we're no longer underground, she thought, her eyes skimming the silvery clouds for traces of the moon. There was something peaceful—and beautiful—about the sky here. The stars appeared closer; they shone brighter than any she'd ever seen. She wasn't sure if it was the same blue sky that blanketed the world above or a different one stitched especially for Diyu. She suspected the latter.

Shadows flickered ahead; behind her the demon guards huffed and puffed to catch up with her.

She didn't wait for them, or for ShiShi. She pushed forward, entering a passageway brightly lit with lanterns and guarded by armed demon sentries. The walls stretched as far as she could see, and the ground gradually sloped upward, creating a hill into which hundreds of stone steps had been carved. She couldn't make out what was at the top of the hill, for she was at the tail end of the longest line she had ever seen—all ghosts!

There had to be thousands, no, *hundreds* of thousands of them.

"What are they waiting for?"

Languai, the first to catch up with her, cackled at her confusion. "To see King Yama. You didn't think you were the only one with an appointment, did you?" He grinned. "You'll be dead just in time to meet him."

The demons all laughed at Mulan's foolishness. Mulan ignored their taunts and turned to ShiShi.

"These are the recent dead," ShiShi murmured. The ghosts' expressions were long and grave or surprised, as if they'd only just discovered that they had died. A good number had arrows in their chests or other terrible wounds of combat; some looked to have been poisoned, and many were very old.

"Wait here," Mulan said to ShiShi so they wouldn't lose their place in the queue.

"Where are you going?" ShiShi barked.

She slipped deeper into the throng, making for a rocky outcrop where she might get a better view up the hill to where King Yama was. The demon sentries were too busy keeping order in the line to acknowledge her: ghosts *were* gossipy, and prone to getting into fights with one another, Mulan noted. Maybe it was because they were bored.

A few dozen places ahead of ShiShi, she thought she recognized some of the Huns that had perished in the avalanche. She didn't see Shan-Yu, though—

"Ping!" someone shouted. "Ping, is that you?"

Mulan scanned the crowd ahead, recognizing the voice of one of the soldiers that had been in her regiment only yesterday. She hadn't been close to him, as she was with Ling, Yao, and Chien-Po, but Captain Li's intense training had created a bond among all his recruits. She jumped off the rock, her voice tight with emotion. "Xiaobo?"

He looked the same as always, a thin black mustache

slanting down to the sides of his chin and a defined bulge protruding from the belly of his armor. He turned around so she could see the arrow in his back. "Got shot by a Hun."

"I'm so sorry," Mulan whispered.

"Don't be." Xiaobo shrugged. "It doesn't hurt anymore. Besides, I've got Lei and Xing to keep me company."

He stepped to the side so Mulan could reunite with two more soldiers from her regiment. In spite of the smiles they wore when they saw her, they too had been felled by arrows. Her chest grew tight.

We left the mountain pass so hastily, we never grieved for our comrades who died in battle. Too many. She glanced at Lei, Xiaobo, and Xing. *I barely got a chance to get to know them.*

"You look like you just got here," Lei remarked. "Don't worry, we'll catch you up to speed."

"All these Huns keep popping up in line." Xing cocked his head back at Huns behind them. "Hundreds of them, all shivering—like they got buried in the snow." He elbowed Mulan, a conspiratorial gleam in his eye. "Does that mean what I think it does?"

She nodded slowly. "They ambushed us, but we managed to defeat them."

Xing's face lit up. "Yes! I knew we'd win."

Unlike his friends, Lei didn't look thrilled. He stared

at the arrow lodged in his belly. "Ping, did you die in the battle, too?"

Mulan decided it was best not to answer that. "I need to speak with King Yama," she said carefully. "Are you waiting for him as well?"

"Yes, and it's the worst." Xing shuddered. "I was pretty good when I was alive—I think. I never overate my share of rice, never gave my ma any trouble, and didn't cry or curse when I got conscripted. Or when Captain Li Shang slapped my knuckles during training." He winced. "That really hurt."

Lei rolled his eyes. "I just hope I won't have to stay too long in Diyu. I'd rather go back to Earth as a cockroach than wait in line any longer."

The line finally moved, and Xiaobo, Lei, and Xing inched forward.

Xiaobo let out a sigh. "We've already waited all day, but we're still way back in line. From the looks of it, we're going to be here forever."

Mulan glanced up at the moon, still faintly visible high above. *I can't wait forever. I only have until the morning.*

"I'm glad I got to see you fellows," she said, about to rest a hand on Xiaobo's shoulder. Remembering he was a ghost now, she drew her hand back.

"Ping, where are you going?"

"My business with King Yama can't wait," she replied, and pushed her way forward up the gently sloping hill. Stealth was not a skill Captain Li had drilled into them during their training, and Mulan was grateful for her light-footedness and smaller figure. The shades didn't pay any attention to her. They were busy talking to one another, and there were more than a few reunions—some happy, some not so friendly.

Her goal was the dais on the top of the hill, furnished with a wooden table piled high with scrolls and books. Was it King Yama, or one of Yama's minions sitting behind the desk? The books blocked her view.

A commotion broke out ahead, and Mulan saw a lion's tail angrily whipping about.

"I am not cutting the line! I may *rightfully* go to the front, because I am not dead!"

"ShiShi!" Mulan muttered, angling her way through the crowd toward the immense lion.

ShiShi grunted when he saw her. "There are you, little soldier."

"I thought I told you to wait in line."

He looked at her sternly. "One doesn't sneak into King Yama's throne room. One strides in proudly and with dignity."

Mulan cast a sidelong glance at the demonic guards standing along the line. "I don't think that's a good idea—"

"King Yama!" ShiShi shouted, his deep voice reverberating across the hollow chamber. "I am the great guardian of the Li family, and I am here regarding an urgent matter. I request an audience with you. King Yama!"

No one responded except the angry ghosts who swarmed around him, shrieking and cursing, but ShiShi powered through them toward the dais.

Mulan grabbed ShiShi's mane, and together they ran up the hill. The shouting and shrieking spread. Angry ghosts snatched at them, but their shadowy fingers slipped right through Mulan's armor.

"Guards!" the ghosts began to shout. "They're cutting the line."

The pandemonium grew until the entire chamber reverberated so loudly Mulan couldn't even understand what the ghosts in front of her face were shouting at her. Then—

"ORDER!"

The cave walls boomed, tiny rocks tumbling down from the ceiling onto the ghosts and demons below.

Mulan's knees quaked.

"I WILL HAVE ORDER IN MY COURT."

Mulan and ShiShi snapped into the line, straightening before the terrible voice. Demon sentries grabbed her and ShiShi.

"BRING THE INTRUDERS TO ME. NOW."

Chapter Eight

King Yama, god and ruler of the Underworld, did not look happy to see them.

His lips, barely visible under his thick peppery beard, twisted into a scowl. His eyebrows, which slanted up like two thick storm clouds and were so long they curled down his temples, furrowed with displeasure.

Mulan didn't know whether she should be awed or frightened. After all, it was the first time she had ever encountered a deity. To her surprise, Yama didn't glow like his subjects, and he looked nothing like the demons. Yet his appearance was monstrous.

Wrinkles contorted his face, and his cheeks were ruddy; his eyes flickered a fiery red and yellow. His neck was thick as the trunk of a willow tree, and his wild black hair was so abundant it rivaled ShiShi's mane. When he stood, as he did now, the top of his heavy gold crown disappeared into the dark space above, and his black and emerald robes flooded down the steps past his desk.

His eyes, hard, calculating, and currently an irritated shade of yellow, bored into Mulan.

It took her a moment to figure out why: she wasn't bowing! Even ShiShi had bent into a deep bow at her side.

Mulan hurriedly copied the lion. As she stared at the ground, King Yama lowered himself back down with a harrumph. His throne, a wooden chair with red-tasseled silk cushions, creaked under his massive weight.

Mulan peeked, lifting her eyes from the ground past the nine steps up to King Yama's dais. She watched Yama open one of the large books on his desk and resume writing in it. Two brass lanterns, shaped like dragons' heads, hovered over his work.

She waited as patiently as she could, expecting King Yama to address her and ShiShi, but the ruler of the Underworld kept writing.

All day and night, King Yama works behind his desk, Mulan's grandmother had told her. *He rarely ventures into the Underworld himself.*

So far, Grandmother Fa's story held up. Yama's

expression was severe, and he seemed grumpy that the papers and scrolls piled higher than his chair.

He didn't look up at them again.

Mulan frowned. She hadn't come all this way to be ignored.

ShiShi was clearly thinking the same thing. The lion had furtively taken a few steps closer to King Yama's throne, and Mulan sidled up next to him.

"Don't think I can't see you," King Yama muttered, his nose still in his book.

Mulan's body snapped up. "Sire, I—"

"Return to the back of the line," King Yama said, scribbling furiously. Ink stained the ends of his long emerald sleeves. "Your indiscretion has been noted. Everyone waits his turn."

"I'm not dead," Mulan said. "And I'm not in line. I'm here to ask—"

King Yama finally looked up from his book, thick brows knitting angrily. "I DON'T CARE," he roared. "Back of the line."

ShiShi glared at Mulan. "Let me do the talking from now on."

With one leap, he bounded up the stairs, stopping just two steps below King Yama's desk. "Your Majesty, you must recognize me. I am the great guardian of the Li family, the protector of the esteemed General Li before he passed into your domain."

"Didn't you hear me?" King Yama pounded his fist on his desk, and the demon guards raised their weapons. "I said, back of the line."

ShiShi opened his mouth, which must have been the last straw—because King Yama gave a thunderous clap with his monstrously large hands.

ShiShi froze midword. His apricot-colored tail grayed, and his mane, spiked from the flurry of danger since meeting King Yama, hardened.

He was stone again, and still as a statue.

"Arrogant guardian," King Yama muttered. "The stone ones are always the worst. So entitled."

Mulan held her breath, her mind reeling, frantically trying to think what she should say or do now. She needed to be careful. She started to ascend the stairs, keeping her head bowed humbly.

"And this one?" the ghost at the front of the line called, pointing at Mulan.

Yama waved his hand. Instantly, his demon guards prepared to jostle Mulan to the back of the line.

But Mulan was too fast. She jumped, balancing atop two demons' spears, stepped onto one of the demon's shoulders, and leapt onto King Yama's dais.

She closed King Yama's book and rested her palms on his desk. The ghosts and demons gasped at her audacity, but Mulan didn't care. *Now* she had King Yama's attention.

Mulan bowed her head as low as she could, unsure of the etiquette for addressing the ruler of the Underworld. She didn't want to anger him further, but she had to make him listen. "Your Majesty, I know you are very busy, but my matter is urgent. I'm here to plead for the life of General Li's son, Li Shang."

King Yama raised a bushy eyebrow. "And you are?"

Mulan swallowed and lifted her hands off his desk. How was she to answer that? Even ShiShi didn't know she was really a girl. Could King Yama, a god himself, see through her disguise?

"Fa P-Ping, sire."

King Yama's huffed. "Ping, you say?" He flipped through another enormous tome on his desk. "There is no record of a Fa Ping in my book."

"That isn't the point," Mulan persisted. She regained her poise. "I need you to look into Li Shang's case. Captain Li Shang, son of—"

"I know who he is," King Yama said. "He suffers from a sword wound inflicted by Shan-Yu." He glanced at an hourglass on his desk. Its streaming sands were inky black. "He'll die in a few hours, when the sun rises."

He turned a page absentmindedly. "As for you, Ping. Didn't anyone warn you that no mortals are permitted in Diyu? Your presence here is forbidden. I will make note of your transgression so the guards can see to it that you return here as a proper ghost. Do you prefer death by burning or dismemberment?"

Mulan steeled herself. "I'm not here to intrude, Your Majesty. I'm here to bring Captain Li Shang back to the land of the living."

At that, King Yama set down his quill and laughed. It was a terrible, terrible laugh that rebounded across the long chamber and silenced the ghosts' whispering and gossiping. "Back to the land of the living? Ha! You're a funny one, Ping, especially for someone who does not exist."

"It's not a joke," said Mulan. "I'm here to bring Captain Li back. It is not yet his time to die."

"And who are you to decide that?" King Yama's amusement quickly shifted into anger. "Hundreds arrive in my realm every hour. *I* am the one who decides whether they stay in Diyu or whether they return to Earth or rise to Heaven. Do you know how much consideration goes into making such decisions? Do you know how difficult it is to decide whether someone should go to Heaven as a reward for his good behavior on Earth, or whether he should stay in Diyu to make amends for that one time he kicked a dog or had too much to drink? Or whether he should make those amends back on Earth in a new life? There is a schedule to keep, boy, and you are wasting my precious time."

I can't give up now, Mulan thought. *Not after ShiShi and I came all this way.*

She'd try a different tactic. "It sounds like a terrible burden," she agreed, thinking fast. "But an important one. Perhaps I could help you. And in exchange for my help, you might . . . consider letting Li Shang go."

"You think you, a mortal, can handle Diyu's records?" King Yama swept his arm across a stack of loose pages. Mulan held up her hands, blocking the papers from smacking her face as Yama had intended. She caught several in her hand and placed them back on his desk.

For such a cantankerous deity, Yama had beautiful calligraphy. It helped ease her fear of him. He couldn't be *that* terrible if all he did was sit behind a desk all day writing names into his book.

Don't get your hopes up, Mulan.

"I apologize," she said. "That was presumptuous of me. But . . . but if you look at hundreds every hour, maybe you've made a mistake here and there."

King Yama's nostrils flared. "A mistake?"

"Captain Li Shang was wounded saving me," Mulan continued, before King Yama could protest further. "If not for me, he wouldn't be dying, and we"—she gestured at herself and at ShiShi, still frozen as stone—"would not be here bothering you.

"But we are here now, because Captain Li Shang is a good man. He's a brave warrior, an outstanding leader, and a loyal friend. China needs him."

"And China will have him back," King Yama replied. "I have taken note of Li Shang's courage and abilities."

Mulan's skin prickled. "What do you mean, China will have him back?"

Yama squinted at his book, tracing his finger across the page. "Ah, yes. Captain Li Shang is scheduled to be reincarnated, quite soon after his death, actually. That is why his spirit is already here in Diyu. He is being prepared for his new life. Consider it an honor."

"China needs him *now*," countered Mulan. "The Huns may be defeated, but there will always be threats against the Emperor—he needs a man like Shang to protect him, to protect China." Her voice quavered. "You already took General Li. Please. Please do not take his son, too."

"I was not given this role because I have compassion," King Yama said bluntly. He returned his attention to his work and scribbled something into his book. "Leave now or face the consequences. I remind you, death by burning or by dismemberment."

Mulan knew this was her dismissal, but she wouldn't budge. She could hear the demon soldiers stirring restlessly behind her, and she wondered if they were too afraid to come this close to King Yama, for they made no move to force her away.

"I came here to save Shang." Mulan clenched her teeth. "I won't leave without him."

Yama set his quill down. He looked like he was going to yell at her again, but instead, he snorted with disbelief. "You're willing to risk everything to save the life of your captain?"

"I am."

King Yama tapped his fingers on his desk. "Your determination intrigues me, Ping. More than that, you've amused me." Yama chuckled, then leaned back in his chair, looking weary. "It's not every day a mortal succeeds in entering my realm and piquing my curiosity, so I will give you a chance." He wagged a finger at Mulan. "But that's all. A chance."

A tiny flutter of hope bloomed in Mulan's chest. She straightened, eager to hear what the ruler of Diyu had to say.

"My realm is vast. There are hundreds of chambers and levels in Diyu. Most evoke terror and despair, but others test you to see if you are worthy. After all, most of the souls that pass into my realm are not meant to stay here forever. That is the case with Captain Li Shang. And you, eventually. You've risked your life to come see me and beg for Li Shang's life. So I will give you the opportunity to do so, as a wager." He paused meaningfully. "If you can find Shang's spirit, and escape my realm with him before sunrise, then you will be free to go."

"All of us?" Mulan clarified.

"Yes. You, Captain Li Shang"—Yama flicked his fingers at ShiShi—"and your overconfident cat."

"But he's—"

King Yama put his hands together for another thunderous clap, startling Mulan so she nearly lost her balance.

At her side, ShiShi let out a quiet whimper. Color returned to his coat, and his eyes slowly regained clarity.

"That . . ." he said with a shudder, "was unpleasant."

"Silence!" Yama shouted. "You are lucky I've relented. Annoy me further, Guardian, and you will not leave my realm. The city of Youdu downstairs could use a new statue."

For once, ShiShi shut his mouth.

"Now," King Yama said, addressing Mulan again. "Where were we? Ah yes, the price you'll have to pay if you lose our wager." He clasped his hands together, looking sly.

"Ping . . ." ShiShi whispered, "be careful."

Mulan ignored ShiShi's warning. "Tell me."

"My realm is a dangerous place, and those who dwell

here are not . . . accustomed to outsiders. Should you die here, or should you fail to escape Diyu with Captain Li's spirit . . . then you—the mysterious Ping with no record in my book—shall stay in Diyu as punishment for trespassing into my realm. You will be my prisoner here. Forever."

Forever. Mulan quailed, seeing the dismal world around her. The line of ghosts stretching endlessly, the scenes of Diyu she had seen from the Bridge of Helplessness.

A shiver ran down her spine, but she bowed her head respectfully. "Thank you for this offer, Your Majesty."

King Yama laughed. "I thought you might want to reconsider—"

"I don't," said Mulan staunchly. "I accept. *We* accept."

Yama blinked, taken aback. "Very well, then."

Yama pointed at the moon, which appeared closer here than it had outside on the bridge. "That is your clock. You have until the sun rises. Time passes differently here than up above, so be mindful. Once you can see only the dark side of the moon, your time is up."

Mulan looked up. The moon was round and bright, but a thin black rim already darkened its edge.

She pushed aside her fears. She had the rest of the night to rescue Shang. They'd battled thousands of Huns together and saved China. Finding him and escaping from the Underworld was just one more battle. She could do this.

King Yama clapped, and his lanterns floated away, illuminating a white stone archway behind his desk.

Mulan studied the archway as she approached it. Etched into the stones were the words ALL OF LIFE IS A DREAM WALKING, ALL OF DEATH IS A GOING HOME.

She recognized the proverb. It was one her schoolteachers had made her memorize and write over and over to practice her calligraphy. She'd never understood its meaning . . . but now, standing at the threshold of the Underworld, something in her throat tightened as she read the familiar words again.

As King Yama's throne room disappeared behind them, Mulan lingered one last moment before the archway. The faint shape of a face—much like those demonic bronze medallions on the vermilion gates—glimmered under the arch, obscuring what lay on the other side. Thick arched brows, a wide nose, puffed cheeks, and angry red-yellow eyes—King Yama.

Mulan glanced at ShiShi and nodded. Then, with a deep breath, she took the first step through the archway. From the arch, Yama's voice rumbled:

"WELCOME TO DIYU."

Chapter Nine

Beyond the archway sprawled a dead bamboo forest. Mulan had seen bamboo stalks before: their stems were supposed to be green as grass, and straight and proud as arrows. Not gray and ashen. Not crooked like lightning bolts.

Mulan glanced back over her shoulder. The archway had disappeared; there was no way back to King Yama's throne room.

"ShiShi, do you know how to find Shang?"

"Do I look like a map to Diyu?" ShiShi growled.

Mulan frowned, not sure why the lion was upset with her. "No, but you're the great guardian. I thought you might know the way."

ShiShi harrumphed, but he didn't reply.

Mulan strode forward. A heavy fog misted the air, making it hard to find a clear path. The thick, crooked canes of dead bamboo were so dense she felt like she was tramping through a forest of wicker baskets. Not a cricket chirped, and not a bird sang.

Whenever Mulan looked up, she saw the stars blink above them—like eyes. Come to think of it, some of these plants—no, *most* of these plants had almost human shapes. In the eerie quiet she imagined she heard whispers emanating from their hollow arms.

She sighed. She had no idea where to even begin looking for Shang. From the Bridge of Helplessness, she'd seen hundreds of different areas within Diyu. Mirrors and fire and deserts and mountains. But here, in this desolate, gray forest—she only saw more and more . . . forest.

Had King Yama tricked her?

She had to keep moving. Or else despair would set in, and she'd lose hope.

But that was why she had ShiShi, wasn't it? Surely, he had to know how to find Shang. Except the lion still wasn't saying anything. He easily matched her pace, but he was being uncharacteristically quiet. Was he still in shock from being turned into stone?

"ShiShi," Mulan tried again, "do you know where we are?"

The lion huffed.

"You're angry with me. Why?"

"Because that was foolish of you," ShiShi snapped, "agreeing to King Yama's wager."

Mulan didn't stop walking. She pushed aside branches, clearing a path for the two of them. "Did you have any better ideas?"

"If you'd just let me talk to him—"

"He turned you into stone."

"That's beside the point! What would your family think of you, gambling away your life like that?" ShiShi scolded. "And your guardian? Do you even have a guardian?"

"I do," Mulan countered. "But you whisked me down into Diyu before I got a chance to tell him."

Besides, she thought, *Mushu is asleep . . . and what he doesn't know won't hurt him.*

Still, ShiShi was right about her family. She swallowed. *Baba will never know what happened to me if I'm stuck here forever. He might think I deserted the army, or that I was killed in battle. That would break his heart. And Mama's.*

"Why are you so concerned, anyway?" she said, pushing her worries as far from her mind as she could. "You're the great guardian of the Li family. Also, you should have told me you didn't know your way around Diyu."

"Why would I?" ShiShi retorted with a snarl. "I served

the Li family faithfully for three centuries, leading its sons to victory and bringing great honor to the family. Every one of my charges was a hero, so they never spent long in the Underworld. Ten generals, two admirals, and three military advisers to the Emperor. My track record was unblemished until General Li was dishonorably ambushed by those Huns—"

"General Li *was* a hero," Mulan interrupted. "His dying in battle does nothing to change that."

Some of ShiShi's anger—and bravado—faded.

"I know that," he said staunchly and marched forward without another word, smashing through branches in his way.

"Shang is a hero, too," she said quietly.

The lion's face drew tight, creases wrinkling his nose. His whiskers stiffened. "Li Shang . . . Li Shang will perish before I even have a chance to begin aiding him."

"Shang isn't dead."

"Not yet, but his father is."

The bitterness in ShiShi's tone made Mulan soften. "You must miss him."

The lion growled. "What would you know about the bond between man and guardian? You've barely experienced one battle. General Li and I fought hundreds together."

"Before becoming a soldier, I was clumsy and impulsive. I didn't know the first thing about fighting. My guardian helped me."

"Li Shang's *training* helped you." ShiShi scoffed. "Who *is* your guardian, anyway?"

"His name is Mushu."

"I've never heard of him. I would have thought your ancestors would have sent the Great Stone Dragon of the Fa family to protect you."

Mulan shrugged. "Mushu's . . . portable." She smiled to herself. "When I first met him, I thought he was a house lizard."

"A house lizard?" ShiShi looked repulsed. "Strange that your ancestors would send such a pitiful guardian to protect you in battle."

"Mushu isn't pitiful. He's—"

"A guardian is a reflection of whom he protects. If your ancestors sent you a lizard, then they must not think highly of you." ShiShi sniffed. "Perhaps it'd be better if I alone sought Shang and brought him home."

Mulan wouldn't let the lion's skepticism upset her. She replied calmly, "You need my help, ShiShi."

ShiShi bared his teeth at her. "I need no one's help. You are not a part of the Li family. I still do not understand why General Li would trust *you*, a mere *recruit*, to bring his son home. Look at you—you're entirely unprepared for the dangers of Diyu. You didn't even bring your sword!"

"I . . . I dropped it when you dragged me down here."

"How committed are you to rescuing Li Shang, little soldier?" ShiShi demanded. "Are you only here out of guilt because he saved you? Or is it the honor you'd bring to your family if you saved him?"

"A little of both," Mulan confessed. She couldn't lie to Shang's guardian—she *did* feel guilty. And she *did* want to make her family proud of her. But ShiShi didn't know *why* that was so important to her—he didn't know how much she wanted to prove she could bring honor to her family, even if it wasn't by impressing the Matchmaker or marrying well. ShiShi didn't even know she was a girl. If he did, he'd probably never have accompanied her to Diyu.

"And even if Captain Li hadn't saved me from Shan-Yu, I still would have come here," she said stoutly. "Shang is my friend, and China needs him. If it's what it takes, I will stay here in Diyu in his place."

ShiShi studied her, his anger fading. "Let's hope you aren't all talk, Ping." He let out a resigned sigh. "I remember your father, Fa Zhou. He fought with General Li many years ago. They were friends. Not good friends, but they respected each other. You remind me of him. But you're far more stubborn. And shorter."

ShiShi meant the words as a gibe, but Mulan smiled, happy to be compared to her father.

"We'll find Shang," she said gently, "but not if we keep arguing over how to do it. We have to work together."

The lion nodded once. "It was a foolish thing to do— bargaining with King Yama," he said again. "But it was brave, and I respect that." He paused. "My visits to Diyu have been brief, but I have centuries of experience. I may have my doubts about you, little soldier, but I'll help you any way I can. *That* I promised General Li."

It was a start. "Thank you."

"Well, first we have to get out of this godforsaken forest." ShiShi snapped another branch with his teeth. "I can barely see where I'm going."

Mulan eyed the surrounding bamboo plants, then looked behind them. The branches had reassembled themselves, obscuring the path they'd taken. She focused on the shapes around them. Some stems knotted one another like webs, some curled down like spiders, and others were straight like ladders.

Her stomach sank. They'd seen this area before.

"Give me your paw."

"What?"

She picked up one of ShiShi's paws, and scraped his claw against a bamboo stem. "We need to keep track of where we're going."

She pointed at a gnarly stalk of bamboo on her right, bent over like a hunchbacked man. "I saw that plant when we first left Yama's throne room. We're going in circles."

"I don't recognize it," ShiShi said stubbornly.

Mulan sighed. *So much for not arguing.* "Do you know anything about where we might find Shang?"

"He isn't fully dead yet, and he's not fully alive. He's a spirit, not yet a ghost."

"What's the difference?"

"Well, he won't be allowed to traipse about Diyu," ShiShi reasoned. "He'll be waiting somewhere until his time comes." He crouched, bending so he hovered over his forelegs. "Climb on my back. We'll move faster, and I don't tire as easily as you humans."

Mulan ignored the barb and leapt onto ShiShi's back. The lion was good as his word. He bounded through the forest. The mist thickened the faster he went, until Mulan couldn't see even a few paces in front of them.

Some minutes later, ShiShi stopped.

"What is it?"

ShiShi growled and shrugged Mulan off. She pulled herself up, recognizing with a sinking heart what had angered ShiShi. They were in front of that bamboo plant again, the one shaped like a hunchbacked man.

Whispers *were* emanating from the stems—there were so many they'd sounded like the wind, but now that she listened carefully, she could hear them coming from individual plants.

"They're alive," Mulan murmured.

"They're ghosts," corrected ShiShi, backing away from the shriveled bamboo. "Ghosts being punished for their human misdeeds on Earth."

A brush of twigs crunched under Mulan's feet. She stepped aside, watching them snake over to their parent plant and reattach themselves. The scratches she'd made were gone, and all the branches ShiShi had cleared had regenerated.

She looked more closely at that hunchbacked shape. The forest's cloudy mist gathered around it more strongly than around the other bamboo. It almost seemed to have a face. The topmost bamboo nodes bent forward, creating what looked like a neck, and she thought she could make out two eyes and a mouth. She pressed her ear against it.

Help me, a voice whispered from the plant just as ShiShi let out a terrible roar.

"I knew it," he rumbled. "Yama tricked us! We're trapped." He raised his paw to smash the plant down, but Mulan raised her arms high to block him.

"Wait," she cried. "I think we keep coming back to this plant for a reason. It said something to me."

Help me, the bamboo repeated.

"If we're going to save Li Shang, we aren't going to do it by listening to a grove of demonic bamboo."

"Just give me one minute," Mulan said. She turned to face the hunchbacked plant. There was something forlorn about its expression—something pained and frustrated.

A man grows most tired while standing still, her father would say when Mulan would complain about having to practice good posture for hours on end. But then she would see her father limping into a room with his cane and automatically straighten her spine. She remembered how difficult it was for him to walk without it—harder still for him to stand straight.

"I think I know what to do," she murmured.

She scanned the area by the hunchbacked plant, looking for a fallen branch. Most of them were cracked, crooked, or twisted. She needed one straight as a rod, one that could serve as a cane. . . .

There!

She knelt and scrabbled through the brush.

"What in the Emperor's name are you doing?" ShiShi rasped.

She ignored him. Mulan studied the hunchbacked bamboo plant again. Its spine curled over, with a branch extending from it that slumped down like a heavy arm. If she could fit the cane just there to raise the spine up—the "man" could stand tall again.

Gingerly, Mulan nudged the rod into place.

"You're wasting our time to do some gardening?"

"Look," she whispered. "Now he's standing tall."

The bamboo began to glow, and then it shook, so violently that the rod Mulan had just inserted flew through the air.

"Stand back!" ShiShi yelled. "We must have unleashed a spirit."

A ghost emerged from the tree, but not the angry, vicious one Mulan and ShiShi had been expected.

"General Li?" ShiShi rasped, half-frozen in shock. Mulan blinked, just as surprised as ShiShi was to see Shang's father.

General Li rubbed his back briefly. "Ah, I thought I was going to be stuck in there for days. Thank you for finding me. I intended to wait for you here by the door, but the bamboo trapped me."

ShiShi was still speechless.

General Li touched the lion's cheek. "It is good to see you, old friend. I am grateful you made it. Both of you."

General Li still glowed with a pale blue aura; he was even more luminous than when she'd seen him on Earth. In fact, he was so translucent she could practically see the bamboo behind him.

"I cannot stay long," Shang's father continued. "King Yama's guards are looking for me."

"Why?" ShiShi said, his chest rising. "What have you done?"

General Li gave his former guardian a mild smile. "Old friend, they are looking for me because I am to ascend to Heaven. They were supposed to escort me to the gates hours ago. But I wanted to stay here in Diyu, to help you."

"We can't find him," Mulan blurted. "I don't even know where to begin looking."

"Diyu is not an easy place to navigate, but Shang is not too far from here." General Li stepped aside.

Behind him, the forest's heavy mist thinned, revealing a watery portal between two bamboo plants marked by bronze demon medallions.

"You'll find him in the Tower of the Last Glance to Home," General Li said, gesturing at the door.

Mulan squinted through the portal and spied a scarlet and emerald tower with a sloping gold-tiled roof and elaborately latticed windows. It spiraled up toward the dark sky like a festival kite still tethered to the ground.

"It is where all ghosts go before they are reincarnated," General Li said. "To reflect and remember home. In the morning, Meng Po—the Lady of Forgetfulness—will bring Shang a cup of tea. Once he drinks, he will forget everything—his family, his friends, even his name. Then he will float back to Earth into a new life. Shang's time in the tower is the last time he will remember any of us."

Mulan swallowed. "I won't let that happen."

"Finding my son will be the easier part," General Li

said. "But the lower you venture into Diyu, the deeper into King Yama's domain you'll go. Look for the doors with the bronze medallions of demon heads."

Mulan nodded. "And the doors? How do I find them?"

"Some of them, you cannot. You will need help. But most levels are marked." General Li gestured at the two plaques on either side of the doorway. Only now did Mulan see the number written underneath each bronze demon head.

"Seventy-nine," she read. "How did we get to the seventy-ninth level of Diyu? I don't even remember—"

"It is easier to descend than ascend," ShiShi interrupted. "The only path out is up."

"What level is King Yama's throne room on?"

"I'm not sure," said General Li, "but ShiShi is right. You must ascend to exit Diyu." He paused. "But it won't be so easy. Diyu is a treacherous place, and it is easy to lose oneself. The ghosts on the bridge are spreading word of your arrival, and many will try to thwart your attempts to save my son—simply for amusement."

"Do you know how we can return to the exit?"

"Sadly, I do not. Few know their way around Diyu. It took me a long time to find this particular door to Shang."

"It's a start," she said gently. "Thank you."

She started to climb onto ShiShi's back, but Shang's father wasn't finished.

"Ping, wait. My son . . . my son is like me in many ways. He'll have accepted his death—he'll believe the honorable path is to die. You must convince him otherwise."

"I will."

"It won't be so easy," General Li said, hesitating. "He may not believe you. Remind him of his childhood." His voice grew hoarse. "Remind him that when he was only six years old, he wanted so much to accompany me to war that he sneaked into my trunk. I didn't realize he was there until I was half a day from home. I told him to walk back, barefoot in the rain, to teach him obedience and patience. It was a harsh punishment, especially for such a little boy, but Shang did not complain.

"I continued on my way, but after a while I turned back and took him home to his mother. Then I told him that one day we *would* fight together, that he would lead my soldiers. Until then, he had to wait."

Mulan pursed her lips. Baba had always told her to wait, too. He'd teased her for being impatient, for wanting to prove her worth. *Except Shang was a boy. He knew he'd get to prove himself one day. And me . . .* Her chest tightened, and she remembered her last dinner at home, the last fight she'd had with her *baba*.

You shouldn't have to go, she'd said.

Mulan!

There are plenty of young men to fight for China.
It is an honor to protect my country and my family.
So you'll die for honor.
I will die doing what's right!
But if you—
I know my place! It is time you learned yours.

She'd been so petulant, so angry. And yet, she didn't regret going in his place. Only that she'd deceived her family.

"Ping," said General Li, breaking her thoughts. "Shang's life is not supposed to end like this. You may think I say that because he is my son, but it is more than that. His heart has always been in protecting his family, his country—his friends. He is too young to die. There is much more good he can do for China. You must make him see that his path is this life."

"I will," she said fiercely. Mulan looked up at Shang's father, meeting his eyes. "I promise I'll find Shang, and I'll bring him back."

Her determination brought a sad but hopeful smile to the general's face. "I believe you. I do not know if I will see you again, Ping. When you find Shang, tell him he has . . . he has honored me greatly. And tell him I'm sorry . . . I'm sorry we never had the chance to fight together."

Mulan's throat dried, and no words could crawl out. She simply bowed her head.

"Go. You have my trust."

Those words again. Why did the words prick at her conscience so much? Shang had spoken them to her only hours ago, honoring her. His words had hurt her then, too. She hadn't deserved them.

She managed a meager smile. "I won't let you down, General."

With a curt nod, General Li stepped behind the mist and was gone.

Mulan turned to the portal, her eyes on the Tower of the Last Glance to Home in the distance, then on the full moon hanging above. The dark band ringing the moon was definitely getting thicker.

She stepped through the door. *I'm coming, Shang.*

Chapter Ten

They found themselves at the bottom of a stony hill, a short distance from the Tower of the Last Glance to Home. There was something lonely about the tower, Mulan felt. Other than its brightly painted walls, its faded scarlet windows and yellow roofs, it reminded her of one of the austere watchtowers she'd seen on paintings of the Great Wall protecting China.

ShiShi was quiet. Mulan supposed seeing the general's spirit in Diyu had had a profound effect on him.

The sky shifted above them, lightening into a dismal gray.

The moon remained, though. It was paler and softer than the moon she was used to seeing in the living world, as if someone had pulled a swathe of gauze over its face.

Mulan inhaled. A familiar, spiced smell lingered in the air. It was faint, but there was no mistaking it.

"Do you smell that?"

ShiShi nodded. "Incense."

From the top of the tower, Mulan thought, gazing up.

At the tower's base was a small, rectangular opening— too narrow for ShiShi to enter.

Mulan and ShiShi exchanged a glance. She'd have to go alone.

The guardian frowned, but didn't argue. "Remember what General Li told you. And don't take your time."

Mulan gave a curt nod.

"Ping," ShiShi added, "don't tell Li Shang about King Yama's deal just yet. Give him some hope. He needs something to live for."

Mulan tilted her head, touched by the lion's thoughtfulness. "All right." She hesitated. "Are you sure you don't want to come?"

"Even if I could, it wouldn't be right."

"Why not?"

"Why?" ShiShi blustered. "Because . . ." He stopped. "Why should I bother explaining to you the intricacies between guardian and man? *Your* guardian is a house lizard. Enough of this. Go, go."

Not needing to be told twice, Mulan hurried up the stairs.

The smell of incense grew stronger, heavier, the higher she went. It used to make her sleepy when she was a child—back then, Grandmother Fa often took her to their family temple to pray for their ancestors. Young Mulan had always had to stifle a yawn when it came to her turn to hold the incense and bow to the ancestors' spirits at the altar.

But now, she was anything but sleepy. Her adrenaline high, she ran faster, ignoring the flickering shadows from the candles tracing her figure as her boots drummed up the cold stone steps.

She wished she'd left her armor downstairs with ShiShi; wearing an extra forty *jin* slowed her down. But she didn't slacken her pace, training her eyes on the wooden door at the top of the stairs. It was slightly ajar, and light slanted out of the opening.

Shang *had* to be there.

Panting, Mulan reached the last step. She caught her breath, collected herself, and stepped into the room. The lighting was dim. Incense burned, the thin sticks staked into a lone tangerine surrounded by candles in bronze cups.

An altar for worshipping the dead, Mulan thought—but that wasn't the sight that made her shiver. Her knees locked in place. Her muscles froze.

Shang leaned against the wall, staring out the window at the world outside. He didn't turn around when she came in. He didn't even seem to hear her.

At first glance, he looked the same as when she had first met him. Thick black hair tied into a neat knot behind his head, cape fastened at the collar and thrown over his shoulders, armor polished and free of tarnish—and blood.

Except—Shang was a spirit.

Mulan's hand jumped to her mouth. *No.*

There was no denying it. Shang glowed a soft, pale blue, and his body flickered like a watery reflection. She could see the window's geometric latticework through his skin.

"Shang," she tried to call; her voice came out strangled and hoarse. The room was small—barely a dozen strides wide and long. She moved toward him, but he didn't budge.

"Shang?"

What was he staring at?

All she saw outside the window was the dreary gray sky. There wasn't a cloud or a bird in sight.

He must see something else.

Worry etched itself in her brow. Shang's eyes were glassy, and not even a muscle in his jaw twitched when she called his name. She wanted to shake his shoulders, but she couldn't even touch him. She tried anyway, resting her hand above his arm. It was like touching warm water.

Am I too late?

"Shang, I'm here. It's Ping."

He must have felt something, because finally, Shang turned.

When he saw her, his brow lifted. It was a small gesture, but Mulan's heart fluttered with relief. He was happy to see her! Then Shang blinked, and his lips twisted into a grimace. He wrung his hands. "Not you, too, Ping."

Mulan's eyes widened, suddenly understanding what Shang must think. "No," she said. "I'm not— I'm alive."

Shang shook his head. "Not if you're here."

"Shang, I'm here to take you home."

"Ping. Look around you. We're in the Underworld."

"Yes," she agreed. "But I'm not dead. Your father's spirit came to me. He brought me your family guardian, ShiShi. He's right downstairs, if you'll just come with me—"

"Ping," Shang said, raising his voice harshly. "This is the last chance I get to see my family. I'd like to be alone."

"I spoke to your father," she repeated. "He said you wouldn't believe me."

"You should have listened." Shang set his gaze back toward the window. "Go. I don't have long here, and I want to remember as much as I can."

"So you know?" she said. "King Yama told you that you're leaving Diyu?"

"I know my body is dying," Shang said flatly. "I know that I have been chosen to return to Earth. It is an honor. I only hope in my next life I can continue protecting China."

"You must protect China in *this* life," Mulan said. "I'm really here, Shang."

"No, Ping." His brows knit, and he wore a pained expression. "If you're here, that means you're dying, too. And I'm sorry to hear it. You should be in your own tower."

Mulan gritted her teeth. She'd forgotten how stubborn Shang could be—almost more stubborn than she was. Almost, but not quite. She wasn't giving up on him.

Help him remember. Help him believe.

"You promised I had your trust, right?" she said softly.

That got Shang's attention. He looked at her uncertainly.

"Your father wants you to live, Shang. I know you think it's dishonorable to try to fight your fate, but you must. We still need you. Your soldiers need you." She paused. "Remember how hopeless we all were in the beginning?"

Shang let out a laugh. It was brusque, but Mulan went on, encouraged. "Do you remember when *we* first met?"

"How could I forget? You were the worst soldier I'd ever seen."

It was Mulan's turn to laugh.

Sometimes she wished she could forget the first time she'd met Shang. Mushu had given her a few questionable lessons on how to behave like a man, so she'd lumbered into the training barracks and somehow gotten into a fight with every other recruit. Shang had arrived to break up the scuffle, and there she was curled up on the ground like a turtle, covering her head so the other soldiers wouldn't batter it. The sight of him had taken her breath away—not because he was tall and imposing and handsome, but because she'd been out of shape and jumped too quickly to her feet.

"I was so afraid of you I didn't even remember my own name," Mulan confessed. It was *mostly* the truth. Honestly, she hadn't even come up with a male name yet. But she *had* been terrified of him. Terrified. And curious.

After all, the expression Shang had worn when they first met—she couldn't tell whether he'd been angry or perplexed. Or both.

What an idiot he must have thought she was.

She was better at reading his expressions now. The crook in his neck—he was listening. The slight bend in his arm when he spoke to her—he was cautious. The parting of his lips now as he waited for her to speak—he was hopeful. Doubt still lingered in his eyes, but he wanted to believe her.

"Are you still afraid of me?" asked Shang. "Especially now that I'm like—this?" He held up his pale blue arms.

"No," said Mulan. "Now I'm just afraid I'll lose my friend. And Yao and Ling and Chien-Po—we're worried that we'll lose our captain. Who else would work us so hard? You have to fight, Shang. It's what *you* taught us to do."

The hardness in his eyes softened. "Is it really you, Ping?"

"I know it's hard to believe. But it is."

"And my father . . . my father truly sent you here—to bring me back."

"He guessed you'd be skeptical. He knows you well." Mulan paused. "He asked me to tell you a story from when you were a child in case you didn't believe me."

"What story?"

"He said when you were six, you sneaked into his trunk and tried to follow him to battle. He caught you, and he promised that one day, you would fight together." Mulan hesitated. "He said he's sorry that never got to happen."

The flinch in Shang's brow was brief, but Mulan caught it. His shoulders tensed and drew up. "Is he here . . . in Diyu? Can I speak to him?"

"I don't know where he is. He said he was to go to Heaven."

Shang's shoulders dropped. He looked relieved, yet sad. "I see."

"He wants you to live, Shang," Mulan went on. "Your family guardian brought me here to take you home. He's downstairs, waiting for us."

Shang lowered his gaze to study her. His eyes wavered as they searched her face—she could tell he *wanted* to believe her. "You can't be real."

"I am," she said. "Shang, you have to believe me. You have to live."

"Why?"

Why, she repeated to herself. Her mind scrambled for an answer. "My father used to tell me about the ancient heroes who protected China against demons. How the gods gave them magical stones or lanterns or swords to help them on their quests. But even then, the heroes weren't invincible. They knew fear and loss, yet they fought anyway, because they knew it was the right thing to do. Because in their hearts, they were brave and true."

She bit her lip, reflecting on her father's stories. The heroes had always inspired her, even if none of them had been girls.

That's not the point now, she reminded herself. *I've got to make Shang want to live.*

"We're just men, Shang. We have no magic, but we have our courage and we have our strength. China needs us. You might have guessed that I was a disappointment to my parents. I was clumsy, and stubborn—and unhappy with myself. I didn't know what I lived for. I didn't know who I was. Sometimes, I still don't." She paused, feeling a lump rise in her throat. "But it isn't always about me. It's about China. My family. My friends.

"I chose to come to Diyu and take you home. You need to make that choice now, too. If you think your path ends here, I'll go. But if you want to keep going, come with me."

She waited for Shang to absorb her words.

"That sounds more like the real Ping," he said finally, peeling himself from the window. He sounded calm, the way he always had been when he commanded his troops, but his next words carried a note of urgency. "So, how do we get out of here?"

Mulan smiled. That was the Shang she knew.

"Follow me," she said, moving for the door. But as soon as Shang stepped out of the room, the walls let out a terrible shudder, and the ground below shook.

"The tower's crumbling!" Shang reached to grab Mulan's arm, but his touch was no more than a shadow. His face twisted with a mix of sadness and frustration, but then he looked at her, jaw set determinedly. "Let's go."

Mulan bolted down the stairs, taking two, three steps at a time. She could hear the stones collapsing, as if someone had taken a giant hammer to the roof. The sound thundered around her.

They were maybe twenty steps from the bottom when

Mulan spied ShiShi pacing at the entrance. They were almost there.

Then the stairs flattened beneath their feet, and down they slid—just seconds ahead of an avalanche of crumbling stones. They were going to crash into the wall!

They kicked at the ground, trying to slow their fall, but it was in vain.

Seeing they were in danger, ShiShi smashed through the entrance and charged in front of Mulan and Shang, breaking their fall and bearing the falling stones on his back. But before he could snatch Mulan in his teeth and take her outside, the tower floor disappeared.

Into the void the three of them plunged.

And ShiShi's roar echoed as they fell, deeper and deeper into Diyu.

Chapter Eleven

Mulan held in her scream. She didn't know how to scream like a man, although she'd mastered talking like one, walking like one, and eating like one. She'd heard Ling and Mushu shriek plenty of times, but never Shang. Shang was always brave; if he felt fear, he used it to find a way to get him and his soldiers out of danger.

So as they fell together down what seemed a never-ending tunnel of darkness and despair, Mulan refused to let this be the moment that revealed her secret, refused to let this be the moment that she gave in to her fear that they all wouldn't make it back home.

She locked her scream in her gut, clutching her sides and biting her lips.

ShiShi was still roaring. His jade pendant whirled in a

flash of green, and he swiped his paws at the air as if wrestling an invisible foe.

Mulan kicked, trying to orient her body so she could see what was beneath her. But she was moving too fast, and the effort only made her dizzy. As they fell deeper into Diyu, she caught a glimpse of different chambers—of roofed houses and burning trees, of craggy wastelands and tempestuous rainstorms. There were whiffs of smoke, the flash of iron chains, and the bloodcurdling screams of ghosts being tortured.

ShiShi landed first, dirt spraying up around him. Shang was next—a silent sprawl, but he groaned, so she knew he was still alive. Well, half-alive.

Mulan braced herself, tucking her head and bending her knees. Her landing was soft—almost cushioned. And furry . . .

"Get off me!" ShiShi grunted. "Off, off. Now!"

Mulan rolled to the side and got off ShiShi's back. The lion was half-covered in dirt, and his orange eyes glowed in whatever dark chamber they'd fallen into. It was certainly a very small chamber; there was barely enough room to fit ShiShi and her.

"Shang?" she shouted, looking frantically about them. She pressed her palm against the stony wall encircling the chamber. No, not a chamber—she could see the sky above them, blue and crisp. She and ShiShi were stuck in a well!

"Ping?" Shang called from above.

"I'm here," she shouted back. "ShiShi is, too!"

Shang peered at them from the top of the well. "Stay there. I'll find a way to get you out."

"We're not staying anywhere," ShiShi retorted. He flicked his tail against the circular wall, then clawed at the stones as he tried to crawl up. It was no use; he couldn't climb them. He tumbled down, his enormous body filling the space of the well bottom.

The guardian tried again and again, to no avail. He kicked his back legs, hitting a wooden bucket, which loudly ricocheted off the wall and hit his tail. He growled, clearly exasperated. "Well, this is unpleasant."

"At least it's empty," said Mulan, tapping the dirt with her shoe. "It could be worse."

ShiShi ground his teeth. "I'm not sure that's much consolation."

Mulan examined the stone walls that enclosed them. The rock was slippery, the grout thin. There was no way she would be able to scale it, even with her nimble fingers. "Shang?" she called up toward the opening. "Do you see anything out there?"

Silence. It seemed Shang had gone to find something to help them.

ShiShi harrumphed. Mulan couldn't help but share his discontent. Mere moments after finding Shang, they'd been separated.

She leaned against the wall, trying to think of another way out.

"Well, little soldier," ShiShi said, "do you have anything up your sleeve this time?"

"I'm working on it," Mulan said. She wondered what purpose this empty well served. Was it an obstacle specifically placed to slow them down? How much time had passed since they'd left King Yama's throne?

ShiShi harrumphed again. "What a way for me to introduce myself to Li Shang—by getting stuck in a well."

Something in his tone broke Mulan out of her reverie. "Is that why you wouldn't come with me to the tower earlier?" she asked the lion after a moment. She lowered her voice. "Because you were worried you'd disappoint Shang somehow?"

ShiShi lowered his head, trying to hide a grimace, his body shifting uncomfortably. Mulan didn't expect a reply from Shang's surly guardian, so it surprised her when he started to speak. "I was General Li's guardian since he was Shang's age. He became more than my charge; he became my friend. And when he died, I promised I'd watch over his son. I *swore* an oath.

"But now? Now that General Li has passed, and his son is in Diyu . . ." ShiShi heaved a sigh, his whiskers drooping. "I would not be surprised if my tenure as a guardian will also pass."

"Shang is lucky to have you," Mulan said, touching the lion's head. "You're brave and . . . confident. You remind me of Mushu sometimes, except you're a lot bigger."

ShiShi shook her hand off him. "I'm nothing like your house lizard."

Mulan bristled at ShiShi's tone. In spite of Mushu's shortcomings and tendency to get her into trouble, she did appreciate him. If she never made it out of Diyu, would Mushu be punished—demoted from guardian?

No, because I am *going to get us out of here.* "ShiShi," she said, "we're going to get Shang out of here. You'll still be a guardian. I promise."

"It isn't only that." ShiShi grimaced again, then let out a sigh. "You aren't the only one who carries the burden of guilt."

Ah. Now Mulan understood. No matter how hard she tried, she couldn't stop blaming herself for what had happened to Shang. It had not occurred to her that ShiShi might feel the same way about General Li. She'd mistaken the guardian's guilt for pride and disappointment.

"Shang would never blame you for what happened to his father," she said gently. "It wasn't your fault."

"Says the soldier who blames himself for Li Shang's death," grumbled ShiShi.

"I feel terrible for my part in what happened to Shang, but I'm not here simply out of guilt," Mulan reminded the lion. "Saving Shang is the right thing to do. I'd do it even if he hadn't been hurt saving me. I'd want to help."

ShiShi raised his head. "I suppose if General Li has faith in you, then I do too, Ping." The lion ground his large, broad teeth, as if he hated how emotional he was being. "Now where is Li Shang? He's taking his time."

Mulan looked up, then eyed the walls of the well curiously. There was a rusted pulley on top, but the rope was no longer there.

"What we could really use is some rope," she said.

"Rope?"

ShiShi shuffled, kicking the old bucket again. This time, Mulan leapt up, peering over at the thin and snakelike object behind him. "Aha!" she cried.

ShiShi craned his neck to look behind him. "Ah, I was wondering why my tail felt so coarse. Is it enough?"

The long rope, tied to the broken wooden bucket, rolled toward Mulan. "It just might work."

She jumped, throwing the bucket as high as she could. It took a few tries, but on the third one, the bucket made it over the well and disappeared. She tugged on the rope, testing its strength. "I'm going to try climbing out."

"What about me?" ShiShi said.

"Hold on." Mulan wrapped the rope around ShiShi's body and tied a tight knot. Then she climbed on top of him and began scaling the well.

"What are you doing?" ShiShi said, his voice bouncing across the walls. "Are you just leaving me behind?"

"Stay there. I'll pull you up once I'm at the top."

She landed on a soft, yielding bed of—flowers? Startled, she sat up and gave a quick stretch before leaping to her feet. An overwhelming aroma of peonies and tangerines and lotus blossoms surrounded her.

"Not what I expected," she murmured to herself, overcome by the beauty of this level. If not for ShiShi still stuck in the well, she would have stopped to take a better look at her surroundings.

"Get me out of here!" the lion roared.

"Shang!" Mulan called, spotting the captain nearby still searching for a way to get them out. He'd managed to find a fallen tree and was lugging it toward them when he saw her.

"Ping, how did you—"

"ShiShi's still stuck inside," she interrupted. "We need your help."

Shang dropped the tree and hurried toward her. Together, they pulled on the rope, heaving ShiShi out of the well.

"At last," ShiShi said, jumping onto the grass. With his claw, he cut the ropes off his body and shook his mane free of dirt. He then stood tall, presenting himself regally to Shang.

"I am the great guardian of the Li family," he boomed.

"I have nurtured the heroes in your family for over a dozen generations, and now—"

"Do you know where we are?" Shang interrupted.

Mulan hid a chuckle. That was Shang—getting right to business.

"No," ShiShi replied with a huff. He looked at their surroundings suspiciously. "We fell a long way. We must be in the heart of Diyu."

"The heart of Diyu is a garden?" Mulan spoke up.

As far as she could see were flowers and trees, all so lush and beautiful Mulan could almost forget she was in the Underworld. Tall grass tickled her waist as she stepped up to a tangerine tree. Behind it was a tinkling brook, teeming with white-and-red-spotted carp.

"Don't eat anything," ShiShi warned her. "Or drink anything either, for that matter."

"Why not?"

"King Yama's playing a game with us. And in his domain, he sets the rules. No unnecessary risks."

Mulan nodded, remembering their trial in the forest. "We need to find a way back up."

"Unless one of you can sprout wings," ShiShi said drily, "I don't see a way of going back up."

She shielded her eyes and looked at the sky. It was blue as the paint the porcelain artists back in her village used—just as brilliant and bright—but there was no sun. If she squinted hard enough, she could make out the moon behind one of the flat white clouds. A quarter of it was now black.

"Don't look so surprised," ShiShi said, noticing Mulan's stricken expression. "You took your time in the tower. And then there was that godforsaken well. At least we have Li Shang now."

She nodded numbly. She had no idea how far they'd fallen from Diyu's gates, and—she couldn't tell how much time they had left until sunrise.

Which, she supposed, had been King Yama's plan all along. There was no way he'd have let them leave Diyu directly from the Tower of the Last Glance to Home.

"There," Shang said, pointing. A gilded pavilion peeked out of the trees, its jade-and-gold-painted roof camouflaged by the lush greenery in the courtyard surrounding it. "Maybe it'll lead elsewhere in Diyu."

"It could lead us deeper into Diyu," his guardian argued.

"Or it could lead up."

"Shang's right," said Mulan. She swept her foot across the dirt, unveiling a brick path that led to the pavilion. "We have to try. Perhaps this pavilion has one of those portals that leads elsewhere."

"I don't like this," ShiShi grumbled, but he followed behind Mulan and Shang, his paws crushing the flowers. "The last time I was invited to a pavilion like that one was with Li Shang's great-great-grandfather. He had the grandest statue of me made and put in the center, and everyone marveled at how glorious I looked. Then it got demolished a few years later during a battle." He moaned. "Terrible memory of such pavilions."

Mulan smothered a chuckle and kept her gaze forward. The pavilion overlooked a pond that was fed by the brook she had noticed earlier. Inside they could see two wooden benches and dark rosewood tables with carvings of foxes on the legs. A pot of tea rested on one table, its steam curling into the air.

"Wait," Shang said, raising a hand before they got too close. "We're not alone."

"I'll go," ShiShi said. "After all, I have the most experience here in Diyu. I can smell demons from a thousand paces away." And before anyone could stop him, he strode to the pavilion, sniffing at the pink and white rosebushes along the path. One of the bushes rustled, and he pounced on it.

"Wait, ShiShi—be careful!"

Too late. As soon as Mulan cried out her warning, a bronze spade popped out of the bush and smashed ShiShi on the head.

Chapter Twelve

"OW!" the lion cried.

Out of the bush emerged a short elderly woman. She wore a round straw hat and a creamy green robe with a yellow sash. The spade gleamed in her hand, and she raised it at ShiShi threateningly. "That'll teach you, you bully of a lion, trying to scare a poor old lady."

"He's with us," Mulan said quickly, stepping in front of ShiShi.

"He's my family guardian," Shang added.

The old lady's eyes twinkled. "Ah, soldiers! You should have said so before. Can't be too careful these days, not with all these demons and ghosts scurrying about. Just the other day, I caught a demon lurking by my plum trees."

"ShiShi isn't a demon," Mulan said.

The old lady tossed the spade into the bushes, then grabbed Mulan by the arm and tapped her armor. Mulan noticed for the first time that the old woman didn't glow or look translucent, like Shang. She seemed almost . . . alive.

The old woman wrinkled her nose. "Fashion has changed since I was last on the hundredth level. Who is the emperor now?"

"Is the hundredth level the highest level?" Mulan asked, ignoring the woman's question. General Li had said the bamboo forest was on the seventy-ninth level, but he hadn't been able to tell her much more. "Is that where the gate is?"

"You're a quick one. Yes, the hundredth level is where King Yama's throne room is."

"What level are we on now? How do we get there?" Shang inquired.

"That isn't so easy." The old woman sighed. "Things here are constantly shifting. It's like a maze. Very easy to get lost. Luckily for you, I know Diyu like the back of my hand."

"Maybe you could help us," suggested Shang.

"Have some tea first," replied the old woman. "All these questions make me thirsty."

"Thank you, ma'am, but—"

"*Lao Lao,*" the old woman interrupted. "You must call me Lao Lao. Everyone thinks of me as their grandmother in

Diyu. We're all family down here. It's been so long since I've had company, especially that of such brave and honorable young men—and with such an impressive-looking guardian, no less!" She touched ShiShi's mane admiringly, which seemed to immediately win over the lion despite his misgivings about her earlier. "Come, come."

Mulan and Shang exchanged a look. "I'm sorry, Lao Lao, but we're in a rush—"

"I won't take no for an answer," the old lady interrupted. Mischief twinkled in her dark, hooded eyes. "And don't tell me you don't have time. In Diyu, we have all the time in the world."

Lao Lao ushered them toward her pavilion.

"Luck must be on our side," said ShiShi happily, still preening over the woman's praise.

"But should we trust her?" Mulan asked. The old woman's energy and short stature reminded Mulan of Grandmother Fa. If not for her white hair, which was so long it reached past her waist, and her pointed chin unlike Grandmother Fa's round one, the resemblance would have been striking. Maybe *too* striking.

"We don't have to *trust* her," said the guardian, "but not everyone in Diyu has ill intentions. Perhaps she can help us get out of here. I'd prefer that over wandering aimlessly about the Underworld."

Shang seemed to share Mulan's concern, but he relented. "It's worth a try."

He entered the pavilion first, and then ShiShi sucked in his breath so he could squeeze himself between the pillars. Following the lion, Mulan ascended the pavilion's delicate steps and walked inside.

It'd been a long time since she had been surrounded by actual furniture: the cushions were silk, the backs of the benches latticed with intricate designs of butterflies and birds, and the round rosewood tables all had candles scented with rose and honeysuckle.

"Sit, sit." The old woman gestured at the benches, and at the cushions on the floor, where ShiShi promptly made himself at home. Mulan noticed the three empty teacups on the table. Had they been expected?

"What a long day," the old woman said, reaching for the pot of tea on the table. "Would you pass me your cup?"

Shang shook his head, and Mulan remembered how he'd tried to take her arm in the tower but couldn't touch her. "I don't think I can—"

"You can touch anything or anyone that belongs in Diyu," Lao Lao told him. "These cups, these benches, the flowers in my garden." She met Mulan's gaze. "But I'm afraid your companions are off limits, so long as they are still living."

Hesitantly, Shang picked up the nearest teacup; his skin was so transparent he could see the flowers painted on the porcelain through his shadowy fingers. He passed it to Lao Lao, who lifted the pot to pour them tea.

"Let me help you with that," Mulan said, rising. "The pot must be heavy."

"No, no. I'm stronger than I look. All that gardening." The old woman tilted the teapot's spout into the first cup. "You soldiers must know about the war that's going on upstairs. I'm afraid my news is rather out of date. King Yama is always extra irritable whenever there's a war. Overcrowding. And work becomes unbearable for him. But I've heard all about you three. Captain Li Shang; his guardian, ShiShi; and Ping, am I correct?"

Shang and ShiShi nodded. Mulan stole another glance at ShiShi's spot across from her. It *was* odd that all the pillows and cushions had been laid out there for him.

"How do you know our names?" Mulan asked.

"It isn't often King Yama allows outsiders from the world above," Lao Lao replied. "You must be a rather special young man, Ping. The boy with no name, some are calling you."

"No name?" Shang repeated. "But his name is Ping."

Mulan fidgeted, remembering the comment King Yama had made when he couldn't find "Fa Ping" in his book. "What about you?" she pressed Lao Lao. "Who are you?"

"Just an old lady lucky enough to have a garden in Diyu."

"You aren't a ghost," Mulan pointed out. "You look alive."

Lao Lao laughed at Mulan's observation. "I'm not a demon, if that's what you're worried about. King Yama and I have . . . an understanding." The old woman winked at Mulan. "Though it seems I'm not the only one he grants special privileges."

Mulan frowned.

ShiShi cleared his throat. "You'll have to forgive him, Lao Lao. It's the little soldier's first time in Diyu. He's a bit edgy."

"I can't blame you, Ping," said Lao Lao with a chuckle. "It can't be easy being the only human traversing the Underworld. You're lucky to have the great Li guardian to guide you. You especially, Captain Li Shang."

ShiShi's fur bristled with pride once more. "Li Shang is the son of the esteemed General Li. I'm going to make him a great hero one day. Once we get out of Diyu, of course."

"Speaking of getting out of Diyu," Mulan interrupted, "Lao Lao, you mentioned that the gate was on the hundredth level."

"Yes," replied Lao Lao. "It is the only way out of here. But most never see that level again once they have entered Diyu. Your best bet is to make it to the ninety-ninth level— the City of the Dead, Youdu—and stay there. The rest of

Diyu is full of hidden dangers. There are endless chambers full of suffering and misery, and beasts from your nightmares. Step into the wrong one, and you may be trapped there forever. But Youdu is quite nice."

Mulan glanced about the pavilion. All six sides were open, so one could enjoy the view of the garden and pond from every angle. She could easily jump out if she wanted, so why did it feel like she'd entered a cage?

"Oh dear," said Lao Lao. "I can see I've alarmed you, Ping. Worry not. This isn't one of the dangerous levels. You're safe here. Besides, nothing in Diyu can harm a ghost."

Mulan frowned again. "If nothing in Diyu can harm the ghosts, then why are there torture chambers throughout the levels?"

"Ah, you're a clever one. Not every ghost must be punished; those who do not pass their time in Youdu."

"And can *they* be harmed?"

"Nothing can harm a ghost unless they are sentenced to be tortured. You see, a ghost's body is like water. They can touch whatever is in Diyu, but they may also pass through it if they choose. It takes some practice, especially flying and such, but most are here long enough to master it." Lao Lao tilted her head. "They also feel nothing—not the pain of a thousand lashes, of flesh being burned, or of eyes being gouged. Not unless they've been assigned to suffer a punishment. King Yama has a knack for determining what one's worst fear is and making them confront it—if they must be punished, that is."

She paused, seeing the worry on Mulan's face. "Your friend *isn't* a ghost. He's close enough, of course, but his body in the real world has not yet died. Until then, almost nothing in Diyu can harm him."

"Almost nothing?" Mulan repeated. "Before you said *nothing.*"

"Did I?" The old woman shrugged. "Ghosts can be trapped or get lost. Those would not be ideal fates for the captain."

"What about Ping?" Shang pressed. "He's not a ghost."

"Ping needs to be careful. Very careful." She plastered on a smile and pushed their cups forward. "Drink, drink. Your tea is getting cold, and you both must be thirsty."

"I'm not," Mulan said, remembering ShiShi's warning. A warning the lion himself was promptly forgetting as he continued to sniff the tea.

"What?" Lao Lao said with a laugh. "You look uneasy, Ping. Are you afraid it's poisoned?"

"Of course not," Mulan said quickly. "We just have a long journey ahead of us, and—"

"All the more reason to drink. A sip or two won't delay you too long." The old woman carried the teapot to them and opened its lid so the tea's aroma could waft to their noses. "Could anything dangerous smell so wonderful? Answer me that."

ShiShi's regal fierceness melted away as he accidentally inhaled the scent of the tea. He sighed. "Oranges. And jasmine. With just a hint of ginger."

Mulan had to admit the tea's aroma was heavenly. The scent wafted into the air, enveloping her in a warm, invisible embrace. The smell made her feel safe.

She looked into her teacup and saw herself smiling rather idiotically. Behind her, one of the brass lanterns hanging from ceiling appeared in the tea's reflection, and she thought she saw King Yama's face appear—as it had on each of the doors they'd found in Diyu.

Maybe there was a portal inside this very pavilion!

She blinked, pushed her teacup away, and turned back to look at the lantern.

King Yama's face disappeared, and the light inside the lantern flickered and danced. The brass caught the light and took on a spectrum of mesmerizing colors.

Mulan blinked, and the lantern returned to how it'd been when she first entered the pavilion. No King Yama, no strange colors.

"Ping?" Lao Lao prodded.

Mulan's jaw hung agape. Her answer, which had been

clear as day only a second ago, fled from her lips. Her brows furrowed. What was the matter with her? She couldn't remember! "Uh, I . . . um . . ."

"Stay and have some tea," the old woman said, placing Mulan's teacup in her palm, "and I'll tell you all about Diyu. I've been here a long time, you know."

Mulan stared at the steaming liquid, watching the dried leaves swirl to the bottom. How beautiful the tea looked, too—she'd never seen tea so colorful. Reds and pinks swirled in with amber and blue—like the mesmerizing patterns on a butterfly.

"Dooo tellll," ShiShi slurred. "I loovee a good story. . . ."

Mulan tore her gaze from the tea. Her head felt light, dizzy. What was it she was trying to remember? A warning, a story—something!

She touched the side of her head, trying to keep it from throbbing. Shang had inhaled the fragrance of the tea; she could tell because his dark eyes looked glassy, and he grimaced as if he were trying to fight off the dizziness, too.

What was it I had to remember? Something about . . . not eating, not drinking in Diyu. Why? Because . . . because it would be taking a risk.

But who had told her this?

ShiShi? Yes, he'd warned her . . . but that wasn't what she struggled to remember. It was something about the tea . . . the tea! General Li had told her that Shang would have to drink a tea that would make him forget his past life. Was that what she'd just smelled? Then the old lady was Meng Po, the Lady of Forgetfulness, and they were in her pavilion!

Mulan's hand trembled, and she almost dropped the cup. She placed her hand over the tea so its smell wouldn't make her forget anymore.

Her mind raced. They had to get out of here, but how?

ShiShi had that dreamy grin on his face. He didn't seem to have moved to drink the tea, to Mulan's relief, but once his stupor wore off, she had no doubt he would.

And Shang.

"It's my special five-flavored tea," Meng Po was saying to him. "Have a sip, Captain."

No, he couldn't drink!

Come on, Mulan. You had no problem being clumsy back home. You spilled tea over the Matchmaker and made a fool of yourself in front of the whole village. Meng Po is not an old lady. She's a cunning servant of King Yama.

Mulan elbowed Shang. Her elbow went straight through his spirit, but it knocked the cup out of his hands. It shattered on the ground.

To her relief, Shang's eyes cleared. She shot him a look. *Play along,* it read.

"I'm so sorry. I'm clumsy. Shang always said I was the worst soldier in the regiment." She faked a laugh. "Didn't you, Shang?"

Shang raised an eyebrow, and then he forced a laugh, too. "Um, the worst."

Meng Po dipped her hand into her pocket, and it resurfaced with yet another cup. "Not to fret. I have plenty of tea." Her voice was still warm, but an undertone of impatience pickled her words. "I'll refill your cup. But Ping, yours is still full. Drink up."

She's a sharp one, Mulan thought. She pretended to sip, but when Meng Po wasn't looking, Mulan threw the cup's contents over her shoulder. She flicked her eyes at Shang, and he nodded.

"How do you make your tea?" Mulan asked, trying to buy time. "It smells so heavenly. Do you grow the leaves yourself? Or do they come from another part of Diyu?"

"I grow them myself," Meng Po said, pouring Shang a fresh cup. "I don't venture out of my garden often."

"Why is that? Are you trapped here?"

"No, no. It's just that I prefer it here. It's so peaceful, you see."

Too peaceful, Mulan thought. *No birds, no insects, only fish.* She leaned over to watch the carp swimming beside the pavilion. *There's something wrong about this place.*

She held her breath. "We really shouldn't keep you any longer."

"Worry not, young Ping, I have all the time in the world."

"She's right," ShiShi agreed. "We should stay here longer. Trust me, most of Diyu isn't half as nice as Lao Lao's pavilion."

Mulan pursed her lips, glancing at the lion worriedly. "Where are we in Diyu?" she asked Meng Po.

"This is the twenty-fourth level. I'm afraid you're quite deep into King Yama's realm."

Mulan's hand jerked, nearly dropping the cup onto her lap. "The twenty-fourth level?"

Alarm flickered in Shang's eyes, but he composed himself quickly. "Gracious Lao Lao, would you be so kind as to tell us the way to the gates?"

"There is only one path out of Diyu," Meng Po replied. "I'll tell you after you drink."

Mulan graced Meng Po with her best blank face. "I already did. It's the best tea I've ever had."

"Is it, now?" Meng Po fanned herself. "If you'd truly drunk it, you wouldn't remember what the best tea was."

Mulan's face grew hot. She stood, lunging to escape the pavilion.

"Stay," Meng Po said sharply. Paper panels unfolded

like scrolls to cover the pavilion's open sides. At once, the pavilion darkened, and Meng Po's eyes narrowed. "Please. It is rude to refuse the hospitality of one's elders."

Mulan swallowed. They were trapped.

"I know who you are," Mulan said through clenched teeth. "You're not anyone's *lao lao*. You're the Lady of Forgetfulness."

Meng Po rose from her seat. Her hooded eyes opened wide, unblinking. "And *you* are the soldier who stole Captain Li Shang from the Tower of the Last Glance to Home. Now drink, or I will be forced to set my demons upon you."

"No."

"My tea is meant to be a consolation. I assure you, it will be much more painful for you—for *both* of you—if you do not drink. You will never make it to the hundredth level."

"You're right. We won't." Mulan snatched the teapot from her hands and tossed the tea at the woman's face. "Not if we stay here."

"Ahh!" Meng Po shrieked, her long white hair dripping with tea.

"Come on, Shang."

Shang was already on his feet. He lifted a rosewood table and hurled it at one of the panels. The paper ripped, and as Shang tore his way through, Mulan smashed ShiShi's teacup with her foot. The lion blinked, stirring from Meng Po's spell.

"Get up!" she shouted. "Lao Lao is Meng Po."

ShiShi bolted to his feet and leapt out of the pavilion. Mulan followed, landing in one of the rosebushes. She pushed her way through the flowers and leaves to the brick path they'd found earlier. Behind her, Meng Po shouted furiously in a language Mulan didn't understand.

She ignored it. They needed to find a portal out of this level, and fast.

Shang was one step ahead of her. "This way," he said, heading north. "Where's ShiShi?"

"He's—" Mulan whirled around to make sure ShiShi was still with them. He wasn't.

She gasped, spotting him behind her—in the garden. "The trees have him."

ShiShi dangled from the top of a tree, his golden fur nearly completely swathed by long sleeves of pointed green leaves. One crooked branch curled over ShiShi's mouth, preventing him from roaring, but when the lion saw Mulan and Shang, he thrashed furiously. He swept his paws at every branch that dared wrestle with him, his sharp claws digging into their arms and shredding their leaves.

Another tree extended a warped arm toward Mulan. She jumped back.

"Ping!" Shang's jaw tightened as he assessed the trees. He stomped on a branch before it could take hold of him. "I'll take care of this. You find the way out."

Mulan bounded away from the tree's clutches, skirting the edge of the rosebushes along Meng Po's courtyard. The pavilion and the pond were the only places untouched by Meng Po's monstrous trees.

The Lady of Forgetfulness had to be behind the trees' attacks. She hadn't moved from her position on the steps of the pavilion, where she was still chanting those strange words.

"Stop it!" Mulan yelled. "Let ShiShi go!"

For a second, Meng Po's dark eyes met Mulan's. She stopped shouting and snapped her fan closed, and the intensity of her gaze made Mulan wonder if she was actually considering Mulan's request. But then, her thin, wrinkled lips curled into a faint smile before she turned her back to Mulan and went inside her pavilion.

Mulan tried to follow the Lady of Forgetfulness, but the pond begun to bubble. Horns emerged, then yellow and red eyes, and the tips of newly sharpened spears.

And now Mulan could guess whom Meng Po had summoned—

The demons.

The demons were coming.

Chapter Thirteen

Mulan dove into the rosebushes, scrabbling for the bronze spade that Meng Po had discarded. To her relief, it was still there. Quickly, she tossed it to Shang.

"Demons!" she shouted. "Coming from the pond. Help ShiShi!"

As the captain hacked at the trees, freeing ShiShi branch by branch, Mulan wrestled against the rosebushes, which had also come alive to attack her. Their stems hissed like snakes and entwined about her ankles.

She glanced quickly to the pond, taking note of the demons who had emerged. There were dozens of them—as many as could fit in the pond. They looked different from the guards she'd met on the Bridge of Helplessness. These demons looked like wolves, and they wore battle armor just like hers; they were soldiers trained to kill.

Mulan gulped, scanning their surroundings. *No cannon to fire this time, and no snow to create an avalanche. I don't even have my sword.*

She kicked away the roses and hurried back toward ShiShi. The lion was almost free from the trees, but one stubborn tangerine tree held on. Its branches wrapped around ShiShi's neck, trying to choke him. While Shang cut at the branches, Mulan pulled ShiShi out of the tree's clutches by his tail, a rescue the guardian didn't seem to appreciate.

"I hate trees," ShiShi snarled at the garden, shaking his mane until the cords holding his jade pendant untangled. "That was Meng Po!"

"We know."

"What a fool she made out of me," ShiShi huffed. "I'll never live this down with the other guardians if they find out. And to think, I was the one who warned you all not to—"

This wasn't the time for ShiShi to pour out his anger at the Lady of Forgetfulness or grieve at how quickly he'd fallen into her trap. Mulan pulled on his mane.

"*Ow!* What are you—"

"Run," urged Mulan. Then she took her own advice and sprinted away from the pond.

Shang held the spade over his shoulder as he ran beside her. Even though he was a spirit, sweat dribbled down his temples. "How many?"

"What—" ShiShi bolted to keep up with Shang and Mulan. "Don't tell me you're all afraid of a few plants," he huffed. "Those trees barely scratched me. They came out of nowhere. It was surprise that got me. Otherwise, they wouldn't have had a—"

"We're not running from the trees," Mulan interrupted, panting. "We're running from the demons."

Looking skeptical, ShiShi glanced back. A horde of demons came into sight, rustling through the bushes and trees. Some looked like the wolf demons Mulan had seen emerge from the pond, and others looked more human— but with red or yellow skin. From her glimpse back, Mulan saw yellow teeth, bloodshot eyes, fur and scales. The wolf demons were fastest. Even though they ran on two feet like humans, they bared glistening fangs. They led the charge, sniffing and howling as they ran.

ShiShi's eyelids peeled back with alarm. He raced to the front of the line, his powerful legs springing off the brick path. "Hurry, Li Shang. Hurry, little soldier. Pick up those puny legs or you'll end up as dinner."

Mulan clenched her jaw, but ShiShi's threat worked. She ran faster.

Not that it mattered. The wolf demons quickly gained

on them, the others not far behind. "I-I say we fight," Mulan said, already nearly out of breath. "We can't run forever."

"Three against thirty," Shang calculated between breaths.

"We've fought against worse!"

Mulan slowed down, forcing the encounter. ShiShi scraped his feet against the bricks. "What are you doing?" he cried. "You cannot kill demons. But they can kill you."

Mulan didn't respond. They couldn't outrun a mass of demons, especially demons who knew the territory better than they did. They had no choice.

And she knew Shang agreed.

"You take this." Shang passed Mulan the bronze spade. He raised his fists, pale blue like the rest of him. "Separate the wolf pack from the rest of the demons. Or else we'll have to fight thirty at once."

Mulan nodded once to show she understood. Then the wolves charged at them. They were fast and vicious and strong, but Mulan and Shang were ready.

Mulan thwacked the first demon on the head. Behind her, ShiShi swung his heavy jade pendant at one, then bit at the next with his sharp teeth. He pounced and jumped, lobbing his enemies off the bricks and into the gardens where Meng Po's trees patiently waited to strangle their next prey. Mulan started tossing her own demons off to the side too.

It shouldn't have surprised her that Shang was the demons' main target. They probably had orders to bring him back to the tower.

Shang had managed to retrieve weapons of his own, but that didn't deter the demons from surrounding him. They howled, jabbing at him with their spears to force him to back up off the path so the trees might have him.

Mulan started toward Shang, but the captain didn't seem to need any assistance. He frowned at the six wolf demons, then gripped his spear and sword in one hand, points at each end. With the weapon at his waist, he spun, swiping at his enemies in a whirlwind the moment they attempted to attack. One particularly smart—or lucky—wolf demon leapt and managed to grab the end of Shang's spear with his teeth. Mulan struck him with her spade and pushed him toward the hungry trees.

Shang shot her a look of thanks. "Twenty more to go. You ready?"

She nodded.

Shang pressed his back against hers and raised his weapons. "Together, then."

The red-skinned demons charged. They were stronger than her, but she was smarter. Mulan countered their spears with her spade and used her smaller size and nimbleness to evade their attacks, feinting and then ducking to swipe at their ankles while Shang often delivered the crushing blow.

The yellow-skinned demons watched from a distance. They didn't join the battle, but their long tongues flicked and they whispered to one another before blowing a horn and calling the others to retreat.

Mulan's hands were raw from clutching the spade tight, but she kept it at her side, watching the demons run off.

"Is it over?"

"I doubt it," Shang said through his teeth.

"We'll be doomed if we stay here," ShiShi grunted. "Demons cannot die. Not by the hand of a ghost or a mortal, anyway. We've wounded them, but they'll regenerate. At least we've bought ourselves time before more appear."

He was right. War drums pounded. They sounded far away, but close enough that the bricks under Mulan's feet quivered. The bushes to their sides rustled, and the trees' arms stretched and crawled across the tall grass. The ground shook—*thump, thump, thump*—with the weight of hundreds of demon soldiers.

"Run!" ShiShi ordered.

This time, Mulan didn't argue. She sprinted.

"The brick path ends just ahead," Shang shouted. "It must be the end of Meng Po's domain."

The path disappeared, and the scenery abruptly changed. Gone were the tangerine and lemon trees, the pleasant fragrance of peonies and plum blossoms. The grass under their feet turned to black rock, and the sky deepened into a dark crimson, with a thick fog obscuring what lay ahead of them.

Suddenly Shang halted. He reached for Mulan, but his fingers went through her arm. "Stop him!" he yelled at ShiShi.

The lion lunged in front of Mulan, blocking her way before she went any farther.

Her breath caught in her lungs. She'd nearly run off the edge of a cliff. In her shock, she dropped the spade. It tumbled down, bouncing against the cliff before it snapped over one of the jagged rocks protruding from the water below.

Mulan winced, watching the spade's bronze pieces sink into the black, murky water. If not for Shang and ShiShi, that would have been her.

"This is as far as we go," ShiShi said.

"We can't fight them off again. Thirty demons is one story. Against a hundred?"

Mulan clenched her fists. She couldn't lose to King Yama, not after finding Shang. She'd promised she'd save him. "There has to be another way."

"I can make the jump," said Shang. "So can Ping."

"That is the River of Hopelessness," ShiShi said sharply. "No one is diving into it."

"We don't have a choice," Shang argued.

More than ever, she was grateful for Shang's training.

Thanks to their speed, they were at least a hundred strides ahead of the demons. Still, it was impossible not to hear the demons catching up. A war drum thudded from their army, out of sync with their thumping footsteps and clashing spears. Mulan, Shang, and ShiShi were cornered.

No, she couldn't let fear and panic distract her. She watched the fog curl underneath the cliff. What secrets was it hiding?

Mulan glanced behind her shoulder to see if the demons were getting closer. But she suddenly saw their way out instead. Above the fog, just under the moon, was a silver mountain.

The slope of the mountain was gentle enough to climb easily. She couldn't see the other side of the mountain, but that didn't matter now.

"Look," Mulan said, pointing at a narrow ridge that looked connected to the mountain ahead. "There's a small cave there at the tip of the ridge." She squinted. "And light inside it. Could be a tunnel that leads to that mountain with the silver grass."

Shang was taller than she was and had a better view of what lay beyond the cave. "I don't think it's grass on that mountain. It looks more like a cemetery."

"You think those are graves?" ShiShi asked darkly. "Look again."

"They're knives," Mulan whispered, seeing the blades shine in the light as the fog cleared. She gulped. "I guess we take the river then."

"No," the lion disagreed. "We take the mountain."

"The mountain will kill us."

"The River of Hopelessness is cursed," ShiShi informed her. "You'll be lost in it forever. And if you *are* lucky enough to escape it, you'll emerge a demon." He tilted his head at Meng Po's oncoming battalion. "Like them."

Mulan relented. There wasn't time to weigh the choices.

Fog and mist cloaked the mountain, obscuring the path toward it. But as Mulan waded through the fog, careful not to misstep and fall off the cliff, she found the narrow cave ahead.

She yanked away the moss blocking the cave's mouth. The tunnel inside was so tight they would have to enter sideways, one at a time. *That, at least, should slow the demons,* she thought.

"You two go first," she said to Shang and ShiShi. The demons were coming, and she'd lost Meng Po's bronze spade to use as a weapon. She took the spear from Shang's hands.

"Wait," said Shang. "What are you—"

"It's you they're after. Not me."

"Go," ShiShi barked after Shang. "We waste time by arguing."

Shang slipped inside first, then ShiShi. Mulan had to shove the lion through the cave with her weight; ShiShi barely fit. She heard him whimper as he inched his way through, nails scraping against the cave walls.

Mulan went next, sidling carefully through the entrance to the dank, musty cave. A few steps into the cave, she bent her head so it wouldn't hit the ceiling. Suddenly, something grabbed her leg and pulled.

She gasped, kicking, and blindly poked her weapon at her assailant.

"Grab my tail!" ShiShi shouted, his voice echoing in the cave.

Mulan reached for it, but even as ShiShi pulled her through, the demons outside still had her foot. Then someone jabbed her ankle with his spear, and Mulan let out a cry of pain.

"Ping!" she heard Shang shout.

Biting her lip to hold in the pain, Mulan hurled her weapon at the demons outside, and ShiShi yanked the rest of her into the cave. The walls trembled, pebbles and stones tumbling from the ceiling.

Mulan covered her head with her hand and limped as fast as she could toward the opening on the other side. Her ankle burned, but she didn't stop to look at it.

The demons tried to follow. The one in the front was too fat to make it through the cave's narrow opening, so he tried stabbing his spear at Mulan while the smaller demons around him tried crawling under his legs into the cave. Their claws scraped the earth as they attempted to scramble inside, but dirt and debris spilled over their eyes.

The cave was collapsing. If Mulan didn't hurry, she'd be trapped inside. As the tunnel widened toward the other side, she barreled through and leapt for the exit. ShiShi grabbed her collar with his teeth and pulled her out.

"Th-that was close," she said, coughing. The fog was thinner on this side of the cave, but it still misted over the ground and hovered about their surroundings. She bent down to catch her breath and rubbed dirt out of her eyes. "Have we lost them?"

"Until they find another way to this side, yes."

With a sigh of relief, Mulan sat up. She tried to get to her feet, but her ankle still burned.

"You're hurt," Shang said.

She touched her foot, pressing the spot the demon had struck with his spear. Blood came back on her fingertips, but nothing was broken. "I'll be fine. It's nothing."

Shang knelt in front of her, examining her ankle, too. "You need to wrap it."

"Later. There isn't time."

"Will you be able to manage this climb?" ShiShi rumbled.

She looked up, only to have her breath catch in her

throat. Just the sight of the Mountain of Knives sent a wave of terror through her.

It was magnificent, in a shocking, terrible sort of way. Thousands of knives and daggers covered the surface, packed so close they looked like silver stalks of grass. Mulan couldn't see their hilts, but the blades were all shiny and clean. Not a smear or speck of blood.

That was somewhat reassuring, she supposed.

Except there was no possible way for her to climb the mountain. Shang could, as nothing in Diyu would harm him. But the knives were staked so close together she couldn't possibly take a step between them, nor could she step *on* them . . . not without impaling herself.

"According to legend, each dagger belongs to a bandit or murderer who is now in Diyu," ShiShi said at her side.

"So they're demons?"

"No, they're ghosts. Even bandits and murderers have some hope of leaving this place. Only those who commit the gravest misdeeds, such as killing one's family or one's ruler, become demons. They have to stay in Diyu forever, since there's no hope of redemption for them. Everyone else becomes a ghost."

Mulan suppressed a shudder. If she failed to bring Shang back to the real world, did that mean King Yama would change her into a demon? Staying in Diyu forever would be bad enough. But to become one of those monsters?

"We must be vigilant," ShiShi went on. "The ghosts are known to haunt the area."

"Great," Shang said drily. "So if we go up this way, we fight ghosts *and* demons?'"

"The demons won't follow us. If we can find a way up."

"And the ghosts?'" Shang inquired.

The lion shrugged. "Another reason to hurry."

Shang didn't seem to like his guardian's strategy. He hesitated. "Ping, are you sure you can do this? It's a steep hike, even without the knives. And your ankle . . . maybe we should find another way."

"There isn't one," she said, hopping to her feet. It hurt to stand on her injured foot, but it wasn't bleeding anymore. She'd manage. "I can do it."

"How?" Shang blurted. "You're not a ghost. You can't step on knives."

Mulan pursed her lips, considering. "I'll come up with something." The scraping sounds in the cave still hadn't stopped. "You go ahead."

"I'm not leaving you behind," Shang argued. "We have to make use of our resources. Maybe your armor—"

"It isn't sturdy enough," Mulan interrupted. "Not by itself."

Clapping her palms over the blade, Mulan pulled the closest knife out of the mountain. "But this would help." She held the blade flat against her boot. Yes, she could bind its flat side of to her foot and bolster it with the armor plates from her shoulders. She'd do the same with her hands. That should be enough to protect her as she climbed. As long as she didn't fall forward or backward . . . or put too much pressure on her injured ankle.

Now she just needed something to tie the blades to her feet and hands. She wished she'd kept the rope from the empty well.

Mulan looked around, then stared at ShiShi's mane. Even after his tussle with Meng Po's trees, ShiShi's elaborate braids had stayed intact. His hair was thick and long—it just might work.

She grabbed the lion's mane and raised her knife. "I'll make it up to you somehow, but this is going to get both of us up the mountain."

ShiShi's orange eyes widened with horror, but he didn't react soon enough. With one swift slice, Mulan cut a handful of the braids and started tying the armor and blades over her hands and feet to protect her from the mountain.

"My mane!" ShiShi cried.

Mulan cast ShiShi an apologetic look, suddenly remembering how she'd cut her own hair before stealing her father's armor. Such a simple action, yet it'd changed everything. She'd severed ties with her old identity and gone from Mulan to Ping, from bride to soldier, from obedient daughter to woman who led her own life.

But what if she'd cut *too* many ties? What if when she went home, her parents no longer recognized her? After all, she wasn't the same Mulan anymore.

Sometimes, she didn't even know who she was. She'd thought going to war would show her, but things were never as easy as that.

Mulan dropped the knife, shaking away her doubts. Shishi's braids felt heavy in her hands. "It'll grow back," she told him as warmly as she could. "And when it does, it'll be even more majestic than it was before."

She tightened the braid over her foot with a knot and gestured at the lion. "Come on, you're next. Give me your foot."

"I don't need to wear any contraption," ShiShi growled. "I am a stone lion, the great guardian of the esteemed Li family. These pitiful knives won't harm me."

"You're not stone anymore."

She started to tie several blades around ShiShi's giant paws. He opened his mouth to argue, but the sound of the demons' drums cut him short.

"They've found us," said Shang.

"Go!" ShiShi said, pushing Mulan toward the mountain with his head as soon as she'd finished ShiShi's blade armor. "I'll follow."

Mulan stared at her hands. She'd turned her gauntlets around so they cushioned her fingers and palms against the flats of the blades she'd tied to her hands. "Here goes nothing."

She took her first step on the mountain, balancing on what had to be the points of half a dozen sharpened blades. Her injured ankle wobbled, and her arms began to flail.

"Focus!" Shang shouted. "Breathe, Ping. Gain control of your breath, gain control of the situation."

Inhale. Exhale. Mulan expelled her breath. She didn't sink, and her foot hadn't been impaled. "That was close."

Beside her, Shang nodded, looking relieved. "Find your center. There you go."

She didn't take time to congratulate herself. She took another step, and another. Shang followed. The knives did nothing to hurt him—he might as well have been stepping on flowers and rocks.

Don't watch him. Watch the ground. Her balance was precarious enough as it was. If she wasn't careful, the knives might cut through ShiShi's braids and unbind her blade-shoes. The key was to pick spots where the knives were staked at a steep, slanted angle, or lay almost horizontal. Mulan aimed for as many of those pockets as she could, stepping on the flats of the blades as if they were stairs and using her palms for extra balance when she needed to.

Even then, it didn't help that most of the knives and daggers were of different heights and widths. Her armor protected her from pricks, but Mulan could feel the effect of brushing against the knives. The sides of her feet, which the blades didn't cover, had already received multiple cuts.

So it didn't help when the knives began to shudder.

Thump. Thump. Thump, pounded faraway drums.

The demons were here. They'd made it through the tunnel, and now, one by one, they burst through the fog. The beat of the drums grew faster and faster, and the demons cackled at the sight of Mulan, Shang, and ShiShi cornered against the Mountain of Knives. They raised their swords and spears, stamping them against the ground as they drew closer.

"Finish the lion and the short one," one of the demons shouted. "Take the spirit to Meng Po!"

The demon soldiers obeyed. They jabbed their spears at ShiShi, and when the lion was too far up to attack, they started throwing their spears and plucking knives out of the mountain to toss at ShiShi and Mulan.

Mulan gasped, almost falling over as she evaded being impaled by a spear. Shang caught the end of the knife tied to her hand and steadied her.

"You all right?"

She nodded, but her lips pursed tight.

"Kill the outsiders!" the demons bellowed below.

Shang's jaw tensed. "You and ShiShi go ahead. I'll distract the demons."

"No," Mulan said, taking another step up. "We all stay together."

"I can't be harmed. You can."

"Li Shang has a point," ShiShi interrupted with a grunt. "Someone needs to keep the demons busy. Or else we're not going to get very far."

"No one gets left behind," Mulan said firmly.

But below, the demons were gaining on them. Some had already started climbing the Mountain of Knives, using their thick armor as shields against the sharp knifepoints. The rest stayed on the ground, continuing to pull knives from the mountain and throw them at Mulan, Shang, and ShiShi.

Knives bounced and clanged against the mountain, one landing dangerously close to Mulan's leg.

"Still want to keep climbing?" ShiShi yelled at her.

"Incoming!" Shang shouted. "Duck!"

Mulan and the guardian flattened as much as they could against the mountain, barely dodging the flying knives.

The drumbeats grew louder, closer. More of the demons were on the mountain now, and they scrambled up with knives in their mouths and swords and spears on their backs. At the speed they were climbing, the demons would catch up to them within minutes.

ShiShi shot Mulan a glare.

"We stay together," she repeated. "No one gets left behind."

"Stubborn Ping." ShiShi harrumphed. "There is a reason I am the great guardian of the Li family. And that is to protect you all." He turned to Shang. "Li Shang, I am sorry I failed your father. I will not do the same to you."

Without any warning, the lion leapt down the mountain, ripping through the fog and landing in front of the demons as the blades that had been tied to him fell away.

"ShiShi, wait!" Mulan shouted. "No!"

The drumbeats stopped.

Chapter Fourteen

There was nothing Mulan could do. ShiShi's fate was eclipsed by the fog below.

She hung her head, holding in a sob.

She'd barely gotten to know the lion. Much as he teased her for being small and for being unworthy of the great task of saving Shang, she knew ShiShi had a mighty heart. Even in those few hours, she'd come to admire his loyalty to Shang, and his bravery. She'd already gotten used to his companionship, had started to think of him as a friend. And now . . .

Shang tried to touch her shoulder, but he settled for resting his hand above hers.

She wanted to tell him that they needed to go down,

needed to help ShiShi. But she knew what Shang would say. *If we do, his sacrifice would be for nothing. We would not honor him.*

And he'd be right.

Mulan glanced up. The half-moon loomed over them, shining bright against the crimson sky.

Her mission was to get Shang out of Diyu. She wasn't about to fail that now. There was no choice but to keep going.

Honorable ShiShi, she thought, swallowing hard, *I know I promised that you would continue to be Shang's guardian. I wish you could have made it out with us, but I won't let your sacrifice be in vain. I will get Shang out of here.*

She turned to the captain. "Keep climbing."

Sometimes Mulan swore she could hear King Yama's laugh emanating from above, taunting her and Shang over ShiShi's loss.

Then she'd realize it was just the pounding of her heart.

She'd lost track of how many times she looked down, sliding her eyes down the slope of the mountain to where they'd started out. Every time, she hoped ShiShi might burst out of the fog with a hearty roar. But he didn't.

Only King Yama's warning thudded in her ears.

Should you die here, you stay here.

She grimaced. That warning had been meant for her,

not ShiShi. The only thing she could do now was make sure they got Shang out of here.

Shang turned, his bare hands pressed against the tips of the knives, so he could face her. Unlike ShiShi, who probably would have filled the silence by rambling about the glories of his past, the captain had been quiet. He had never been a man of many words, and she caught him opening and closing his mouth, as if he were debating what to say.

"You all right?" Shang asked, finally breaking the silence. His voice was gentle, and it took Mulan a moment to realize he was trying to comfort her over ShiShi's loss.

Mulan parted her lips. Was she all right? ShiShi was gone, the moon was half-dark, and she still hadn't told Shang about her agreement with Yama. She needed to, but somehow the Mountain of Knives didn't feel like the place to have the discussion. Not so soon after ShiShi's loss. She'd tell him once they reached the top.

"I will be," was all she said.

Shang's thick brows knit with concern.

Her chest tightened. *Funny he should worry about me when he's the one who's dying.*

"It was a brave thing he did," said Shang slowly. "I can see why my father entrusted him to you."

"He was supposed to be your guardian once we got out."

"I know." Shang swallowed. "When my father was alive, he used to warn me that I relied too much on myself and not on others. I thought that was what it meant to be strong— I never saw him ask for help, never saw him *need* anyone. I wanted to be like him: the great leader of China's finest troops. I didn't know he had a friend with him all along, helping him."

Mulan nodded, touched by the earnestness in his voice.

"Do you have a guardian?"

"My ancestors sent me someone." Mulan stepped up with one foot, heaved the rest of her body to lift the other leg. Even if her ankle hadn't been swelling, she'd have to climb slowly. At least the pain was subsiding. "When we get out of here, I'll introduce you."

"I'd like that."

Mulan allowed herself a small smile. *Good. He's talking like we're going to get out of here.*

Shang motioned for her to resume hiking up the mountain. The slope was less steep than it'd been earlier, and in some places, the path was nearly flat.

"Come on," he said. "If we can't make it up to the top of this tiny hill, all my hours spent training you will have been for nothing."

"Tiny hill?" Mulan said. "I'd hardly call this a hill."

But his words worked. Her determination renewed, she

returned to trudging up this horrific Mountain of Knives. Her toes curled against the ski blades as they clanged against the pointed knives. The armor under her hands and feet grew heavy. Sweat dribbled down the back of her neck. But Mulan didn't stop. Up, up, up.

She couldn't stop thinking about what Shang had confided earlier, and what a comfort the words had been to her. She'd always admired him as a leader and soldier— someone who always knew what to do in battle. But she was beginning to admire him even more as a person. She doubted he could tell a lie to save his life. The few times she'd caught him not knowing what to say, he had stammered or averted his gaze. He never resorted to bending the truth . . . unlike her.

Was it wrong of her to deceive him, especially when he trusted her so much? If he ever found out the truth about her . . .

Stop it. Mulan sighed. *Friend or not, he can't find out the truth.*

Strange; it was easier to forget *here* than up in the real world that she was pretending to be a man. In Diyu, a realm of ghosts and demons and monsters, keeping her guise as Ping was the last of Mulan's worries.

You can't forget, she reminded herself. *No matter how much you might want to.*

"Ping?" Shang said, glancing back and seeing that she still lagged far behind. "Is your ankle bothering you?"

"No." She forced a throaty laugh, the one she'd perfected to be "manly" enough to pass as Ping. "Stop worrying about me and don't wait up. I've got this."

Shang didn't move. Mulan ignored him and kept climbing. Finally, when she caught up with him, he followed.

The higher they climbed, the quieter it became. Maybe ShiShi had exaggerated about the ghosts. They were nearly at the top, and she hadn't encountered a single one.

She inhaled. That was a good thing. Best to savor one's luck, not question it, especially when in the Underworld.

Every few steps, Shang waited for her. It was hard not to see the concern creased on his brow. The climb up was far more difficult for her than for him. For her, each step was a highly calculated risk. If she put too much weight on one foot, or leaned backward or forward too much, she could be impaled.

Meanwhile, Shang easily leapt from knife to knife. It almost looked fun, if not for the fact that he was a spirit hovering close to death. Mulan didn't dare pick up her pace.

They still had a ways to go before reaching the top, but luckily, the path was not too steep. Mulan tried to focus on her footing and not on looking up or down.

Both directions made her nervous. If she looked up,

she could see the impossible landscape of cliffs hanging in midair, supported by little else other than the clouds. If she looked down, she saw the thousands of knives staked into the mountain. Every now and then, as they climbed higher, she spotted bloodstains on the blades. She tried not to wonder if it was human blood . . . or demon blood. It wasn't clear which would better.

Neither spoke for a long time. The knives on her hands and feet were getting heavy, and Mulan estimated they were almost up the mountain.

She wiped her forehead. "I'm grateful you never made this a training drill. The pole with those medallions was hard enough."

Shang chuckled. "Climbing a mountain of knives? I'll keep it in mind for future exercises."

Mulan groaned. "Future exercises? The war is over."

"You can never be too careful. China will always face the threat of invaders."

"That'll be for you to deal with, Captain Li Shang," she teased. "After I get you out of here, I'm going home."

Shang opened his mouth to reply, but the mountain's summit came into view. Shang shielded his eyes from the light and went ahead to inspect the area. "There are no more knives up here. Just grass. We're almost there."

The news made Mulan climb faster. She couldn't wait to be at the top. Blood speckled the sides of her hands, and she could only imagine the condition of her feet. Every step hurt more than she cared to admit, and even after what felt like hours on this mountain, every time she remembered she was literally walking on knives, her nerves sent a pang of panic to her mind. Her temples pulsed, and her forehead dripped with sweat.

So when her fingertips touched that glorious grass lining the mountain's summit, Mulan gathered her breath in her chest and swept her leg up over the edge. It wasn't as easy as it sounded, especially since she still needed to avoid all those knives with their blades sticking out of the mountain's rock face.

But there was one knife—no, it was too long to be a knife. One *sword* that'd been stabbed into the mountain, blade first. It looked special, and any other time, Mulan might have taken an extra long look at it. But now all she noticed was that its golden hilt stuck out from the thin metal knives around it. Perfect to use as a step to haul herself up to the summit.

She rolled onto the grass. She didn't care that it was brown and withering and crinkled under her back. "We made it!"

Shang chuckled. "My climb wasn't as hard as yours." He hesitated. "We should take a break here. Consider our next step."

"Good plan."

Mulan sat up and observed where they were. A plain of sorts. One that looked like it hadn't been visited or tended in a long time, given how dead the grass was both in the plains and on the hills. She'd take a dead hill over a mountain of knives any day.

She unfastened the binds over her hands, then cut the braids on her feet. She clutched the remains of ShiShi's mane, tied it to one of the daggers, and staked it into the ground. Not quite the regal memorial he deserved, but it would have to do. She sighed. There seemed to be little else on this mountain.

Then, remembering that strange sword just to her side, she leaned over the mountain edge to inspect it. The hilt was dull with age, but still gold, with short wings at the base of the blade that pointed forward. It had to be hundreds of years old.

Mulan was about to leave it, but there was something inscribed on the blade itself. She could see only the first word. It was the same as in her name: *Fa*. Flower.

Curious now, she reached down and tried to wrench the sword free. It was stuck tight.

"Let me help." Shang knelt beside her and clasped the edge of the hilt. Together, they pulled. Out slid the sword. The weight of it nearly tipped Mulan over the mountain, but she caught herself in time and backed up away from the ledge.

Catching her breath, she laid the sword on the grass, wiping it clean of dirt and grime. The characters on the blade glittered in the moonlight.

"'The flower that blooms in adversity is the most rare and beautiful of all.'" Mulan's brow furrowed. "This doesn't seem like something that would belong in Diyu."

Still, *Fa* was in her name. Maybe it was a sign she should keep it. A sword could come in handy. After all, she'd left her own sword back in the real world. She hoped it'd still be there when she returned.

She peeled off one of her gauntlets and yanked a sleeve off her tunic, then wrapped it around the sword. She got up. Little cuts and pricks smeared her hands with blood, but it didn't hurt. Not yet. "Where to now, Captain?"

Shang said nothing. He was looking at her bare arm and her hands. The blood had dried on her fingers and palms, but they still looked like a mess.

"I'm fine," Mulan said, quickly putting her hands behind her back. Her ankle still hurt where the demon had struck her with his spear, but the bleeding had stopped there, too.

Shang, on the other hand, hadn't even suffered a scratch. His shoes brushed against the ground like shadows, barely touching the earth. He wasn't even tired. She knew it bothered him. It was a reminder that he was practically dead.

Mulan's shoulders fell. This was the first time they'd been alone—and not fleeing demons—since she'd found him in the tower.

She sat on a flat rock overlooking the Mountain of Knives, letting her boots sink into the soft, dry dirt. "How do you feel?" Mulan asked Shang. "Are you hurt anywhere?"

"I feel nothing," he replied numbly. He touched his abdomen, where his physical body had been slashed. "Even this pain is gone. The wound's healed. I guess ghosts don't carry their wounds with them."

Mulan remembered the Imperial soldiers she'd seen standing in line to see King Yama, how they'd still had arrows protruding from their bodies. They'd looked the same as Shang—bodies glowing and nearly translucent—but even from Mulan's short moments with them, she'd gotten the sense that they had already accepted their fate. Shang, on the other hand, seemed different. It was almost as if he still had a string tethering his spirit to Earth. Once it was cut, though . . . no, that was why she was here. To take him back.

"You're not a ghost," she said.

"I know." Shang hesitated. "I never thanked you, Ping, for coming to Diyu to look for me."

A flush heated Mulan's cheeks. She blamed it on the exertion required to keep climbing this mountain—even though she'd finished climbing minutes ago. She pretended to be preoccupied with rolling up her shortened sleeve. Its threads were frayed now, and tickled her arm. "Trust me, I'd rather be here than up there. It was cold, and I could hear Yao snoring even from my tent."

That got a laugh out of Shang.

Mulan grinned. "Chien-Po made a soup for everyone. I tried to get you to drink some, but you wouldn't." Her smile faded, and a wash of cold suddenly made her shiver.

"I . . . I couldn't break your fever, and you were burning up. Everyone said you were going to die." She inhaled a ragged breath. "I stayed with you, hoping you'd get better, but I must have drifted off to sleep. Then I saw your father's ghost with you at camp. At first I thought I was dreaming, but it was really him. I promised him I would bring you home."

Shang was silent. "I'm sorry I didn't believe you earlier."

"I can't blame you for that." She hugged her knees to her chest and laughed through her nose. "There's a lot to take in after coming to this place. Soldier demons, angry trees, lavish tea pavilions, and mountains of knives. I hardly believe it myself." She started to get up, but Shang stopped her.

"You need to bandage your feet, Ping. There's more walking to do."

"We should get going."

"We can take a minute for you to dress your wounds," Shang said, in a voice that wasn't to be contested, so Mulan sat back on the flat rock and attended to her injury.

"You know, Ping, I'm glad my father got to meet you. He always wanted another son, but . . . he and my mother never had any other children who lived."

Shang sucked in his breath. Mulan had rarely heard him talk about his family before. He'd always kept it private. "I know he must be grateful I've found a friend like you."

Someone he can trust, Mulan finished for him in her thoughts. She tightened her bandage. "What will you do after the war, Shang?"

"I haven't really thought about it," Shang admitted. "I've been away for so many years. I suppose I'll visit my mother first." He paused ruefully. "She'll be lonely now that my father is gone."

"She must be very proud of you," said Mulan gently. "Will you stay at home?"

"Not for long." Shang's spirit might be pale blue, but she detected a faint blush reddening his cheeks.

"What is it?"

Shang shook his head, pursing his lips tight. His back became stiff as bamboo.

"Come on, tell me," Mulan teased. "Or I'll assume the

worst. I'm guessing . . . she's a terrible cook? No? Hmm . . . maybe she reads tea leaves. There's a woman in my village who's very superstitious. She won't wash her hair on anyone's birthday, and—"

Shang arched an eyebrow, the only indication that he was curious what else she might come up with. *And* that she was completely wrong.

"I won't tell anyone. I promise. Your secret's safe with me."

His shoulders dropped out of resignation. "My mother has it in her mind that I need to find a . . . a bride." He sounded nervous. "It was never a priority of mine, not with the war. But now that my father has passed, I am the head of the family. It is my duty to carry on the family line."

It was Mulan's turn to raise an eyebrow. "You don't sound excited about this."

Shang shifted his weight from one foot to the other. "Before I left for battle, my mother tried introducing me to a few girls. But they were only after my family's name." He paused, clearly at a loss of what else to say.

Mulan hid a smile. She'd rarely seen him like this. How funny that Shang always knew what to do in a fight, and how to train a man to be the best soldier possible, yet faced with a personal conversation about his life he became almost . . . shy.

"I'm listening," she said. "What were they like?"

"All they could do was flutter their fans and bat their eyes. The matchmaker Mother hired bragged that they were perfect porcelain dolls. What she didn't say was they had no minds of their own." Shang grimaced at the memory without looking at her. The sides of his neck pinked with embarrassment. "They'd say anything to make me like them."

How familiar that sounds. Mulan put her hands on her hips. "Not all girls are like that. You have to look at it from their perspective, too. Girls are raised to be pretty and graceful, and *quiet*." She made a face. "They aren't allowed to speak their minds, and they don't have a choice in who they marry. My parents were lucky that they fell in love, but their marriage was arranged, too. And my mother, she doesn't even belong to her family anymore after they got married. It wasn't my mother's decision, but her family's. They told her that a woman's only role in life is to bear sons."

Shang leaned forward. "You sound quite passionate about this."

His closeness made Mulan hunch back. Remembering who she was pretending to be, she felt her cheeks burn. "I just . . . I mean, I bet there are some girls who'd make better soldiers than boys. If they were given the chance."

"A female soldier? That's the craziest thing I've heard."

"Girls can be strong, too."

"Not like us, Ping."

Mulan hid a smile. "You'd be surprised."

"Well," Shang said. "As much as I'd love to meet a female soldier, it won't happen in my lifetime. It's against the law."

"Yes, it is." Mulan swallowed hard. "But that doesn't mean girls can't be clever or strong."

"You're right. My mother is quite sharp. My father always respected that about her." He paused. "Even then, my father was a man of tradition. So is my mother. I never thought to question that a woman should not belong to her husband's family." Shang tilted his head, looking thoughtful. "It doesn't seem fair, now that I think about it."

"It isn't."

"Perhaps when I marry, I'll combine the ancestral temples so my bride won't have to leave her family."

Mulan couldn't help feeling touched. "Really?"

"Then again, I've yet to meet a girl I can actually talk to."

"You need a girl with a brain," Mulan found herself saying without realizing it. "One who speaks her mind."

"Do you know one like that?"

She looked down at her bandages again, hoping Shang didn't hear her pulse getting faster. "I might," she said, trying her best to sound like she was still teasing him.

Mulan, she scolded herself. *What's wrong with you?*

"I'd need to know what else you value in a girl," she said to Shang, ignoring the strange stirring in her chest. "A lovely face with shining eyes? A sweet, melodious voice? Someone who's delicate and graceful as a flower?"

Shang reddened, and Mulan laughed. She was having fun teasing the captain, something she'd never gotten to do before. "Chien-Po wants a girl who can cook well. Yao is the one who wants someone who adores him. Hmmm . . . I'd guess you'd want someone capable." She wrinkled her nose. "Someone who can take care of the household when you're at war."

"Taking care of the household is like commanding an army. My mother could be a general in her own right." He chuckled, then became serious again.

Mulan lifted a shoulder. "What else?"

"What else?" Shang repeated. He exhaled. "Someone who's smart and brave, and kind. Someone I can trust. Someone who's honest."

Mulan's tongue grew heavy. *Honest.* Shang might think Ping was honest, but he wouldn't think the same of Mulan.

Why do you care what Shang thinks? Mulan berated herself. *You're Ping, his friend. You're not one of these village girls chasing after him. Besides, if you ever make it home, you'll have other things to worry about. Like whether Mama and Baba will even welcome you back.*

Still, she couldn't forget Mushu's sly comment. *You like*

him, don't you? he'd asked one night, after observing Mulan try to comfort Shang.

She'd denied it then, and she denied it now. She'd only been concerned about Shang! After all, he was her commanding officer, and he'd just received a rebuke from Chi Fu about his capability to lead. That didn't mean she *liked* him.

But the swoop in her stomach when she looked up at the captain hinted otherwise. She ignored it, mentally stomping the feeling away, along with her earlier desire to tease him about what he looked for in a girl. Suddenly that subject was the last thing she wanted to talk about. Especially since he'd never look at her that way. He couldn't.

"So who's this mystery girl you might know?" Shang asked wryly. "Is it your sister?"

Mulan choked. "My sister? Who said I had a—"

"Chi Fu did."

"He did?"

"Well, he knew Fa Zhou had a daughter. None of us knew he also had a son."

Mulan stared at her hands, then leaned down to finish wrapping her ankle. She could not look at Shang right now. "Uh, my father doesn't talk about me much."

"That's what you told us." Shang chuckled. "Remembering how you were back then, I can understand why. When you go home now, I know he'll be very proud of you."

"I hope so."

"You're a hero, Ping. I'm guessing when you go home, girls will line up for your attention."

"Ha!" Mulan laughed awkwardly. "I don't know about that. It's not really on my mind."

Shang cleared his throat. "So tell me . . . about your sister. Is she—"

"I finished wrapping my ankle," Mulan interrupted abruptly. "We should get going. We must be getting closer to the gates. Maybe you'll wake up just in time for breakfast."

Her brusqueness took him aback. She could tell from the way Shang's brows jumped up and his lips parted. If they'd been talking about anything else, Mulan might have apologized for interrupting him. But the more he pressed her about her family life, the more uneasy she became.

Thankfully, he recovered quickly and nodded. "All right."

"Wait." Mulan said it before she registered what she was doing. She grabbed a handful of grass and let the stalks fly in the wind. She didn't know when they'd get another chance to talk like this. "I need to tell you something."

"Yes?"

Mulan paused, and that flush crept back onto her cheeks again. She wanted to tell him who she really was. Not Ping, not Ping's sister. Mulan. Just Mulan.

But she could already picture how betrayed Shang would be.

I never sought out to earn Shang's trust. Why do I care so much what he thinks about me? Is it because I'm trying to prove that I'm someone worthy of that trust? Yes, that's part of it.

But also . . .

Her stomach fluttered—an uncomfortable, unfamiliar sensation. *Also,* she scolded herself, *I'm an idiot. Keep to the plan. I can't afford to have anyone finding out who I really am. It could get Baba in trouble. And disgrace the family.*

That flutter in her stomach sank. *Not to mention, Shang would hate me . . . if he found out the truth. He'd never trust me again.*

"Never mind," she said bitterly, glancing at the moon. "We should get going."

"You keep looking up at the sky, Ping." Shang craned his neck to look up. "Do you think everyone up there is still asleep?"

"Up there? As in, the soldiers in our camp?"

Shang nodded. "I feel like I've been here for years. Yet, if my body is still alive, it can't have been more than a few hours."

"Didn't you meet Yama?"

"No," said Shang. "The last thing I remember was talking to you. When I woke, I was here—in that tower. I thought I was already dead."

"You aren't. Time runs differently down here."

"If that's the case, why are we in such a rush?"

Her mouth went dry. All this time she'd wanted to confess she was really Mulan, she'd forgotten to tell him the importance of getting back before morning!

"Because . . . I made a deal with King Yama."

"A deal?" His brow furrowed. "What kind of deal?"

"If we don't reach the gates by sunrise," said Mulan, her voice shaking, "you'll die."

Shang was quiet. "I see. What about you?"

She faltered. He wouldn't like this part, but she needed to tell him. "If we don't make it out, I . . . I stay here. As his prisoner."

The captain's expression leapt with shock. "What? Ping, you can't be serious. You can't be risking your life to—"

"It was the only way," she interrupted. "You did the same for me."

Shang pursed his lips tight. His shoulders tensed, heavy with the news she'd just told him, but he knew it was too late to argue. Now he, too, glanced at the moon. "Then we make our way to the gates. Let's go, Ping—"

A familiar roar cut him off.

Chapter Fifteen

ShiShi pounced in front of them, making the earth shudder from the impact of his landing. "I told you the great guardian of the Li family would not be defeated by a pack of demons!" ShiShi proclaimed.

Mulan was nearly speechless. "You're back!"

"Of course I'm back. Did you expect to make it out of Diyu without me?"

Overcome with relief, Mulan embraced the lion. "We thought you were dead."

Her hug caught ShiShi off guard. "Careful with the mane." He made a face and shook his hair until Mulan had to back away. "It's still in shreds after what you did to it."

"Sorry."

"How did you escape the demons?" Shang asked.

"Hmph. Those squirrels are no match for a great stone lion such as myself." ShiShi squared his shoulders proudly. "Oh, there were hundreds of them, maybe thousands, even—"

Shang raised an eyebrow. "Thousands?"

"Fine. A *hundred*. Don't interrupt. A lion always lands on his feet. And when I did, I ripped their spears apart with my jaws and roared my mightiest roar! Most of them ran away after that. Then I chased the rest around the Mountain of Knives until there was nowhere to go. Those gloating fools thought they had me, but I spied a portal underneath one of the knives. It led me here, to level fifty-one."

Level fifty-one, Mulan thought. *Still a long way to go.*

ShiShi's tail swirled behind him as he circled Mulan and Shang. "I must say, I'm surprised to see you two loitering about. Why are you still here? I told you to hurry. This area is rife with ghosts."

"We didn't see any," she insisted. "How did you—"

"That's odd," the lion guardian interrupted. "I could have sworn that I've heard that many ghosts amass just below this mountain."

Mulan froze, hearing the whispers now. They were faint, but getting closer. And worse, there were many of them.

"What was that sound?" came whispers from the knives. "It sounded like a lion."

An angry voice. "It woke me."

"It's the outsider."

"The outsider?"

"The boy with no name."

"Find him! Tell the others."

The ghosts glided up the mountain, their movement causing a gust in the air and making the knives whistle. A chorus of harsh squeaks and shrieks ripped the air.

Unlike the ones Mulan had encountered on the Bridge of Helplessness, these ghosts looked dangerous. And angry. A few were decapitated and carried their heads under their arms; others were missing eyes and fingers and teeth. Their auras were all varying shades of red.

Mulan, Shang, and ShiShi backed up onto the grass, but it was too late. Before they could get any farther, a band of ghosts blocked their path.

"The outsider from the real world," rasped one of the bandit ghosts. He grinned at Mulan, revealing his missing front teeth. "I heard about him. He crossed the bridge. He wouldn't heed the warnings."

Another bandit ghost appeared. His belt was lined with a dozen knives, and he was missing his fourth finger and left eye. "You know what we do to those who don't heed our warning."

"Call the others. Tell them we found the trespasser."

Laughter. It rang across the knives, bouncing off them

like bells that chimed far, far into the distance while also sinking into Mulan's bones. The ghosts scattered across the mountain, retrieving their knives and daggers.

"Ah, my blade hasn't sung with the flesh of a mortal man since I was alive," one said, sharpening his knives against each other.

"Don't run, outsider. We'll make you one of us in due time."

The ghosts laughed. As they crowded together, blood and death singing in their hollow eyes, a pang of dread sharpened in the pit of Mulan's stomach.

"Bandits and murderers," Mulan murmured, repeating ShiShi's warning.

And just her luck, they were all after her.

Chapter Sixteen

There was nowhere to run. The bandit ghosts surrounded them on every side. Even if Mulan decided to fling herself off the cliff, the Mountain of Knives waited below. They couldn't fight, either—only Shang could intercept the ghosts. Mulan's sword and ShiShi's claws would go right through them.

Whispers still echoed from the knives, word rapidly spreading across Diyu that the "outsider from the real world" had climbed the Mountain of the Knives.

Mulan clenched her jaw. More ghosts flooded the plains, arriving in whirlwinds of pale, glowing reds, yellows, oranges, and greens. The newly arrived ghosts weren't bandits or murderers tied to the Mountain of Knives. Most were dressed like ordinary citizens. They'd come to witness the spectacle of a mortal making his way up Diyu.

A ghost with iron-rimmed spectacles landed on the grass. Mulan recognized him immediately as one of the ghosts who'd been on the Bridge of Helplessness—the one with the orange aura who'd warned her that he and the others would be watching. Jiao.

Jiao carried a scroll under his arm, and his ghostly fingers were stained with ink. He reminded her of Chi Fu, except without the long whiskers.

Behind his spectacles, the ghost's beady black eyes narrowed at her. "We heard about what happened with your meeting with King Yama. You should never have crossed the bridge, outsider."

The others ghosts agreed. "You'll never get out now."

Widening her stance, Mulan reached for the ancient sword at her side and unwrapped it. She raised it at the ghosts. "Leave us alone."

ShiShi leapt forward to address the ghosts. He bared his sharp teeth as he said, "The boy here has an agreement with King Yama. Let us pass."

"I was there," screeched one of the ghosts. "He cut the line!"

"I heard what King Yama said," another chimed in. "King Yama never promised that we couldn't interfere."

"It isn't fair that an outsider is in Diyu," another ghost

murmured. "It isn't fair he gets to see what awaits him in the afterlife."

"He must die."

"We'll take him to the river."

"You will do no such thing," ShiShi bellowed. "Anyone who wishes to harm Ping will have to go through me."

The ghosts scoffed and did just that. They passed through ShiShi, and the poor lion guardian looked as if he were going to be ill. His fur paled and stood up, and he shuddered.

Shang stepped in front of Mulan, but she shook her head. "Let me deal with this."

Mulan faced the ghosts with her sword at her side. "I understand you're all upset with me, but I'm here only to—"

"We don't care why you're here." The ghosts lunged. "No mortals allowed!"

As Mulan instinctively raised her blade to block them, a white, pearlescent light emanated from the sword, so bright the ghosts shrank away.

Mulan blinked, unsure of where the sword's power had come from. She glanced at ShiShi, but he simply lifted his chin to encourage her. Shang did the same with a nod.

"No sword can harm us," Jiao reminded the others. He sneered. "We're already dead."

At that, Mulan tilted forward. A mischievous grin

spread across her face, and the ghosts squirmed. "If that's true, why are you all so afraid of it?"

One of the bandit ghosts sharpened his knife across his belt and twirled it from finger to finger. "I'll deal with the boy."

Mulan arced her sword at him before he dared come close. The ghost leapt back, seeing she had cut through his belt and scratched his arm. His aura flashed a bright, burning red. "What in the— That's impossible." He wiped the blood from his skin. It shimmered like the rest of him. "That's no ordinary sword."

Commotion ensued as the bandits argued over who would attack her next. Mulan inched away, disappearing behind a throng of green-glowing ghosts. They were calmer than the bandits; they hardly noticed her.

She exhaled, wondering whether she should be thankful the ghosts were so disorganized. There had to be thousands of them here, laughing and gossiping as if this were the site of a village reunion. Most of them floated in the air, completely unaware of Mulan's presence. Now if only she could get Shang and ShiShi out of here.

"It's been so long since I've seen you. Are you staying in Youdu?"

"Not yet. Hopefully in the next century or two. I hear property there has gotten expensive."

"It has. There's a war in the living world. Lots of soldiers keep arriving. Some of them are too young to have committed any crimes, so Yama doesn't sentence them with any torture. They go straight to the City of the Dead. Youdu's getting so crowded. I think there's a batch of us scheduled for Heaven later this week, though."

"Is that the mortal down there? He looks a little like my younger brother."

"Poor thing. No way he's getting out of here alive."

"Unless someone decides to help him." The ghosts looked at each other and laughed. "Not us!"

Mulan stopped listening to the conversation. *There are so many ghosts here—some look like they've been here for centuries.* She glanced around. *I wonder if any of them might be related to me. Grandmother Fa always said to respect my ancestors . . . for if I needed help in Diyu, they would come. She never said I needed to be a ghost myself.*

"The mortal's down here!" one of the floating ghosts shouted. "Come get him!"

"Call for your ancestors," Mulan told Shang as the bandits headed their way. "Maybe they can help us."

"Ancestors?" ShiShi blubbered. "Why would we—"

"Good thinking, Ping," said Shang. He began to yell, "Is anyone here of the Li family? I need your help!"

"Is anyone here of the Fa family?" Mulan shouted,

slipping through another crowd of ghosts. "I belong to the Fa family!"

The bandits surrounded her. "Appealing to your ancestors won't help you, outsider." The ghost without teeth sneered. "Now be brave, soldier. It won't hurt. And you'll get to skip standing in King Yama's line. Again."

Shang opened his arms. "You won't touch him."

"Step aside, Captain." The bandit ghost cocked his head. "This isn't your battle to fight. My quarrel isn't with you."

"Yes," warned the ghost's colleague. "You're about to be reincarnated, so I wouldn't taint your soul with bloodshed."

Shang lunged. "You want to fight Ping, then you fight me, too."

"You can't kill me, boy. I'm already a ghost."

"Is anyone here of the Fa family?" Mulan shouted one last time. "I belong to the Fa family!"

"We are of the Fa family!" a shrill voice hollered back.

Mulan's ears perked, searching for the ghost that'd spoken.

"Don't touch the boy, you thugs! He belongs to our family!"

To Mulan's surprise, the bandits actually hesitated—and the ghost who'd shouted was a young woman, pushing her way through the crowd. Two men followed her, and Mulan assumed they were also her ancestors.

"Fa Mei, what do you think you're doing?" said the thin ghost tailing Mulan's ancestor. "Stay quiet!"

"We should help him," Fa Mei said. Her black hair fell to her waist, knotted into a simple braid adorned with white jasmine flowers. Rouge painted her lips, and her skin was lightly powdered white as parchment. Without all that makeup, she might have resembled Mulan.

"I agree," said the second ghost with Fa Mei. "We should help him. He's family."

"Uncles! Auntie!" Mulan cried, calling for the three approaching ghosts. "Please help. It's me, Fa . . ." Her voice faltered. She couldn't say Fa Mulan. "Fa Zhou's son."

"Get out of the way," Fa Mei said, fluttering the bandits to the side. "This is family business. You know the rules. . . . You don't interfere with family business."

The bandits glared at Mulan, but they backed away—a little.

Mulan's three ancestors straightened. Now that they were closer, Mulan could make out their appearances better. Fa Mei was a young woman dressed in expensive silks, and next to her was an elderly man who was rather rotund and a bald man with a cane who slightly resembled her father. They flew to Mulan's side.

"Fa Zhou's son, did you say?"

"Yes," Mulan gasped. "Please help us get out of here."

The bald ghost stroked his chin. "I think we should help, Liwei. What do you think?"

"The boy's an outsider, Ren. We can't trust him."

"We don't even know why he's here."

"He won't be an outsider for long if you leave him like this," ShiShi snapped at the ancestors. "He'll be dead."

"Help us," Shang said.

Fa Liwei, the older ghost, steepled his thick fingers. "Prove that you're family, first."

Mulan let out an exasperated sigh. "I already told you I am."

"If you're really family, you should have brought a gift."

"Gossip's like money hereabouts," Fa Mei said in a sing-song voice. "Everyone's dying for some news."

That made little sense to Mulan, but she nodded as if she understood. Gossip never failed to interest the ghosts, she remembered the demon guards telling her. "I can tell you what's happening with the Fa family right now."

"And why King Yama can't find you in the record books?" Ren added. The bald ghost patted the small bulge in his robe's left pocket.

Shang tossed Mulan a sidelong glance. A question perched on his lips.

Mulan frowned. No, she couldn't tell them that. "Why don't I tell about why I'm here instead? Like the other ghosts say, it's not every day a mortal comes to Diyu."

Her ancestors made a face. "It's a start. All right, we'll get you out of here."

"Leave it to me," said Mei. She floated toward the bandits and wagged her fan at them. "You bullies leave my cousin alone," she said shrilly. "We'll deal with him. He's family, after all."

The toothless bandit frowned. "But he's an outsider."

"And King Yama let him stay," Mei retorted. "If you want Yama to be mad at you, keep threatening to throw the boy into the river."

The bandits lunged at Mulan anyway, but she countered their attack with her sword. Metal clashed against metal, and a piercing scrape stung the air. With two rapid thrusts, Mulan surprised even herself to see she'd disarmed the ghosts. Their knives clattered at their sides—in pieces.

The bandits backed off, thunderstruck. "You got lucky, outsider."

"We'll be watching you."

Then they plunged down the Mountain of Knives until they were out of sight.

"What are you all looking at?" Liwei barked at the other ghosts. "Go home. The family reunion is over."

The ghosts grumbled, and some spat on the ground. But to Mulan's relief, they listened. Away they floated, the majority of them zipping down deeper into Diyu. Jiao, the ghost with the spectacles, was the last to leave. His thin face sagged with disappointment as he watched the bandits retreat to the Mountain of Knives. He sent Mulan a glare, one that promised this wasn't the end.

She ignored him and turned to Mei, Liwei, and Ren. "Honorable ancestors, thank you for helping us."

"That was a magnificent display of skill," Mei purred. "It's our honor to help family."

Liwei wasn't as impressed. "That is, if you really *are* family." He hovered around Mulan, examining her as if she were a caterpillar in a jar. "There haven't been many deaths in the Fa family recently, so my news is years out of date, but I seem to recall Fa Zhou only had that little g—"

Mulan cleared her throat. "Let's talk on the road," she said in her best, manliest tone. "Honorable ancestors, I appreciate the chance to speak with you—but Captain Li Shang, his guardian, and I are in a hurry. We need to reach the Gates of Diyu before sunrise so we may return to the living world."

"Sunrise?" Mei exclaimed. "You should have told us that earlier. You won't make it to the top before sunrise." She pulled her hair apart and began to rebraid it. "You might as well stay here with your family and chat."

Mulan frowned. "I thought you could help us."

Ren pressed his hands together, looking serene. His robe was worn and tattered; if Mulan were to guess, he'd been a monk while he was alive. But what was a monk doing in the depths of Diyu?

"There's a shortcut," he said. "I'll show it to you."

The other ancestors glanced at him. "Ren, are you sure that's a good idea?"

"Of course." Ren waved off their concerns with bravado.

"What is it?" Shang said.

"Liwei and Mei are simply worried because you'll have to pass through a few of Diyu's . . . unsavory parts."

"Unsavory?" Shang repeated.

Fa Mei smiled at Shang in a way that made Mulan uncomfortable. "We are in the Underworld, Captain. You didn't think King Yama would make it easy for you, did you?"

Shang squared his shoulders. "He's not going to win." He shot Mulan a determined yet grateful look. "Ping isn't going to have to stay."

"That's not what all the other ghosts think."

"Enough banter," said Ren, lifting his cane. "Follow me. Quickly, before the bandits change their minds."

Mulan, Shang, and ShiShi hurried after Ren. The ghost seemed to take their time constraint seriously, for he barreled across the land, moving far quicker than someone with a cane ought to.

Then again, he was a ghost.

"Where are we going?" Mulan asked. Beyond the plains, there wasn't much other than a tight cluster of hills; they leaned against each other like sand dunes, so closely knit they choked any view of the horizon. "We need to go up."

"I know. Patience, young Ping. You'll see."

Mulan breathed a sigh and followed. They'd need all the help they could get if they were going to get out of here before sunrise. Their time was already halfway up: the moon was half-bright, half-dark against the velvety sky.

"Isn't it beautiful?" Mei asked, catching Mulan staring. "Even though living in the Underworld can sometimes be a chore, the view of the moon here's better than anywhere you'll find in the real world."

Mulan couldn't disagree.

"Don't lag behind," Liwei said, pushing past Mei. "That goes for you, too, boy with no name."

"Why do they keep calling you that?" Shang asked, following at her side.

"Um, wh-why?" Mulan stuttered. "Beats me."

"It's strange your ancestors are treating you so badly, Ping. Those two, Liwei and Mei"—he gestured at the ghosts, who were clearly whispering about Mulan together—"they don't seem to want to help you."

How could she tell him her ancestors *had* a good reason not to want to help? Because they were right—she wasn't who she said she was. They didn't know *Ping*.

But she couldn't tell Shang that.

"I don't mean to offend your ancestors," Shang added, misreading her silence. "If you trust them, I will, too."

"You *should* trust them," Mulan said, hoping he wouldn't catch how her voice faltered at the end. *More than you trust me.*

Because, if she was honest with herself, how could Shang trust her if he didn't even know her real name?

Chapter Seventeen

Mulan's ancestors halted before the last hill. It was lower than the others, and freckled with white and yellow dandelions across the grass. Ren poked at the hill with his cane, and Mulan saw multiple demon-head medallions appear, speckling the dry grass with red, glowing eyes.

Underneath the teeth of two of the bronze medallions were rings—door handles. With one tug, Ren parted them, revealing a door under the grass. He walked straight into the hill. Mei was next.

ShiShi balked. "This could be a trap. I wouldn't—"

"Relax, guardian," said Liwei. "It's a portal that'll take you to the ninety-seventh level. That's as high as we're allowed to go anyway."

"I'll go first," Mulan said to ShiShi.

Before he could protest, she slipped into the hill, her foot landing on a narrow brick path.

Inside the hill was another hive much like the one she'd seen from the bridge when she'd first entered the gates. It was like looking up an endless well, except each stone was a different chamber. Most were bleak, rocky, cavernous rooms, but others held forests and stone deserts and tempestuous thunderstorms. Mulan saw demons laboring over a stone furnace in one, and a village of ghosts in another. She tried searching for any sign of the vermilion gates at the very top of the hive, but her eyes couldn't see so far.

Taking her place behind Ren, Mulan followed the thin brick path as it wound up and up the cave. Often, the path forked into a maze of winding, serpentine lanes, so Mulan reminded herself to be grateful Ren knew the way.

Shang followed, then ShiShi—who landed so wide he almost fell off the brick path. It was then Mulan noticed the pathway beneath her was floating. Beneath them was an infinite tunnel of darkness.

"This isn't very promising," the lion muttered, throwing a glance about the cave's interior.

"It isn't the most scenic route," said Ren, "but it's fast. And the demons won't think to look for you here—only veterans of Diyu know all the shortcuts."

"Would you care to explain why *you* are a veteran of Diyu?" ShiShi grumbled. "I'd think a monk shouldn't be here at all."

"I had a few . . . shortcomings," Ren admitted. "But I'm bound for Heaven soon, as you can see by my aura."

What kind of shortcomings? Mulan wondered. She would have asked, but Ren was the only one of her ancestors who hadn't questioned her identity. She thought it fair not to do the same of him.

Still, for a monk, his pockets jangled rather noisily.

Maybe it's full of pebbles. Or stones. Who knows what ghosts in Diyu collect?

Mulan pushed aside her doubts and focused on her surroundings.

The smells changed rapidly. Wafts of wood fire and cinnamon, and sometimes dead fish; Mulan also heard shouts and screams from far away. When there were stairs, they were narrow and rough. ShiShi climbed them five at a time, keeping pace with Mulan's ancestors, who had no trouble floating up and up.

"The stairs are for the demons," Ren explained.

Mei snorted. "It helps keep them in shape. Most of them get lazy after a thousand years."

"Can all ghosts fly?" Mulan asked.

"The longer you've been here, the better you are at it."

Ren tilted his head at Shang. "I'm guessing you haven't mastered your unearthly talents yet."

"Err, no."

"You won't have to," Ren said matter-of-factly. "You're not staying here long."

"How can you tell?" Shang asked. "I don't look any different from you."

"Our colors." Ren compared his ghostly aura to Shang's. They were nearly the same shade of blue, Mulan noted. Most of the ghosts she'd seen had been either yellow or red. His aura was green, almost blue—like the eye of a peacock feather.

"Once you turn blue, it means you're either going to be reincarnated or you're bound for Heaven. I'm guessing you're the former. Those bound for Heaven usually don't stick around the lower parts of Diyu."

"The bandit ghosts were red," Mulan remembered. "What does that mean?"

"Red means you have a long time to serve. Behavior in Diyu is closely monitored, just as it was in the real world. King Yama's put a stamp on all of us. Only he knows how long we have here. But our colors are a hint. When we get closer to blue, that means our time is coming up. Or we've done something to deserve getting out of this place."

"The Li family has no one lingering in Diyu." ShiShi

grunted. "Clearly, the Fa family isn't as distinguished. Why are *you* all here?"

Mei glowered at the lion. "What do you mean, why are *we* all here?"

Liwei peered at her, his jowls sagging over his neck. "You know what he means. Not everyone in the Fa family's been honorable, you know. I'd say *some* of us bring the family name down more than others." He stroked his chin, studded with short white hairs. "How many husbands did you have again, Mei?"

"You're one to talk about reputation," Mei retorted. "You think you get to take the high road because your parents were acupuncturists? Why don't you tell them why that business didn't survive? Oh, because *you* killed one of the patients."

"It was an accident!"

Listening to them, Mulan wanted to roll her eyes. "Are they always like this?" she asked Ren.

"Try living with them for centuries," Ren replied with a dry chuckle. "Careful," he said, looking up. "Watch your head, cousin Ping."

Mulan hunched over, thankful for the warning. The ceiling lowered sharply, and ShiShi was the first and only one to hit his head.

"Serves you right," Mei trilled at the lion.

Shang straightened his back once the ceiling returned to its normal height. "Where are we?"

"We have to make a few detours," Liwei said, stifling a yawn. His heavy eyelids blinked at Mulan. "I hope they'll be inspiring for you, young Ping. If I'd seen all this, I would have lived my life quite differently."

"We're passing the Chamber of Rocks on your left," Mei narrated. "Don't stop and stare."

Mulan and Shang looked, but ShiShi grunted and didn't bother slowing down. Inside the Chamber of Rocks were hundreds of ghosts, all chained to black lacquered columns. Each ghost carried a rock above his head so heavy that if it fell, it would certainly crush him. Mulan couldn't look at them without feeling pity.

"Don't mind them," said Mei. "I had to do it for a while, too. Twelve years, thirty-four days, and five hours." She shuddered. "It's best not to pay them any heed."

"Is this how ghosts are punished?" Mulan asked.

"If you deserve it," said Mei airily. "Or if King Yama's in a bad mood when you greet him."

"I did my time on the Ice Mountain," Liwei said, somewhat proudly. "Trust me, it's much more agonizing than the Chamber of Rocks. Though there is another, fourth Fa ancestor in Diyu. Unfortunately, he's still in the Valley of Eternal Misery. We were on our way to visit him when you three made such a commotion on the Mountain of Knives."

Mulan pursed her lips. "Well, I thank you most graciously, Auntie and Uncles, for guiding us."

"Please don't call me Auntie," said Mei. Her aura was pale yellow, like the steamed egg cake she'd started nibbling. "I can't be more than a year or two older than you."

"Fa Mei died young," said Fa Liwei. "It would have been tragic, had she not been such a shrew to her husbands."

Mei whacked him with her fan. "You should talk." She faced Mulan and Shang, then jabbed the end of her fan into Liwei's stomach. "This one died from indigestion. He choked on a fish bone."

"At least I was old."

"Old and fat," Mei retorted.

"Please," Ren said, holding his arms wide. "Enough bickering."

"Definitely motivation for you two to be good on earth," ShiShi muttered to Mulan and Shang. "Or else you'll have to spend centuries with idiots such as these."

"ShiShi, they're my ancestors."

"Even worse."

"Ah, here we are," Ren announced, coming across a bronze bell in the middle of the path. "Will you do the honors?"

Mulan struck the bell with the side of her sword.

"I meant to ask you where you got that sword from," ShiShi said, staring at the blade.

"I found it on the Mountain of Knives. Why?" Mulan tilted her head. But Ren made another turn and peeled open another hidden door. Shadowy light flared in her eyes.

"Here we are," Ren announced. "The ninety-seventh level, mostly occupied by the Hall of Echoing Forests."

It didn't look like a hall. Mulan was beginning to learn that Diyu's structure was different from anything in the real world. Here, mountains could float on clouds, and rivers could course through the sky. Everything here existed to suit King Yama's whims.

A soft hum buzzed from the trees, and every few beats, the leaves rustled in an erratic rhythm. The sky was dimmer here, and shadows danced across the forest canopy. The trees were withered and shriveled, with branches that looked like bones and leaves shaped like teeth. But aside from that, the forest wasn't so different from the bamboo grove where Mulan and ShiShi had first arrived.

"How do we get to the hundredth level from here?"

"Follow the moonlight." Ren pointed at the beam of silvery light across the trees. "Didn't King Yama tell you that?"

Mulan gazed up. "He didn't tell me anything."

"It won't be easy finding the gateway to the next level, but if you follow the light it'll at least bring you to the right vicinity. If you can find the gate latches shaped like King Yama's face, they should lead you to another stairway. Just be careful of demons."

Fa Mei frowned. "Aren't you forgetting to warn them about the Caul—"

"No," Ren interrupted. He cleared his throat and fumbled with his sleeves, his poise disappearing for an instant. "No," he repeated. "There's nothing to worry about. I'm afraid this is as far as we can take you."

"What didn't you warn us about?" Mulan said.

Ren laughed, a little too loudly for Mulan's liking. "Mei was just being paranoid. The Chamber of Boiling Despair *used* to be on your path—"

"Some call it the Cauldron," inserted Mei.

"—but Diyu's chambers and levels move constantly, and you shouldn't have any trouble with it."

"Shouldn't?" Shang echoed.

"I wouldn't send my own blood into the Cauldron," Ren assured them hastily. "After all, it is such a joy for me to see one of my descendants alive and well."

Mulan thought she heard Liwei or Mei snort, but maybe she'd just imagined it. When she glanced at them, they both avoided her gaze.

"Watch the moon and you'll be fine," Ren promised. "You're so close to the top already. You'll certainly make it."

The moon was north of them, still half-bright and half devoured by darkness. No change in their timing. That was good.

"I guess we should be on our way." Eager to resume their journey, Mulan started to bow to each of her ancestors.

"Not so fast," said Mei. She sat on a tree stump, elegantly adjusting her shimmering silk skirts so they didn't touch the dirt. "Ping, you said you'd update us on family news."

Mulan swallowed. *Right.* "There isn't much to report," she said lamely. "The family's all doing great."

Mei threw her hands up in the air. "That isn't an update. I want to hear why you're here. The other ghosts say there's no mention of you at all in King Yama's book. That means you don't even exist."

"We don't have time for stories," ShiShi interjected gruffly. His attention was on something within the trees. "We're on a tight schedule."

"She didn't ask you, lion," said Liwei.

Mei reached into her pocket and took out another steamed egg cake, this one topped with a dark red date. "How about a treat for the loyal guardian?"

ShiShi's fur bristled, and his tail became stiff and straight. "Absolutely not. I won't be fooled into accepting food from you."

"Fine, your loss." Mei took a bite. "Mmm. So delicious. I always thought guardians had a weakness for sweets."

"Or spirits." Liwei snickered. "Where do you think all those gourds of rice wine go when you leave them for your ancestors at the altar?"

ShiShi scoffed and returned his attention to the forest. He still looked preoccupied by something in the trees. Mulan looked over, and all she caught was a flash of red fur. It disappeared behind the brambles before she could make out what it was.

ShiShi crouched, tail whirling behind him. "On second thought," he said, his anger suddenly gone, "I suppose I can give the family reunion a few minutes."

"ShiShi?"

"You stay with Ping, Li Shang." ShiShi strode off into the woods. "Don't wait for me. I'll find you."

Mulan raised a hand after him. "Wait, where are you—"

"He probably saw a fox," said Ren. "They run rampant in this area."

"What a peculiar beast." Mei stuffed the rest of the egg cake ShiShi had refused into her face.

Shang looked at Mulan, confused. "Ping, is there really no record of you in Yama's book?"

Mulan's tongue sat heavy in her mouth. She didn't know what to say.

"Oh, that's right," Mei said, licking her fingers clean of crumbs. "I still don't remember Fa Zhou having a son." She frowned. "And I *would* have remembered."

"You do have a knack for keeping track of the men in our family," Liwei said drily. "Or rather, getting them into trouble."

Ren glared at them before returning his attention to Mulan. "Now that the lighting is better, let me take a look at you, cousin Ping."

Ren patted Mulan's face. It was like being brushed by the wind, and when he squeezed her cheeks, she thought she felt a pinch.

"See?" he said to the others. "Cousin Ping has Fa Zhou's teeth and forehead. Fa Li's hair and eyes. A bit soft on the jaw and cheeks, but he's still a growing boy, I suppose."

"I see the resemblance," Mei agreed. She peered at Mulan from beneath her long eyelashes. "But he's far shorter than Fa Zhou is. And smaller, too. Not even a hair on his chin."

"You know, they're right." Shang smothered a laugh. "You're lucky. You never have to shave."

"Hmph." Liwei circled Mulan with his hands behind his back. "I still think you're hiding something. If we find out you lied to take advantage of us, we'll throw you into the river ourselves. It isn't far from here, you know."

"How dare you call Ping a liar," Shang said, inserting himself between Mulan and the three ghosts. "Ping risked his life to rescue me. Did any of you have that sort of honor? I think not. Otherwise, you wouldn't be here."

Liwei whistled, then floated over to inspect Shang. "And who are you to speak of family honor to us?"

"That's Captain Li Shang," Mei whispered to her relative.

Liwei's eyebrows rose. "Of the famous military Li family?"

"An honorable clan indeed." Mei batted her eyelashes at Shang. "My first husband was a military man, too. He was killed in battle a week after we got married. I accidentally put flour in his cannons instead of gunpowder, and I forgot to sharpen his sword. I was so lonely." Mei straightened the collar on Shang's cape, and Mulan couldn't help feeling a twinge of jealousy. "I'll bet you wouldn't let a little accident like that kill you. You're so strong and tough."

Shang recoiled, looking flustered.

"Look," Mulan said, stepping between Mei and Shang, "I *am* here to bring Captain Li Shang back to the real world. I made a promise to his father."

"I think it more likely you're a demon," Liwei announced, going back to Mulan. "A demon in disguise sent by Meng Po to trap him in Diyu forever."

"What?" Mulan spluttered. "I'm not a demon."

"So you say. Demons are liars. Seems you and they have that in common."

"I'm not a demon," she repeated. "And why would Meng Po want to trap Shang here anyway? He's to be reincarnated."

"Meng Po's army isn't what it used to be," Liwei reasoned. "A decorated captain from the Emperor's army would make a fine addition to her warriors."

"That's ridiculous," Shang said. "Ping risked his life to come here and save me."

"I suppose," Liwei allowed. "But either way, *cousin* Ping, if what you say about coming into the Underworld is true, it's against the rules to be here."

"Maybe we shouldn't be helping him after all," Mei said with a gasp. "I only have a century left until I'm invited to Youdu. I can't afford to have my sentence extended just for helping a poor relation."

Liwei nodded, a scowl forming on his round face. "I can't imagine the dishonor Ping is bringing upon our family for trespassing into Diyu. . . . That is, if we really *are* his family."

"I am your family," Mulan insisted. "I've always respected my ancestors."

"Have you, now?" Mei crossed her arms. "I've never heard your prayers to us."

Mulan gulped, wishing she'd heeded Grandmother Fa's advice to be more attentive to her ancestors when she prayed at the family shrine. Maybe if she'd paid more attention to them in the past, she could have trusted Ren, Mei, and Liwei with her secret. They would have helped her.

"Fa Zhou doesn't talk about his son much," Shang informed Mulan's ancestors. "So leave Ping alone."

Mulan's heart warmed. She didn't need anyone to stand up for her, but the way Shang defended her—as if he'd personally taken the insult to heart . . . there was something nice about it.

He's just defending his friend, Mulan scolded herself. She pushed those warm feelings aside.

"The only reason we came to his aid was because we wanted news." Mei pouted. "*And* we thought helping you three might shorten our sentences here in Diyu. For good behavior, you know. Not *all* of us have Ren's luck."

Mulan glanced at Ren, who had been strangely quiet during the whole exchange. He didn't add anything. "I'm not going to shame the family," she informed Mei and Liwei. "I know what I'm doing."

"Do you now?" Liwei snorted. "No wonder your parents try to forget you exist."

Shang stiffened. "Ping is one of the brightest men I know. He single-handedly saved China."

"If Ping is so great, why wouldn't Fa Zhou talk about him?" Liwei inquired. "Is there something wrong with the boy?" He flew up to Mulan. "Something isn't right about this story."

"I always thought Fa Zhou only had one child," Mei chirped. "That girl, Fa Mu . . . rats, I always forget her name. Fa . . ."

"Mulan," Ren finished for her.

"Right." Liwei eyed Mulan in a way she didn't like, as if he'd figured out her secret. "A clever girl, at least from what her grandfather said when he passed into Diyu."

Mulan gulped. "You spoke to my grandfather?"

"He stayed in Diyu for a few days, long enough to tell us some stories. He mentioned nothing about Mulan having a brother."

"I remember this," Mei chimed in. "Fa Zhou had just hurt his leg in battle. Grandfather Fa told us Fa Zhou'd been discharged from the army and had promised to spend more time with his daughter."

Shang's brows knit. "What about Ping?"

"Grandfather didn't talk much about me, either," Mulan said hurriedly. She took extra care to keep her voice low and deep. "The family doesn't like me very much. I was always getting into trouble—you know how things are . . . as a boy, haha!"

Mei nibbled on yet another egg cake. "But he gave Mulan that dog. I remember now."

"Yes, because Fa Li was so sad she could not bear Fa Zhou a son . . . your grandfather brought Mulan a dog. He said they'd named it Little Brother."

Just remembering the story made Mulan's throat tight. She'd forgotten about it until now. Grandfather Fa had passed away only a month after he'd given her Little Brother.

"And surely, if you've been fighting in the war with Captain Li Shang," Liwei reasoned, "you cannot be that much younger than Mulan."

"That's enough, Liwei," said Ren, poking his cane at the ghost. "The boy doesn't look like a liar."

"You're one to talk," Liwei muttered. "Maybe he takes after you."

Mulan frowned, wondering what Liwei meant by that.

"There is a tunnel ahead, beyond the forest," said Ren, arching his neck high while he ignored Liwei's comment. "Take the leftmost path always. Then you'll have to pass a few chambers before reaching the City of the Dead—Youdu."

"A few chambers?" Shang said. "Can you be more specific?"

"You'll know them when you see them," said Ren cagily. He folded his hands together and bowed. "May your quest be successful and bring honor to the Fa family."

Mei dusted her sleeves. "We hope to see you here . . . eventually." She winked at Shang. "And if you end up staying, you know where to find us."

Liwei frowned, still skeptical of Mulan's relationship to the Fa family. He leaned toward Shang, and said—just loud enough for Mulan to hear—"Remember what I said, Captain Li. I'd be careful if I were you. You don't know who you can trust down here."

"Thank you for your concern, Ancestor Fa Liwei," Shang said coldly. "But I can trust Ping."

"Fine." Liwei shrugged. "As long as you're sure it's Ping. The Lady of Forgetfulness has a powerful way with illusions."

"That's enough," Ren said brusquely. "Please excuse my grandnephew, Captain Li. His many decades in Diyu have hardened him."

Shang gave a stiff bow. "I understand."

Mulan bowed, too, ignoring Liwei's unfriendly glare. "Honorable Fa Liwei, Fa Ren, and Fa Mei. Thank you for your help. Farewell."

Out of respect, Mulan stayed to watch the ghosts fly off in different directions. Once they were gone, she found that Shang had already started treading through the grass.

Apprehension swelled in her throat. He hadn't waited for her.

Mulan hurried to catch up with him. "We shouldn't wander off too far. ShiShi said he'd find us. Shang?"

Shang took a while to reply. His lips were pursed, and he wouldn't look at her. "I'm looking for him." He bent to examine the lion's paw prints in the dirt. "His tracks stop here."

"Hey," Mulan said, reaching out to try to touch his arm. "What's the matter?"

Shang pulled himself away. "Nothing."

"You . . . you don't believe what they said about me, do you, Shang?"

"Of course I don't. I'm just . . . looking out for ShiShi." Shang cleared his throat awkwardly, then started walking faster. He parted the three branches with his arms, making for the hills that would lead them closer to the gates.

The captain was a terrible liar. She could tell her ancestors' conversation had gotten Shang thinking.

Great, she thought, her shoulders sinking. *Great.*

Mulan felt her lungs constrict. She'd tried so hard for the past few months to hide who she really was. To become Ping the brave and capable soldier and bury Mulan under the facade of armor and a deep voice.

She'd been so happy to earn Shang's trust, and now . . . she'd lost it.

And she had a feeling that even if she told him the truth, she'd never gain it back.

Chapter Eighteen

Pain burst from Mulan's ankle as she ran to catch up with Shang, but she ignored it. The captain wasn't slowing down for her; he didn't even look back to make sure she was still behind him.

"Shang?" she called after him. "Shang. Please. Talk to me."

Finally Shang whirled around, his red cape bright against the dead foliage. "Are you really Ping?"

Mulan winced, both from her ankle and from Shang's question. "Who else would I be?"

"You could be a demon. I wouldn't be able to tell."

"I asked you to trust me," she said, limping. "Remember? In the Tower of the Last Glance to Home."

"I trust the Ping I trained," said Shang stubbornly. "The Ping I know wouldn't lie to me."

Mulan didn't reply. How could she? Guilt gnawed at her. Deep down, she knew he was right. She had been lying to him. But how could she tell him the truth, knowing what he'd think of her if she did?

"Look at me," she said. "I'm no demon."

Shang sighed, looking worn and defeated. "It's just . . . it *is* odd. I'd forgotten about it until now, but Chi Fu couldn't find any record of you either. He started looking into it during your training, but after I decided to send you home, he relinquished his search. Then everything happened so quickly. . . . You and the rest of the troops improved, and we were called into battle."

"Shang . . ."

"Just tell me, Ping. Look me in the eye and tell me that your ancestors are wrong and simply didn't know about you. I'll never doubt you again."

I can't tell him the truth, she thought miserably. *What I did—stealing Baba's conscription notice and dressing up as him—was against the law. I could be executed for high treason, and Mama and Baba would be in trouble, too.* She pressed her back against the closest tree, lifted her ankle to let it rest. *But if Shang trusts me, shouldn't I trust him?*

She slid her back against the tree until she was almost

sitting on the ground. What could she say? She valued Shang's trust. Ever since that first day she'd reported to duty, she'd looked up to him—first as a leader, then as a friend.

And now?

She let out a silent sigh and stole a glimpse at the captain. He didn't say anything, but she could feel the change in their friendship. He doubted her.

She picked herself up, shuffled her feet against the dead leaves. "Who else *would* I be?" she said, laughing uneasily.

"Ping," said Shang thinly. "It's a simple question. Are you, or aren't you, the son of Fa Zhou and Fa Li?"

"I'm . . ." Mulan twisted her hands. She couldn't lie to him—not to his face like this. Yet she couldn't tell him the truth either. "I'm—"

Shang backed away from her. "All I need is a yes or no."

"Shang, I can explain," Mulan pleaded, but she could see from his eyes she'd lost him.

He snapped a thick tree branch behind him, broke it in half with his fists. She'd never seen him so angry before, so hurt. "Who are you, then?"

"I'm . . . I'm—"

His eyes narrowed. "You say my father sent for you." Shang circled her. "But mortals can't come into the Underworld. How are you here?"

"I told you," Mulan said. "I made a deal with King Yama—"

"The ghosts said King Yama couldn't find any mention of you in his book," Shang said, still gripping the broken branches tight in his fists. "Have you been lying to me, Ping? Or were you never Ping to begin with?"

"I—"

Mulan didn't know whether to be relieved or dismayed that ShiShi reappeared just that instant. The lion, completely oblivious to Mulan and Shang's argument, pounced out of a thicket, landing in front of the pair with a thud.

"I thought you two would be farther along by now," he rebuked them.

"This isn't a good time, ShiShi," Shang said through his teeth. "We're in the middle of a discussion."

"No time to talk," the lion answered. "My instincts were right. Meng Po is still looking for you, Li Shang. I found traces of her tea in the dirt not far from here. Before long, the area will be overrun with her demons. We must—"

"Not now, ShiShi," said Shang, seething.

"Yes, now! She's eluded us. She could be anything, or anyone."

"Even Ping?" Shang said coldly.

"What?" The lion's fur bristled. "What is going on here?"

"N-nothing," Mulan stammered. "Shang, we really

should listen to Shi—" She stopped, noticing Shang's eyes were as cold as ice. Her shoulders fell.

Can you blame him? You're not who you said you were.

"Did either of you hear what I just said?" ShiShi barked. "Meng Po is looking for us. So get off your lumbering feet and run!"

Shang folded his arms and drew himself tall so he towered over Mulan. "I'm not going anywhere until this . . . this *imposter* tells me who he really is."

"Imposter?" the lion repeated, standing between the two. "What is this nonsense? Come out with it—both of you."

"Ping's ancestors don't have any recollection of his existence," said Shang.

Mulan stared at the ground.

"I always knew ghosts were trouble." ShiShi dug his paws into the dirt, clearly vexed with both of them. "Ping's ancestors probably just haven't heard of him."

"I thought so, too," Shang allowed. "But Ping is hiding something." He glared at Mulan, and despite the hardness of his expression, there was a trace of disappointment in his eyes. "At least, *this* Ping. For all I know, the real Ping is still at camp watching me die."

"I am the *real* Ping," Mulan insisted. She turned to ShiShi. "Please, tell him."

A low grumble escaped the lion's throat. He looked left

and right, taking in their surroundings. The trees echoed, whistling with the quiet wind. "The boy is telling the truth, Li Shang. Your father sent him to Diyu; he asked *me* to guide him here. I have been with him since."

The arrogant guardian's face became wise and expressive, and now Mulan understood how he'd been General Li's trusted companion for so many years.

"If you want to doubt anyone, it should be me. I was your father's guardian for almost thirty years, yet I was unable to protect him from being killed by Shan-Yu. Because of my failure, tragedy has befallen your family." ShiShi lowered his head, as if the jade pendant he wore weighed him down. "I'd planned to seek you out, to protect you as your guardian next, but I was too late."

Shang stiffened. His shoulders drew in tight, and Mulan could tell he was trying to hold back the emotion of remembering his father's death.

"Do not misunderstand me," said the lion. "There is no dishonor in falling in battle. Not in your father's case, nor in yours. My shame is not that both of you died in battle. My shame is that I failed to protect you and your father, and I seek to salvage what little honor I have left.

"Your friend Ping, however, is different. At first I thought he'd only promised to come to Diyu out of guilt, because you'd risked your life to save him. But I see now I was wrong about him."

ShiShi's defense of her only made Mulan feel worse. The truth—that she was a woman—froze in her throat.

"Ping is a true friend," ShiShi continued. "Do not let his silly ancestors muddle your thinking. Have more faith, Li Shang. Ping risked his own life to come down into the Underworld. He battled hundreds, maybe even *thousands*, of ghosts to seek an audience with King Yama in his throne room, and even convinced Yama himself to give him a chance to save you!"

"I know that," Shang said, shoulders drooping ever so slightly.

"You do?" ShiShi huffed.

"Ping told me."

"Then?" the lion growled. "How can you be so ungrateful? If Ping cannot leave with you before sunrise, he will become King Yama's prisoner for all eternity. Only a true friend would make such a sacrifice."

Shang fell silent. He stared hard into the ground and wouldn't look up. His lips were drawn into a thin line.

"Your father was the same when he was young, Li Shang," ShiShi continued, more gently now. "He was so proud it became difficult for him to see past someone's flaws. But he learned over time, thanks to my help."

The guardian inched closer to Shang. "You have your father's pride. He was hard on you as a commander and a teacher and father, and you are his son through and through. But that does not mean you should be hard on your friends—on the people you can trust and rely on. If Ping has a secret to hide, let him hide it. He has already proven himself to be trustworthy, so he must have his reasons."

A shadow drifted over Shang's face, darkening his aura's shimmery blue light. He leaned against the tree for what felt like a long time. Finally, he lifted his head and walked over to Mulan.

"Whatever secret you have," Shang said solemnly, "I trust you keep it for the right reason, and I will honor that."

Behind him, ShiShi backed away to give them some space, and he nodded for Mulan to accept the captain's apology. But Mulan couldn't.

Why couldn't she?

She looked up. Shang's eyes burned with that intense earnestness she had grown to admire. That gaze ensnared her now.

He'll never trust me if he doesn't know the truth. She grimaced and squeezed her fists. *I can't lie to him anymore. Even if he hates me, he deserves to know.*

She opened her hands. "Shang, you've never once lied

to me. ShiShi's right—you've been tough on me and the other soldiers back home, but it's always been to make us a team . . . and to build trust among us."

She bit her lower lip, a habit the village gossip had once told her was unladylike and unattractive. Strange; all her life she'd striven to become a proper young woman, to make her family proud of her. These past few months, she'd spent doing the opposite. Trying to pass as a man, a soldier.

Her worst fear had been that she'd be caught impersonating someone who didn't exist. She never imagined she'd tell anyone of her own free will. She swallowed. "So you . . . you should know it's true. I'm not . . . Ping."

"If you're not Ping, then who are you?" Shang asked.

"I'm . . ." Mulan sucked in her breath. Her voice shook, and she worried her heart might burst out of its armor.

She set down her sword, rubbed the sweat off her palms onto her bare arm. Then she reached for her hair and undid the knot. The black sheet of hair tumbled down, brushing just against her shoulder blades.

"My ancestors were right," she said, surprised by how calm her voice was. "My parents never had a son. There is no Ping."

She raised her eyes to meet Shang's. "There is only—Mulan."

Chapter Nineteen

Shang's lips parted slightly, but he didn't say anything. Then, slowly, muscle by muscle, she saw the betrayal register on his face. The warmth in his brown eyes chilled, his neck turned rigid, and his lips thinned into a flat, tight line.

"You—" Shang clenched his jaw. "That's impossible. You can't be a—"

"A woman?" Mulan finished for him. She said, quietly, "I told you some girls could fight."

Shang didn't laugh. His face darkened as a shadow washed out the pale blue light from his body.

Mulan knew he wouldn't take it well, but she hadn't thought about the effect seeing him like this would have on her. A hard lump swelled in her throat, and her heart pounded so intensely she would have sworn Shang could hear it.

"Please," she said, "hear me out. It's not what you—"

"Why should I listen to you?" Shang said, stung. His fists curled at his sides. "You lied to me."

"I'm the same person."

"No, you're not."

"Shang . . ."

Shang flinched at his name. "*Captain* Li."

Mulan turned to ShiShi. The guardian's head was low, so she couldn't see his reaction to her confession. But she could guess—he wouldn't look her in the eye, and his whiskers tilted down in a doleful expression.

"I did it to save my father," Mulan told Shang softly. "Please understand that everything I—that *Ping*—did was true and in service to the Emperor's army. I never meant to hurt you."

Shang didn't reply.

"Please understand," Mulan tried again. She moved closer to him, until her shadow brushed against his glowing silhouette. "I wanted to spare my father. I hoped to make him proud of me, the way you and your father—"

Shang recoiled, his rigidness snapping. "Do not speak of my father. You lied to him, too."

"I had no choice!" Mulan bit back another protest.

"You should understand, Shang. I was trying to save you. He—"

"Understand? That I couldn't save my father when he needed me, so I should understand that you lied and deceived the entire army so you could save yours?"

"That's not what I'm saying," appealed Mulan.

"Then what?"

"That's enough," ShiShi said, finally speaking up. Mulan turned to the lion.

"Listen to her, Li Shang. Do not let your emotions overwhelm you. Whether she is Ping or Mulan, a true friend is rare."

"ShiShi," Shang growled. "You are my father's guardian, not mine."

"I *am* your guardian," replied the lion. "You are being stubborn. Do not let pride blind you into forsaking your friend."

"You trusted Ping," Mulan said. "Why is Mulan any different?"

Shang turned away. He wouldn't look at her. "I thank you for accompanying my guardian to find me in the Underworld." His voice was distant, polite, as if they were strangers. "I relieve you of your duty here, and I discharge you from your obligation to the army. ShiShi and I will complete the journey out of Diyu. I ask that you find your own way."

His words were like a punch to the stomach. Mulan paled. "Shang . . ."

"The penalty for impersonating an Imperial soldier is death," Shang said coldly. "I don't want to see you again. If I do, I'll have no choice but to follow the law."

Mulan's chest tightened. Before she bowed her head, she thought she saw a flicker of emotion waver in Shang's eyes. But he kept his chin lifted, and without turning back, he headed into the forest.

ShiShi rose to his feet and began to trail Shang, but he lingered for a moment, then went up to Mulan.

The lion took a deep breath through his nose. "Worry not. I will get him out of Diyu before the sun rises."

She nodded. Mulan was afraid if she said anything else, her voice might break.

He paused. "Remember to follow the moon, little soldier."

She waited until ShiShi and Shang were out of sight. Then she crumpled onto her knees, sinking into the dirt.

It hurt to breathe. It hurt, like someone had taken her heart and squeezed it dry. Tears pricked the corner of her eyes, but Mulan wiped them away with the back of her hand.

She wouldn't cry.

What did I expect? That he'd learn the truth and then congratulate me for fooling them all? For being a girl strong and brave enough to fight alongside men?

Mulan sniffed again. No. But she had thought he might . . . understand.

He doesn't. That's clear as day. Who could blame him? I said so myself—all anyone expects of a girl is to be obedient and raise sons. Girls aren't meant to go to war. Why should I have expected Shang to think differently?

Mulan dug her hands into the soil. The realization that she'd have to go home in disgrace made her chest tighten. So much for her dreams to bring honor back to her family.

Everything had fallen apart.

Not only that—if she was being truly honest with herself, she was disappointed.

I wish he'd understood.

She clutched at her chest and took a deep breath. It didn't help with the pain, but it helped clear her mind.

Deep down, she knew Shang's threat to kill her was just that—a threat. But she knew he'd meant what he said about never seeing her again. And that stung.

Mulan watched the dirt slip through her fingers, and then she got up. She had to keep moving. Even if she dreaded what her parents would think of her now, if she stayed here any longer she'd lose all hope of ever seeing them again.

It was dark. The moonlight was barely strong enough to breed shadows, and as she fumbled through the woods she wished she'd brought a lantern so she might see ShiShi's paw prints in the dirt.

The trees swayed around her, and the wind picked up in strength, carrying a rush of leaves into the air. The leaves swept across Mulan's face and arms, the teeth along their edges lightly scratching against her sleeves.

You lied to me, something whispered. *You lied to me.*

Mulan froze. "Shang?"

Shang . . . the voice echoed.

"The Hall of Echoing Forests," Mulan reminded herself grimly. "Just what I need."

Mulan shivered, ignoring the trees as they began to speak. *Who are you? Ping? Who are you? I trusted you. Trusted . . . you . . .*

She grimaced. If anything, the whispering trees made her move faster. "I have to get out of here."

By now she'd lost all sign of Shang and ShiShi. They'd disappeared into the thick of the forest, leaving her alone with the trees. Cloaked in the shadows, the trees could easily have passed for monsters with barbed arms and swooping wings.

But they didn't scare Mulan. As she made her way through the forest, it was loneliness that sharpened in her gut, not fear.

She'd grown up with few friends. She'd played with the neighborhood boys, chasing pigeons and catching fireflies with them until it was no longer considered proper. By then, the girls in the village scorned her. In front of her mother and father, they pretended to be polite, but Mulan knew what they said about her behind her back.

Ill-bred and ill-mannered.

She has the temper of a firecracker and the grace of a bull.

It's a miracle she even looks like a girl—look at the hay in her hair, and the dirt on her face. What a discredit to her mother!

The insults had never bothered Mulan too much. Back then, her mother comforted her by telling her to ignore what people said, and talking to her father would always make her feel better. And she'd had Khan for company . . . then, later, Mushu and Cri-Kee. But here, in this vast forest—she was alone.

She hadn't been so alone in a long time.

Mulan picked up her feet. She had to get moving. Even if Shang no longer thought of her as a friend, even if he hated her—she still cared for him. And their fates were still intertwined. If she didn't get out of Diyu, Shang would remain a spirit.

The wind intensified. It had never been so strong before. It warped the trees' song, turning the humming into a low hiss.

Mulan shielded her face, then gathered her hair and tied it back up. The pain in her ankle hadn't gotten better. She'd put too much pressure on it earlier climbing the Mountain of Knives and running after Shang. Now it begged her for rest.

I can rest when I'm out of here, she told herself. Ignoring the terrible voices hissing after her from the trees, she pressed against their trunks for support. Step by step, she trod through the forest, following the moonlight for that tunnel Ren had promised was on this level.

The moon's beacon was merely a slant of light touching upon the forest's dark canopy. It illuminated the path toward the tunnel. Gradually, the trees thinned out, and Mulan reached a small clearing in the woods.

A tunnel awaited her in the clearing. No, not just one tunnel. *Three.*

This couldn't be right. Which one did she take?

The tunnels lay over the earth like three enormous hollow logs. Ivy crawled over their sides, but not a leaf or branch dangled over the tunnels' entrances.

Mulan peered into each, but the paths inside were shadowy and dark. She couldn't see where any of them led.

She examined the ground, hoping to find a clue of which tunnel Shang and ShiShi had taken, but she saw nothing.

No footsteps, no paw prints. Had Shang and ShiShi even come this way?

With a deep breath, she traced the outer walls of the tunnel. The stone was cold and unmarked. There were no bronze medallions of King Yama's head, the marker Mulan had looked for on every other portal to another level.

Another gust of wind assaulted Mulan, bringing a tempest of leaves to batter her face. She pushed the leaves away, and a deep, rumbling sound echoed from the tunnels.

You're never going to get out of here, a voice whispered. *You're lost.*

That wasn't an echo. "Who's there?" Mulan shouted.

You're going to die here in Diyu. Alone.

She spun to face the trees behind her. They still swayed, their leaves swishing and swooshing with the wind.

Mulan shoved aside the voices. "Ren said to always take the leftmost path," she said, forcing herself to focus. "I guess that counts for the tunnels, too."

She stepped toward the first tunnel, sure of her choice.

Then something in the ivy brushes rustled, and Mulan halted. Her hand went to her sword. "Who's there? Come out."

"That's the wrong tunnel," said a soothing feminine voice. "You might want to rethink that path."

Mulan blinked.

"Down here," the voice spoke again.

Mulan shifted her gaze down, to the side of the tunnel.

There stood a russet-furred fox with unblinking jade eyes. She had to be the most striking fox Mulan had ever seen. Her fur was glossy and smooth, her tail striped with touches of gold. She was caught under a boulder.

"Help me," the fox whimpered. "Please. My tail is stuck."

Mulan knelt, gauging the situation. The boulder was heavy—far too heavy for her to lift or push. She stuck her sword under it for leverage, then heaved.

"Thank you, thank you, soldier." The fox slipped out and swished her tail back and forth, making sure she hadn't lost a hair. "I owe you a debt of gratitude."

"No," Mulan said. Her tone was flat, and she realized she probably sounded very rude. She sighed. "No," she said again, "it's the least I could do."

"Then the least I can do is tell you that demons are looking for you," replied the fox, grooming her tail. "They were here just minutes ago searching for intruders."

Mulan froze. "Demons? Here?"

The fox nodded. "When they saw me, they decided to have some fun and trap me under the boulder. If not for you, who knows how long I would have been here, languishing among these singing trees."

"Did they find anyone?" Mulan asked urgently.

"Not yet. You look lost, soldier."

Mulan swallowed the hard lump in her throat. She didn't trust creatures of Diyu, and this fox—no matter how innocent sounding—was no different. Besides, she needed to hurry, in case the demons found Shang and ShiShi. "I'm not, thank you."

She quickened her pace and headed for the tunnel, but the fox followed. "If you're trying to reach the hundredth level, this isn't the correct tunnel. You need to be in the left-most tunnel."

Mulan slowed. That was what Ren had told her. Maybe the fox wasn't trying to lead her astray. "Isn't this it?"

"No, but I can show you the way," the fox said helpfully. "It isn't far."

The fox scampered back into the forest. After some hesitation, Mulan followed, but she kept her sword in her hand just in case.

The fox was right. There *was* another tunnel back in the forest. There was a grove hidden behind a large willow tree. And this one had a medallion of King Yama's frowning face floating in the middle of the entrance.

She'd never been so relieved to see anyone frown at her.

"Thank you," Mulan said, breathing hard. "If not for you, I would have missed this."

"Of course. It's my pleasure. Where are you going?"

Mulan hesitated. Her grandmother had always told her to beware of foxes. In all the tales she'd heard as a child, they were full of tricks and up to no good. Her instincts told her to be careful, but her emotions were high and her defenses were low. "I'm trying to get to the gates."

"I can come with you, if you like." The fox smiled at Mulan, her jade-green eyes still unblinking. "You shouldn't go alone, soldier. Not when you look so glum. What is the matter?"

"Nothing you can help me with."

"Well, at least let me guide you through the tunnel. It can be quite a maze, and there are certain chambers within you'll want to avoid."

"Thank you," Mulan said, "but I can manage."

"I have to go this way anyway," the fox insisted. "How about I take you as far as I need to go?"

There was no arguing. The fox scurried off into the dark tunnels ahead, and Mulan had no choice but to follow.

Chapter Twenty

The tunnel's steps were high and uneven; Mulan lost count of how many times she nearly tripped. Sometimes the ceilings were low, and other times they were so high she wondered where they could possibly be walking under. All this forced her to be alert, which she decided was a good thing, if only because it kept her mind off Shang.

Rocks, pebbles, and leaves littered the ground. She could see little else. The shadows here were dense, and the darkness was the excuse she gave herself every time she took a careless step. Deep down, she knew her heart was elsewhere.

"We're almost there," the fox said. "Just a bit more."

Mulan followed without a word. If she inhaled deeply

enough, she caught a hint of ash in the wind, as if from something burning far, far away. She remembered the blazing fires she'd seen in the chambers they'd passed with her ancestors and wondered whether she'd be sent to one someday for lying about who she was.

If I am, it'd be worth it. Mulan clenched her fists. *Even if I could go back and change everything, I wouldn't. I'd still have gone to war for Baba.*

"Why so sad?" The fox's green eyes gleamed in the darkness. "You're so close to defeating King Yama and reaching the exit. Yet you almost look like you'd rather stay here forever."

Mulan snapped out of her thoughts. "You know about my deal with King Yama?"

"The demons mentioned it when they were looking for you." The fox's pointy ears perked. "They mentioned a spirit and a lion, too. Why aren't you with them?"

Instead of answering, Mulan pressed her palm against the tunnel's granite walls. The stone was even colder inside the tunnel. Touching it sent a shiver down her spine.

"Because they found out who I really am," she said quietly. "They found out I've been lying to them."

The fox stopped swaying her tail. "But you've such an honest face, soldier. I can't believe that you would lie to your friends."

"Looks are deceiving, then," Mulan said. Liwei had been right to doubt her. She wished she could see her ancestors now and apologize to them, and at least tell them the truth.

"I can see the wound is fresh," said the fox, "so I won't press you about it. But I might understand better than you think. We foxes have the reputation of being crafty. Even if we're telling the truth, we're called out for being liars."

"That's not what happened," said Mulan.

"Then?"

She let go of the tension in her shoulders. "It's a long story."

"Hmm. I know just what will cheer you up."

Before Mulan could ask what, the fox made a sharp turn left through a tight, winding passageway. The smell of flowers wafted to Mulan's nose, and she sniffed.

"Isn't it glorious?" the fox said, her voice echoing down the tunnel as she ran ahead. "Through here. We're almost there."

"Wait!" Mulan cried, running to catch up. "Wait! Is that the way out? Where did you—"

Her breath caught in her throat as she emerged from the tunnel. "Go?" she whispered, finishing the question to herself.

The fox was gone, but Mulan had arrived in a garden.

Instinctively, she held back before taking another step.

No, this wasn't Meng Po's garden. There were no rosebushes or tangerine and lemon trees, no wild grasses growing tall as her waist. No demons lurking beside the pond.

This garden was peaceful and calm. Pink cherry blossoms and violet plum blossoms graced the sweeping trees. The petals fell like snowflakes, dancing and swirling until they touched the soft, verdant grass.

There was something familiar about this place.

Her eyes traveled down the flat stone steps. She knew this path, knew those stones. The third one from the bottom had a crack in the middle—from when she was five and the neighbor's boy convinced her there were worms on the other side of the stones. She'd hammered the stone in half, eager to catch a few worms to play with.

There weren't any, of course, but her mother had helped her find some dragonflies by the pond instead, and they'd spent an afternoon counting them in the garden.

Mulan smiled wistfully at the memory. *This can't be the same garden. I'm in Diyu.*

Yet no painter could have re-created what she saw more convincingly. Every detail was as she remembered. At the bottom of the stone-cobbled path was a pond with rose-flushed lilies, and a marble bench under the cherry tree.

She used to play by the pond when she was a little girl, catching frogs and fireflies in wine jugs and feeding the fish leftover rice husks and sesame seeds until her mother scolded her.

And beyond the moon gate was—

Mulan's hand jumped to her mouth.

Home.

That smell of home—of Baba's incense from the family temple, sharp with amber and cedar; of noodles in Grandmother Fa's special pork broth; of jasmine flowers that Mama used to scent her skin.

Forgetting her doubts, Mulan dashed down the steps and through the moon gate, past the great stone dragon statue and wooden fences to her family's home. She slid open the faded red door and called, "Mama? Baba? Nai Nai?"

No answer.

The house was empty.

Slowly, Mulan walked down the main hall. Her boots tapped against the cherrywood floor, which had been swept clean. Her grandmother did it every morning over her mother's protests and offers to help.

"Sweeping away the bad luck gives me something to do," Grandmother Fa always responded. "And having something to do keeps me young."

Mulan kept walking. Something inside her yearned to touch everything she saw, but she was afraid it would all vanish if she did.

Four scrolls hung on the east-facing wall, their edges slightly wrinkled with age. Her great-grandfather had spent years painting the scrolls. Each one portrayed a different season—spring, summer, autumn, and winter—in their family garden.

Mulan stopped in front of the scroll of spring, studying her ancestor's confident brushstrokes and the delicate cherry blossoms forever captured in midbloom. Her fingers crept up, skimming the painting from the top of the trees to the bright yellow carp swimming in the pond. The garden outside still looked the same.

She took a step back, her boot creaking against the wooden floor.

This isn't real, she reminded herself. *This isn't real.*

Even if it wasn't, she felt some guilt about wearing her boots inside her family's home. Dirt from her soles smudged the wooden floor panels, and she could almost hear her mother scolding her for wearing shoes inside the house.

She started to head out, but she passed her room. It was the same as she'd left it: a pile of cushions by her bed for Little Brother to sleep on, a stack of poetry and famous literature on her desk that she was supposed to study to become a "model bride," and the lavender shawl and silk robes she'd worn the day before she left home. The jade comb Mulan had left in exchange for the conscription notice caught her eye; it now rested in front of her mirror.

Mulan's gaze lingered on the comb, on its green teeth and the pearl-colored flower nestled on its shoulder. She wanted to hold it, to put it in her hair and show her family—to show *everyone*—she *was* worthy. After all, her surname, Fa, meant *flower*. She needed to show them that she had bloomed to be worthy of her family name.

But no one was here, and she didn't want to face her reflection. Who knew what it would show, especially in Diyu?

She isn't a boy, her mother had told her father once. *She shouldn't be riding horses and letting her hair loose. The neighbors will talk. She won't find a good husband—*

Let her, Fa Zhou had consoled his wife. *When she leaves this household as a bride, she'll no longer be able to do these things.*

Mulan hadn't understood what he meant then. She hadn't understood the significance of what it meant for her to be the only girl in the village who skipped learning ribbon dances to ride Khan through the village rice fields, who chased after chickens and helped herd the cows instead of learning the zither or practicing her painting, who was allowed to have opinions—at all.

She'd taken the freedom of her childhood for granted.

When she turned fourteen, everything changed.

I know this will be a hard change to make, Fa Li had told her, *but it's for your own good. Men want a girl who is quiet and demure, polite and poised—not someone who speaks out of turn and runs wild about the garden. A girl who can't make a good match won't bring honor to the family. And worse yet, she'll have nothing: not respect, or money of her own, or a home.* She'd touched Mulan's cheek with a resigned sigh. *I don't want that fate for you, Mulan.*

Every morning for a year, her mother tied a rod of bamboo to Mulan's spine to remind her to stand straight, stuffed her mouth with persimmon seeds to remind her to speak softly, and helped Mulan practice wearing heeled shoes by tying ribbons to her feet and guiding her along the garden.

Oh, how she'd wanted to please her mother, and especially her father. She hadn't wanted to let them down. But maybe she hadn't tried enough. For despite Fa Li's careful preparation, she had failed the Matchmaker's exam. The look of hopefulness on her father's face that day—the thought that she'd disappointed him still haunted her.

Then fate had taken its turn, and Mulan had thrown everything away to become a soldier. To learn how to punch and kick and hold a sword and shield, to shoot arrows and run and yell. To save her country, and bring honor home to her family.

How much she had wanted them to be proud of her.

But when I go home—to my real home—will Mama and Baba forgive me for leaving? Or will there be nothing but disappointment on Baba's face when he sees me?

Heart heavy with emotion, she turned to go.

As she passed a line of milky-white paper windows in the hall, she looked through one and noticed movement in the garden. Someone was sitting on the bench outside!

Could it be her grandmother? From this distance, Mulan couldn't be sure.

She hurried out of the house, her shoes tapping against the stone steps—sometimes two at a time—for the garden. Once she reached the moon gate, Mulan caught her breath and winced at the pain from her ankle. Then she looked up.

On the marble bench was Meng Po, fanning herself with her feathered fan. A bushy, striped fox tail peeked out from under her skirt, and a pot of incense burned at her side.

Mulan gasped. "It was you! You tricked me."

Meng Po opened her hands. "Sit with me, young Ping."

"No." Mulan reached for her sword.

"Put away your weapon," Meng Po said calmly. "I'm not here to hurt you."

"I don't believe you. I know what you are." Mulan pointed the blade at the cup of tea Meng Po cradled on her palm. "I know what's in that tea."

"I was not lying when I told you my tea was a consolation," Meng Po intoned. "Most consider the tea of forgetfulness a gift. It is a blessing to forget the troubles of one's past."

"Not to me."

"Then strike me with your sword and be on your way. I will not fight you."

A gust of wind blew, and a swirl of cherry blossoms brushed against the top of Mulan's head. Her anger melted.

She squeezed the hilt. Try as she might, she couldn't fight Meng Po. The old woman was unarmed.

She doesn't need weapons. She's an enchantress.

Still, Mulan couldn't do it. "Let me go," she said tiredly. "I need to find my fr—" She couldn't call them her *friends* anymore, not after what had happened. Not when they hated her. "I need to find Captain Li and his guardian."

"They are safe," Meng Po said. "They are on their way to the gates."

"You sent your demons after them," Mulan retorted. "How can they be safe?"

Meng Po reached for the pot of incense and set it on her lap. "Trust me."

"I might as well trust a fox," said Mulan bitterly. "This is all an illusion."

"And what is wrong with that?" Meng Po blew the

incense's smoke in Mulan's direction. "Isn't life but a dream?"

Mulan coughed, fanning the smoke away with her hand. "I'm not here to discuss philosophy with you."

"What better place to discuss it than in the Underworld?" Meng Po said. "All of life is a dream walking—"

"All of death is a going home," Mulan finished, reciting the words written in King Yama's throne room. She inhaled, the garden's sweet floral smell stirring the sadness in her heart.

"You *are* home, Fa Mulan."

"This isn't home." Mulan opened her arms at the illusion around them. "This is *your* doing."

"This is where you belong. Up there, in the real world, no one understands you for who you are. Not even yourself. But here, here you can be your true self."

"How would you know anything about my true self?"

Meng Po cast a sly, sidelong glance at Mulan's sword. "Come, I'll show you."

Before Mulan could protest, Meng Po took her wrist and guided her to the edge of the pool. Mulan's watery reflection stared back at her: a girl with bloodshot, swollen eyes, pale cheeks, and bruises all over her arms and legs.

But that wasn't all Mulan saw. She saw a young woman who'd thrown her heart into becoming a warrior, who'd fought battle after battle, whether it was to please her family and honor their expectations, or to protect China from invaders.

And the one friend she'd thought might understand—hadn't.

She'd lost him.

And she'd learned a cold lesson. She couldn't be herself.

"I've failed," Mulan whispered. "I thought I could prove that I was someone worthwhile, but I was wrong."

Meng Po knelt beside her. "I can change that, child."

In the old woman's hand was a white porcelain cup of tea. It rested between the lines of her palm, a tempest of steam swirling into the air.

Mulan's instinct was to throw the tea into the pond, but the Lady of Forgetfulness's power was too strong. Wind carried the tea's steam over to Mulan's nostrils. She held her breath, refusing to breathe it in.

"Haven't you ever wondered what life would be like if they were proud of you?" Meng Po asked.

Mulan refused to reply. She watched her reflection in the pond ripple.

"I can give that to you. If you drink. Everything will be much easier."

Mulan stiffened. Meng Po's offer was tempting, much as she didn't want to admit it. Against her better judgment, she leaned toward the Lady of Forgetfulness, accidentally inhaling a waft of the tea. The smell was overwhelming, and it calmed her immediately.

Meng Po's eyes mesmerized her. "It was cruel of your friends to leave you, to not even try to understand. *I* understand, Fa Mulan."

Mulan frowned at her. "How can you? You've never lived in the world above. You're the Lady of Forgetfulness."

Wrinkles dimpled the old woman's cheeks as she laughed. "You say that as though I were a monster."

"Not a monster," Mulan said, shaking her head. "But you're not human. You're a creature of Diyu."

"I wasn't always what you see here," Meng Po said. "You're right, I have been here a long, long time. It has changed me, no doubt. Yet I still remember who I was once before. Regardless of my past, I sensed you carried a secret the moment I saw you. Even King Yama and your ancestors did not. I understand you better than you know."

"That's what the fox—*you* said earlier. You were trying to trick me."

"Too many doubts cloud your mind," said Meng Po, ignoring the accusation. Her voice soothed Mulan, even as she tried to fight it. "Too much fear and restlessness. You will never complete your journey if you continue like this. Drink to clear your doubts. Drink so you will have the strength to go home."

Mulan's hands trembled as she took the cup of tea. She meant to throw it into the pond, but its weight was surprisingly heavy on her palm. The tea leaves churned inside the porcelain lips, spinning and spinning. Mulan held the cup far from her face, but she couldn't resist looking at it.

Her vision blurred. When she looked up, she was no longer in the garden. She was home again, except this time she wasn't alone.

"Mulan?" called her father's voice.

Chapter Twenty-One

Her head reeled. *What just happened?*

"Mulan?" her father called again. He sounded nearby, but that was impossible. "Are you listening to me?"

Mulan blinked, and everything cleared. She was sitting at the dining table with her parents. Little Brother yapped at her side, eager for a bone.

"Little Brother," Mulan said, laughing as her dog jumped to lick her face.

Her father cleared his throat, and Mulan held her breath when she saw him.

Fa Zhou looked the same as when she'd last seen him. A smile perched on his narrow face, even though he was pretending to look displeased with her for not listening. "Ahem."

I know this isn't real, Mulan thought, staring at her father. No disappointment or anger lurked in his expression. *Would it be so terrible if I pretended just for a moment it was?*

Just seeing Fa Zhou helped banish some of her sadness . . . at least temporarily. *I'm not going to think about Shang or ShiShi or what life will really be like when I go home. Let me just enjoy this.*

"Mama, Baba," Mulan breathed. "I'm . . . home."

Fa Li put her hands on her hips. Jade earrings dangled by her cheeks as she said, "And not a second too soon. I'm glad you decided not to be late to dinner for once."

Mulan turned to her father, who was quiet as usual but wore a proud smile. She loved that expression on his face. The corners of his eyes wrinkled, lifting his face with a touch of humor. "Your mother has some news for you."

"News?"

Fa Li knelt, taking her place at the table. Normally, she didn't let Little Brother sit beside Mulan at the dining table, but she didn't say anything about it today. "Eat, first. Eat, eat, before the food gets cold."

Mulan picked up her chopsticks and dipped them into the soup. The noodles inside were yellow as wheat, with chunks of beef and pork and crunchy stalks of green spinach. Her stomach growled, but she picked up one of the chunks and gave it to Little Brother instead. She was too curious to eat.

She folded her hands on her lap. Her armor was gone, she noted absentmindedly. Her hair was long again, brushing against her back. And she wore a crisp silk robe, tied at the waist by a red satin sash. "What's going on?"

Fa Li beamed. "We heard back from the Matchmaker this morning. She was very impressed with your examination yesterday."

"We are very proud," Fa Zhou said. "She's made a good match for you, Mulan."

"What?" Mulan was glad she hadn't eaten any noodles, because she likely would have choked. "I thought I failed the exam."

"Failed?" Fa Li sipped her tea. "After so many weeks of studying and preparing? And after Baba prayed so hard to the ancestors? No daughter of ours would fail. The Matchmaker said she had a difficult time deciding on a husband for you because there were so many young men who'd make a fine match."

"What about the war?" Mulan blurted.

Fa Zhou placed his chopsticks to the side of his bowl. "What about it?"

"Baba, you were conscripted to go to war. The Emperor's counsel called your name in front of everyone in the village. Don't you remember?"

Fa Zhou chewed on his noodles, then patted his mouth dry with his sleeve. "The war is over. We won."

Worry creased Fa Li's forehead. "Are you not feeling all right, Mulan?"

What is going on?

Mulan knelt deeper onto the cushion under her legs. "I'm not sure. I feel a little dizzy."

"That's because you should eat something." Her mother gestured at the food with her chopsticks. "All this running around—at least there's no hay in your hair this evening, Mulan. But you're so thin. Eat something to replenish your energy. And drink your tea. Baba's already on his second cup."

The smell of Fa Zhou's medicinal tea reminded Mulan of his poor health. Six cups a day, the doctor had told him— three in the morning, and three in the evening.

Mulan sobered. There was nothing she wanted more than to make Baba happy. She warmed her hands over the cup. She *was* thirsty—and hungry, yet something held her back from joining her parents as they ate and drank.

This isn't real, a voice nagged at Mulan. The reminder shot a pang of loneliness through her. *I should leave.*

She started to get up, but Grandmother Fa appeared, carrying a plate of orange slices and steamed pork buns. She set them in the center of the table, then plopped onto the cushion opposite Mulan's father. Her eyes were different, Mulan noticed. Darker, more hooded.

That's just because she's sitting in the shadows.

"This is what you wanted, isn't it?" said her grand-mother cheerfully. "To make us proud? You've done it."

Forgetting her plan to leave, Mulan relaxed and nodded.

Her family looked so happy. She'd never seen them so proud of her before. This *was* what she'd always wanted. To uphold the family honor, to do her duty as a daughter.

This moment was perfect. It was everything she could have asked for.

So why did she feel so hollow inside?

She turned to her father. The glow on Fa Zhou's face and the tenderness in his eyes melted her. That emptiness in her stomach twisted. *This is what you wanted. Embrace it.*

"Eat something, Mulan. You're making me nervous just sitting there."

Little Brother barked in agreement.

Mulan reached for one of the steamed buns in the center of the table and pulled apart its soft white dough. She laid it on her plate, then reached for her tea again and inhaled its hot steam. The hollowness inside her faded, and that nagging voice reminding her things weren't real—blurred into the distance.

"So," she said, "tell me what the Matchmaker said."

"She was very impressed with you. It took her a while to find a suitable match, but there's a young man from the capital who she believes would be perfect. He comes from a good family, your stars align harmoniously, and he has a bright future ahead of him."

That told Mulan absolutely nothing. Suddenly she wondered why she'd wanted this so much—to be given away to a stranger to marry. Couldn't a woman be worth something without having to be a bride?

She bit back her comments. *I can't change the law. I can't own land or even speak my mind. Mama and Baba only want what's best for me.*

"What's his name?" Mulan asked, trying her hardest to sound interested.

The gate outside shuddered, and two sets of footsteps echoed across the courtyard, growing haltingly closer.

Fa Li froze. "Who could that be? We're not expecting anyone."

Mulan tumbled off her cushion. She was already up. "Bandits?"

"Sit down, Mulan," said Fa Zhou. "I'll deal with it."

Mulan pretended not to hear. Gripping her chopsticks in her fist, she crouched beside the window behind the dining table and peered outside.

No, not bandits.

A soldier. He was surprisingly light-footed for being so tall and strapping, and stranger still, he'd arrived with an enormous lion with a disheveled mane. At first she thought he was stealing one of the stone statues from their ancestral temple, but then the lion moved, his tail curving behind him like a cat's.

Mulan's fear became curiosity. "Is that a real lion?" she called out, pointing at the beast. "I've never seen one in the village before."

"Mulan!" Fa Li whispered harshly. "What are you doing, shouting out to intruders?"

"It's just a soldier. And his pet . . . lion."

"They're trespassing on our property." Fa Li nodded to Fa Zhou. "You ought to get your sword."

"There's no need," said Mulan quickly. "I'll just tell him to go away."

"Close the window and return to dinner. Right now, Mulan."

With reluctance, Mulan started to reach for the curtains hanging above the window, but the intruder's handsome face twisted with shock when he saw her.

Mulan tilted her head. She couldn't make out his face; shadows cloaked it, even when he stepped closer to the lanterns hanging from their roof. Yet something about him looked familiar. But why?

"Pi— Mulan," he cried. "You're—"

Grandmother Fa sidled up next to Mulan by the window. Her smile slid into a frown. "What are you doing here, soldier? Go away before I shoo you out."

The soldier ignored Mulan's grandmother. "It's Shang," he said, trying again. "Don't you remember me?"

"Ignore the man and come back to dinner," Grandmother Fa said. "That steamed bun smells delicious."

"It's Shang," the soldier said again, running closer to the house. He tapped on the window. "Please, listen to me."

Mulan parted the window's wooden shutters just a little.

"She's in one of Meng Po's illusions," said a new voice. It was deeper, and it seemed to be coming from the stone lion behind the soldier. "She probably can't see you."

"I know." Shang's voice sounded tense. "Come back with us. You're in danger here."

"Danger?" Grandmother Fa snorted. "This is her home. Go away before we call for the guards." She reached over Mulan and slammed the window shut. The curtains folded over the paper screens. "We should send the intruder away, don't you think?"

Fa Zhou nodded. His face had become blank as a stone. He got up obediently to follow the order, while Grandmother Fa grabbed Mulan's wrist, dragging her back to the table.

"Wait." Mulan twisted away and ran for the window again. Lightning pricked the sky, and it began to rain. Yet the soldier shielded his eyes as if the rain were coming from the ground, not from the sky. As if the rain were sand, not water.

"Shang," she said. Something about the name brought a flutter to her stomach. "Why am I in danger?"

"Because of her." Shang pointed at Grandmother Fa. "She's the Lady of Forgetfulness." He gritted his teeth, white against the dark shadows of his face. "Did you drink her tea? Is that why you don't remember me?"

Mulan stared at the cups of tea back on the dining table. "Why should I remember you?"

"We went to battle together—against the Huns," Shang said urgently. "I trained you."

"Impossible!" Grandmother Fa tsked. "Stop listening to this idiot, Mulan. Come back to dinner. Your father will take care of him."

"No!" Thunder rumbled, drowning Shang's words, so he had to shout, "You called yourself Ping, remember?"

Mulan touched her temples. *A little.* She remembered being afraid, and hiding among dozens of soldiers. She remembered not wanting to fail.

"We fought together," Shang continued. "We fought against Shan-Yu, and I was wounded. You came here—you came to Diyu to find me."

Mulan parted her lips. "I'm sorry. I don't . . ."

"You were my friend," Shang said. He took a step forward, crossing through the window and wall until he was in the house. His shadowy hand reached out to touch Mulan's arm.

The memories came back in waves. The snow. Mushu. Shoving Yao aside and taking the cannon. Firing it into the mountain. Fighting the Huns. Captain Li Shang, and ShiShi . . . falling down and down into Diyu.

"Captain?" Mulan whispered. "What are you doing here? You came back for me."

"I'm not leaving you behind. If you stay, I stay, too."

"But I thought . . ."

Shang looked at her bashfully. "I was wrong. Man or woman, you're still my friend."

A flood of warmth rushed across Mulan. Then she started, realizing that her family—or rather, the illusions of them—still watched her. Unblinking and unmoving, Fa Zhou and Fa Li sat frozen in their places. Little Brother's tongue hung out of his mouth, suspended as he tried to bite the bone she'd left for him under the table.

Only Grandmother Fa stood, tapping her foot impatiently.

"You're not my family," said Mulan, at last recognizing what had been different about her grandmother. "You're Meng Po."

Meng Po's eyes darkened. Thunder rumbled, then the rain abruptly stopped. "What I said earlier was true, child," she warned Mulan. "You will never reach the hundredth level. Drink, so you may escape King Yama's punishment. Drink and stay here. I'll give you the family you've always wanted. The one that loves you and is proud of you."

"No," said Mulan. "I won't drink." Drawing her sword,

she swept it across the table, flinging the teacups and dishes off until they shattered against the wooden floor.

Mulan raised her sword to Meng Po's throat. "Now let us out."

The Lady of Forgetfulness touched the glowing blade. Her brows furrowed for an instant, and she looked up at Mulan, appearing more intrigued than angry. Then her expression washed away, becoming unreadable as before. "As you wish. But this was your last chance."

The walls of her family home flickered and faded. In its place was a vast desert, so empty Mulan could see nothing but its unchanging landscape in every direction. A few crooked trees, faraway dunes that melded into the gray horizon, and blasts of wind and sand. She dropped her chopsticks—no more than two twigs.

Still wearing Grandmother Fa's face, Meng Po laughed. Then, before Shang or ShiShi could seize her, she vanished into the sand.

Chapter Twenty-Two

Gone was her family's garden, the cherry and plum trees, the pond with the pink water lilies, the marble bench and moon gate, and the house, along with her mother, father, and Little Brother. They'd all vanished. Not even the smell of incense remained.

Mulan's knees weakened. She stared down at her boots, taking in the bandage around her ankle that was starting to peel off, the water stains on her armor, the gauntlets covering her knuckles. She touched her hair. It was short again, tied back into its knot on her head.

"Are you all right?" asked Shang.

Mulan nodded mutely, but inside, her heart thudded in her ears. Shang was back. But why?

He didn't look angry at her anymore. If anything, he looked rather ill.

"Are *you* all right?"

"Am I—" Shang fumbled. "I should be asking if *you're* all right."

"You already did."

"Oh. Yes." He started toward her awkwardly, then stopped and twisted his hands behind himself, as if he were holding back.

ShiShi watched Mulan closely. "What did you see?"

"My home, my family," said Mulan faintly. "Everything was so real. I could smell the pork in my grandmother's steamed buns. I could even feel the fur on Little Brother's back."

"Meng Po's enchantment is strong," said ShiShi, trying to console her. "She used your memories against you."

"She nearly succeeded. Seeing my family again . . . Everyone was there—my mother, my father, my grandmother. I left home without permission, so to see them happy to have me back—to see them proud of me . . ." Mulan shivered. "I wanted it to be real. I wanted it so much I almost started to believe it."

"But you didn't," ShiShi said. "You freed yourself from her magic."

"I might not have," confessed Mulan. She dug her foot

into the sand, watching it wrinkle under her weight. Only moments ago, the ground had been wood. "If I'd stayed a little longer . . ."

"No," Shang said. "You wouldn't have."

"I don't know about that."

"I know," he said firmly. "The only reason she found you in the first place is because of me. It's my fault. We should have stayed together, yet I left you. I abandoned my friend, who would never have done the same to me." He lingered on that note sadly. "I'd understand if you never forgave me, but . . . can you?"

Mulan crossed her arms and pretended to think about it. "For not trusting me, or for saying women can't make as good soldiers as men?"

"Both."

Mulan had never seen the captain look so vulnerable and ashamed. It touched her. "I might be persuaded."

"Despite all his courage and brawn, he can be a daft one." ShiShi sounded proud about Shang's change of heart. "His father was similar at this age, but—Li Shang has a big heart."

A trace of hopefulness lifted Shang's expression. "I was wrong to judge you so quickly. I was ungrateful. You risked your life to come here and find me." His eyes met hers. "I promised that I trusted you, and that should not change whether you're a man or woman. You are my friend whether you are Ping or Mulan."

She smiled. "Thank you, Shang. You're my friend, too."

The captain exhaled with relief. "I'm glad."

ShiShi clambered over a rock, motioning for them to follow. As Mulan walked beside him, the lion shook his head at her. "In all my years serving the Li family, you certainly are a first, Mulan."

"Why is that?"

"I've seen many men dress as girls to evade serving in the army, but never any women who dressed as boys so they *could* serve." ShiShi chuckled. "What a story this will make for the other guardians. What about *your* guardian? Does he know you're a woman?"

"Your guardian's a man?" said Shang with a frown. His face twisted into a grimace as he considered this. "So he . . . he sleeps next to you at camp? In your tent?"

"He's a dragon. And yes, he sleeps in my tent. But what else would you expect? Everyone else in the army is a man." Mulan's shoulders shook with laughter, seeing Shang's frown turn into a beet-red revelation.

"I'm sorry I left you," Shang said quietly. "I turned back to look for you—in the forest, but we couldn't find you." He inhaled. "I became worried."

"But he was too stubborn to admit it," ShiShi added.

"Still, Li Shang would have come to his senses sooner or later, little soldier, but you can thank *me* for making it sooner. I reminded him how much you sacrificed to get here."

Shang flinched at his guardian's gentle reprimand, but his gaze didn't leave Mulan. "I also remembered what you told me in the tower. How you were a disappointment to your parents, and you were unhappy with yourself. I didn't completely understand what you'd meant then. But I understand a little better now. Everything I said earlier . . . I didn't mean it, and I regret it."

"I'm sorry, too," Mulan replied. "I didn't mean to lie to you."

"I know," said Shang. "But you did it to save your father. I would have done the same if I were in your position."

She raised an eyebrow. "Really?"

"Well," Shang fumbled, "I mean, if—if I were a g-girl, but it's hard to imagine that. I mean, I'd like to think I would have."

"It's not as hard as you think. Getting the voice down is the toughest part of it." Mulan chuckled and heaved herself up a craggy boulder fallen in their path.

"Tougher than my drills?" Shang joked.

She laughed. "Maybe not," she allowed. "I was so afraid you'd see right through me and send me home."

Shang laughed with her, but he sounded nervous. "I

would never have guessed. You—" He clamped his lips tight. "Y-you're strong," he stammered, "and I'm not just saying that. I mean it. You . . . you fight good."

ShiShi rolled his eyes. "Come, you two, move faster. There'll be time enough for you to gape at one another *after* we leave Diyu."

"I'm not—"

Mulan stifled another laugh, then sobered. "We must be far from the hundredth level. How deep into Diyu did Meng Po lead me?"

"Not too deep. ShiShi and I found a door in the desert while we were looking for you. It looks like a portal."

"One that should take us back to the City of the Dead," ShiShi said, nodding his head to quicken their pace. "From there, we'll find the gates."

Mulan's heart lifted. "So we're close."

Shang started to walk next to Mulan, but ShiShi stepped between them. "Not close enough."

Mulan was both relieved and disappointed ShiShi had inserted himself between them. She couldn't explain it, but now that Shang knew she was a girl, she felt shy around him.

Stop that, she scolded herself. *You're a soldier!*

Trying hard not to look at Shang, she listened to ShiShi tell the story of how he'd guided one of the Li ancestors to become a great hero who helped the Emperor unify China.

He'd risen from being the son of a penniless rice farmer to become an admired warrior, respected for his keen battle strategy, surprise tactics, and mercy on his defeated opponents.

"He was a legend for hundreds of years," finished ShiShi. "People even wrote songs about him, and sang them from village to village." The lion puffed up his chest with pride. "The tune was quite catchy, I remember. Shall I sing it?"

"No!" Mulan and Shang said at the same time.

ShiShi harrumphed. "Well, I—"

"I want to know *your* story, Mulan," Shang interrupted. "Tell me about your family. Your father—Fa Zhou—he was in the army with my father. And he is married to—"

"My mother is Fa Li," Mulan supplied. "She was the daughter of a civil servant in the Imperial City. She greatly honors the classics, so it always upset her that I could never memorize them."

Shang smiled. "I can understand that." He straightened again. "So you have no brother?"

"No, my ancestors were right. It's just me. My parents tried to have a boy, but they couldn't have any other children." She'd never talked about this with anyone before, not even Mushu. "I don't think my father minded much, but it was hard on my mother."

Shang was quiet. He was listening.

"I wasn't the ideal daughter. I was too clumsy to be of use around the house, and too independent to stay at home weaving and playing the zither all day. The only way I could uphold the family honor was to marry well. But on the day I met the Matchmaker, I accidentally set her on fire."

"Really?" A laugh escaped Shang, then he quickly cleared his throat. "I mean, that's terrible."

Mulan grinned at him. "I would have laughed, too, if I hadn't been so terrified. I know I disappointed my family. I'm an embarrassment to them. I guess I didn't want to be trapped in a marriage." She sighed. "At the same time, I wanted to be a good daughter.

"When Chi Fu came to my village and called my father back to the army, I saw it as my chance. I decided to go to save my father, but at the same time . . . a small part of me wanted to escape." She had never admitted that out loud before. "I wanted to prove that I could be more."

"You *are* more," Shang said, slowing down to speak with her. "I meant what I said earlier about you being a hero." He faltered. "I learned something today. No matter whether you're a girl or a demon or a ghost, you are my friend . . . Mulan."

Mulan held her breath. Hearing him say her name—her real name—was strange, yet nice. Her heart lifted, and she warmed. "So you're not going to discharge me?"

"No," Shang said firmly. "A good soldier is hard to find. China needs you."

"China needs both of us," said Mulan. "Together."

They stopped, suddenly approaching the break in the desert's arid landscape. Just as Shang and ShiShi had promised, there was a wooden door planted at the middle of the desert.

Just a door. No walls, no tunnels, no path leading up to it. Mulan stepped around the door, but there was nothing behind it. The only promising sign was the bronze medallion of King Yama's face nailed into the center of the door.

"There was a placard earlier," Shang said. "Something about Youdu. We didn't have time to dust it off and read it."

Mulan swept the sand off Yama's nose and teeth, revealing a small metal placard beneath the bronze cast. Etched onto the placard was the number ninety-seven.

"We're back at the ninety-seventh level," Mulan said, growing excited. "We *are* close."

"Does it say anything else?"

Mulan rubbed the placard with her sleeve. "Nothing here. Wait." She squinted, using the light emanating from Shang's body to illuminate whatever had been carved on the door.

"Let me try," said the captain, kneeling beside Mulan. His light glimmered against the placard. "It looks like a warning here. *Do not enter. . . .*"

"I can't make out the rest. Something about *pillar* . . . *fire*, and *Youdu*."

"Enough of this," ShiShi said. "Youdu is this way. I'm certain of it. Open the door, Li Shang."

Grabbing the latch hanging from King Yama's bronze head, Shang pulled the door open. It swung to the side with a creak.

Steam hissed on the other side of the door. Mulan took a careful step into the new chamber, pressing the back of her hand to her mouth as she adjusted to the sweltering temperature.

Smoke thickened the air, and the heat prickled her skin. A draft of hot air skimmed the pebbles on the ground, sifting away the pale yellow sand on Mulan's boots. Thick black dust quickly coated her clothes and shoes.

"This doesn't look like the City of the Dead," she said. The ground was black as coal, and when she kicked the dirt, it spilled off the sides of a steep slope. In every direction, clusters of tall, thin tube vents sprang from the ground, steam hissing from their chimneys.

They were on a mountain, she realized. No, a volcano, given the glassy streams of lava running down its sides. Smoke obscured the horizon, but Mulan could make out the flat peak not too far up.

At last, she saw the River of Hopelessness again. This

time, its magical waters coursed in midair, a ribbon of black silk looping through the clouds—so high it intersected the volcano at its peak.

Yet as her eyes followed the river, she saw that the peak was the only place it flowed on land. On the side facing them, the river streamed lower, snaking over the sides of the mountain. Not too far ahead, in fact, it loomed so low that its width obscured her view of the sky. She could almost feel the spray of its icy waters on her face.

As they began their climb up the volcano, she was sure the earth wobbled. No, quaked.

Mulan and Shang exchanged a worried look.

The ground rumbled again. Mulan stumbled but caught her balance. She stole a glimpse over her shoulder, but she had a sinking feeling she knew what she would see.

Sure enough, the wooden door had vanished.

"It looks like that's where we have to go," said Shang grimly. He pointed at the volcano's peak, where a black stone pillar stretched into the sky.

"Maybe that's what the door was trying to tell us," ShiShi said. "That has to be the way to Youdu."

"I don't know," Shang said hesitantly. "I say we turn around."

"We can't," said ShiShi, cocking his head at the vanished door. The lion's sharp eyes focused on the black pillar crowning the top of the volcano. "There are stairs cut into that pillar that spiral upward. I'll wager we have to climb it to reach the next level."

Shang opened his mouth to say something, but orange light suddenly reflected in his eyes, followed by an explosive blast from the sky. Mulan spun, and her heels rocked back as a blast of fire hurtled down from the clouds.

"Take cover!" Shang shouted.

Mulan dove. If not for the River of Hopelessness thrashing above her, the fireball would have scorched her. Instead, it slammed into the river's waters and sizzled with a hiss.

Shakily, she pulled herself to her feet. "What was that?"

"I don't know," said Shang. "It looked like fire falling from the sky."

"Maybe it was just lightning," ShiShi suggested, but his deep voice trembled.

"Maybe." Shang waited. "It seems to have stopped."

"I don't think it was lightning," Mulan said. "I'm beginning to think that warning was on the door for a reason."

"Then we make for the pillar now," Shang said. "Stay close behind me, and stay under the river."

Mulan nodded, but she knew he was trying to sound brave for her and ShiShi's sakes. Anyone could see that the River of Hopelessness would shield them only for a short while.

They'd have to make the best of it. Once they reached the volcano's summit, the river wouldn't be their shield at all. It'd be their obstacle. For on the summit, it no longer floated above; it slammed into the mountaintop, gushing across the mouth of the volcano. Even from where she stood, Mulan could hear the river cutting across the rock with enormous power, like a jagged piece of metal ripping through sand. She couldn't see its waters swirling across the peak, not yet. But what she could see was the river spilling off the peak, cascading down into a great black waterfall.

The sight of it all prompted a new worry to crawl inside her gut.

The pillar was on the peak. If the river crashed there, it would likely obstruct their path. They might have to cross it.

Worry about that later, Mulan. We have to reach the top first.

Sweat prickled her neck and forehead. Her palms were warm, her gauntlets clinging to the backs of her hand. With each breath, the air grew thicker and thicker.

The smell of incense was long gone, but Mulan sensed something else in the air. "Do you smell that?"

"Smoke," Shang murmured.

"And firewood," added ShiShi.

The higher they climbed, the stronger the wind became.

The path was rocky and steep, with boulders and storms of pebbles tumbling down as they went up. But after the Mountain of Knives, Mulan hiked up without much trouble. The only difficulties were avoiding the fireballs and not stepping into the glistening streams of lava.

Halfway up the volcano, they moved out of the river's protection; it coursed left, looping higher into the clouds.

They'd need to be careful. Mulan covered her mouth with her hand, trying to shield herself from the gray snow spilling from the sky.

ShiShi had to shake his mane free of the stuff every few steps. "Confounded snow," he growled. "Only in Diyu would it snow on a volcano."

"It's not snow," Mulan said, catching a handful and sifting it through her fingers. "It's ash."

"Ash?" ShiShi sniffed. "There's far too much to be ash. Next you'll say all these rocks on the ground aren't rocks."

She bent to pick up one of the black sticks that'd started appearing all around them. At first she'd thought they were oddly shaped rocks, but as soon as she saw the skull—

"They're bones," she whispered. "Demon bones. What could kill demons in Diyu?"

She wasn't sure she wanted to know.

ShiShi sniffed. His round, golden eyes blinked, and he looked worried.

"What is it?" Shang asked.

"We should turn back."

"You just said we couldn't."

"I changed my mind," said the lion hastily. "Come now, let's find another way."

"We're so close," Mulan argued. The moon was nearly black. Only a thin crescent still glimmered in the sky. "We don't have time to turn back. We're almost there."

"Listen to me, girl," ShiShi barked. "You don't want to face what is on the top of this volcano. Trust me."

Another fiery blast sliced the air. The impact knocked Mulan off her feet, just missing her. The blast of fire smoked and sizzled, charring the rocks and bones with its heat.

Then came another burst, and another.

"Run!" ShiShi bellowed. "He's seen us."

"Who?"

Before Mulan could get her answer, an earth-shattering roar ripped through their conversation, sending spikes of fear down her spine.

ShiShi scraped his claws into the ground to balance himself. His fur stood on its ends. "Huoguai," he whispered. "A fire demon."

A wall of fire sprang up from the ground, separating her from Shang and ShiShi. The burst of heat sent Mulan reeling back, and the flames temporarily blinded her. She had never seen fire so powerful and alive. It danced, overwhelming the sky with its brightness and intensity. Black clouds of smoke on the top of the wall bloomed up into the night.

"Shang? ShiShi?"

The fire rippled and crackled, snuffing out the sound of her voice.

Mulan gritted her teeth. The wall was too high to vault across, the flames far too strong to put out. The blaze was so thick she couldn't even see Shang or ShiShi on the other side.

"What do you want?" she shouted at the fire.

The fire swayed, as if laughing.

"Who are you?"

Within the blaze's walls formed the terrible Huoguai. His head blazed with fire, his scaled body red as blood. A fierce, pointed tail whipped behind him, its movement sharp like a stab of lightning. And on his back were wings made of smoke.

Huoguai opened his wings, spreading them from one edge of the wall to the other. Smoke wisped from his wings, but underneath was a web of bone and muscle. With a violent shudder, he clapped his wings back. The wall of fire crashed down, a blinding sheet of flames. Molten rubble sprang up with a hiss. The earth boomed.

Mulan stumbled wildly as the ground cracked. The

fallen wall was now a sea of flames. It spread hungrily, washing out everything in its path.

Light sparked in Huoguai's hollow black eyes. He gathered his wings, surged from the sea of fire, and snatched Mulan with one sharp talon on his hand. He closed his fist around her waist. Up and up he flew, as the world beneath her crumbled, taking Shang and ShiShi with it.

Chapter Twenty-Three

Mulan writhed, wrestling Huoguai's claws for a way out of his grip. His fingers were thick and bulbous as a tiger's, and his talons alone were bigger than her hands. He was all scales and smoke. Touching his skin scalded her. Breathing pinched her lungs.

She desperately reached for the sword at her hip. No use. Even if she could get to it, Huoguai had wrapped his fingers so tight around her waist he could easily have snapped her in half.

They swooped up. The volcano's rocky face rushed in front of her, followed by a wave of heat. When the smoke cleared, she could see the volcano's expanse from their height in the sky. Here, the river no longer hung in the sky.

It gushed over the mountain, blanketing its shiny orange and red streams of lava. As her feet dangled precipitously over its waters, she spotted the black pillar on the other side of the river.

Huoguai had flown them to the peak.

She squirmed again, trying to twist her way out so she could see her friends. "Let me go!" she shouted. "Let me—"

Her shouts became a gasp when the fire demon suddenly dropped her.

It wasn't a fatally high drop, but it was painful. Mulan landed on a harsh bed of rock and bones. Her sword clattered next to her on the volcano's wide rim. She lifted her head first, then her hands and legs. Nothing was broken, but she winced as she moved her ankle. The fall hadn't helped it. If not for her armor, she might have hit one of the rocks and suffered worse.

She looked up. The sky was bloodshot, and she saw Huoguai disappear into the clouds, his wings beating a powerful torrent of embers and ash swept up from the volcano.

The ground steamed, the pale gold ribbons in the rock shiny with heat. Around her were more charred bones, cracked demon skulls, and battered shields and spearheads. Smoke hissed from the rocks, and molten stone bubbled within the cracks in the ground. Craters as wide as ponds dimpled the surface, boiling with the earth's red-hot soup.

Columns of black rock veined with glowing red lava protruded from the summit.

The Chamber of Boiling Despair, she remembered with a shudder. *This is what Mei tried to warn us about. This volcano must be the Cauldron.*

From below, she'd thought that the volcano's peak was flat. Now that she was at the top, she realized she'd been wrong. The ground sloped inward like a bowl. Like the cauldron it'd been named for.

And she'd landed on its rim.

Mulan pulled herself up and reached for her sword. Bruises splotched her body, but she ignored the pain and ran to the edge of the rim to search for Shang and ShiShi.

No sign of them. Or of Huoguai.

Smoke curled everywhere, obscuring her vision.

She clenched her fists. The last time she'd seen Shang and ShiShi, the demon's fire had ruptured the ground. Maybe they had fallen deeper into Diyu. Maybe they were dead.

They're still alive, Mulan told herself. *They have to be.*

But even if Shang and ShiShi were alive, could she find them from up on the peak? Why had Huoguai dropped her off here?

Probably so he can come back for me later, she thought with a shiver.

Fear wrenched Mulan's gut. How could she defeat a demon powerful enough to split the earth, and strong enough to toss them about as if they were mere checkers pieces?

She coughed, holding her sleeve up to her mouth to keep the ash out of her lungs. She needed to get to the pillar. Reaching it had been their goal before they'd gotten separated, and if there were hope of reuniting with her friends, it'd be there.

As some of the smoke cleared, Mulan took a good, hard look at the pillar. As she'd feared, the pillar was on the opposite side of the River of Hopelessness. Its swirling waters surged across the center of the Cauldron, then plunged off the edge in a black, looming waterfall. Shrill screams resonated from its depths.

Maybe there's a way around it, she thought with a gulp.

The smoke thickened. Mulan coughed and trod onward, fanning the air with her hands. She spotted an old shield left behind and picked it up. Scorch marks blackened the iron surface, but at least it would protect her as she searched for her friends.

Fire lit the sky.

"Huoguai," Mulan said, recognizing the swirls of smoke and fire. They were coming from below. She ran to the brink of the Cauldron to get a better look.

Her heart jumped when she spotted Shang and ShiShi on a ledge halfway up the Cauldron. They hadn't fallen after all!

"Shang!" she shouted. "I'm here!"

Shang, who'd just picked up a spear, heard her. "Mulan! We're—"

From out of the shadow, Huoguai drew himself up. Against the mountain, Mulan took account of his staggering size. His feet were planted on the ledge, but the tips of his wings nearly reached the top of the Cauldron. Mulan ducked before he grabbed her again. Huoguai raised his wings and punched the side of the mountain. Boulders flew. ShiShi roared, his claws scraping against the ground with a terrible screech. Shang managed to keep his balance. He held his spear above his head, and with one strong swoop, he threw it at Huoguai's head.

The weapon lodged itself in the demon's left eye. With a thundering scream, Huoguai plucked the spear out of his eye and burned the weapon in his hands. The spear's ashes skated across the wind.

Huoguai turned to Shang and ShiShi and opened his mouth again, breathing another terrible blaze. The flames snaked across the side of the volcano. They couldn't harm Shang. But ShiShi let out a yelp when the fire singed his mane.

Huoguai flew at them. Fiery rocks ripped from the sky, rocketing down to smash Shang and ShiShi. He was playing with them, Mulan realized. Huoguai had countless opportunities to kill ShiShi—and her. But by separating them and toying with them, he was drawing out the inevitable.

That was why he had dropped her off on the peak—on the *wrong* side of the peak. To torment her, and remind her that time was running out.

Set against the bloodshot sky, the moon tantalized Mulan with its closeness. It was nearly cloaked in shadow, a sliver of its silvery light burnished with the demon's fire.

She had to do something.

Huoguai lifted his wing and struck at the captain, hurling him deeper into the Underworld. How Mulan wished Shang had learned to float and fly! As the ground shook, he tumbled down the mountain along with ShiShi. If they fell into the river . . .

"Hey!" Mulan shouted to the demon. "It's me you want. Not them."

The fire demon's coal-black eyes turned to her. They glowed like embers, and the fire in his hands strengthened. Mulan ducked behind her shield, barely evading the column of flames Huoguai blasted her way.

He didn't stop. Mulan held her shield tight to her chest, bending her head behind it. She smelled her hair burning and snuffed out the ends. Mulan counted the rhythm of the demon's attacks. When she gathered enough courage, she waited for the rest between blasts, then ran.

Keep his attention away from Shang and ShiShi, she thought frantically as she dashed across the summit. *Give them time to climb back to safety.*

Huoguai's hands flared, hurling streams of fire her way. The ground quaked again. Mulan couldn't afford to stumble. She widened her stride, pushing through the sharp twinges of pain in her ankle and running until she reached the end of the Cauldron's rim.

Then the blasts of fire stopped. The glow in Huoguai's black eyes disappeared. His eyes darkened, hollow and cold. He lowered his hand, and instead his body shook in laughter. The wind rippled, and the sky thundered.

Mulan backed up until she stood on the brink of the Cauldron. One more step back, and she'd tumble into the river. *Not good.*

The river smothered the Cauldron's mouth, a giant crater in the center of the peak, but smaller craters had formed along the rim. They bubbled and spurted now with bright, hot lava.

Mulan stumbled forward, her balance wobbling as the ground trembled.

Demon soldiers surged up from the craters and rocks!

They barged onto the volcano, surrounding Mulan and closing in on her.

Unlike King Yama's or Meng Po's demons, the fire demon's soldiers wore no armor. Their faces were scorched red like Huoguai's, but their eyes were gray and vacant, their noses hollow—like skulls. Born from the Cauldron to do Huoguai's bidding, they looked more like monsters than animals—their chests bore scabs and burns like art or markers of identification. Some carried swords, others carried spears, and more than a few carried thick chain whips. The closest demon lashed his whip against the rock, unleashing a gust of searing debris that flew into Mulan's face.

"Ahh!" Mulan cried as the debris stung her cheeks. She blocked her face with her hand, then glanced back at the edge of the Cauldron. The river cut off her path down the mountain.

Nowhere to run. But if she stayed here, could she fight the demons and win—while having time to reach the pillar?

The demons sneered at her. "Not even the ghosts come here," one growled. "What brings you, mortal soldier? Are you in the mood to die?"

"He looks afraid. Look at the quaking legs. A bit scrawny."

"Don't complain. It isn't often Huoguai gives us a feast."

"I'm going to slice his arms and drink his blood."

"I'm going to roast him on a spit."

"Save me his eyeballs. I love eyeballs. It's been so long since I've had some."

"Too long," his comrade agreed. "The last one carried a sword, too."

"More like a toothpick."

"I could use a new toothpick."

Mulan thought fast. The only way off this volcano was to jump off. Even if there weren't streams of lava and jagged, toothy precipices awaiting her below, leaving the Cauldron wouldn't have been an option. She needed to get across the river.

Not far away, she heard Shang's lion guardian scraping his way up the opposite side of the mountain. She could barely see him; the river's murky waters separated them like a wall. Smoke clung to his ruffled fur, and his sharp nails cut across the black mountain face.

"ShiShi!" Mulan cried.

ShiShi lifted his head when he heard her. His eyes widened when he saw the demons behind her.

"Behind you!" the lion yelled. "Use your sword!" Wind muffled his next words. All she could hear was something about "magic" and "demons."

One of the demon's chains wrapped over Mulan's waist, pulling her away from the edge. She rocked back on her heels, digging them into the dirt to slow herself from being dragged.

She hacked at the metal chain with her blade. Tossing its remains on the ground with a clatter, she stared defiantly at the demons. She didn't know which one had tried to pull her back, but their message was clear. Time to fight.

She staggered to regain her balance and tightened her grip on her sword. The hilt was warm from the fire and heat. The characters engraved on the steel shone.

Use your sword, ShiShi had said. What was that supposed to mean? She'd been fighting with it all this time. What did she need to do differently?

Mulan rubbed the steam off her blade. "The flower that blooms in adversity is the most rare and beautiful of all," she murmured, reading the quotation engraved on it again. The words didn't give her any secret key to defeating the demons.

She returned her attention to the demons. One in the front row spat, his webbed feet sinking deep into the sizzling ground. The rest lashed at her feet with their chains, taunting her as she jumped out of the way. She staggered back, almost slipping thanks to a pile of bones.

"Look at him dance." They laughed. "Don't fall off the cliff, human. You need to roast a bit first."

She inhaled and glanced at her reflection in her sword. Dirt smudged her cheeks. Sweat dribbled down her temples, and her arms writhed with fatigue. She looked tired—and afraid.

Not exactly the rare and beautiful flower this sword's been waiting for, thought Mulan. *But if I think like that, I'm never going to defeat these demons.*

She looked down at her hands. They were clasping the sword so tight her knuckles were white. She swallowed. *I can't be afraid. If I am, all is lost.*

The sword had glowed earlier, when Mulan faced the bandit ghosts. What had she done to invoke its power?

I'd been trying to protect my friends, she remembered. *The bandits attacked, and I just raised the sword without knowing its power.*

Maybe that was the key. Skill wasn't enough to bring the sword alive; it was her courage and strength—her need to save Shang and ShiShi from Huoguai, and take Shang back to the real world where he was still needed. Instinct had overcome doubt.

With a nod to herself, she raised the sword high above her head. *I need to get to Huoguai so I can protect my friends,* she thought. *Help me, please.*

As before, slowly the sword began to glow. Mulan faced her opponents, her confidence returning. "You want to fight? Then come get me."

The demons hissed. They grunted and shuffled their feet, preparing to charge. But as they lunged for Mulan, her blade burned brighter than the lava spitting from the ground, brighter even than Huoguai's fire.

The demons recoiled at its brightness. "Stop! I can't see!"

Pressing her sword's hilt against her ribs, she charged between two of the demons, slashing their sides with her blade. Ash spilled from the demons' guts, and they howled with surprise.

Mulan dodged as they attacked her blindly. A few ran too far, tripping over the edge of the rim and tumbling off the mountainside.

"Look away!" one of the demons shouted, blocking his view of her sword with his shield. "He has the sword, the Sword of the Blazing Sun."

"The hero of legend has returned!" the demons screeched.

"The hero with the Sword of the Blazing Sun!"

Mulan's ears perked. The hero with the Sword of the Blazing Sun? Her father used to tell her a story about a hero, half man and half god, who had lived thousands of years ago, when monsters and demons still roamed China's lands. The Emperor had asked the demigod, who was known everywhere in China for his great fighting prowess, to expunge the monsters that terrorized China and send them into Diyu. The Emperor, who also had powers from the heavens, gave the demigod a magical sword that glowed with the light of the sun. It could cut through anything, even the swords of demons and ghosts. But only the demigod could unlock its power.

Mulan had always thought the story was only a legend. But could it be that the sword she'd found was the same one? Maybe the demigod had left it in Diyu when he died. In her tales of the Underworld, Grandmother Fa always mentioned that even heroes and famous warriors spent time in Diyu.

It's not like you can ask any anyone your questions right now, Mulan scolded herself. *Focus on the fight!*

She stomped on one of the demon's chains. The rest of the demons stepped back, putting a good distance between them and her.

Making use of the break, Mulan untied the knot on her head. Her hair tumbled down again, brushing against the nape of her neck. She unfastened her armor, freeing her shoulders of their heavy burden.

The demons watched her in disbelief. "A girl?"

"I am Mulan." She raised her sword high. She'd never fought as herself before—as a woman, not a woman pretending to be a man. No more hiding, no more pretending. No more fears that she'd endanger herself and her family.

She was who she'd always wanted to be.

Even if that feeling could only last here in Diyu—even if they made it back to the real world and she had to go back to pretending to be Ping, Mulan knew she'd never forget it. Taking off that mask was exhilarating; it spurred her courage.

Her sword blazed brighter than ever before. The demons raised their shields to protect themselves from her sword's glare. "I am trying to reach the portal with my friends," Mulan shouted over their cries. "I give you this one opportunity to leave in peace."

"You think we're afraid of a girl?"

"No one wants to accept my offer?" Mulan scraped her boots against the rock. "Your loss."

With a unanimous howl, the demons charged.

Have courage.

She half closed her eyes, remembering her months training under Shang's command. He'd taught his soldiers to outrun an onslaught of burning arrows, to turn a simple wooden pole into a deadly weapon, to fire arrows into pomegranates in midair.

All achievements she'd thought were impossible. Until they weren't.

Speed, endurance, strength. Precision, focus, confidence, Mulan told herself. *I am the coursing river, the raging fire. I am the warrior.*

She waited until the demons were close enough that she could smell their rotten breath. *Now!* Mulan thrust her sword into the lava streaming through the rock and heaved upward, swooping the burning embers into the demons' eyes.

They screamed, wailing in pain and flailing for their

eyes. A few still attacked, shoving their swords and spears blindly in her direction. Mulan picked her first target. She swept a foot forward and lunged, countered one demon's attack, and then kicked him in the shin and tripped him. He fell over the ledge.

Like with the ghost bandits, she slashed through the demons' spears and whips and swords. This surprised Huoguai's soldiers, and she destroyed as many of their weapons as she could before the demons had recovered from her initial attack.

Larger demons appeared, emerging from the boiling craters. They looked much like the others, except they had odd numbers of eyes and arms and ears that looked stitched together out of different creatures—part bear, part tiger, part snake.

She gripped her shield, kept it high over her chest. The demons were large and powerful. They attacked high, above her ribs and side. Their only weakness was their lack of speed. Mulan needed to use her smaller size to her advantage. She was able to evade most of their attacks with her nimble footwork and quick thinking. She even managed to make two of the demons accidentally strike each other by ducking right before they swung at her. But she knew it was only a matter of time before they defeated her.

Her wrists started to tire from the thrusting and blocking. The arm carrying her shield shuddered every time a spear or sword jabbed at it. Her muscles tightened, and her grip faltered. Someone's chain whip lashed her arm, and she cried out in pain.

Ignoring the searing pain in her arm, Mulan dropped the shield. She couldn't carry it anymore. She'd have to use only her sword.

The demons could sense her tiring. They flanked her, three on each side.

"She's weak," they said. "Let's finish her off!"

They attacked, but she was ready for them. She ducked and drew a sharp arc across their calves. Ash poured out instead of blood. From their screams, she knew she'd hurt them.

Hurting them wasn't the goal. Stopping them was.

She was gaining ground. Holding her palm to the flat of her blade, she pushed the closest demon into the bubbling crater. Another whipped her back with his chain.

Mulan arched in pain, feeling the searing lash cut into her flesh. The demon laughed, and down came his chain again. This time, Mulan jumped to the side and blocked the chain with her sword, catching it in the blade. She yanked the chain away and coiled it over her wrist.

Shang should've included these in our training, she thought as she caught her breath. *If I get out of here, I'll bring it up.*

She charged at the closest two demons, wrapping the

chain around their legs as she dodged their attacks. Then, as they stumbled toward her, she blocked their attacks and pushed them off the Cauldron. One by one, they fell, but Mulan didn't give herself a moment to rejoice. She'd learned from that mistake the first time—with Shan-Yu.

One last demon awaited her. It was just her luck that he was also the biggest. She threw her shoulders back so she looked bigger than she was and copied ShiShi's best, most intimidating snarl.

The demon roared in response. His sword was as broad as her face, and it whooshed in the air whenever he swung. Mulan darted away as he attacked, dodging and crouching as the demon heaved his sword at her head. As he charged, she pivoted away from the brink and ducked, only letting herself breathe when the demon slipped and tumbled off the Cauldron.

Panting, Mulan bent over her knees. Her sweat dripped onto the ground. Quickly, she caught her breath and scoured the area for signs of Shang and ShiShi.

She trained her eyes on Huoguai's wings gliding above the volcano, then on Shang's luminous blue form, and ShiShi's tattered golden mane. The fire demon must have been after Shang and ShiShi this entire time, but to her relief, her friends had managed to evade him and climb back up onto the top of the Cauldron. They were on the other side—the *right* side of the river. The pillar leading up to Youdu was just behind them.

So why weren't they leaving?

"Go!" Mulan shouted. "This is your chance!"

The wind swallowed her words, but Shang turned to her. His brow furrowed.

We're not leaving without you, his expression read.

"No," Mulan said under her breath. But she knew Shang was stubborn, just as stubborn as she.

Her friends couldn't defeat Huoguai without her help, but she couldn't help them from here. She had to cross the River of Hopelessness. Somehow.

Quickly, Mulan charted a path toward the river, running from rock to rock and hiding behind them so she wouldn't attract the fire demon's attention. Getting to the river was the easy part. How she'd cross it was another story.

She'd have to figure it out, and soon. Before Huoguai killed Shang and ShiShi, or threw them into the river's treacherous black waters—and everything was lost.

Chapter Twenty-Four

Mulan could not find a way to cross the river and reach her friends. Here on the Cauldron, the river was too wide, the waters too treacherous. There was no way to swim across, and nothing she could use to build a raft.

On the other side of the Cauldron, Shang rammed another spear into Huoguai's wings, then swiped the spear right, creating a tear that Mulan could hear even over the river's thundering waters. With a savage shriek, Huoguai jolted into the air and ignited his injured wing with his breath. When the flames smoldered out, he was whole again.

Smoke unfurled from his wings—a gathering storm. With a flash, Huoguai opened them and swooped for Shang.

The captain jumped, barely missing him.

Huoguai dangled in midair before diving again. Fire coursed through his veins, rippling across his red, inflamed head and muscular arms. His tail plunged down upon the rocks, smashing them and everything around them. Compared to Huoguai, even ShiShi seemed tiny. As the lion raced out of the demon's path of destruction, Mulan saw Shang prepare for another attack.

I have to help them, Mulan thought in a panic. *I have to get across.*

But how? This chamber was a desolate place. Nothing but bones, abandoned weapons, craters, rocks, those tubelike columns—

The columns!

They jutted from the earth, thin and pointed, almost like the stalactites in the cave that led to Diyu. Mulan started for the tallest one around. It was at least twice her height, which was about half as wide as the river. Just thin enough it might work. Shoulders heaving, she lifted her sword and struck the column at its base.

It was lighter than it looked. Not the sturdiest pole, either. Too chalky. Any other time, she might have worried about it snapping in two, but it would have to do.

Mulan backed up and tied her sword to her side. Holding the stone pole at her shoulders, half of it above her head, she sprinted as fast as could for the edge of the River of Hopelessness.

Seconds stretched.

Kicking one knee up to drive her higher into the air, she jumped and pushed the end of the pole down into the river, feeling it stick to the crater's surface. The icy water stung the back of her legs, forcing a gasp out of her lungs. She only had moments before the pole would topple.

If she fell in, she'd be lost in Diyu forever.

She snapped her hands and legs together. The river pounded, thrashing at her ankles. The screams she'd heard earlier grew louder, resonating from the ghosts trapped in the water. She didn't dare look down. Her eyes were fixed on the other side of the river.

All that mattered was getting across. Getting to Shang and ShiShi.

Her arms burned as she swung her body forward, gathering momentum. With a grunt, she threw herself as far across as she could reach. Mist from the river folded over her, blurring her vision. That was the most terrifying part—not being able to see. Not knowing whether to treasure this moment as her precious last. Whether the river would devour her next breath, whether she'd never see her friends again.

Then it was over. Her body slammed onto the other side of the Cauldron.

ShiShi grabbed her by his teeth, pulled her away from

the edge. He pressed her against the back of a rock. "Hide before he sees you."

"We need to get to the pillar," Mulan said, shivering. Her hands still gripped the pole tight. She dropped it and allowed herself one breath to recover. "I can distract him."

"No," said Shang. "Huoguai will see you. He's guarding the pillar. Any time we try to get close, he attacks. He's too strong."

"He has to have a weakness—"

"Move!" Shang shouted.

ShiShi shoved Mulan to the side. Seconds later, a boulder plunged from above, smashing the very spot she'd been.

"I'm afraid this is where it ends, little soldier." The lion guardian gulped. "It was a valiant effort."

"No." Mulan wiped her face. Spray from the river slicked her palms, and an idea struck.

ShiShi peeked out of their hiding spot, looking distressed. "He's coming."

"The river," she murmured.

"What did you say?" asked ShiShi, jumping as the ground hissed. "I cannot hear with all the world collapsing around us."

"We've got to lure him into the river."

The lion growled. "Are you insane, girl?"

"It makes sense," Shang murmured. "We need to split up. You two head for the pillar. I'll lure him to the river."

"What if he throws you in?" Mulan protested. "You can't fly."

Shang's expression softened. "Trust me."

"Wait—" Mulan got up. "I'm coming with you."

He nodded at Mulan, as if she were his equal instead of his recruit. "Together, then."

As soon as he said it, there was a thunderous crash, and their hiding spot crumpled. High above, Huoguai laughed.

ShiShi growled and ran to catch up with Mulan and Shang. "Wait for me!"

Mulan shouted to catch Huoguai's attention. "I'm here. Your soldiers didn't kill me."

"And I'm here!" Shang shouted from the opposite side of the ledge.

The captain leaned over the edge of the Cauldron, dangerously close to the river. As the black waters spilled down the volcano's side, Huoguai batted his wings, diving to hurl Shang into the river.

"Now!" Mulan shouted. At her command, everyone launched their attack. ShiShi threw a boulder at Huoguai's wing, and Mulan threw her sword at the other wing.

Huoguai flailed, thrashing against the river's murky surface. He gathered himself and leapt into the sky, hanging low to recover.

Mulan ran toward Huoguai, pulled her sword from his

wing, and slammed the hilt into his belly until he tumbled back toward the river. Huoguai hissed.

With a lurch, he snapped his tail over Mulan's waist, taking her with him.

"Mulan!" Shang shouted.

Mulan didn't waste time kicking and clawing at the demon. She had her sword in hand this time. She swung it at the demon's wings and ankles, but Huoguai didn't stop. His wings beat against the powerful wind, and at last she saw that they hung over the river; she could see the waterfall's black waters gushing down and down, past the clouds into Diyu's abyss. She stopped attacking him with her sword and gulped.

"Mulan!" Shang cried from the edge of the river. "Mulan, jump!"

Shang had found what was left of her vaulting stick. Holding it over his head, he stood precariously close to the river.

"Grab the pole!" ShiShi shrieked.

She started kicking the air, using her weight against Huoguai so the demon juddered back toward the Cauldron—and toward Shang.

But then Huoguai stopped fighting her. Instead, he tightened his tail over her waist and reached out with his claws to toss Shang into the river. Shang leapt out of the way, but Mulan panicked. Her getting onto the Cauldron wasn't worth the risk of losing Shang. Knowing she needed to do something before Huoguai reached the captain, she stabbed her sword into the demon's tail.

Huoguai shrieked. He lost control for one precious second, and Mulan uncurled his tail from her waist and reached for his wings, grabbing onto whatever she could as Huoguai veered out of control, flames spiraling out of his fingers and tail. He clawed at his wings, trying to pluck Mulan off as he regained control of his flight. His tail slashed and whipped, spurting waves of fire.

Inspired, Mulan grabbed the tip of his tail and thrust its flames at his wing. Smoke blustered into the air, and she could smell Huoguai's wings charring. It might not hurt him, but it distracted him. Before he could stop her, Mulan reached for the sword still lodged in his tail, plucked it out, and stabbed it into his wing. She could feel the blade pierce Huoguai's thick muscle, the sharp edge scraping against bone. Without hesitation, she ripped her sword down, slicing off half his wing.

With a deafening cry, Huoguai began to fall. He spiraled, careening down toward the river. Mulan clung to his remaining wing, trying to steer him toward the Cauldron so she could jump back onto land. But he fought back, fixing them for the river and its waterfall. His tail whipped at her, trying to grab her so they'd both go down.

She had no choice but to jump anyway.

She knew she wouldn't make it. She could see Shang holding out the pole, ShiShi beside him, his arms out-stretched to catch her. But even if she could make it to land, the river was in her way. She would fall right into its stream, onto the crest of the waterfall, and then plummet down its cascading black waters.

Shang saw this, too. Teeth gritted, he bolted to his feet and leapt over the waterfall, extending the pole that extra length Mulan needed so she wouldn't fall.

It happened so fast. Mulan slammed onto the pole, landing hard on her chest. The impact drew a gasp from her lungs, and as soon as she caught her breath, she tried to wrap her arms around the pole and kick up her legs onto its support.

"Hold on!" Shang shouted.

Her body slipped, but Mulan seized the pole again with her hands.

Shang was floating above the waterfall!

"Hold on," he shouted again. "I'm going to pull you in."

The river beat at them. Shang, unused to his ghostly abilities, wobbled.

Mulan gasped as the pole quaked and her feet dipped into the river's icy waters. Below her, she saw Huoguai still spinning in and out of the waterfall. It would be a long, long drop down.

"Look at me, not Huoguai," said Shang, his pale blue figure shimmering as he hovered over the river. "I've got you. Hang on."

The wind fought them. They began to dip toward the river, and Mulan's stomach swooped. "Are you sure you know how to fly?"

"I don't. Hang on!"

Mulan dangled off the pole. Dust spilled from its rocky surface. A sinking feeling lurched in her chest, and she started inching her hands across to the center of the pole, where it was stronger.

"It's not going to hold me!"

"Almost there," Shang said, leaning his body toward the Cauldron. "Hang on. Just a little longer."

Mulan tried not to look up at the pole. She could feel it collapsing under her grip.

Shang was so close to the Cauldron his cape brushed against the rocky bank. Just one more step, and ShiShi would have pulled them to the ground. They would have been safe.

Then the pole snapped in two. Mulan screamed.

Chapter Twenty-Five

She flailed, her fingers slipping through Shang's. He couldn't grab her; he was a spirit, little more than a shadow. A powerful rush of water surged behind her back. The river was ready to take her.

He might not be able to touch her, but the Lady of Forgetfulness had said he could touch anything that belonged in Diyu—like her sword.

"Grab my sword!" Mulan shouted.

Just in time, Shang reached for the blade hanging at her side. "I've got you," he said, teeth clenched and jaw tight.

Still clasping the sword, he hauled her up until her arms folded over the Cauldron's rocky shoulder. Mulan rolled onto the dome, pressed her hand against the edge of the cliff, and looked down.

At the very bottom of the waterfall, trapped within the river's black waters, was Huoguai. Smoke cascaded over the demon's face as he struggled against the crashing waves. Then he was gone, washed away.

She let out a sigh of relief. "That was close."

"Of all the foolish things to do," said Shang, shaking his head. "You nearly got yourself killed."

Mulan grinned. "Couldn't let Huoguai throw you into the bottom of Diyu."

"Well, it worked. You defeated him."

"We both did." She inhaled to slow her heartbeat. Her grin softened into a smile. "And you flew just now."

"I . . . I don't know how I did it," Shang stammered. "I was worried about you. When I saw you about to fall into the river . . . I just . . . jumped."

"You could have fallen in the river yourself."

"It was worth the risk. You're important." Shang flinched, realizing he'd said something he hadn't meant to. He cleared his throat, shuffling his feet uncomfortably. "I mean, you're one of my soldiers. You did the same for me. Just now. Thank you."

"You're welcome." Mulan couldn't help it; her smile widened at how uncomfortable Shang looked. Something about the way he'd said she was *important* melted her inside.

"Are you all right?" he asked.

"My pride is battered," ShiShi answered for her. The lion huffed, untangling his burnt mane with displeasure. "But I'm intact."

Shang returned her sword to her. "You're hurt," he said, gesturing at Mulan's bruises.

"Worry about me later," she said, gathering her breath. "Look."

She pointed at the sky. Now that Huoguai had been defeated, the world around them brightened. The streaks of crimson behind the clouds faded, and the sky turned blue as the clearest summer day. Even the smoke cleared, and the hissing from the craters and chimney rocks became silent.

At last, there was no fire demon guarding the pillar. The moon shone on its dark stones, the slanted light hitting upon a metal placard posted at the base of the tower. Mulan and her friends approached it wearily.

" 'To Youdu,' " Shang read. " 'The City of the Dead.' " He paused. "Is that where the ghosts . . . live? Before they ascend to Heaven?"

"Most of them," ShiShi replied.

"Most?"

"The citizens in Youdu are mostly there because they don't deserve the torture chambers of Diyu but also don't deserve Heaven quite yet."

"But some ghosts never make it to Youdu?"

"The very good ones," ShiShi replied, "and the very bad ones."

Shang said nothing, but his brow was tense, deep in contemplation.

He must be worried we won't make it, Mulan thought. *We wasted too much time fighting Huoguai.*

She jumped to her feet, ignoring the pain bubbling in her side and arm.

"Come on," she said. "You can't both be that eager to stay on this level."

"I'd be faster if you weren't in my way," ShiShi said, harrumphing as he navigated the narrow steps. "Need I remind you I have four legs compared to your two?" He tailed her, bounding up three steps at a time.

She pressed a hand against the pillar's wall, using it to steady herself as she climbed the spiraling steps. She wiped her dusty fingers on her pants, and glanced back at Shang.

The captain followed, easily keeping up. But unlike ShiShi, who huffed and grumbled all the way up, Shang was quiet. Often, he looked up at the blackening moon.

Mulan followed his gaze to the sky. Something glimmered just above the pillar, catching the fading light of the moon and reflecting it onto the sky. At first she thought it might be a star, but Diyu had no stars.

Could it be a mirror? she wondered. She'd seen

something like it on the Bridge of Helplessness. But she hadn't thought much of it then, and she didn't think much of it now.

After all, what could a mirror possibly have to do with their journey to the Gates of Diyu?

Chapter Twenty-Six

Mulan was starting to get used to the stark scenery changes that happened whenever they passed through one of King Yama's special portals. But when she pushed open the door, she wasn't prepared to arrive inside a rather peaceful and quiet temple.

Golden-eyed green dragons swirled around the columns, and round yellow lanterns swung from the tiered, tiled roofs. In the center of the temple was an enormous gold statue of King Yama. Yama's pupils alone were bigger than cabbages, and his beard glistened, clearly newly polished—but its size and opulence weren't what struck Mulan as strange.

"I've never seen King Yama smile," ShiShi muttered,

frowning at the grinning statue and echoing her thoughts. "I'm guessing this statue was sculpted before the gods tasked him with reigning over the Underworld."

"Where was he before?"

"Legends say he was a great scholar," ShiShi replied. "One who was just and fair, and had a brilliant mind for bookkeeping. So the Eight Immortals put him here, to keep records of the Underworld for all eternity."

Mulan felt a pang of sympathy for Yama. That was no easy task. "No wonder he's always scowling."

"Indeed."

Surrounding Yama's statue were countless sticks of incense, bowls of oranges, and cups of rice wine, all made in offering. And on the wall were hundreds of round bronze King Yama medallions.

"That's a sign," Mulan said, striding up to the wall. "These medallions are on every one of the doors we've crossed."

"Or they could simply be a tribute to King Yama," ShiShi replied, shaking his fur clean of ash. "I doubt we'd find the portal so easily."

Maybe he was right. Hanging from each of the medallions was a little metal placard, not too different from the ones that had been nailed on King Yama's doors. Except delicate red tassels dangled from these placards, which looked much like the wish cards she'd seen in temples back in her village.

Mulan reached for one of them. *Please let me reunite with my mother in Heaven.*

I beg you, King Yama, please do not send my brother to the Cauldron.

I pray you take care of my family, King Yama. Let my sons and daughters live to a ripe old age.

Mulan set down the placards, moved. They *were* wishes, wishes made by the ghosts living in Youdu.

She caught Shang looking at the wishes, too. He skimmed through them one by one, as if he were looking for one he'd recognize.

The lion frowned, coming across his reflection in one of the grayish puddles beside the large water gourds. ShiShi glared at Yama's statue. "I swear I can hear him laughing at me."

Mulan listened. She did hear a rumble, but it wasn't from the statue. "I think that's just the noise coming from outside."

She wandered to the front of the room, past the open door. The sky was the darkest blue, but it was bright, as bright as the sky she'd seen on the Bridge of Helplessness. Stars wove across its canvas so that Mulan could almost make out the celestial tigers, birds, tortoises, and dragons she'd read about as a child.

To her surprise, she saw Shang leaning against the wall. He was staring at the moon again. "Shang?"

"Hmm?"

"You keep looking at the moon."

"It looks different here," he replied. "Bigger, brighter. But more shadows." He raised his chin to the eastern part of the sky. "Is that the bridge you crossed into Diyu?"

"The Bridge of Helplessness," Mulan named it, recognizing the stone bridge winding through the clouds. Maybe the exit wasn't in the temple after all.

She hurried down the stairs into the city. "The bridge is on the hundredth level. If we can see it from here, there must be a way to it."

"Finally." ShiShi huffed after them. "I could use some fresh air. Where to?"

Mulan halted at the street, unsure of the answer herself.

"Follow the moon," Ren had said. But here in Youdu, the moon shone everywhere. And, as she soon noticed, *every* door in the city had King Yama's face on it.

Great, she thought. She hiked up her shoulders, refusing to give up hope.

"We ask," she said. "There has to be someone here who knows the way."

The problem was, there were too many people to ask. The city stretched as far as she could see. Youdu was certainly colorful, with its bright kites and blue-tiled roofs and sun-shaped lanterns. Peddlers lined the dirt-paved streets, and wagons full of cucumbers and fish and oranges trotted to and fro, jostling against pushcarts and rickshaws and ghosts carrying buckets of flour or water. Pig-faced demons butchered chickens and ducks, ghosts played mah-jongg on the roofs, and a trio of wiry-bearded ghosts rolled dumplings in the corner to sell.

"We don't have enough time to interrogate every ghost and demon," ShiShi said. "The sun will rise soon in the real world. The moon is already—"

"I know," Mulan said, glancing at the sky. Only a sliver of the moon remained. The rest was covered in shadow. "Give me a minute to think. If this is the last level before the gates, getting out of here must be all anyone thinks about. Someone has to know."

Mulan went up to the first ghost she saw, a man carrying a basket of carrots. "Excuse me, sir. Do you know how to get to—"

"Watch where you're standing," he spat. "You're in everyone's way."

Mulan frowned, but she bowed her head. "Sorry. I'm just trying to find the path to the hundredth level."

Another ghost overheard their conversation and smirked. "Aren't we all?" she said. "You'll get there when King Yama decides you're ready."

According to their wager, that would be never. "That's the only way?" Mulan pressed. "What about the bridge?"

The ghosts didn't bother looking up at the sky. "What about it?"

"There's no door?"

The ghost woman shrugged. "The Chamber of Mirrors is rumored to be on this level."

"The Chamber of Mirrors?" cut in another ghost. Mulan's conversation was drawing a small but eager crowd of eavesdroppers. "Even if it were on this level, why would you want to take its test?"

"Better to wait," agreed the ghost carrying the carrots. "I heard if you don't pass the test, King Yama traps you in the mirror forever."

"Where is it?" Mulan asked.

"If I were to guess, it'd be near the Courtyard of Worldly Justice." The ghost woman pointed north, toward the towering pagodas and pavilions peeking out from behind the squat city buildings. "But I'd think twice before looking for it, if I were you."

"No one leaves the Chamber of Mirrors," one of the ghosts said darkly. "You should wait. Your turn will be called."

"After all, there's no rush." Another ghost threw her a narrow look.

That was her cue to leave. "The Chamber of Mirrors," Mulan repeated. "Thank you!"

She dipped out of the crowd and regrouped with Shang and ShiShi, who'd been waiting for her by the fruit stalls. She was about to ask Shang if he could fly up to the roof and get a view of the Chamber of Mirrors, but noticed his attention was elsewhere.

A dull ache rose in her throat. They'd defeated Huoguai, and they had only one level to go before they reached the gates. Yet ever since they'd left the Cauldron, Shang hadn't been himself. Yes, he wasn't the type of man to wear his emotions on his sleeve, but usually when he was pensive it was because he was considering strategy—or analyzing weaknesses to help them win a battle. Now that most of the battles had been fought . . . why did he act like he'd over-looked something important?

Worried, Mulan went up to him. "Shang—"

"You're back," interrupted ShiShi, oblivious to what-ever was going on in the captain's mind. "What did you find out?"

Mulan dropped her hand to the side. "We need to find the Chamber of Mirrors."

"Any idea where?"

"One of the ghosts said we should start in the Courtyard of Worldly Justice."

ShiShi nodded and took the lead down the bustling

street. Mulan walked beside Shang. "What's the matter?" she asked quietly.

Shang pursed his lips. "Nothing."

"Are you worried we won't make it out in time?" she said, sidestepping a crowd of merchant ghosts. "We will."

"That's not it."

His eyes flickered, and Mulan glanced back to see what had caught Shang's attention. An elderly ghost with a trimmed beard and a red cape just like General Li's.

Now Mulan understood. "It's your father, isn't it? You think he might be here?"

"No," Shang said. "You told me that he was hiding from King Yama before he went to Heaven, and I believe you. I just . . ."

"What?"

"I just hoped I might see him. Before we left Diyu."

His confession struck a chord of emotion in her. So *that* was what had been on his mind. Sorrow pinched her heart. They'd been in such a hurry to leave Diyu it hadn't even occurred to her Shang might want to see his father. And now that they were almost out, it must have been difficult for him to leave his father behind without saying goodbye. "We could look for him."

"There isn't time. Youdu is too vast. Besides, my father may already be in Heaven."

She swallowed, not knowing how to comfort him. In

front of them, ShiShi started to slow down. She could tell from his raised ears that he was listening.

"Tell me about your father, Shang," she said. "We only spoke briefly."

Shang hesitated. "Growing up, I . . . I hardly ever saw him. And when I did, I was always so afraid that I would do something wrong or not live up to his expectations." He drew in a deep breath. "I wish I could have spent more time with him. He was always away on duty. I suppose I wanted to be a soldier so I could see him more. So I could make him proud of me. But now I'll never have that chance."

ShiShi stopped walking. "Your father *is* proud of you," the lion said somberly. "He was your age when I came to him as a guardian. He was stubborn, just like you. Fearless, just like you. How we fought! Your father rarely listened to me, but he was a man of integrity and grit and pride.

"His death has been difficult on me, too. There is so much of your father in you, Li Shang. Every time I look at you, I see him. And that will ease the pain of losing him, a little each day."

A glow flickered in Shang's eyes. Mulan could tell he was deeply moved, but fighting not to show it. She touched his arm. Even though he couldn't feel it, she wanted him to know that she was here for him, too.

"Thank you," Shang said quietly. "Thank you both."

According to the street signs, they'd stopped a few blocks

from the Courtyard of Worldly Justice. ShiShi started moving again, but Shang pointed at a ghost gambling on one of the sloping rooftops.

"Isn't that your ancestor, Mulan?"

Sure enough, it was. Although Ren now donned a straw hat, covering his bald scalp, she recognized his thin silhouette and religious robes.

"Ren?" Mulan called. "Cousin Ren?"

Her ancestor's eyes widened when he saw her. Mumbling something to his friends, he stuffed his gambling tiles into his pocket and opened a fan to hide his face.

"Ren, I know that's you." Mulan jumped onto one of the wooden beams supporting the house Ren and his friends were on and started to climb.

Seeing her approach, Ren panicked and started to flee to the nearest roof. But Mulan was too quick. She saw he'd left his cane behind, and she used it now to trip him.

"Aiyah!" he cried. Sheepishly, her ancestor floated down from the roof. "Why, cousin Ping, what a surprise to see you here."

Shang grabbed Ren by the collar and lifted him. "I thought you said the ninety-seventh level was the highest one you could go to."

Ren mustered a nervous chuckle. "To be fair, Captain, it was Liwei who said that."

That wasn't good enough for Shang. "You lied to us."

"Um, well . . . you see, Captain. It's quite a long story." Ren's hands went to his neck as Shang tightened his hold on his collar. "Ack! And rather difficult to tell since I'm . . . choking."

Mulan put her hands on her hips. "Let him go, Shang."

Shang dropped Ren. The ghost again tried to flee, but Shang stepped on his robe.

"Save your breath," said the captain. "Unless you really think you can outrun me."

"Point taken." Ren dusted off his robe and straightened his collar.

But now he had to face Mulan. Anger simmered inside her as she remembered how much danger Ren had put them in—by not warning them about the Cauldron, and even insisting that it was off their path! They might not have made it out in time, and worse yet, they could have been killed.

She crossed her arms. "What kind of monk are you, Ren, to lie to us?"

"H-honestly, cousin Ping," Ren stammered, "I didn't think you'd find me up here." He tried to collect himself. "You see, I have an unfortunate gambling habit, and I owe Jiao over there a good sum."

Mulan looked up and saw Jiao—the ghost with the glasses from the Bridge of Helplessness. His mouth slid into a crooked grin, and he waved.

"Many of the ghosts started to bet on how far you'd get through Diyu before being killed." Ren rolled up his sleeves. "And I made a wager with Jiao on whether or not you'd beat Huoguai." Seeing Shang's glare, he cleared his throat nervously. "I bet you would, of course. Ghosts have a habit of gambling, you see. Helps pass the time. But I can't leave this place if I have any outstanding debts. . . ."

No wonder Jiao and so many ghosts had tried to thwart them. It wasn't about being angry at all; it was about winning bets!

"Let me guess," Mulan said, passing him back his cane. "Jiao also bet that we wouldn't make it to the top. And he said that if you misled us, he'd forgive your debts."

"I didn't mislead you."

Mulan crossed her arms. "You purposefully sent us to the Cauldron when there could have been another way."

"It wasn't purposeful!" Ren insisted. Leaning on his cane, he took off his hat and pressed it against his chest. "I did warn you that you'd have to cross a few unsavory chambers."

"You didn't warn us about Huoguai," said Shang through his teeth.

Ren winced. "I hoped you might bypass him. . . ."

"Bypass a fire demon?" ShiShi growled. "You must be dreaming."

"It was the fastest way," Ren insisted, cowering under ShiShi's and Shang's glares. The monk pressed his hands together and composed himself. "Besides, I had faith you would defeat him."

ShiShi harrumphed. "Did you, now?"

Ren held his hat as a shield. "Cousin Ping," he appealed. "You are so clever, after all. Most everyone is quite happy that you've vanquished him. It'll make traveling around Diyu so much easier."

"So now she's a hero, thanks to you?" ShiShi cried. "You could have gotten us all killed."

"She?" Ren repeated.

Mulan sighed. Best to come clean to her ancestor. "I *am* Fa Mulan. I made up the name Ping so no one would become suspicious when I took Baba's place in the army."

Ren drew a sharp breath. "So you lied to your ancestors. Sounds familiar."

"She lied to do a good deed," said Shang sharply, "not so she could pay off her gambling debts. You two aren't the same. Not at all."

Mulan let her hands drop to her sides. "Ren, we need your help. We need to get to the hundredth level. Do you know the way?"

"I'm afraid I don't," Ren said, putting his hat back on. "Truly. You see, this is where ghosts wait until they ascend to Heaven or return to Earth. You only go up when King Yama says you can."

"We don't have time to wait," ShiShi barked.

Mulan was calmer. "One of the ghosts mentioned something about the Chamber of Mirrors."

Ren made a face. "You want to go there?"

"You know where it is?"

"Everyone does. It's in the West Pearl Quarter." Ren must have seen the hope spark in her eyes, for he quickly added, "But don't get too excited. Legend has it that anyone who goes inside never comes out again."

"It's worth a try. Can you take us there?"

"It's a little ways away. I can show you . . . if you would be so kind as to, um, stop stepping on my robe, Captain Li Shang."

Shang glared at him and lifted his foot.

Ren gulped, then started off with a nod. For a ghost with a cane, he moved quickly. He threaded the marketplace deeper into Youdu until they reached a cobblestone path surrounded by grand, gold-tiled pagodas. A line of ghosts curled outside the tallest building.

"What are they in line for?" Mulan said, half running and half walking to keep up.

"That's the Hall of Justice," replied Ren, gesturing at the tallest pagoda, which had a large gong swinging in the middle of its courtyard. "They're waiting for Yama to call them to Heaven."

At Mulan's side, Shang looked intently at the line, but there was no sign of General Li.

Ren made a sharp right into an alleyway, then across another square and up seven steps until they arrived at an antique store with a tattered red-brown awning.

" 'The Chamber of Mirrors,' " ShiShi read on the store's door. "This is a shop!"

"I warned you it was just a legend," Ren replied. "Now let's go before the shopkeeper sees us and—"

Ren never finished his sentence. The shopkeeper, an elderly man wearing a black scholar's hat, appeared at the door. "What are you hooligans doing, loitering in front of my store? Can't you see we're closed?"

"We are looking for a way out of Diyu," Mulan said. "I was hoping you could help."

The shopkeeper tilted his glasses up his nose and cocked his head at Mulan. "Help a mortal? Mortals are not permitted in Youdu. I'm afraid I'll have to sound the alarm."

"No, don't!" Ren cried, throwing himself into the door to keep the shopkeeper from reaching for the bell inside. "Zhen, this is a special case. She's my relation."

At the sight of Ren, the shopkeeper stepped fully outside. To Mulan's surprise, most of his body was covered with short brown fur—like a monkey. He even had a tail.

"Fa Ren," said Zhen the shopkeeper with a click of his tongue. "So, after seventy-nine years you finally decide to come back and pay your debts. You owe me eight gold coins."

"That's not why I'm here," Ren said. "But I'll have the money. Soon."

"Will you, now?" Zhen glared at the three of them, focusing especially on ShiShi. "There is no exit anywhere on this level. Now go away before I call the guards."

Zhen spun around to reenter his shop, but Mulan caught the door before he closed it.

"This is the Chamber of Mirrors, isn't it? All the ghosts in the marketplace said the way out of Diyu is through here."

"Why, of all the impertinent—" Zhen growled at her, but Mulan wouldn't let go of the door. "Everyone gets out of Diyu the same way. You die, you do your time, and then you wait by the Hall of Justice for King Yama to call your name."

"I see," Shang said, tilting his head to the side thoughtfully. "It is quite strange that a scholar should be in charge of an antique store."

"Yes," agreed ShiShi. "I would have thought a man of such impeccable learning would have been more favored by King Yama. You can't earn one of those official hats unless you are brilliant."

"Maybe he did something to anger King Yama?" Shang suggested. "Otherwise, he wouldn't be working in this empty antique store. Look, there aren't even any customers."

"It's not *just* an antique store." Zhen pursed his lips, and it became clear he'd said too much. "Go away. The store is closed."

"Look, Zhen," entreated Ren, "don't punish the girl because of me."

"You said she's your relation!" Zhen glared at Ren. "Given your reputation, that knowledge doesn't instill much confidence in me."

"Just hear her out."

"I don't need to," Zhen said sharply. "She's not going to pass the Chamber of Mirrors."

"How do you know if you don't give me a chance?" interrupted Mulan. "Please. If we can't leave Diyu, Captain Li Shang will die."

"And she will be trapped here forever," Shang added. "As a demon."

Mulan watched Zhen make a face. The possibility of anyone turning into a demon seemed to strike a chord in him. She straightened, leveling her gaze at him. "So, I ask you . . . is the Chamber of Mirrors the way out of Diyu?"

Zhen tapped his fingers on the end of his tail. "I've heard about your story, soldier. You and your friends battled many demons to get here—even defeated Huoguai. But in the Chamber of Mirrors, you only battle the demons within." He poked her in the arm. "Very few have come out alive, least of all victorious."

A chill rippled down Mulan's spine. A battle against herself? How could that even be possible?

"I want to go in," she said, determined.

Zhen peered at her. She stared back, unwilling to give up.

"Interesting." Finally, the shopkeeper let out a sound that was somewhere between a sigh and a laugh. "Fine, I'll let you inside. But be warned . . . the chamber was constructed with powerful magic. It will only let you out when it deems you are ready."

Mulan nodded, and Zhen widened the door behind him a notch so she could slip inside.

"Only she can pass," Zhen said, blocking Shang and ShiShi from entering.

"I'm going with her," insisted Shang.

Zhen shook his head. "Apologies, Captain, but these are the rules. There's an inn down the street that makes quite passable soup dumplings and serves spirits as well as guardians. You'll have a while to stay, I understand."

"It'll be fine," Mulan reassured him.

"I don't like this," said Shang. "What if it's a trick?"

"It isn't."

"No weapons," Zhen said brusquely, gesturing at the sword hanging at her side.

She swallowed and untied her sword, placing it in Zhen's waiting hands.

"You should say your goodbyes," he said, unsmiling.

Mulan frowned and faced ShiShi, Ren, and Shang. The captain's teeth were gritted, and his fists clenched.

"I'll see you soon," she said, her gaze lingering a touch longer on Shang. *I hope.*

Without another word, Mulan slid open the wooden door and went inside.

Her heart hammering, she entered the Chamber of Mirrors. Faint bursts of light flickered above her, dancing in a soft wave—like those lights she had seen on the Bridge of Helplessness!

As soon as she reached up to try to touch the lights, the door thudded behind her and locked with a click.

She whirled around.

Zhen was gone. So was the door she'd just entered. And the lights that had welcomed her into the chamber vanished, plunging her deep into darkness.

She was trapped.

Chapter Twenty-Seven

Trying to remain calm, Mulan took three careful steps deeper into the chamber. So far, there were no hissing rocks, sprawling trees, or golden pavilions in the distance. No, for once the chamber was an actual room, one long and hollow enough for the sound of her footsteps and breathing to echo when she moved. Except, from the looks of it, there was no way out.

Seconds passed, and her apprehension grew. Inside the chamber was dark as a winter's night, so she couldn't tell how large or deep it was. She blindly stretched out her hands, walking until she touched a wall. It was smooth and cold, like glass. She bent down. The floor was glass, too.

Mirrors, she realized as her sight slowly adjusted to the

dark. Mirrors surrounded her from the ceiling to the walls to the floor. Yet not one of them reflected her.

Come in, the mirrors whispered. *Come closer. Closer.*

"Who are you?" she said aloud. "Show yourself. I'm ready."

The voices laughed, then grew in strength and number. *Are you, now?*

No one is ready. Not even you, Fa Mulan.

Mulan spun. There was no one in the room with her. Only herself—and the mirrors.

She grimaced. Was this a game?

"Where are you?"

Inside, the voices beckoned. *Come closer. Look into our eyes. Then we can begin.*

She couldn't pinpoint any particular mirror the voices were coming from, but a soft brown light emanated from one to her left. It was shaped like a tomb and reminded Mulan of the graves in her family's ancestral temple. A thin stripe of bronze embellished the edges of the mirror, and as she approached, the glass clouded and swirled.

Mulan's father appeared. He leaned on his cane, and when he saw her, his brows knit together in surprise and confusion. "Ah, Mulan. You've returned from the war."

Mulan stiffened. Another illusion. Her pulse quickened, remembering how easy it'd been for her to fall for Meng Po's deception. How she'd yearned to make her family proud of her, even if it had been an illusion.

Not this time, she said, steeling herself to face the reflection of Fa Zhou. This time, she'd play along. But she wouldn't forget. "Yes, Father."

"And?" Fa Zhou leaned forward on his cane. The gray patches of hair along his temples were whiter than Mulan remembered. "What have you to say to us?"

"The Huns are defeated. The Emperor is safe." Mulan bowed. "I return, your obedient daughter."

"Obedient?" Fa Zhou's narrow face tightened into a frown. "Your mother thought you had perished in battle."

Mulan's shoulders dropped. She'd imagined this conversation with her family countless times. She'd pictured the day she returned home from war—would her father be proud of her? Or would he be disappointed that she'd deceived him? Some nights, she couldn't sleep for the worry that her father would look at her the way this false Fa Zhou looked at her now.

As if no one in the world could have disappointed him so much.

Don't let him get to you, she reminded herself. *Just play along.*

"I didn't," she said quietly.

"You show yourself here, unannounced, after leaving

without a word. After stealing my armor and taking my place in the army. Given what you have done, what makes you think your mother and I would accept you back into this family?"

"I was trying to save you."

"It would have been better if you had let me go."

"You would have died!"

Fa Zhou pounded his cane on the ground. "Better I die with honor than live with the disgrace my only child has brought upon this house."

His words stung, even though Mulan knew this was all magic, just an illusion of her father that the Chamber of Mirrors wanted her to see.

She stormed toward the walls, trying to find a way out. No matter where she turned, Fa Zhou followed her, appearing in the glass. She couldn't escape him.

"These are lies," she said. "My father would never say this."

Wouldn't he? the voices from the glass whispered. They were in her mind now. Oh, how her head throbbed. The question tugged at her heart.

"He wouldn't." She shook her head, recalling her last day at home. It'd been burned into her memory. After failing her examination with the Matchmaker, she'd gone to the garden to be alone. She'd been inconsolable until her father found her and sat next to her.

My, my, what beautiful blooms we have this year, he'd remarked. *But look, this one is late. I bet when it blooms, it will be the most beautiful of all.*

Her father always knew how to comfort her. Mulan still repeated those words to herself sometimes.

As if the Fa Zhou in the mirror could read her thoughts, he held out a blossom in his hand. The limp petals sagged onto his palm, dried and withered.

"I was wrong." He crushed the flower in his fist. "The blossom will never bloom. It is dead to me."

Mulan watched the petals flake onto the ground. Anger swelled in her chest, so tight it became hard to breathe. How dare this projection of Fa Zhou ruin what had been one of her most tender memories of her father?

"My father encouraged me to see the strength within," Mulan told the mirror crisply. "When I was a little girl, he told me that life is a journey, one whose path diverges due to the choices I made. He told me not to worry about how difficult a path might look, for the only one worth following was the one that my heart chose." She waited, but the Fa Zhou in the mirror said nothing. "My father would understand what I did. He believes in me."

"I did believe in you," Fa Zhou replied coldly. "But that was because I trusted you. Do you know how worried your mother was when we found you had left home? Do you know how much danger you put your family in when you impersonated my son—my son who does not exist? It does not matter if your intentions were honorable. The risks you took were too great, and they cannot be forgiven."

Was that really what Baba would think? Mulan swallowed. Doubt swarmed inside her, and no matter how she tried to quell it, she could not.

Her mother appeared beside him, carrying a tray of tea. Distress lined her face, and she wouldn't look Mulan in the eye.

"Baba is right," Fa Li added, passing Fa Zhou a cup of the tea. "Everyone saw the Emperor's counsel give him the conscription notice. The neighbors have been wondering why your father is not serving."

Mulan glanced at her father. He sat quietly, holding his teacup but not drinking. He wouldn't look at her.

"A secret like that cannot be kept forever," her mother finished.

"I did not mean to—"

"War broke your father's body," Fa Li interrupted again. "But you have broken his heart, Mulan."

Her mother's words were like a punch to Mulan's stomach. Mulan felt her knees lock and her breath catch. It was true her father's health was weak. She'd always prided herself in helping her mother take care of him—making sure he had company on his morning walks about the garden, that he wore an extra robe over his clothes when it was cold, and that he ate enough cabbage and carrots and celery at dinner.

But she'd never stopped to worry about how her decision to leave home might affect his heart.

Fa Zhou choked on his tea then. Fa Li dropped the rest of the tray and rushed to help him.

"See how weak he is?" her mother rebuked Mulan. "It is because of you. You should not have come back."

"No!" Mulan bolted up to the mirrors, but her parents disappeared from the glass.

She clenched her fists. "This is all a lie. My parents won't renounce me when I go back. They won't."

Why should this fate be so unbelievable? the mysterious voices taunted. *You disappointed them, Mulan. First when you could not make a match. Then when you ran from your failure.*

"I was trying to help them."

You went for yourself, the mirrors hissed. *You told Captain Li Shang that, and it was the truth. You left home out of selfishness.*

You will never find acceptance. Not at home, not in the army, not anywhere. That is your fate, Fa Mulan.

Before she could reply, the empty mirrors fogged and misted. This time, the entire chamber came alive, every mirror capturing Fa Zhou and Fa Li's neighbors until their entire village occupied the room. The villagers whispered to one another, just loud enough for Mulan to hear.

"That's her. She's back."

The whispers grew louder.

"Do you see what she's wearing?" The women scoffed. "Trousers!"

"And her hair, so short. Do you see the way she walks? With her chin up like she owns the world. Such impudence."

"My daughter would get an earful if she went out looking and strutting about like that."

Mulan didn't flinch, not even as the insults brought back the pangs of loneliness she'd felt in the Hall of Echoing Forests. No matter how real everything looked, she'd been in Diyu long enough not to fall for the enchantment. But what was the test here? How was she supposed to get out of here . . . by letting them insult her? Or by fighting back?

"I used to think she was just clumsy," her family's baker said.

"She's a discredit to her father's name."

"Who does she think she is? Her father was a legendary warrior."

"It's a shame they never had a boy."

"Do you remember how Fa Zhou used to let the girl go wild? Even gave her a horse. Look what's come of that."

"I still can't believe she ran away to join the army."

"Maybe they put her up to it. The old man can barely walk anymore. Wouldn't surprise me if he was behind the whole idea."

"My father had nothing to do with my going to war," Mulan shouted back. "It was my choice."

"A woman doesn't get a choice. If the Emperor had wanted women in his army, he would have said so. You're a traitor."

This isn't real, she reminded herself. *This isn't real.*

The villagers weren't listening. "Did you think the Emperor would honor you, even if you saved China? When he finds out what you've done, he'll have you killed."

"You're a traitor."

"I'm not a traitor," Mulan cried. "I did it for my father."

"Traitor! Traitor!"

The villagers yelled, their accusations growing so loud Mulan couldn't distinguish one from another. She let them scream at her. She could bear it.

Then, a little girl threw a bouquet of withered flowers at Mulan.

The action, so quick and unexpected, stunned her. She stared at the little girl, whose black hair was braided to the side and adorned with a simple blossom.

She looks so much like me, Mulan thought, *when I was her age.*

"How could you, Fa Mulan?" said the little girl, sounding more sad than angry. "How could you lie to your parents and dishonor them that way?"

"I didn't mean to," Mulan whispered. "I didn't."

Seeing they'd hurt her, more children appeared, flinging withered flowers at Mulan.

They'll never understand, she thought. *Every time I try to explain myself, they twist my words.*

Breaking through the crowd, Mulan ran. The villagers parted for her, sneering and hissing as she fled. There wasn't far to go before she hit the wall. But when she looked up, she found herself back at the training camp with the other soldiers.

She turned back. Gone was the village, and even her home. There were only mountains in the distance, and a line of familiar-looking pitched tents. And an armory of swords, bows, and arrows.

Shang appeared. His lip curled with disdain when he saw her. "What are you doing here? I told you to go home."

Mulan stood her ground. She raised her chin at the captain. Another one of the chamber's illusions. "Why do you think I'm here? I *am* trying to go home."

Shang stared her down. If not for the hard glass under Mulan's feet, she might have forgotten he wasn't real, that he was simply a projection of the Shang waiting for her outside—for her to free them. With every passing second, everything in the Chamber of Mirrors felt more and more real, from the sweat on Shang's forehead to the wrinkles on his shirt. Even the flags behind him fluttered with the wind, and Mulan thought she could smell pine from the trees in the nearby forest.

Shang grimaced. "To think I considered you my friend. I've never been more wrong about anyone in my life."

"I am your friend."

"Friend?" Shang laughed. "You nearly got me killed with your foolish maneuver on the Tung-Shao Pass. Shan-Yu was right in front of you, and you missed him! Do you know why you couldn't defeat him?"

"Because you're a girl!" said her friend Yao, coming up from behind her.

With him were the rest of the soldiers, Mulan's friends.

Ling wrinkled his nose at her. "I can't believe we trained together."

"Girls can't be soldiers," Shang yelled. The men shouted in agreement. "They're weak, and they cry at the first sign of danger."

Shang raised his hand, and a gust of wind pushed her to the other side of the field. "Get out of here. You aren't fit to serve the Emperor."

Mulan tumbled, falling on her backside. The soldiers

laughed, Ling and Yao particularly loudly. Even Chien-Po couldn't bear to look at her.

"I'm not going anywhere," she said, getting up. "I belong here."

"You belong nowhere," Shang said sharply. "To betray the Emperor is to betray China. Your life is meaningless."

Mulan swallowed. Even if he wasn't the real Shang, what he said was true. The Emperor *would* have her killed if he knew. "You've said all this before. But you didn't mean it."

"Didn't I?" Shang scowled. "The penalty for what you've done is death."

Yao grabbed a bow and raised it at Mulan. "Say the word, boss."

Shang paused, and Mulan thought maybe, *maybe* she'd gotten through to him. Maybe making everyone see that she wasn't worthless was the key to getting out of this chamber.

Yao, Chien-Po, and Ling pointed their arrows at her.

She couldn't even hear the thudding of her heart. The soldiers' disapproving chorus drowned out her shouts. "No!" Mulan cried again. "Shang, you can't! This isn't real."

"I know it isn't," said Shang. To her horror, the captain's body paled, becoming blue and luminous. He strode out of the mirror to show her he wasn't a reflection like everyone else. "But I am."

"No," she whispered.

"Only one of us leaves Diyu alive," he said, his jaw tightening with resolve. "I'm afraid it's not going to be you."

Then Shang's eyes, glassy as the mirrors surrounding them, hardened. "FIRE!"

Chapter Twenty-Eight

All at once, the mirrors exploded. Thousands of tiny glass shards ripped across the room, flying off in all directions. Mulan crossed her fists in front of her face, blocking her head from the oncoming storm of mirror pieces. Sharp fragments nicked her cheeks and sliced through her sleeves and pants. She tried to fight off the flying shards with her gauntlets, but there were too many of them. The glass beneath her cracked, and the ceiling collapsed. She ducked and covered her head with her hands.

"Stop!" she shouted. "Shang, please!"

The captain lowered his hand. The storm ceased, and the soldiers drew back their weapons. "Had enough?"

Mulan shakily rose to her feet and saw her reflection in

the pieces of glass at her feet. She touched her cheek. Blood smeared her fingers. She recoiled.

Had Shang really just given an order to kill her? The Shang she knew would never hurt her.

"Shang," she said, her voice quavering, "I don't know what you've been told, but my deal with King Yama is for *all* of us. You, me, and ShiShi. We have to work together and find a way out of here."

"Zhen told me how to get out of here," said Shang, crossing his arms. "You fight your inner demons, Mulan. And mine is that the friend I trusted most lied to me. The only way I can vanquish that is if you take my place in Diyu."

There was a trace of regret in his face. It softened his features for one fleeting moment, long enough to make Mulan's heart lurch. Maybe it *was* him.

Then his expression hardened. "China needs me, Mulan. More than it needs you. So this is how it must be." He turned to the soldiers behind him, motioning for them to prepare for another attack.

Mulan kicked her leg back into a lunge and raised her fists. She wasn't going down without a fight. She'd find a way out of here—for both of them.

Her father appeared at Shang's side. "You should never have come back."

Her mother and grandmother echoed Fa Zhou. Then

the villagers and the rest of the soldiers. Mulan even saw the Matchmaker among them.

"You are a disgrace!" the Matchmaker yelled. She turned to the other villagers, her bright red lips curling into a smirk. "I knew she was trouble."

"How dare you show your face back here!"

"You will never bring your family honor."

As the shouts intensified, Mulan's cheeks grew hot with shame and anger. Her heart pounded, her skin tingled with sweat. This was one of her greatest fears: to go home and be reviled by her parents, their village, and her friends—for bringing shame upon her family name.

I fought for you all, she wanted to yell. *What does it matter if I'm a girl? I held my own. I saved our army from the Huns.*

But she pursed her lips tight and reined in her anger.

This is a hallucination, Mulan told herself. *Don't listen to them. Don't lose control.*

She couldn't even understand what they were shouting anymore. The commotion grew so loud that all she could make out was her name.

Find a way out, she reminded herself. It was hard to see where the walls were. The frames around the mirrors had disappeared, and if she hadn't known better, Mulan might have believed she were actually outside and not trapped in a chamber of mirrors.

She ventured closer to the walls, but Shang obstructed her way. She tried to move past him, but he was too fast.

"A life for a life," Shang said. "King Yama can't afford to let both of us leave Diyu. Only one of us gets to go, and it isn't going to be you."

"Watch me." She bolted left, running for the mountains behind the tents. She thought she saw a way out—a brightly lit path that led toward the distant moon. If she could reach it—

Another wave of shards shot out of the mirrors. As soon as Mulan heard the glass whizzing across the chamber, she slammed her body to the ground. The glass fragments looked sharper this time. They were thinner, too, with sharp points that glimmered as they flew.

They hurt like needles. Just pricks at first, but as more and more shards bit into her flesh, the pain seared into her arms and legs. Some pierced her skin, and others cut her only as they flew past. As glass shattered all around her, echoing and echoing in her ears, Mulan realized she had no idea how to get out of here.

In the Chamber of Mirrors, you only battle the demons within, Zhen had warned her.

Even if everything in this chamber was an illusion, the gashes on her cheeks and arms were real. The staggering pain from her battered body—that was real too. If she didn't fight back, she *would* die here.

So she got up, shielding her face with her arm. The shards flew at her so fast there was no time to blink. Only fight. She raised her arms and jabbed at the glass pieces. She didn't hold in her fear. Every time a fragment pierced her, Mulan let out a cry. Then she channeled that pain into anger and determination to live. She kicked and whirled, swooping her legs up to evade the flying glass pieces.

Without a shield, she couldn't possibly protect herself from every angle. She wouldn't last long against the mirrors, not unless she broke them. Her tactic had been to defend herself, but that wouldn't work forever. Even when she aimed her kicks and punches back at the mirrors, more shards fired her way. She picked up a larger piece of glass and held it against herself. The shield was brittle; it wouldn't last long.

Shang watched from a corner of the chamber, arms crossed and shoulders square. "Give up, Mulan. You'll never get out of here."

Teeth gritted, Mulan smashed an oncoming shard with her raised gauntlet. The impact hurt her wrists. Everywhere hurt, really. Her shoulders ached, and glass pierced her knees and legs. Only adrenaline kept her going. "I could do this all day."

"You don't have all day," Shang replied. "And neither do I."

He turned, heading for that lit path toward the moon—toward freedom. He was leaving without her!

Mulan's chest tightened. She couldn't forget the anguish on Shang's face when Huoguai had taken her, when he thought she'd perish by falling into the waterfall. Shang, the *real* Shang, cared for her. He wouldn't betray her like this.

"Wait!" Not caring about the shards anymore, Mulan ran after Shang, ignoring the blasts of pain as the glass smashed against her armor. Weakly, she reached for his arm. "Wait."

All at once, the camp and the mountains and the trees vanished, blanketing the chamber with a blank darkness. The reflections of her parents, her friends, and the villagers disappeared.

Only Shang remained. He stood in the middle of the moonlit path. His eyes were hard. "You don't give up, do you?"

"I'm not leaving without you," said Mulan. She reached for his hand, but a gust of wind shuttled her away from the captain. No matter how she tried to make up the distance, another gust tore them apart.

She blocked her face with her arm until the wind passed. When she looked up again, King Yama's soldier demons surrounded them. She recognized Languai, the blue one who'd led her across the Bridge of Helplessness. He stood in the front next to Shang, whom his soldiers had tied to a tree.

Before she could begin to fathom what was happening, Languai thrust a wooden bow into her hand. "Kill Captain Li," he ordered. "Then you may leave Diyu."

The bow was nocked with a jagged shard of glass. Its sharp point glinted in the chamber's dim light.

"No," Mulan whispered. But the demons began to growl at her.

"Kill him, kill him," they chanted.

"The only way you'll leave this place is if I die," said Shang. "I wouldn't hesitate if I were in your place."

She lowered the bow and arrow to her side. Was it really him? Deep in her heart, she knew it wasn't. The real Shang was waiting for her to pass whatever tests awaited her in the Chamber of Mirrors. But maybe that *was* the test—or rather, the *price* she had to pay to cross this chamber.

"If it is true that only one of us may leave, then I will stay."

Shang pressed his lips into a thin, cold line. "Even if it means you're trapped here forever?"

"King Yama won't be merciful," added Languai.

A chill nestled in the nape of her neck, but Mulan didn't shiver. It didn't matter whether this was only a test, or whether this was real. Her determination to save her friend wouldn't waver. If this was the end of her journey, so be it.

"I made a promise to myself that I'd bring you home," said Mulan, stepping closer to Shang. She straightened. "If I have to break it, then—"

She raised the bow, drawing the string taut. As she pointed the glass arrow at Shang, she saw the captain hold his breath. She waited a beat before releasing the arrow. She couldn't afford to miss.

"Then I'll save you." Her voice cracked as she spoke. "No matter the cost."

With a snap, the arrow tore across the chamber. During its flight, its glass edges caught all the light of the moon shining above, reflecting a thousand colors. It was a beautiful sight, one that kept Mulan from daring to breathe before the arrow found its target—

And ripped through the rope around Shang's shoulders, setting him free.

Nearly collapsing with relief, Mulan barely noticed as the bow dissolved in her hand. Everything else disappeared around her: the demons, the tree, the rope—even the glass arrow shattered at Shang's feet.

Shang's blue aura shimmered, darkening so Mulan couldn't really tell whether it was the captain who spoke, or someone else: "You have passed this first test," rang the low, hollow voice. "You swore you would risk your own life to save your friend, and even in the face of betrayal, you kept your promise." The captain's shadow began to fade. "Now, do you know yourself? We shall see."

When he was gone, Mulan let out a deep breath.

A test. Her lungs nearly gave out with relief. *That wasn't really Shang. It was just a test.*

Glass crunched under her boot. Her knees quivered, so she carefully lowered herself onto the ground to gather herself. Thousands of her reflections stared back at her from the smashed glass pieces.

She was bloodied and bruised. There had to be dozens of tiny shards lodged in her body, and one particularly large piece in her thigh. Mulan winced when she saw it, but she knew what she had to do.

She wrapped her hands over the shard.

One, two three.

With one swift thrust, she pulled the mirror fragment out of her leg.

Pain shot up to her temples. Gasping, she hugged herself, clenching her teeth until the sharp gnawing in the leg dulled. Then she pressed on the wound to stop the bleeding.

As the pain slowly passed, Mulan pushed her hair out of her eyes, then glanced behind her shoulder. Shang had said she could advance, but the chamber was empty. Was the test over?

No.

The voice sounded like her own, but it didn't come from her thoughts.

"Who's there?" Mulan limped to her feet. Glass scattered down from her clothes and hair with a soft rattle.

The debris on the ground thinned and wobbled, turning into watery, silver-colored pools that gushed across the room, healing the mirrors she had broken.

In every mirror was a reflection of Mulan.

Look hard at yourself, her reflections said.

Mulan looked. She took in her chapped lips, her unevenly cut black hair, the gashes and bruises on her arms, and her fraying sleeves and dirtied uniform.

Which is the real Mulan? The girl in a uniform pretending to be a soldier, or the girl in a dress pretending to be a bride?

"Neither," Mulan whispered.

Correct. Both are lies.

Mulan flinched. "I'm not a liar."

You are nothing. No matter how hard you try, no one will ever see you for who you are.

Mulan turned, but another reflection intercepted her.

Your father is right, the mirrors taunted. *Shang is right. They're all right. You'll never be anyone worthwhile. How can you be? You broke Baba's heart when you left, you selfish girl.*

"I didn't mean to. I didn't think—"

Yes, you didn't think. Just as you didn't think when you ran off to set off the cannon. You *got Shang killed. You are the reason he's in the Underworld.*

"I'm going to save him."

No you aren't. Her reflections laughed. *Why do you think King Yama really let you down here?*

Mulan swallowed, holding in the pain from her cuts. "Why?"

Your deceitful heart, Fa Mulan. King Yama recognized it the moment he saw you. You belong in Diyu.

Mulan's reflections smiled, their faces slowly contorting and twisting. Their black hair whitened, skin shriveling and graying like a corpse's. Finally, their eyes blinked open, glowing a bright and terrible red.

This is your fate, Mulan. Your next life will be eternity as a demon. What a warrior you'll make for King Yama.

Horror washed over her. Mulan gritted her teeth. "If I lose my wager against him, then I have no control over what my fate is. But I have not lost yet. I can still get out of here and bring Captain Li Shang back to the living world."

You can't if you're trapped here.

You can't if you die here.

"Then show me the way out!"

One of her demonic reflections loomed over the ceiling.

We'll give you a hint, Fa Mulan, she said. *Choose one of us. One of us is your true self. Find her.*

The mirrors fluttered, shifting until each became a different portrayal of Mulan.

Each mirror is a door. Only one will take you to the gates. The others will take you to the pit of Diyu. But be swift. You don't have much time left.

The moon appeared above her. The thin crescent was little more than a sliver now.

Mulan turned to her task and frowned. The reflections all looked different. In some, she wore her father's armor, and in others, she was dressed as a girl, carrying a silk fan, her hair tied in an elaborate chignon as it had been to see the Matchmaker. It was the reflections' faces that riveted Mulan's attention.

"Which one?" she murmured, stepping up to the closest mirror. The girl inside had bloodshot, swollen eyes and sniffled every other beat, but she copied Mulan's gestures and movements like a true reflection.

I am Fa Mulan, the girl said suddenly. She sounded exactly like Mulan, except the sadness and bitterness in her words came from someone who'd lost all hope. *I disguised myself as a boy to fight in the war. In my pursuit of honor and glory, I broke my family's heart.*

Mulan swallowed. Was this her? How could she tell?

"It's true," she said slowly, "I disobeyed my father by going off into the army. But I didn't do it for my own honor or glory. I did it to save him."

Was it her imagination, or did the darkness tick deeper into the moon? It was nearly gone.

Mulan moved on to the next mirror, shaken by her first encounter with her reflection. How would she pick from all these mirrors before time ran out?

No, I am Fa Mulan, said the next reflection. *I ran away from home because I was a failure. I was afraid of facing my parents' disappointment. I was a coward.*

Was *this* her? In a way, yes. As much as the first reflection had been her.

"I *was* afraid," Mulan admitted. "But I left home so Baba wouldn't have to. I left home to save him—and myself."

The next mirror held a reflection of Mulan in full armor, with blood on her hands. *I am Fa Mulan. Because of me, Captain Li Shang is dying. Because I disobeyed him during battle, he must pay with his life.*

Mulan balked at how the reflection's words struck her heart, and she fought to give a calm reply. "Yes, Shang followed me because I disobeyed his orders . . . because I stole the cannon. I saw a chance to save China, and so I took it."

He only saved you because you succeeded, said the reflection. *Otherwise, he would have let you die.*

"He saved me because he is brave. Because he is my friend."

This wouldn't do. She didn't have time to listen to every reflection. Mulan circled the room, listening to the girls in the mirrors confess their regrets and guilt.

I don't deserve to go home.

I'm a coward.

I can't bear to go home. Baba and Mama will be so angry with me.

Mulan had heard all this before from the villagers and the soldiers. It wouldn't help her here. She needed to wash out the voices, to pay attention to her own.

Choose me, another reflection implored her. *I've always been pretending to be someone I'm not. First the perfect bride so someone might marry me, then the perfect soldier so I might bring honor home. I need to accept there is no perfect path for me.*

Her reflection's plea tugged at Mulan's heart.

No, that wasn't her. She did have those doubts, but they didn't make up who she was.

"Hurry, Mulan," she muttered to herself. She paced the room, trying to ignore the shaking in her knees, the lightness in her head. "Think. Think!"

What is there to see in my reflection? she wondered. *A girl pretending to be someone else? A girl walking off the path that was set for her?*

Who am I?

It was a question she'd asked herself a thousand times. She'd never been forced to find an answer, not even when she'd left home to join the army as Ping.

Yet now everything depended on her answer.

She took a deep breath. Did she know any of these girls who were in the mirrors? One had accused her of breaking her family's heart; another had accused her of being a coward. Did she see herself in any of them?

"Yes," Mulan whispered. "I've tried so hard to hide, to run away from who I don't want to be. I never stopped to look at my reflection and tell it who I *want* to be."

She spread her arms across the room. Her voice echoed from wall to wall. "Maybe I didn't go for my father. Maybe what I really wanted to prove was that I could do things right, so that when I looked in the mirror, I'd see someone worthwhile.

"I want to honor my family by being a good daughter," she continued, "but I also want the freedom to be myself, to say and do what I think is right, even if that means deviating from the path that is expected of me. For so long, I've been scared—scared of what my parents will think when I go home, scared of what my friends in the army would think if they found out I'm a girl. I'm not scared anymore. It doesn't matter if I'm pretending to be Ping or if I'm Mulan.

As long as I am true to myself, then my reflection will show who I really am."

Then who are you? the mirrors hissed. *Make your choice.*

Mulan spun, taking in all the mirrors.

Make your choice, they whispered.

She stopped in the middle of the chamber and paused at the mirror on the ground. Her reflection pooled at her feet, like the pond back in family's garden. And inside, a girl peered back at her.

Her reflection's hair was short, but she wore a simple violet robe tied at the waist with a blue sash. At her hip was her father's sword, and tucked in her hair—a blossom from their family's cherry tree.

Mulan knelt and lowered her fingers to the glass. It rippled at her touch. "This one. This is me."

A beat. *Are you sure?* asked the girl in the mirror.

"Yes," said Mulan firmly. "It doesn't matter whether I'm a girl dressed like a bride, or a girl dressed like a soldier. I know my heart."

Mulan flattened her hand against the glass, facing her reflection. Together, they said, "I am Fa Mulan, a girl who would sacrifice her life for her family and for China. I am a girl who journeyed into the Underworld to save her friend from dying. I am a girl who has fought battle after battle to finally recognize herself in the mirror. And now I do."

The mirror beneath cracked, splitting between her feet. Its sides sprang up, engulfing Mulan within a long, winding staircase.

She tumbled down three, four steps. Above her, the mirrors folded back into place, leaving her in the blank darkness.

With a deep breath, Mulan arose and began to tread down the murky path of stairs, knowing with each step that she drew closer either to the pit of the Underworld, or to her freedom.

Chapter Twenty-Nine

Mulan had been certain she had selected the right mirror, but doubt tugged at her confidence when she stepped out of the glass and found herself in the middle of a lush bamboo forest.

Faint, gauzy sunlight blurred her vision, and the sweet smell of morning dew tickled her nostrils.

Her heart sank.

Sunrise. Had she run out of time?

She blinked until her vision cleared. If she *had* picked the wrong mirror, then this forest was the last thing she'd expected to encounter in the pit of Diyu. Verdant bamboo plants surrounded her, a forest like the one she and ShiShi had arrived in after they'd left King Yama's throne room.

Mulan spun. Yes, this was that first chamber they'd entered in Diyu. Except that forest had been withered and dead. Here, everything bloomed with life. Birds sang above her, chirping and whistling as they flitted across the leaves adorning the tops of the bamboo plants. Insects buzzed. A gold-striped butterfly landed on Mulan's shoulder.

The butterfly fluttered away, up and up. Her eyes followed it, lifting toward the sky. The sun glimmered, and the moon was nowhere to be seen. Mulan searched desperately for it, but the bamboo stems blocked her view, stretching so high they wove a jade-colored net over the sky.

"The moon sleeps," came a gentle voice. "Your quest is over."

Mulan turned, facing a young woman she had never seen before. She was regal and tall, dressed in a soft pink silk gown that rippled like the gentle currents of a river. Her black hair was intricately coiled into braids and rolls pinned with pearls and sparkling rubies and sapphires. Only her eyes, full of mischief, looked familiar.

Mulan's brows knit. She recognized those eyes. "Meng Po?"

A grin crossed over the young woman's lips. She nodded. "Well done. This is my true form."

"Does that mean . . ." Mulan faltered. Her throat grew tight. "That I've—"

"You've won," said Meng Po, bowing her head. "You've passed the Chamber of Mirrors." She held out her empty arms. "I have no more tea to offer you, and no more tricks. You have defeated me, Fa Mulan."

Mulan eyed the Lady of Forgetfulness suspiciously. "I defeated you? Then why are you here? My wager was with King Yama."

"So it was, but King Yama is too busy to oversee Diyu's internal affairs. That is my duty, you see. I ensure that there is order in the Underworld. So when I learned that you had arrived to save Captain Li Shang from death, I took it upon myself to investigate you and deter you. I must apologize for my methods, but we cannot have just anyone coming in and out of Diyu to rescue the dead. That would disrupt the very balance of Heaven, Earth, and Diyu."

Mulan felt a rush of understanding. "You must have been angry with me."

"You challenged me," Meng Po allowed. "Which happens very . . . very rarely. I was angrier with King Yama for allowing a mortal into the Underworld." Her mischievous eyes sparkled. "But I agree that the captain still has much to do on Earth in this life, so a part of me is relieved that you have succeeded."

"Where is he?"

Meng Po stepped aside, revealing a path behind her.

Mulan was sure it hadn't been there moments ago, but now, nestled among the bamboo was a thin bridge overlooking a clear, tinkling stream. Two phoenixes guarded the left and right side of the bridge's entrance, their fiery wings magnificent against the sunlight.

"Is that the Bridge of Helplessness?" Mulan asked.

Meng Po chuckled. "No. You'll not see the Bridge of Helplessness on your journey out of Diyu. This is a different bridge, the Bridge of Serenity. Your friends are waiting on the other side."

Mulan nodded and turned for the bridge.

"A word before you go," Meng Po requested. "I may not have a chance to speak with you again, not for many years."

Mulan paused. "Yes?"

"You made a worthy opponent, Fa Mulan. I have worn a thousand faces, but even I did not see through your disguise right away." Meng Po folded her arms, her long sleeves drifting in the wind. "You surprised me, and given I've made my home among the ghosts and creatures of the Underworld, that is a difficult achievement indeed."

Mulan's lips parted, but she didn't know what to say.

Meng Po raised her arms.

At once, the gashes on Mulan's skin healed. Her wounds closed, and the dull pain in her ankle vanished. The rips and tears on her sleeves mended themselves, and her soldier's uniform, which had seen battle on Earth as well as in the Underworld, began to shimmer—until the simple muslin and linen cloth became a rich, forest-green silk. Her tunic lengthened, stretching until it flared behind her calves. Fitted over her chest was the finest armor, emblazoned with pink lotus blossoms and a red dragon.

"There," said Meng Po, rubbing her hands together. "That's a more appropriate uniform for such a warrior such as yourself."

Mulan stared at herself in awe. "Thank you, Meng Po, but I can't wear this. I'm returning to the army. And . . ." She stopped. "And . . . they don't know I'm a woman."

"I know, I know." Meng Po chuckled. "I was about to tell you not to grow too attached. My magic is based in illusion, after all . . . but you shouldn't reunite with your friends and see King Yama in those rags. Now—" Meng Po gestured at Mulan's sword, which had reappeared at her hip in an exquisitely carved wooden scabbard. "Tell me where you found this sword."

Mulan passed it to her. "On the Mountain of Knives."

"I have not seen it in many years." Meng Po marveled at the blade, running her fingers across the words emblazoned on the steel.

"It doesn't seem like something that belongs in Diyu. ShiShi said it had magic."

"Indeed it does," Meng Po said slyly. "Is that all you know about it?"

Mulan touched her chin, remembering. "My father once told me about demigod who lived long, long ago. He was a hero who wielded a magical sword. One like this."

"Your father was right," Meng Po agreed. "Except that hero was not a man, but a woman. Me."

Mulan inhaled. "So the sword is yours."

"Indeed." Meng Po smiled. "My father was a god, and my mother was human. If I had been a boy, I would have been invited to live in Heaven. But the gods saw no use for another half-breed girl. So I sought to prove myself to my father, and I did so by serving in the Emperor's army. I was a woman, but I was also half-immortal. The Emperor could not refuse my service, but that did not mean the men respected me. Not at first, anyway. I earned it over many trials and many years."

" 'The flower that blooms in adversity is the most rare and beautiful of all,' " Mulan murmured.

Meng Po nodded. "My days as a warrior are long past. Eventually, my father did invite me to join him in Heaven. But there are plenty of immortals in Heaven, so many that they are often forgotten on Earth. I wanted to be remembered, and I wanted to be useful. So I chose to live here in Diyu among the ghosts and demons and creatures I banished from Earth, and to help King Yama maintain order in the Underworld."

So the "hero of legend" the demons on the Cauldron had been talking about was Meng Po! Mulan would never have guessed. She could scarcely believe this woman was the same person who'd tried to trick her multiple times in Diyu. She also couldn't believe she was warming up to her.

"But I thought only a demigod could unlock the sword's power," Mulan said.

"That is not true," replied Meng Po. "Only someone with a hero's heart could do that. A heart like yours, Mulan." She paused before continuing, "Your heart has been tested, and you have come far. But not every fight is fought on the battlefield. There will be more to come, for you and those who follow you. Do not let yourself be forgotten, Fa Mulan. And do not forget—you are not alone."

"Thank you, Meng Po."

The Lady of Forgetfulness passed the sword to Mulan, but Mulan shook her head. "It's yours, not mine. I have my father's sword waiting for me back in the real world."

Meng Po smiled again. "Then take this, as a memory of the battles you have fought here."

The sword disappeared, and in its place was a magnolia blossom. Its petals were soft and pink like the blush of a peach.

Meng Po tucked the blossom behind Mulan's ear. "There. A reminder that where there is beauty, there is also strength and courage and resilience."

"Thank you," Mulan whispered.

Meng Po gently tilted Mulan's chin up. Wistfulness touched her face. "King Yama will have a difficult time judging you. I'll wager he's relieved he won't have to do it today."

"What do you mean?" asked Mulan, confused.

"We here have a saying: only the brave may enter, but only the worthy may leave. You have achieved something few others have, Mulan, and shown us that your heart is true. You and your friends will have many more trials to face on Earth, and I can only wonder what King Yama will do with you when one day, you return to Diyu for judgment. Whether he will send you to me to be reincarnated—for it is clear you are a hero who could do much on Earth in yet another life—or whether he will reward you with passage to Heaven."

She lingered a beat in thought. "I suppose we'll just have to wait. Until then, I wish you and Captain Li good fortune back in the land of the living."

Her skirts billowed as she stepped away from the bridge. "Now go. Your friends will be waiting for you with King Yama."

With that, Meng Po drew up her skirt and changed into a crane. Fluttering her wings, she soared high into the sky.

Mulan watched her until she vanished behind the sun with a flash of light.

Mulan tilted her head down and faced the bridge. The phoenixes guarding the entrance flared open their wings.

For the first time since she could remember, a strange feeling of peace came over her.

She was going home.

Chapter Thirty

Shang was the first one to see Mulan emerge from the bridge. Waiting beside King Yama and ShiShi, he stood against the hollow curve of one of Diyu's stone caverns, shifting from foot to foot as if he'd been waiting hours.

But once he saw her, the worried creases on his forehead smoothed and his brow lifted, and he made his way toward her.

Maybe it was from the long walk across the bridge, and all the battles she'd fought in Diyu, but the sight of him quickened her pulse. She drew in a shallow breath.

There was something different about Shang. He looked whole, yet his body still shimmered with an otherworldly aura. A different sort of aura, though. One that no longer burned like the pale blue of a fire's heart, but instead glimmered like watery rays of sunlight.

A flush deepened his cheeks. He must have realized she'd seen him staring at her. Still, the grimace he'd worn stretched into the widest smile she'd ever seen from the stern captain.

Her stomach fluttered. She wanted to run up to him—to jump with relief and joy, and grab his hand, even—but she held back.

There was something behind the fluttering in her stomach, behind the shiver tingling down her spine. Mulan knew deep down what it was. Mushu had been right. She *did* like Shang; she had for a long time . . . and being here in Diyu with him had only drawn them closer and intensified her feelings for him.

But now she needed to reason those feelings away. Despite everything they'd been through, Shang would be the only person in the army who knew the truth about her. They hadn't discussed what that would mean when they returned to the real world.

You'll be friends, Mulan told herself. *What else would change?*

"You're here," Shang said, unaware of her thoughts. The broad smile remained on his lips.

Mulan couldn't help grinning back. "You're here, too."

"I'm glad," they both said at the same time. Then Mulan laughed to break the awkwardness, and as if they were both thinking the same thing, they each took a hasty step back.

"You look good," Shang blurted. His face turned increasingly red, and it took Mulan a moment to realize why. He'd never seen her dressed like a girl before. "I . . . I like your hair down. It suits you."

Mulan stifled a laugh, and instead smiled at him. "Thanks."

"There you are," ShiShi rumbled, interrupting the two. "We thought you'd never get out of that chamber. You certainly took your time."

"You try saying that next time *you* go into the Chamber of Mirrors," said Mulan good-naturedly. Best not to recount how she'd almost died inside; not now, anyway. "I encountered Meng Po right after I passed."

"Meng Po!"

"She's not so bad." Mulan touched the magnolia blossom in her hair. "She gave me this flower when I returned her sword. . . . It appeared back at my side after I left the Chamber of Mirrors. Turns out, the Sword of the Blazing Sun belongs to her."

"To Meng Po?" Shang repeated. "But how? She nearly got us killed—"

King Yama stomped his foot. Mulan had been so excited to reunite with her friends she hadn't even acknowledged him.

Now she saw him standing behind her friends with one of his enormous tomes under his arm. For once, he wasn't scowling, but he didn't look pleased, either. Then again, Mulan supposed he never looked happy . . . except as a statue in Youdu's temple.

"I'll tell you about it later," she whispered to Shang.

Surrounded by his demon guards, the ruler of the Underworld stood before the great vermilion gates of Diyu. Once he saw Mulan finally approach him, he clapped his large, wide hands. The sound made the cave walls tremble.

"Your Majesty," Mulan said, bowing deeply, "I found Captain Li Shang, and I've brought him back to you before sunrise."

"You cut it rather close," King Yama said gruffly. "But fair is fair."

"So we're free to go?"

"Not yet." Yama pulled at the ends of his beard. He looked ever so slightly anxious. "You say you saw Meng Po? Did she seem . . . upset?"

"Upset?"

"That you foiled her plans to keep you here!" King Yama rumbled. His round eyes flicked to Shang and ShiShi. "You all get to leave Diyu, but I still have to deal with her, you know. For all eternity."

"She wasn't angry," Mulan assured him. "She gave us all her blessing."

"Good," King Yama said, calming down.

"I thought I sensed her mark on your new attire," ShiShi grumbled to Mulan. He tore at his mane, and at the braids that had come apart. "She could've spent some of her magic on me. Look at me. I can't go back to the real world looking like this. I'll be the laughingstock of all the Li ancestors."

She chuckled. "Stop being so vain. You look fine."

King Yama whistled at ShiShi, beckoning the lion to his side.

ShiShi straightened, assuming the king of the Underworld was about to honor him in some way, but King Yama simply propped his great tome over ShiShi's back.

The lion grunted. "I'm not a book stand."

King Yama disregarded the guardian's complaints and flipped through the book until he found Shang's name. Grasping the ink brush tucked behind his ear, Yama dipped its bristles into the porcelain inkpot floating at his side, then scratched out *Captain Li Shang* from the book.

"There," he said. He reached for a paper fan inside his pocket and waved it at the ink to dry. "All done." He wagged his brush at Shang. "Next time, look before you throw yourself in front of the enemy's sword."

"Yes, sir."

"Good. Now get out of here. I've a schedule to keep."

"Not yet," came a chorus of familiar voices.

Mulan's ancestors!

Ren, Mei, and Liwei appeared, escorted by the blue demon guard who'd first accompanied Mulan into Diyu. Languai scowled when he saw Mulan, but that was probably just his normal facial expression. When their eyes met, he nodded his head in an acknowledgement of respect.

"Of all the millions of souls in Diyu, what luck you had to run into these three." King Yama frowned at the Fa ghosts, particularly at Mei—who batted her eyelashes at him. "Now thank them and say goodbye. Be quick about it. I'm in a generous mood, but that doesn't mean you can dawdle."

"He really never does smile," Mei muttered. She puckered her red lips into a pout, then faced Mulan. "It's good to see you again, Ping . . . I mean, Mulan." She slapped Mulan's shoulder with a fan. "I *knew* you weren't a boy."

"I'm sorry for my deception," Mulan replied. "But I had to . . . for Baba."

"You should have told us." Liwei wrinkled his nose, and for a moment, Mulan worried that he still was angry with her. Finally, he nodded. "But family is family. At least now I know you're really one of us."

"Family is family," Mulan repeated with a smile. "Thank you, Honorable Ancestor Fa Liwei."

"If you want to thank us, pray that we reach Heaven soon," Mei added. "It's been centuries since anyone's included us in their prayers."

"I will," said Mulan, warmed by her ancestors' acceptance. "I promise."

With that, Mei and Liwei parted for Diyu again, but Ren lingered. The monk shuffled his feet, looking nervous as he approached Mulan.

"I paid off my debts thanks to you," he said. "I knew you'd make it through the Chamber of Mirrors."

"I'm glad." She softened. "You were a great help to us, Ren. What will happen to you now?"

A beam brightened Ren's face. "King Yama thinks I can make up for my past misdeeds in a new life."

"Congratulations," she said, truly happy for her ancestor. "Will you go soon?"

"I'll wait in line at the Hall of Justice once I see you off. Might take a few days, or weeks. Good time to reflect."

"On?"

Ren patted his head. "Let's just say I wasn't the most exemplary monk when I was alive. I wanted to be an actor, but my mother wouldn't allow it. So I needed money to fund my own troupe, and I turned to gambling. When Mother found out, she sent me to the temple."

"Let me guess—you didn't stop once you became a monk?"

He cast her a sly grin. "I couldn't help myself. I was kicked out of the monastery a few months before I died. But with hindsight, my bad habits helped me make a life here in Diyu." Ren straightened, and a wave of calm washed over him. "And helped me stay here long enough to meet my descendant, Fa Mulan the hero."

Mulan blushed. She still wasn't used to being called a hero, especially not as her real self.

"I hope our paths cross again in the real world." Ren folded his hands together, then stepped back until Languai caught his arm. He and the guard faded back into Diyu, and another ghost took their place at the end of the cavern.

"Father," Mulan heard Shang gasp.

Sure enough, it was General Li. His chest swelled with pride, and he glowed even brighter than before; even his armor gleamed. He walked toward them slowly, never taking his eyes off his son until he had approached King Yama.

King Yama frowned. "So that's where you've been," he grumbled to the general. "My soldiers have been searching everywhere for you."

General Li bowed to King Yama. "Your Majesty, my humblest apologies for evading your soldiers."

"You trespassed into the mortal world," King Yama said sternly. "That is forbidden. I should revoke my decision to send you to Heaven."

"Please, Your Majesty," said Mulan. "It was my fault. I offered to go."

"I said I *should*," huffed King Yama. "I didn't say I *would*. I told you I'm in a generous mood."

General Li hid a smile. "I am ready to ascend to Heaven. Only give me a last moment with my son."

King Yama heaved a sigh. "Go. Go. Hurry before I change my mind."

General Li bowed once more before addressing ShiShi, his former guardian. "Farewell, old friend. Watch over my son for me."

ShiShi nodded once. He lowered his head before Mulan could see the tears forming at the edges of his round orange eyes.

General Li continued to Mulan. "And I must thank you as well, Ping. You look different than I remembered."

Mulan looked up at the general nervously. "That is because I am not Ping," she confessed. "My name is Mulan."

General Li blinked, confused.

"She is Fa Zhou's daughter," ShiShi explained, before Mulan could do it herself. "She impersonated a man to serve in the Emperor's army, and to spare her father from having to fight."

"A female warrior," murmured the general. After a moment's thought, he chuckled. "Audacious, but I cannot say I disapprove. What a soldier Shang's mother might have made. She could have defeated the Huns with her fierceness alone." General Li made a face.

His laugh faded, and he straightened, taking on the authoritative stance of the revered general he'd been in life. "Now I must thank you, Fa Mulan. Few men would have had the cunning and bravery to save my son from Diyu. Fa Zhou is lucky to have a daughter such as you."

Mulan's throat swelled, and her eyes grew misty like ShiShi's. To hear General Li say her father would be proud of her, and know he truly meant it—left her speechless.

"Thank you, sir," she said, realizing everyone was waiting for her reply. "Your words mean a great deal to me."

"I can't imagine it was easy for my son to discover his best soldier is a woman. I'll trust you to keep my son's pride in line."

Mulan pressed her lips together to keep from smiling. "I'll do my best."

Now, finally, General Li turned to Shang. "My son," he said quietly. "China thanks you for what you have done, but your role in protecting the Emperor is not finished."

Shang bowed. Mulan couldn't see his face, but his voice trembled. "Yes, Father."

"Take care of your mother." General Li placed both hands on his son's shoulders. "And listen to ShiShi." The general mustered a faint smile. "He has a big head and thinks he's *always* right, but over time, you'll learn he usually is. There is much wisdom you can learn from him. If you do so, you will not make the same mistakes I made when I was your age. You will become a better man than I. That is all I can hope for."

Shang opened his mouth as if to protest, then closed it and nodded. "I will, Father." He paused. "Thank you for coming back and saying goodbye. I will not let you down."

"Then my heart is full. I will watch you from Heaven." General Li clasped Shang's hand, lingering until Yama let out a warning cough. The general nodded, let go of his son's hand, and returned to King Yama's side.

"When you cross the gates," said Yama, "keep walking. No matter what."

His voice echoed across the cavern, and when Mulan turned back she realized he—and General Li—had vanished.

The bronze bell hanging above the gates chimed. Mulan's eyes lifted toward the sound. She'd never noticed the bell before; it hung, suspended in the air by nothing at all. But that no longer surprised her.

She was almost sad to leave this place behind—to return to the real world where ghosts and demons and magic did not tread. Where bridges didn't hover in the air, and rivers didn't stream across the clouds. Where old women didn't turn out to be powerful enchantresses, and mirrors couldn't speak to one's very soul.

As the bell continued to blare, the round demonic faces carved into the gates' vermilion-painted wood clattered their square metal teeth, their red eyes searing to life. The knocking grew louder and louder, until the entire cave shuddered.

Then, with a deep and throaty rumble, the gates began to part.

Chapter Thirty-One

Sunlight pierced the crack between the gates, bathing the entire cavern with a soft white glow. Mulan shielded her eyes and stepped closer to the rumbling gates. She could see dawn outside, the sun glittering as it rose above the horizon.

"It's morning," she murmured. Mulan tilted her chin, letting the light bathe her face and warm her. "You know, I've never been so happy to see the sun."

"That's the way I used to feel after each battle," replied Shang. "Just grateful to see another day."

She knew exactly what he meant.

Behind them, ShiShi hadn't budged from his spot.

"Aren't you coming?" Mulan said, waving him toward her. She chuckled. "Don't tell me you're still worried about your mane. I'll help you braid it again before you have to face Shang's ancestors."

The lion straightened, gathering his tail so it curled by his side. In a deep and solemn tone, he said, "This is the last you will see of me, Fa Mulan. I wish to make a proper farewell."

Mulan's hand dropped to her side. Her good humor faltered. "You're not coming with us?"

"Not through these gates," ShiShi said. "I promised General Li I would aid you in saving his son. That journey is over now, and after I report to the Li ancestors, I must assume my duties as Li Shang's guardian."

Mulan had become so fond of Shang's guardian. It had never occurred to her that the lion wouldn't continue to be part of her life after their journey to Diyu together. Now that ShiShi said he had to go, emotion flared in her chest. Her shoulders sank. "So I'll never see you again?"

"Not in this lifetime," ShiShi said sadly. Then he tilted his head, his nose twitching thoughtfully. "That is, unless you somehow become part of the Li fam—"

"Unless you see him," Shang hastily cut in, "through me. ShiShi will always be with me, and you will always be my friend, Mulan."

Mulan did not know why a knowing smile touched ShiShi's mouth, but she ignored it and embraced the lion instead. The gesture took the guardian by surprise, for he let out a small, strangled cry. Then he relaxed and patted Mulan's back with a paw.

"You're stronger than you look, little soldier. I will miss you."

"Thank you for everything," she whispered in ShiShi's ear.

She let him go, and somewhat bashfully, ShiShi shook his mane, seeing that his hairs stood tall and bristly. "I wish you well, Fa Mulan." He nodded at Shang, too. "I wish you both well."

The lion stepped into the light shining from outside the gates. Little by little, his golden coat grayed, his fur smoothed into stone, and his round persimmon eyes hardened.

As the gates finished opening, the light swelled and washed over ShiShi's statue until—in a flash—he was gone.

Mulan swallowed hard. She turned to Shang. "Ready?"

"Wait."

She looked up at him, curious what he had to say. "Yes?"

"When we go back, you'll be Ping again." Looking flustered, he stared at his hands. "I was just . . . I was just getting used to calling you Mulan." Shang hesitated. Color deepened his face. "I also realized I never thanked you for saving me."

"You did."

"I thanked Ping." A lift in his brows framed the gentleness in his eyes. "Not Mulan."

There it was again. That warm buzzing in her heart.

Her pulse sped up. She didn't dare breathe or blink, afraid she might give away all the emotions bursting inside her now. She became suddenly aware of everything—the slip of hair tickling her shoulder, the heaviness of her lashes when she blinked, the tingle in her veins as blood rushed to her head. The hammering of her heart against the counterpoint of her unsteady breaths.

"So." Shang cleared his throat. He took a step closer to her, his hand outstretched. For a moment, she thought—no, she *hoped* he might reach for her hand. If he had, he took it back at the last moment. He wasn't human again yet, so it would have passed through her anyway. "Thank you, Mulan."

Warmth radiated inside Mulan. "I should thank you, too," she said softly. "Saving you helped me find out who I really am."

Shang looked confused, but she simply smiled.

"Will you two hurry up?" King Yama's voice bellowed from above. The cavern walls boomed. "I'm not going to keep the gates open forever."

They were standing in the gates' shadow when it struck Mulan that Shang had finally stopped glowing. The closer they approached to the gates, the more color returned to his face.

"What is it?" Shang asked, catching her watching him.

Emotion overwhelmed her. "You're becoming alive again," Mulan breathed.

Little by little, his eyes warmed into that dusky shade of brown she'd come to miss. A shadow traced the outline of his body, from the curve in his neck to the powerful slope of his shoulders. As his glimmering blue aura faded, his hair blackened, and his skin, bronzed from years of training under the sun, glowed with life.

She had no idea what came over her—impulse or instinct—but she reached for Shang's hand.

He looked surprised, and for an instant she wondered whether it was because he could feel her touch, or because she had reached for him. Maybe both.

Shang's stance loosened, and he drew her close, not letting go of her hand. "I told you once you were the craziest man I'd ever met. I guess I have to change that to the craziest woman."

Mulan laughed. "You're delaying us from leaving Diyu to tell me that?"

"And that Ping was right about his sister."

Now Mulan lifted her chin, curious. "Why is that?"

"She's strong and kind and beautiful and brave. . . ."

"And also speaks her mind," Mulan reminded him.

". . . Honest, in the way that counts most."

"And she occasionally disobeys orders," Mulan warned him, "even from her commanding officer."

". . . She has discerning judgment."

Mulan smiled. Tentatively, she reached for a wisp of hair that clung to Shang's temple. She brushed it aside gently, and Shang caught her hand in his and brought it to his chest.

Mulan's skin tingled.

"I'll never meet another girl like her," he said. "Now that the war is over, I'd be a fool to let her out of my sight."

A surge of warmth swept over Mulan. She felt herself glow, felt the heat in her heart ripple through her veins and rush to her head. It was the strangest sensation. At first she strained to maintain control, for maybe she'd misunderstood Shang. Oh, she couldn't tell. The ground was spinning and her heart was pounding so madly, maybe she'd imagined everything he'd said. But from the way he held on to her hand, the way he looked at her, waiting tensely for her answer, she knew she hadn't imagined it. So she couldn't control the giddiness of her heart, the swoop in her stomach, or the tremble in her knees. And her face broke into a smile.

Then, before King Yama interrupted them again, Mulan turned to face the gates. It was bright outside, unlike the darkness that had wrapped her and ShiShi during their terrifying fall into the Underworld. Meng Po had promised many more trials would await her and Shang, but whatever they were, she knew they'd face them together.

And it was together that they passed through the Gates of Diyu.

Light exploded, so blinding and bright that Mulan had to shield her eyes with her free hand.

Keep walking, she thought, remembering King Yama's instruction.

Each step grew more difficult to take. Fierce winds knocked them off their feet. An invisible force tossed them into the air. She couldn't tell whether they were rising or falling. The wind was so strong Mulan could barely breathe.

But she could feel Shang's hand over hers. He interlaced his fingers with hers and tightened his grasp so they wouldn't be blown apart. He squeezed her hand and winked, an assurance they would be all right.

They started moving faster. A powerful gust roared and thrust them up and up. The winds swirled, and everything spun. Air juddered beneath Mulan's feet, and like tidal waves, the wind folded over them, flinging them apart.

"Shang!" she screamed.

They reached for one another, but the wind was too strong. They were moving too fast. A flash of white from above stung her eyes. The light grew brighter and brighter, swallowing them in its brilliance.

Shang's face was the last thing she saw before the world tilted, and everything went black.

Chapter Thirty-Two

Mulan's eyes snapped open. She bolted up, accidentally hitting the back of her head against the pole behind her. Pain shot up her spine, and she groaned.

Her vision was blurry, still blinded by that intense light from the gates, and traces of the bell's distant ringing still hummed in her ears.

But she didn't need to see to know where she was. The ground under her boots was moist and cool, with the soft crunch of newly melted snow. The frost that had glazed the pole behind her—only hours before—was gone. And outside, she heard Yao and Ling making rooster sounds, a call for everyone to wake.

There was no doubt about it. She was back in her tent, back at camp with the rest of Shang's troops.

Mulan rubbed her eyes and gathered her legs to her chest. The wooden bowl with the remnants of Chien-Po's soup clattered at her side. Everything was just as she'd left it.

She quickly pulled herself to her feet. "Shang?" she whispered.

No answer.

Mulan heard a whistle-like snore escape from behind her shield. Gently, she lifted it and peeked underneath.

Mushu. Still asleep.

She decided to let the dragon rest.

Pockets of sunshine flickered through the tent, freckling Mulan's armor with tiny dots of light. The rest of the tent was still dark, but the shadows gathered most heavily in the center—where Shang's cot was.

And there, she saw Shang's still figure, just as she'd left him.

Her shoulders drooped with disappointment. Had it all been a dream?

She breathed into her hands. It wasn't as cold anymore, but her hands trembled. She flexed her fingers to warm her muscles, then noticed the bandages around her ankle were gone. She lifted the hem of her pants. The wound the demons had given her was gone, and the scratches on her hand had vanished, too. Even her uniform was back to the way it had been before, and her father's sword rested against the tent folds next to Khan's saddle.

And yet . . .

Feeling something soft and feathery in her pocket, Mulan reached inside and pulled out a delicate pink flower. The magnolia blossom Meng Po had given her.

She uncurled her fist and inhaled. Did she dare hope that meant Shang *was* better?

Please. Let him be well.

The ringing in her ears faded, and now she heard quiet but steady breathing coming from the middle of the tent.

She took a few steps to his bedside, then knelt and folded her arms on the stool by his head. Seeing him, she let out a ragged breath. He was still asleep, but his hands were folded above his blanket over his chest. She was sure she'd tucked them at his sides before.

Twisting her hands to warm them, she reached out her fingers to touch his forehead.

His skin was cool. His fever was gone.

Mulan felt the blood rush to her ears, but she didn't dare shout out to the rest of the soldiers outside. Not yet. She needed to be sure.

Her hands still shaking, she lifted his blanket and checked the gash on his abdomen.

No infection. The flesh around his wound was still inflamed and pink, with flecks of dark dried blood around the gash. But a thick red line had formed in the middle, the makings of a scar. The wound had closed!

Shang coughed. His voice was hoarse, but he half opened one eye. "I . . . I thought I told you to leave me behind."

Mulan's hand jumped to her mouth. She nearly choked with relief. "Shang!"

His face scrunched, brows knitting together as the sunlight returned with its full intensity. He blinked again, both pupils focusing on her. Color bloomed in his cheeks, almost like the flush on his face when he'd seen her cross the Bridge of Serenity, but here Mulan took it as a sign that he was feeling better.

Shang propped himself up using his elbows.

"Slowly," she said, hiding a smile as she put her hand behind his back to help him. "How do you feel?"

"Disoriented," replied Shang. "But better. Much better."

He pressed the back of his hand against his forehead, wiping away the sweat. He stretched as he sat up, his chest broadening and the muscles in his arms flexing under his sleeves. Mulan blushed for noticing.

"Good." She turned, afraid Shang might see. Breathlessly, she touched her face, its heat giving away the beam radiating on her cheeks. It took all her restraint not to fling out her arms and hug Shang.

She didn't know why she was being so shy. He'd told her in Diyu how he felt about her. Yet when she looked at him again, Shang quickly averted his gaze, as if she'd caught him staring at her.

"How long was I asleep?" he asked hastily.

"A little more than a day."

Shang pulled his blanket over his lap and leaned forward. He wouldn't look at her, she noticed. And he hadn't said a word about them being back in the real world.

He's acting strange. Did he not remember what had happened in Diyu? Did he not remember that she was Mulan, not Ping?

A twinge of disappointment tightened in her chest. That meant he didn't remember seeing his father, didn't remember ShiShi or the moments they had shared . . . the closeness they'd developed after she'd told him the truth about herself.

Didn't remember what he'd told her just before they crossed the gates—about not letting her go.

A lump hardened in her throat. Her hands moved, reaching for a canteen, but she was hardly aware of what she was doing. She felt suddenly cold, as if the world had changed in some irrevocable way, and only she knew it.

Stop it, Mulan. It didn't matter that Shang didn't remember their time in Diyu. It didn't even matter if her entire journey in Diyu had only been a dream.

Shang was better.

That was the most important thing. He wasn't going to die.

Even if he no longer remembered she was Mulan, not Ping, the bond they'd shared in Diyu had been real. She would find a way for them to be close again.

But how? Now that the war was over, she and Shang wouldn't have much time left together. After they paid their respects to the Emperor, she'd go home to face her parents, and Shang would return to his home as well . . . and face his mother and her plans to marry him off.

Her shoulders sank. She couldn't lie to herself by pretending that thought didn't bother her.

No matter what, she wouldn't make the same mistake again. She would tell him the truth about who she was. Soon.

Joy surfaced to her emotions again, but it was more bittersweet this time. She swallowed so her voice wouldn't crack when she spoke. "I'm sorry."

"Sorry for what?"

Lying to you, almost killing you. She blustered, "I don't know what I would have done if you'd died. Thank you for saving me from Shan-Yu."

He smiled at her, tenderly enough to make her cheeks warm again. "You would have done the same for me."

Her heart skipped. Mulan took a moment to find her breath. "I'm glad you're better, Shang. The rest of the troops will be, too." She stood, deciding she should leave before she sounded too awkward. "I'm going to tell everyone the good news."

Shang's stomach growled.

"*And* I'll see if Chien-Po has breakfast ready."

Before he could say anything else, she fled the tent, shouting the news. "Captain Li Shang is awake, everyone! Shang is awake!"

Chapter Thirty-Three

The snow had melted overnight. Patches of grass sprinkled the ground, and Mulan even saw flowers sprouting from the earth. Around her, the soldiers sprang to their feet and hastily dressed so they could see Captain Li Shang's recovery for themselves. Yao and Ling clamored around Chien-Po, arguing over who would get to bring Shang his breakfast.

"Ping should bring it," Chien-Po said, wiping excess soup off the sides of the bowl with his sleeve. "We should all let the captain rest."

"When can we see him?" Ling asked.

"I'll ask," Mulan said, taking the bowl. She paused in front of the tent, where all the soldiers had eagerly gathered. "He just woke up, so give him a moment."

Yao shooed the soldiers away. "Yeah. Give him a moment."

Chi Fu, however, was insistent on seeing Shang. Carrying his head high, he strode to the front of the tent and rapped Mulan's shoulder with his scroll before she could go inside. "I demand to speak to the captain."

"He's resting," said Mulan cheerfully. Not even Chi Fu's demands could annoy her this morning.

"Resting?" Chi Fu scoffed. "A likely story. You must be delusional, Ping. Given how severely Captain Li Shang was wounded, I'll hardly bet he's—"

"Recovered?" Shang finished for the Emperor's adviser, crouching to exit the tent. "Yes, I'm recovered. And I highly suggest everyone eats a full breakfast this morning. We have a long day's march ahead to the Imperial City."

The soldiers fell silent. Even Chi Fu stopped talking. His jaw fell, hanging agape.

"It's a miracle," the soldiers whispered to one another. "He's alive."

Knowing she was grinning like an idiot, Mulan passed Shang his breakfast. "Welcome back, Captain Li."

"Well, this *is* a surprise," Chi Fu said, pulling on one of his whiskers. "How did this happen?"

Shang rested his hand on Mulan's shoulder. "Ping took care of me. He didn't leave me behind, like you *told* him to."

Chi Fu crossed his arms. "That boy nearly got you killed!"

"He saved us from Shan-Yu," Shang reminded him. "I expect the Emperor will want to know which soldier we owe our lives to."

"Fine." Chi Fu glared at Mulan. "But don't expect me to write you a glowing report."

"I won't," Mulan said, stifling a laugh.

As Chi Fu walked away, Ling slurped the rest of his soup and muttered to Mulan, "Even his compliments sound like insults."

"Yeah," said Yao, "but for once, I don't want to punch his face. I'm too happy the captain's alive."

Mulan laughed, and pressed her own bowl to her lips. "Me too. Me too."

How good it was to be back among her friends.

Mulan fitted her saddle onto Khan's back. On the horizon, she could almost make out the Imperial City's red walls and blue roofs.

"Hurry up with breakfast," she heard Shang call to the men. He'd emerged from the tent, fully dressed as if nothing had ever happened to him. How strong he looked as he strode across the camp, carrying a box of supplies they'd take with them to the Imperial City.

"We leave in five minutes. The Emperor is waiting."

Mulan tightened the cord strapping her saddle to Khan's back. At her feet, a familiar shadow approached, growing smaller and smaller as he drew near.

"You sneaky, sneaky girl," Mushu said, grinning. "Are you going to tell me what miracle you worked on the captain last night?"

"I don't know what you're talking about."

"I know a man about to croak when I see one," retorted the dragon. "And Captain Li Shang was as good as dead."

Mulan mustered a nervous laugh. "I don't know. I fell asleep."

Her guardian peered at her suspiciously. "You know, in spite of dressing up as a man and all that, you're not a very good liar."

"I did!" Mulan protested. She picked Cri-Kee off Mushu's back. "Maybe he has a lucky cricket."

Cri-Kee chirped in agreement.

Mushu crossed his arms. "I still think you're hiding something from me. I don't like it, Mulan. Not one bit. You know you're not supposed to lie to your guardian."

"It's a long story. I'll tell you later."

"Later?"

"Tonight," she amended. "After we finish marching."

The dragon nodded. "Deal."

While they marched, Mulan walking Khan by his reins

in the middle of the line, she watched Shang. For someone who'd been at death's door only a day ago, he led the soldiers admirably. They cheered around him, singing and whistling as they marched. Shang didn't join in. She could tell his injury still bothered him, for every now and then he limped when he walked. But he wouldn't accept her or anyone's help, which didn't surprise her.

Still, he was being quiet. Unusually quiet, even for him. He hadn't smiled since breakfast.

"What's wrong with the captain?" Yao said, nudging Mulan in the rib. "He doesn't look happy to be alive."

"He *is* happy," Ling contradicted. "Look, he's not frowning. When he's not frowning, he's happy."

"What do you think, Chien-Po?" Yao asked.

"Hmm." Chien-Po pressed his hands together. "He looks like he's contemplating something."

Chien-Po's right, Mulan thought, casting her gaze on Shang. Chi Fu was at his side, prattling on and on about all the honors the Emperor was bound to bestow upon him for his excellent record keeping and military counsel, no doubt. Shang didn't look like he heard a word of it. He didn't even look like he was pretending to listen.

He looks preoccupied.

Mulan wondered what Shang was thinking about. She had to restrain herself from going up to him and asking. She'd gotten used to being at his side, but now that they were back in the living world, she constantly had to remind herself that he was her superior officer. She couldn't just go up to him and ask him what was on his mind. Not in front of the other soldiers, anyway.

So it surprised her when, in the middle of the day, after hours of marching, he came to find her.

He tapped her shoulder.

"Can I talk to you?" Shang said.

Seeing that the rest of the soldiers were at Mulan's side, he cleared his throat and assumed a more authoritative tone. "Ping, walk with me. Chien-Po will lead the troops for now. Don't slow down."

Mulan passed Khan's reins to Ling. She saw Mushu try to follow her, but she gave a tiny shake of her head. Yao and Chien-Po sent curious glances her way, too, but Mulan ignored them and followed Shang.

He didn't say anything for a long time. The two simply walked, putting space between themselves and the rest of the soldiers.

"What's on your mind, Captain?" Mulan finally asked.

Shang blinked. He sighed. "Too much. I barely know how to sort it all. The war is over, the Huns are defeated, and . . ."

"And?" she prodded gently.

"Honestly, I don't know how I'm alive." Shang hesitated. "The wound I got from Shan-Yu should have killed me. Yet here I am, walking, not even two days after he attacked me. Even the pain is mostly gone."

The desire to tell him everything tugged at Mulan. She ignored it. Shang would think she was crazy.

"It's a miracle, like the soldiers say," she replied instead.

"Maybe," Shang allowed. "But part of me wonders—" He restarted the thought. "I had a fever . . . and slipped in and out of consciousness. My memory of everything is hazy. I mean, I heard and saw things that I don't even know were real."

Mulan's heart lurched. Could it be? She pursed her lips, trying hard not to give anything away. "What do you remember?"

"I . . . I remember being so sure I was going to die that I asked you to go to my mother, and . . . and—"

Oh. "And take your ashes to her," Mulan finished quietly. "Yes, that happened."

He still didn't look at her. Instead, he frowned. "Then I had the strangest dream, Mu—" He stopped. "Ping. You're going to think I'm crazy."

Had he almost just called her by her true name? Mulan stifled a gasp. She nearly forgot to keep walking—her legs felt suddenly light, along with the rest of her.

"Tell me," she said, trying to keep her voice steady. "I'm listening."

"I heard my father's voice. I couldn't really understand

what he was saying, because . . . because I was dying, and I was a spirit in the Underworld. I was trapped there, in this tower with stone walls. But I could hear him speaking to me, and when I looked outside the tower walls, I could see my entire family. My entire life again."

Mulan slowed her steps. Her heart pounded so fiercely it became a struggle not to burst out at Shang with questions, not to tell him she'd been there, that it had all been real. "What happened then?"

"Then you arrived with a lion at your side to save me."

Her pulse sped up. "A lion?"

"You did. It felt so real. There were demons and ghosts, and chambers of fire and knives and mirrors."

"Funny," Mulan whispered. "I had that same dream."

Shang turned to her, meeting her gaze. In that moment, his expression was the most tender she'd ever seen it. "You did?"

Instead of replying, she reached into her pocket, folding her hand over the magnolia blossom Meng Po had given her. Her memories of Diyu were already fading, but there were certain things she would never forget.

"Yes," she whispered, holding out the flower for him to see. "I was there."

"What do you remember?"

"You were a spirit, waiting for your body on Earth to die. Your guardian and I came to rescue you. He had a fur coat the color of honey, and eyes as wide and round as oranges." She smiled. "He also had the ego of a peacock, but his heart was big. We all fought a woman who could change her shape from a fox to a butterfly, and who brewed tea that could make you forget your own name. And we outsmarted a fire demon. Sounds crazy, doesn't it?"

Shang's eyes flickered. "Go on."

"Then you reunited with your father at the gates," Mulan said softly. "He told you he'd be watching you from Heaven. Then a great bell chimed—I can still hear its ringing in my ears." She laughed. "And we woke up back where we started."

"How did you—"

"It wasn't a dream," she replied. "It was real. All of it."

Comprehension dawned on Shang's face. "But that means, you're . . . you're—"

She waited, not daring to hope.

"You're Mulan. Fa Mulan."

Relief flooded her. She took an unsteady step forward, then parted her lips. "That's right," she whispered.

He inhaled, his shoulders settling down. "When I woke up, I thought it'd been a dream. But when I saw you, all I could remember was that you were Mulan, not Ping. That's why I couldn't look at you. I thought I had to be crazy for thinking that."

"You aren't."

"And now it's coming back. Most of it. The important parts."

"The important parts?"

His brow creased. "There was something else I wanted to tell you when we were in Diyu, but I never had the chance."

"What is it?"

"With your permission, I'd like to tell the Emperor that our best soldier—the soldier who saved us and defeated Shan-Yu—is a woman."

Mulan blinked, not sure she'd heard correctly. "It's against the rules, Shang. He'll—"

"He will honor you," Shang replied, knowing what she was about to say. "You saved China, Mulan. It doesn't matter whether you're a man or a woman. You're a hero. I know he'll see it that way. When he does, the rest of China will, too."

He paused. "Who knows? Soon, China may have its first female commander—perhaps even general one day."

"General Fa Mulan?" she said with a laugh. "I don't know about that."

"It has a ring to it," Shang said softly. He cleared his throat and rubbed the back of his neck. "It just struck me how glad I am that I followed you up that hill," Shang continued. "If I hadn't been attacked by Shan-Yu, none of this might have happened."

Mulan's lips formed a coy smile. "You mean I never would have gone to Diyu, and you would never have been rescued by Ping's sister?"

"That," agreed Shang, "and I might never have discovered how I felt about . . . about you."

Her breath hitched. She couldn't take another step. Her feet had frozen, rooting themselves to the dusty road beneath her shoes.

"I meant what I said in front of the gates," said Shang softly. "I'll never meet another girl like you." He shuffled his feet and went on quickly, getting to the point: "You told me in Diyu that you set your matchmaker on fire. Does that mean she never made you a match? I mean, do you have someone waiting for you at home?"

Mulan's mouth curved. She had an idea where this was going now, and she had to press her lips tight to keep from smiling. "I have my parents and my grandmother."

"Would they object if I visited?"

"Object?" A laugh tumbled out of her throat. "They might never let you leave."

At that, Shang grinned.

Hearing her laugh, Yao, Ling, Chien-Po turned back and waved.

"They must be wondering what we're talking about," she said, waving back.

She touched her cheek. It was hot, and she could only

imagine how flushed she must look. Her friends—and especially Mushu—would be very curious about why Shang had made her blush. She'd tell them, but not yet. For now, maybe she could blame it on a good run.

"Come on," said Mulan to Shang, still glowing. "I'll race you back."

Together, they ran to catch up with the soldiers. They'd march to the Imperial City, to be honored by the Emperor. Then home, to begin the next chapter of their lives.

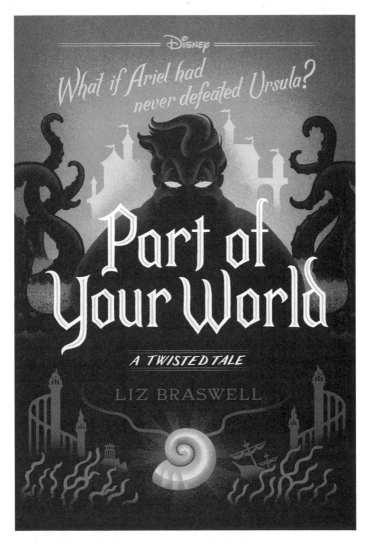

Turn the page to start reading Liz Braswell's
twist on *The Little Mermaid*.

Prologue

In the foothills of the Ibrian Mountains . . .

Cahe Vehswo was in the field repairing a wooden fence. It was less to keep the wolves out than to keep the stupid sheep *in*, where the only slightly smarter child-shepherds could watch them.

It was a beautiful day, almost sparkling. The pines weren't yet brittle from late summer heat and the deciduous trees were in full glory, their dark green leaves crackling in the wind. The mountains were dressed in midseason blooms and tinkly little waterfalls. The clouds in the sky were ridiculously puffy.

The only off note in nature's symphony was a strange stink when the wind came up from the southern lowlands: burning animal fat, or garbage, or rot.

Everyone in the hamlet was out doing chores in such forgiving weather; rebuilding grapevine trellises, chopping wood, cleaning out the cheese barrels. No one was quarreling—yet—and life on their remote hillside seemed good.

Then Cahe saw something unlikely coming up the old road, the King's Road. It was a phalanx of soldiers, marching in a surprisingly solid and orderly fashion considering how far they were from whatever capital they had come. With their plumes, their buttons that shone like tiny golden suns, and their surprisingly clean jackets, there was almost a parade-like air around them. If not for their grim, haughty looks and the strange flag they flew.

An order was cried; the men stopped. The captain, resplendent in a bright blue cap and jacket, rode up to Cahe along with his one other mounted soldier, who carried their flag.

"Peasant," he called out—somewhat rudely, Cahe thought. "Is this the township of Serria?"

"No," the farmer started to say, then remembered long-forgotten rules for dealing with people who had shiny buttons, big hats—and guns. "Begging your pardon, sir, but that's farther along, on the other side of Devil's Pass. People call this Adam's Rock."

"No matter," the captain said. "We claim this village and its surrounding lands in the name of Tirulia!"

He cried out the last bit, but the words bounced and drifted and faded into nothing against the giant mountains beyond, the dusty fields below, the occasional olive tree, the uninterested cow. Villagers stopped their work and drifted over to see what was going on.

"Begging your pardon again, sir," Cahe said politely. "But we're considered part of—and pay our taxes to—Alamber."

"*Whatever your situation was before,* you are now citizens of Tirulia, and pay homage to Prince Eric and Princess Vanessa."

"Well, I don't know how the king of Alamber will take it."

"That is no concern of yours," the captain said frostily. "Soon the king of Alamber will just be a memory, and all Alamber a mere province in the great Tirulian empire."

"You *say* Tirulia," Cahe mused, leaning on the fence to make his statement sound casual. "We know it. We buy their salted cod and trade our cheese with them. Their girls like to wear aprons with braided ties. Perde, son of Javer, sought his fortune down south on a fishing ship and wound up marrying a local girl there."

"Fascinating," the captain said, removing one hand from his tight grip on the reins to fix his mustache. "And what is the point of all this?"

Cahe pointed at the banner that flapped in the breeze.

"That is not the flag of Tirulia."

In place of the sun and sea and ship on a field of blue that was familiar even to these isolated people, there was a stark white background on which a black-tentacled octopus with no eyes gibbered menacingly. It looked almost alive, ready to grab whatever came too close.

"Princess Vanessa thought it was time to . . . update the sigil of house Tirulia," the captain said, a little defensively. "We still represent Tirulia and the interests of Prince Eric, acting for his father, the king, and his mother, the queen."

"I see." Another villager started to speak up, but Cahe put a hand on his arm to stop him. "Well, what can we do, then? You have guns. We have them, too—to hunt with—but they are put away until the boars come down from the oak forests again. So . . . as long as the right tax man comes around and we don't wind up paying twice, sure. We're part of Tirulia now, as you say."

The captain blinked. He narrowed his eyes at Cahe, expecting a trick. The farmer regarded him mildly back.

"You have chosen a wise course, peasant," the captain finally said. *All hail Tirulia.*

The folk of Adam's Rock murmured a ragtag and unenthusiastic response: *all hail Tirulia.*

"We shall be back through this way again after we subdue Serria. Prepare your finest quarters for us after our triumph over them and all of Alamber!"

And with that the captain shouted something unintelligible and militaristic and trotted off, the flag bearer quickly catching up.

As soon as they were out of earshot, Cahe shook his head wearily.

"Call a meeting," he sighed. "Pass the word around . . . we need to gather the girls and send them off into the hills for mushroom gathering or whatever—for several weeks. All the military-aged boys should go into the wilds with the sheep. Or to hunt. Also, everyone should probably bury whatever gold or valuables they have someplace they won't be found."

"But why did you just give in to him?" the man next to Cahe demanded. "We could have sent word to Alamber. If we'd just told the soldiers no, we wouldn't have to do *any* of this, acting like cowards and sending our children away into safety. . . ."

"I did it because I could smell the wind. Can't you?" Cahe answered, nodding toward the south.

Just beyond the next ridge, where the Veralean Mountains began to smooth out toward the lowlands, a column of smoke rose. It was wider and more turbulent than what would come from a bonfire, black and ashy and ugly as sin.

"Garhaggio?" someone asked incredulously. It did indeed look like the smoke was coming from there. From the volume and blackness there could have only been scorched earth and embers where that village had been just the day before.

"I bet *they* told the captain no," Cahe said.

"Such causeless destruction!" a woman lamented. "What terrible people this Prince Eric and Princess Vanessa must be!"

Eric

Eric woke up.

He was having that dream again.

It came to him at the strangest times—when reviewing the menu for a formal dinner with Chef Louis, for instance, or listening to the castle treasurers discuss the ups and downs of dealing with international bankers. Or when his beautiful princess went on and on about her little intrigues.

All right: it was when he was bored and tired. If a room was stuffy and he was sleepy and could barely keep his eyes open.

Or right before he fell asleep properly, in bed—that moment between still being awake and deep in dreams. The same split-second when he often heard angelic choirs sing-ing unimaginably beautiful hymns. He could only listen, too frozen in half-sleep to jump up and quickly scribble it down before he forgot.

But sometimes, instead of the choirs, he had this:

That he was not Prince Eric wed to Vanessa, the beautiful princess. That there had been some terrible mistake. That there was another girl, a beautiful girl with no voice, who could sing.

No—

There was a beautiful girl who could sing, who somehow lost her voice forever on the terrible day when Eric fell asleep. He had been dreaming ever since.

There were mermaids in this other world.

He had known one. Her father was a god. Eric's princess was an evil witch. And Eric had touched greatness but been tricked, and now here he was, dreaming. . . .

He looked down suddenly, in a panic. His arms were crossed on his desk over pages of musical notation, supporting his dozing head. Had he spilled any ink? Had he blurred any notes? A rest could be turned into a tie if the ink smeared that way . . . and that would ruin everything. . . .

He held the papers up to the moonlight. There was a little smudging, there, right where the chorus was supposed to come in with a D major triad. But it wasn't so bad.

His eyes drifted from the pages to the moon, which shone clearly through his unglazed window. A bright star kept it company. A faint breeze blew, causing the thick leaves of the trees below to make shoe-like clacking noises against the castle wall. It carried with it whatever scents it had picked up on its way from the sea: sandalwood, sand, oranges, dust. Dry things, stuff of the land.

Eric looked back at his music, tried to recapture the sound and feel of the ocean that had played in his head before waking, aquamarine and sweet.

Then he dipped his pen in ink and began to scribble madly, refusing to rest until the sun came up.

Scuttle

It seemed as if all of Tirulia were crowded into the amphi-theatre. Every seat was filled, from the velvet-cushioned couches of the nobles up front to the high, unshaded stone benches in the far back. More people spilled out into the streets beyond. No one was going to miss the first perfor-mance of a new opera by their beloved Mad Prince Eric.

It was like a festival day; everyone wore whatever color-ful thing and sparkly gem they had. Castle guards stood in polished boots along the aisles, making sure no fights broke out among the spectators. Vendors walked among the crowds both inside and out selling the bubbly, cold white wine Tiru-lia was known for along with savory little treats: bread topped with triangles of cheese and olive oil, paper cones filled with crispy fried baby squid, sticks threaded with honey-preserved chestnuts that glittered in the sunlight.

It would all have made a fabulous mosaic of movement and colors and dazzle from above.

And it did for a certain old seagull named Scuttle, who was quite enjoying the view.

He and a few of his great-grandgulls (sent along to watch him) perched on the rail above the highest, cheapest seats in the theatre. While the younger ones kept their sharp eyes alert for dropped morsels, ready to dive down at the tiniest crumb of bread, Scuttle contented himself with just watching the pomp and muttering to himself. Only one great-grandgull remained by his side, trying to understand what he saw in the human spectacle below.

The costumes were lavish, the orchestra full, the sets cunningly painted to look more than real: when a prince produced a play, wealth showed.

And when that prince came out to take his seat in the royal box, arm in arm with his beautiful princess, the crowd went mad, howling and cheering for their royal artist. Sometimes called the Dreamer Prince and even the Melancholic Prince for his faraway looks and tendency toward wistfulness, Eric looked momentarily cheered by this expression of love from his kingdom, and waved back with the beginnings of a real smile.

Vanessa gave one of her grins, inscrutable and slightly disturbing, and pulled him along to sit down. With her other hand she stroked the large nautilus necklace she always wore—a strangely plain and natural-looking ornament for the extravagant princess.

The orchestra tuned, and began.

YA
YA FICTION LIM
Lim, Elizabeth.
Reflection.
08/03/2022